THE
SWAN'S
NEST

∞

ALSO BY LAURA MCNEAL

The Practice House

The Incident on the Bridge

Dark Water

BY LAURA AND TOM MCNEAL

Crooked

Zipped

Crushed

The Decoding of Lana Morris

THE
SWAN'S
NEST

A NOVEL BY

Laura McNeal

ALGONQUIN BOOKS OF CHAPEL HILL 2024

Published by
Algonquin Books of Chapel Hill
Post Office Box 2225
Chapel Hill, North Carolina 27515-2225

an imprint of Workman Publishing
a division of Hachette Book Group, Inc.
1290 Avenue of the Americas,
New York, NY 10104

The Algonquin Books of Chapel Hill name and logo are
registered trademarks of Hachette Book Group, Inc.

Robert Browning's letter to Elizabeth Barrett Browning reprinted courtesy
of Armstrong Browning Library, Baylor University, Waco, Texas, and
Wellesley College, Margaret Clapp Library, Special Collections.

Printed in the United States of America.
Design by Steve Godwin.

The publisher is not responsible for websites
(or their content) that are not owned by the publisher.

This is a work of fiction. While, as in all fiction, the literary perceptions and
insights are based on experience, all names, characters, places, and incidents
either are products of the author's imagination or are used fictitiously.

Library of Congress Cataloging-in-Publication Data

Names: McNeal, Laura, author.
Title: The swan's nest / a novel by Laura McNeal.
Description: First edition. | Chapel Hill, North Carolina :
Algonquin Books of Chapel Hill, 2024. |
Identifiers: LCCN 2023055236 (print) | LCCN 2023055237 (e-book) |
ISBN 9781643753201 (hardcover) | ISBN 9781643756042 (e-book)
Subjects: LCSH: Browning, Robert, 1812–1889—Fiction. | Browning, Elizabeth Barrett,
1806–1861—Fiction. | LCGFT: Biographical fiction. | Novels.
Classification: LCC PS3613.C585936 S93 2024 (print) |
LCC PS3613.C585936 (e-book) | DDC 813/.6—dc23/eng/20231204
LC record available at https://lccn.loc.gov/2023055236
LC e-book record available at https://lccn.loc.gov/2023055237

10 9 8 7 6 5 4 3 2 1
First Edition

for Tom

"He will kiss me on the mouth
Then, and lead me as a lover
    Through the crowds that praise his deeds:
And, when soul-tied by one troth,
    Unto *him* I will discover
That swan's nest among the reeds."

—ELIZABETH BARRETT,
XIV of "The Romance of the Swan's Nest,"
Poems of 1844

THE
SWAN'S
NEST

PART ONE

∽

England

ONE

∞

SHE WAS STUCK when she wrote it. Stuck in her third-floor room, which was stuck in the narrow, crowded house, which was stuck on Wimpole Street, which was stuck in the fog.

It had been twenty-two years since she could run or walk outside without fear of the sickness returning. They said it was good she was a genius. She could bring the world into her mind, and couldn't she write whatever she could read? *It's a disease of the spine*, the doctor said. *It's your heart,* the doctor said. *It's your bowels, it's what you eat, it's what you don't eat, it's what you do, it's what you don't do, it's the air, it's the heat, it's the cold, it's the writing—stop writing!* In Sidmouth, she was better, then worse. In Torquay, she was better, then worse. In London, there were no purifying gusts of sea air, no wide views, only smoke and the fumes from the pulverized manure of passing horses. She stayed in and turned into what they called her: poetess, hermitess, invalid, Miss Barrett.

But Mr. Browning went places. France, Italy, Belgium, Russia. His poems took you into other minds: a Spanish monk's, a murderer's, an Italian duke's, a French boy's. He knew, somehow, their thoughts and diction, and yet people didn't understand what he was doing. They complained that he was obscure and difficult. His poems weren't difficult at all. They were mesmerizing.

She wanted to light something on fire and hold the torch over Browning's head. Not in a review but somewhere better, more subtle, so she put his name in the mouth of her lovesick narrator, who was also, as it happened, a poet. "Or from Browning," said her poet, "some 'Pomegranate,' which, /

If cut deep down the middle, / Shows a heart within blood-tinctured, of a veined humanity."

It felt, when she did it, like a riddle she had written just for him. Browning would know why she had chosen a pomegranate, and why she had compared the color to the blood of a human heart.

But maybe he didn't read her work. August passed without a word. September, October, November, December. The darkness of fall, with its long nights, became the darkness of winter. She tucked Mr. Browning's silence into the space where you put things you did not think about, and she began to translate Aeschylus's *Prometheus Bound* again.

TWO

∞

WHEN ROBERT CAME back from Italy and learned Miss Barrett had done him a favor, and the favor was in a book a friend had sent to his sister, who had not mentioned it, he was shocked. He was also annoyed.

"I wasn't rude about it," Sarianna said. "I wrote to Mr. Kenyon right away and thanked him."

Sarianna thought at first she knew right where she'd put the gift, but it actually took her a long time to find where she'd stuffed it—two whole volumes, called simply *Poems*, by Miss Barrett.

"Did you read them?"

"I was busy, and then I forgot."

"If you had mentioned it I could have at least sent her a line," Robert said.

"Why would I write to you in Italy about such a thing? To tell you how nicely Moxon was binding other people's poems?"

He couldn't deny it hurt a little to see all that leather and gilding for Miss Barrett while his new poems, *Bells and Pomegranates*, came out in cheap pamphlets. Clearly, it wasn't that *poetry* wasn't selling.

He already liked her. That far-off place you could reach only in lyric was the place she inhabited, and from there she seemed to be speaking—was he mad, or was it Kenyon's suggestion?—directly to him.

When beneath the palace lattice,
You ride slow as you have done,

And you see a face there—that is
Not the old familiar one—

Perhaps Miss Barrett had seen him below her window that day when he and Kenyon were walking by and Kenyon stopped to ask if he could introduce Robert to her. After five minutes Kenyon came back out of the house to say Miss Barrett was too ill. Robert had no reason to think it was a lie, but poets were probably always stopping by Miss Barrett's house, hoping to meet her, asking for introductions or mentions or reviews.

He went poem to poem in search of what Kenyon said was there. He wouldn't ordinarily confuse the narrator with the author—that was a mistake people made with his own poems, and he chided them for it. But when Catarina said "Come, O lover, Close and cover," he looked for the message that might be for him alone, and when a little girl named Ellie stood alone in the reeds, he looked again, thinking Ellie = Elizabeth.

And then he found it.

Browning.

In the poem, a servant was reading aloud to the woman he loved, and the poems he chose, among Petrarch's and Wordsworth's, were *Browning's*. Miss Barrett had read not only his new poems but *Sordello*, which no one seemed to like or understand. The allusion was deft and unmistakable.

He touched the words on the page. Held it closer to the lamp. Closed the book, opened it again. It was after midnight, but the page didn't change. The words were still there, saying the same thing he thought they said.

All this time—almost half a year—she had heard nothing from him. She had sent him a message in the cleverest, most flattering way, and he had said nothing in return. She must have thought he didn't care.

The clock said ten after one, but he must write to her at once and undo the harm.

I love your verses with all my heart, Dear Miss Barrett, he began.

so into me it has gone, and part of me it has become, this great living poetry of yours, not a flower of which but took root and grew.

. . . In addressing myself to you—your own self, and for the first time, my feeling rises altogether. I do, as I say, love these books with all my heart—and I love you, too.

He closed the book, put out the light, and stayed awake, eyes open, wide open, in the dark.

THREE

∞

THERE WAS NOTHING in the first post for him that morning. He went out riding York in the cold, pushing the horse to go farther, the better to use up time. When he came back, his mother was walking tree to tree, as she liked to do, nursing this branch and that.

"You ought to go inside," he said. "How long have you been out here?"

She fingered the bark of a tree that had broken in half. "Your sister is out of sorts," she said. "Rinny is ashamed of her dress."

She must mean for the party tonight at Mr. Talfourd's. "Why?" *Any letters?* he wanted to ask.

There was no wind, and the clouds held either rain or snow. His parents had been thrilled at first to think of Sarianna meeting Dickens—it was why they'd said she could go with Robbie to the party—but then his mother had begun to worry about the others Rinny would meet, what worldly ideas and material extravagance she would encounter. Now his mother would also worry about the weather.

She leaned on her walking stick and turned her eyes on him, the right lid palsied, the left one its clear blue self. She tried to smile and dab at the weeping eye at the same time. "The second post has come. Did you see Miss Barrett wrote back to you?" she asked.

The bark of the nearest pear tree glistened under ice as he touched one of the branches, making the ice melt under his thumb.

"She must have been pleased with what you said. Might she be at the party?"

"No." If Miss Barrett were well, he could ask her to dance and tell her again how sorry he was for the lapse of time. "She doesn't go out."

"Why not?"

"I don't think she can walk."

They were close enough to the house to see Sarianna take a bowl from the warming shelf and with a frown, study what was inside. By the time he and his mother came in, she was rinsing mud off potatoes.

"How was York?" Sarianna asked.

"Spooked by everything."

Sarianna wanted to ride York, too, as long as they were keeping him for Uncle Reuben, but York was too young and unpredictable.

There it was on the table, his name written by Miss Barrett's hand. He took it up and slipped it into his pocket.

"Miss Barrett didn't waste any time, did she?" Sarianna said. "Go on. Open it."

"I don't want to be late."

"You're not going to read it?"

"I'll read it, but we need to hurry. The weather will slow us down."

"Perhaps you should stay home," their mother said. "It's too cold."

"I'll not make any dangerous friends," Sarianna said. "You don't give me credit."

It was too dark on the stairs to read the words, but there were lines all over the front, on the back, on the next page, on the back of that one. He went to his room and lit the lamp.

Such a letter, she said, *from such a hand*. She did not blame him for the long silence. He had not wounded her pride. She was inviting him to write again. In fact, to write to her, if he would, and talk about such faults as rise to the surface in her poems. *Such faults as rise*. As if he could find any fault in her Catarina or her Ellie.

How strangely formal she was, and yet generous. *I will say that while I live to follow this divine art of poetry, in proportion to my love for it and my devotion to it, I must be a devout admirer and student of your works. This is in my heart to say to you—and I say it.*

He dressed for the party without being the same self: the broken-down, the humiliated. The one who wrote a horribly obtuse poem that his father paid to print and that no one bought and Tennyson mocked. Miss

Barrett was his *admirer and student*. Miss Barrett, his admirer and student. Ha!

"Off we go," he said to Rinny. His mother was fiddling with the back of her wool wrap and Rinny inched her gloves on. The right index finger had a hole, so she ripped them off again, went in search of others. The letter was in his pocket, heating him like a brick in a cold bed. As soon as he could, he would steal away from the party and write Miss Barrett an equally formal and yet generous reply. He would *relish, adore, cherish*—

"I do wish you'd stay home," their mother said.

His sister's teeth were clenched, her lips pale. Her old excitement was gone and he didn't know why.

"Nonsense," he said. "You mustn't worry so much. I'll take care of her every moment."

"I hope it stops snowing."

"It will," Robert said. "Don't worry. Come, Rinny. Let's meet the great man."

FOUR

∞

ELIZABETH WAS GLAD she'd written back to Mr. Browning so quickly. It was the best way—to write as soon as you heard from someone. Otherwise, the letter became a chore.

"We're off," Henrietta said, dressed for a party.

"But it's snowing," Elizabeth said. "George came in all melted."

"Not anymore. Guess who'll be at Talfourd's."

"The adoring Mr. H.?"

"I certainly hope not. I never want to see him again."

Elizabeth said she was glad to hear it, and she smiled brightly in expectation, waiting for news of who would be at Talfourd's.

Henrietta said the name carefully, almost as if she wished to take back the news. "Dickens."

The armor of contentment would cease to feel light and natural if not worn at all times, and it was such a bore to ruin everyone's good time with your envy. "Ah!" Elizabeth said. "How thrilling!"

"I mean to give that man Browning a word, as well."

"What kind of word? Don't."

"I must."

"Addles, I have written him. Don't. He'll think I'm showing his letters everywhere."

"Everywhere? To your sister?"

"Don't accuse him of anything. Don't speak to him."

"I will only attempt to discover what kind of game he thinks this is."

"He would never play any sort of game."

"Then I will find that out." Henrietta blew a kiss and went through the door.

"Addles!" Elizabeth called, but Henrietta shouted, "George is waiting!" and went clattering down the stairs, leaving the room with the noise, loud at first, then loudly quiet, of everyone else going about their business. Something invisible ticked. It ticked and time passed but it held her inside it and made her think what to do with it. She had written Mr. Browning a nice, light blanket, pressing down here and there on errant sparks, words, like *love*, that could be misunderstood, and now Henrietta was running, as Henrietta always did, with her hands on fire. *"I saw your letter, Mr. Browning, to my sister."*

If Elizabeth were not always in this room—avoiding coughs, avoiding strain, the year before, the year to come, the year unending—if she were well, and she were at the party, what would Mr. Browning say to her? She could speak to him herself. She knew what he looked like because he was one of the five poets whose pictures she had cut from *A New Spirit of the Age* and had Henrietta arrange on the Wall of Esteem, as she called it. It would be embarrassing in every way if Mr. Browning found out he was on her bedroom wall. He would misunderstand. He was simply a colleague, a reminder that she was not alone in her aloneness. "I admire you," she could think as she considered him among the other writers on the Wall of Esteem. "I admire you, and I admire you, Miss Martineau, and you, Mr. Wordsworth, and you, Mr. Carlyle, and you, Mr. Tennyson."

And I admire you, Miss Barrett, Mr. Browning might say, if they met at the party, though what his letter had said was *I love your verses with all my heart, dear Miss Barrett* and *I love you, too*. Words like that from a man who wrote lines that felt not hammered into shape but born alive. She'd had to read his letter again. And again. To be sure. To feel afresh the amazement. She could read it again tonight, if she wanted, or read the lines she loved most in his poem *Sordello*. It was ten thousand times better to read Mr. Browning and write Mr. Browning than to be a woman in a body, in a dress, in a hot, crowded, noisy room. At a dinner party, you never stopped thinking about your face or the face of the person you were talking to. Horrifying impediments: faces.

The door downstairs banged shut, and Henrietta's voice carried in the cold as she and George climbed into the carriage, and then the wheels took them. The vision of Henrietta accosting Mr. Browning filled all the space around her. What if Henrietta said, "Mr. Browning! I have seen your face on my sister's wall."

Elizabeth took a blank page, inked her pen, and wrote a note to Henrietta.

> *Tell him nothing. Please, Addles. Tell him nothing. I beg you.*
> *Yr. dearest*
> *Ba*

She rang the bell; her dog raised his head, and Elizabeth said he might as well put it back down because there was nothing left on the tray. Flush put his head back on his paw, disappointed, but Wilson appeared.

"Shall I take the tray, Miss?"

Up went Flush's head.

"I need this message to go to Henrietta."

"Now, Miss?"

"Yes. Could Billy take it?"

"He's gone home."

She could not send Wilson, and she could not ask Mrs. Orme to do it, nor her sister Arabel.

"Perhaps Miss Arabel," Wilson said.

Arabel would have to hire a hack and bear the cost of going there, if she could leave the house without their father noticing, which was unlikely at this hour.

"Or Mr. Alfred," Wilson said. "He's downstairs with Miss Arabel."

To her brother she could not bear to say why the message was so important.

"Never mind," Elizabeth said, "it doesn't matter."

"Are you sure, Miss?"

She nodded, unsure.

"I'll be back with tea soon."

The room ticked.

FIVE

∞

THE SNOWFLAKES FELL in smaller and smaller pieces, as if the sky were
a box that contained only crumbs. The bits settled on Robert's face and
gloves, and when they reached the pasture, an owl sat watching them from
the dead elm. Robert pointed to it without a word. They stayed quiet, staring back at it, until it lifted its great self and flew away.

"Will Mr. Kenyon be there?" she asked.

"I expect so," Robert said.

"Does he know you wrote Miss Barrett about the poem?"

"No."

"You ought to tell him."

"She will tell him if he wants to know."

"I don't want him to think it's my fault it took you so long."

"He won't think that. It wasn't your fault at all. I was in Italy."

"What did you write to her?" Sarianna asked.

"How much I admire her poems."

"Do you? Even the romances and romaunts?"

"Yes."

"It isn't what you do or want to do, though."

"Yes, it is. In its essence. I was completely caught up in them."

"I'm so glad."

"Can I tell you, Rinny," he said. "I wish I could write her back this
minute."

"We can go back home."

"No, no. I just wanted you to know how happy I feel. I'll write her later. It will be a wonderful party."

They passed the stable where York slept, the deep black circle of the pond, the cobnut tree. There were no other walkers, not even when they neared the station, where the steam engine was already belching clouds of smoke, and the doors to the cars were open, and a man in uniform stood beside a brass pole.

"Sit here," Robert said, giving her the side by the window so she could watch the countryside brick up into bridges and tunnels and tall houses and lighted taverns.

"This is better than I thought," she said. "It's clean in here."

"Yes, it is, I suppose."

When the train got up to speed, she smiled like a little girl and held on to the armrest.

"Do you like it?" he asked.

"Very much. I'm never walking anywhere again." She stared attentively out the window for a while, trying to see where they were, but she saw nothing she recognized in the dark.

"When will you go back, do you think?" Sarianna asked. "To Italy, I mean."

"When I have the means. If I have them."

"Would you settle there? Forever?"

"If I could. I would still visit you."

"How much money would it take?"

"Not much. It's much cheaper there."

"If the new poems sold?"

"Ha." The first time he'd seen *Bells and Pomegranates* on cheap paper, as if they were some reporter's account of a murder in Cheapside, he knew his light was fizzling out already, or had been a phantom light in his own head, merely the reflection, in the mirror of his delusion, of the great writers' fires.

"We want you to stay home," Sarianna was saying. "Mother, especially. So don't write anything hugely profitable and move to Italy."

"You have my word. I will avoid profit like the plague."

SIX

∞

THE TALFOURDS' HOUSE was ablaze. It was, by far, Henrietta's favorite house on Russell Square, and the Talfourds were her favorite hosts. "Is that Mr. Browning?" she asked her brother. "With Mr. Chorley?"

"Yes," George said, and George waved to Mr. Kenyon, who was making his way across the room with two cups of punch.

"I want to tell Mr. Browning that I read his poem."

George laughed. "*Sordomello*? The whole thing? I don't believe you."

"Not that one." Perhaps she ought not to have mentioned it. George, of all people, must not hear about Mr. Browning's love letter. "George," she said, seeing someone else now, "is that Miss Goss?" It had been a long time, but Lenore Goss's face was the same, or perhaps it was the posture that was the same. Insouciantly erect, proudly displaying her turquoise dress. She saw Henrietta, lifted her glass, and began to walk with annoying self-possession in their direction.

"How good to see you both," Miss Goss said. "How long has it been?"

"An eternity," Henrietta said. "I haven't seen you since you came to Hope End. George was in dresses then, I think."

"I was not," George said.

"How old were you?"

"Nine, I think we calculated," Miss Goss said to George.

"Then you have met each other already in town?"

"Oh, yes," Miss Goss said. "We know all the same people."

Henrietta tried not to let her eyes flit from Lenore's face to her necklace to her gown, appraising elements, noticing how expensive and fashionable each gem and ribbon was, how fine and unblemished was her skin. "Where are you living now?"

"Here on the square," Miss Goss said.

"It must be lovely to have a park."

"It is," Miss Goss said.

Henrietta tried to read George's manner, which was not the stiff cheer of everyday George. There was a meaningful suppression, and it was answered by something in Miss Goss, who suppressed herself, too. Henrietta was about to ask another question when Mrs. Talfourd burst into their circle.

"Hetty!" Mrs. Talfourd said. "Alice wants you to practice with her before dinner."

Henrietta, Lenore, and George turned to watch the Talfourds' wolf-hound place his paws on Alice's hips and receive an oyster. Every man in the room, it seemed at that moment, was staring at Alice, and Henrietta felt a pang as she remembered her first party and thinking that she was about to be chosen and wed and made terribly happy forevermore. Parties were different at sixteen.

"She is uncommonly pretty, Rachel," Henrietta said.

"Luckily, she doesn't know it yet. Before Alice sweeps you away to the library, could you—" Mrs. Talfourd paused, pulling Henrietta away as she apologized to George and Lenore. "Where did she go, now? Robert Browning has brought his sister, and I think she's hardly been anywhere at all, though she must be at least thirty. I hope she hasn't hidden herself somewhere. If you could be so good as to draw her out a little."

Henrietta studied the clusters of guests half-shouting at one another in the drawing room, and at the same time she tried to watch George and Miss Goss, who were walking away together. Mrs. Talfourd said, "Here we are," and smiled her broad, unaffected smile. The young woman Mrs. Talfourd presented to Henrietta wore a plain, high-cut dress adorned only with a sagging gold pin. Her brown hair was loose and curly, and her expression had settled somewhere between frightened and brave. It was her eyebrows, Henrietta decided, that one would emphasize in a portrait, and that little squint of her eyes that said she didn't care what you thought. If only

Henrietta could shade them just right, the viewer would see Miss Browning was a little handsome.

Henrietta gave Miss Browning her warmest smile. "I suppose we both must go about being introduced as 'the poet's sister.'"

"I have not much occasion," Miss Browning said. She kept touching the little gold bird pinned to her bodice. Her dress had been mended—neatly—at the place near the armhole where you could never disguise a patching no matter how clever your maid was with a needle. Her dress was too high at the throat, and too plain. And her hair was parted in the wrong place.

"I've just read one of your brother's poems," Henrietta said, hoping they would not get into a deep discussion of it. She had asked Ba to tell her what it meant so she would not say anything silly.

"And I, your sister's," Miss Browning said. "I was just telling Robbie how I adore *Lady Geraldine's Courtship*."

"I adore it, too," Henrietta said. "It's so romantic and it ends happily."

They were at a loss then.

"This is a lovely home," Miss Browning said.

"Isn't it?" Henrietta said. "It's my favorite in all of London."

The crowds around them surged and parted, shouted and kissed, and Henrietta asked Miss Browning where her brother was.

"There," Miss Browning said. "In the yellow gloves."

His upper body was of normal or possibly abnormal length and his legs were a little too short. If she were sketching him, she might lie about that a little, unless she thought him foolish, and then she would let his legs be what they were. Mr. Browning used his hands and arms as he talked, and he laughed a lot, and the people around him laughed, too, with evident ease, as if they were in no hurry to get away. His teeth—she caught him mid-smile—were nicely straight, so that was a relief. His beard was less prissy in person than it had seemed in the portrait Ba had. It was a little untamed, which was how Henrietta liked beards. Also, his nose was not as large as it appeared in profile, and she very, very much liked his eyes, which were blue. His clothes were neat and smart. Why, she wondered, did his sister not look smart, too?

"Did you come by coach?" Henrietta asked Miss Browning.

"The train."

"Really! Was it far?"

"Not very. From Deptford."

Henrietta had no idea where Deptford was. "Is the air better?" she asked.

"Oh, yes. We have a little land in Hatcham."

"What do you grow?"

"Pears and apples."

"We lived in the country when we were growing up," Henrietta said. "We all miss it terribly, especially now, when the city is so gruesome. Though I confess I found the society meager. Is it just the two of you?"

"My brother, our parents, and I."

"How economical. My mother had eight boys. And only three girls to keep all the boys in hand. It must be very clean and good-smelling and all that, in Hatcham. Please tell me you have none of these awful fogs."

"I'm afraid we do, sometimes."

"What I would give to walk out, as we could at our old house, and be among cows and woods, a church just over the hill—it made me want to sketch all day. We had hops. A few pears and apples, not much. Is it there, among your fruit trees, that Mr. Browning gets his ideas?" She must ask Kenyon what Mr. Browning's father did.

"Sometimes. He is just returned from Italy. He was there four months."

"Oh?" Ba would like that. She read a book set in Italy every single year, the same book, over and over. *Corinne ou l'Italie*, by Madame de Staël, who seemed insufferable to Henrietta, but since it was about a lady poet who was always standing up and rhyming like some kind of acrobat, improvising on whatever topic people suggested, perhaps Ba could get Mr. Browning to read it.

Miss Browning touched the gold bird and let it fall back down. So, Henrietta thought, there was money enough for Mr. Browning to go to Italy for months on end, but not enough for his sister to go as well. Or to have a new dress.

"I am his copyist, though, when he is home," Miss Browning said. She was obviously proud of this, raising her head a little higher.

"My sister would never trust me to copy anything for her!" Henrietta said. A serving man was carrying a platter through the room, heaped high with something round and bready and still warm, from the smell of it. She was starving. She wondered if she should suggest moving near the oysters.

"If you would please tell her," Miss Browning said, "how much it meant—the compliment to Robbie. It was so unexpected, and I think it has buoyed his spirits tremendously."

"Oh, these poets," Henrietta said. She did not want everyone—especially Mr. Browning and his family—thinking her sister had *intended* to make Mr. Browning write a love letter. That Elizabeth had *invited* such a torrent. "Mr. Kenyon tells me," she said, "that writers like to celebrate and toast one another in their books. Does it not seem like a club sometimes?" She gestured toward Mr. Browning and the group that encircled him, which included Mr. Talfourd, whose play she had not liked, though others had said it was brilliant. "Your brother seems quite at home in it, I must say."

"It seems so," Miss Browning said.

"My sister is not of that stripe. Even before she was ill, she hated parties. And balls. And dancing. She is most alive in a book, really, or with her family. I think it's her sensitivity. She feels everything so much more than other people." Henrietta tipped her glass up and discovered she'd already finished the punch. A single sweet drop rolled down into her mouth as she glimpsed Mr. Browning telling the end of a story that made half a dozen people laugh and laugh. This was the man who had written, without even *seeing* Ba, without knowing her *at all*, "I love your verses with all my heart, dear Miss Barrett, and I love you, too." He might be one of those men who was always declaring that he loved someone. He looked boisterous enough. Henrietta wanted to say, *Does your brother often make love to women he has never met?*

"Do you like to polka?" she asked Miss Browning and then returned Alice Talfourd's hopeful wave.

Miss Browning shook her head.

"I must—please excuse me,' Henrietta said. "I'm being summoned by Miss Talfourd. I hope I will see you later, Miss Browning."

ROBERT SLIPPED INTO a room that he had thought was Talfourd's study, but it was a sort of stage, he saw now, with a curtain rod fixed to the ceiling and velvet drapes hanging down and closed. He scanned the semidarkness for a writing table. It would only take a moment to tell Miss Barrett where he was and what he had interrupted to write a reply. He would say he could not wait another moment to respond.

My dear Miss Barrett, how can I—

But this wasn't Talfourd's study, and there was no writing table, only crudely painted scenery of a castle and a big wooden chair. Before he could reverse his steps and go back out, he heard a door on the other side of the curtain open and shut.

"I want to see the letters," a man said. It was the familiar hoarse voice and low cough of George Barrett.

"I don't have the letters here," a woman said.

"Then," George said, "I can come to your house in the morning."

Robert would have to make his presence known. He stepped toward the curtain, preparing a joke about dramatic monologues, but the woman said, "I must ask Miss Hawthorne first. I have to think how to proceed," and George said, "But why? I thought she came here to present her claim," and he cleared his throat again.

It was too late now. The stage where Robert stood was dark, and the part of the room where George and the woman stood was lighter because there were windows open to the street. He calculated the steps to the door through which he had entered: three. If he could make it without a sound, he would still have to turn the knob. Had it been a noisy door? He couldn't remember.

"She did," the woman said. "I told her I would test the waters and test them I have."

"Who paid for their passage? Was it you?"

"No. I didn't know anything about it until she came to my door," the woman said. "Mrs. Waddell and I were friends when I was there, and I suppose she remembered my little speeches about what ought to be done to make things right."

"What made her think sending a Black woman to England would do that?"

"When a man has forced himself upon a helpless—"

"Which man?" George asked.

"It pains me as much as it does you."

"He wouldn't do that, and you ought to know it."

"The letters she has were written by Sam."

Robert didn't know who any of these people were.

"And that's what Sam says? That he forced himself upon a helpless woman?"

"No. Her helplessness is an economic fact. She was a housekeeper."

"So?"

"I have been there, and you have not. When an Englishman in Jamaica has a mistress, he calls her his housekeeper. He sets her up in a little house. They have children together. These children may or may not be provided for in the same way that a servant here might be provided for in a will, by which I mean they are given a token amount, and, before abolition, they would also, perhaps, have been manumitted. The Englishman who does this in Jamaica nearly always has an English wife. But as you know, your brother was single. There are other arrangements even worse, naturally, just as there are here. Crimes of all kinds, for which the men are never punished, unless they are Black."

This was met with silence, in which Robert pieced together the facts. Sam must be George's brother, which meant he was Miss Barrett's brother. The Barretts were in sugar, as Kenyon was, as many were, and their sugar plantation must be in Jamaica. George spoke again, wearily. "Could we not stick to the facts in Sam's case—facts being things that may be proven?"

"They were living together. He'd left Cinnamon Hill so that he could do as he liked without the interference of your uncle and aunt. Not that his uncle was blameless. He was guilty of the same revolting—"

"Too far, Lenore." George's voice had changed, and the other half of the unwelcome mystery was revealed: the woman speaking was Lenore Goss.

"It's in the will. The will did not go far enough, in my opinion," Miss Goss said.

They fell silent. Robert heard nothing for a few miserable seconds. Then George said, "I'll come in the morning. I'll see you at nine," and he coughed once, as if placing a period.

"She will not be ready. It's too soon," Miss Goss said.

"Then you should not have brought your wild claims to my house."

The door on the other side of the curtain opened, a brighter light touched the floor visible between the curtain panels, and the door closed again, darkening the floor. Robert waited for the footsteps in the hall to recede, and he waited a bit longer. Feeling very much like a child who has been stealing food from the kitchen at night, he stepped toward the door, no longer being especially careful, and he heard something. Footsteps, a rustling, and the other knob of the invisible door. Of course. Miss Goss would not have left the room in George's company. Robert stood still. He closed his eyes. What a fool he would seem, or worse. But Miss Goss did not throw the curtains aside and demand to know what he was doing, spying on them. He heard a door open, then close, then nothing. Only after a long pause did he return to the ballroom.

THERE WAS SOMETHING exhilarating and dangerous about meeting a man alone in a room, even if that man was George. A little flicker, as if you might, and he might, but this was George, Lenore said to herself, and George wouldn't. When Lenore's driver had stopped that morning beside number 50 Wimpole Street, a house like every other on the street, she was surprised to see, just a dull front of oxblood bricks and identical drapes, but the man who opened the door wore livery, as if to contradict the impression that the Barretts were ordinary people. It was astounding, quite astounding, that the Barretts of Cinnamon Hill lived in such a plain, ugly house. Was it even big enough for what must be at least nine grown-ups? You could add up the boys in the family because (and this was only one of the many odd things about Mr. Barrett) the two youngest were named for their place in the family: Septimus was number seven and Occyta was number eight. Even without the two eldest, Edward having drowned and Sam having died in Jamaica, and without their mother, who had died when Occyta was a baby, there were three girls, all well on in their thirties, and six boys, though Stormie might be in Jamaica now, as he had been when Lenore was there. The enormous estate in Herefordshire where she'd met them for the first time, ominously called Hope End, had been sold to pay debts, she knew, but that was ages ago. Some of Lenore's friends said that what sugar was bringing now would pay only the medical bills of the poetess, and the bills of Mr. Barrett's lawyers took all the rest, the lawsuit having become a sort of parasite, but people would say anything.

"Is Mr. Barrett in?" Lenore had asked the serving man. "George Barrett, I mean."

The servant said he was sorry, but no, Mr. Barrett was not at home, and he took her card.

She let him close the door on her, and she returned to her carriage, but she did not go home. She told her driver she would wait a bit, and she sat inside the coach with a blanket on her knees to see if any of the Barrett siblings might show up. She could see the steps of the house, and the windows that reflected the street, and a silver bowl beside a fringed drape. It was cold, and her driver was probably colder still, so she could not wait long, but she did not have long to wait. George Barrett was a fast walker, and he was making good time as he rounded the corner. When he felt himself unobserved, he was very severe. You wouldn't even guess that he was gentle inside, that his fierce eyebrows and sideburns could make you want to reach out a hand, smooth his cheek, try to make the light eyes look frankly into your own and do something besides their duty.

Lenore threw off the blanket and unlatched the door. He didn't hear her call to him as he began to ascend his steps, in a hurry to get warm, or in a hurry because he was George. His shiny hat was perfectly correct, as were all his clothes, and she felt a misgiving as she stepped out, walked up the steps, and reached for his arm. He would not like her coming to see him at his house.

"George," she said again.

He turned, saw it was she, and smiled a little, but not much, because he was worried about how it would look. He glanced up and down the street.

"I have a piece of serious business," she said.

"With me?"

"Not directly. But I hoped you might persuade your father to give me a brief audience."

She knew he wouldn't like that, and he didn't. He was his father's most faithful son. Everything that Sam had chafed at, George willingly and honorably performed, the sober and loyal, the tried and true.

They entered through the front door together, and the servant took George's hat and coat and left them alone in the hall. Lenore had never been in it, and yet she had a strange moment of transport back to Jamaica. The girl in the painting just above George—Pinkie Barrett, an aunt—stood on the pinnacle of a very English hill, graceful and slim in a white lawn dress and a pink sash, arm raised as if a partner would appear and dance with her, but instead she had died in Lady Somebody's school.

"Wasn't that at Cinnamon Hill?" Lenore asked George.

"My father had it brought here." George cleared his throat several times, and he ran his hand along his right sideburn as if it hurt him.

"Are you ill?" she asked.

"Not at all. The air sticks in my throat."

"It's especially bad this year."

"So they say."

At parties they sought each other out and disagreed but in a friendly way. George was always saying that Lenore would come around, one day, to see that all her agitation against trade and commerce and power was fruitless, and she was always saying that he would be disillusioned someday. She thought she saw, sometimes, a sort of yearning in his face when they danced. She often expected him to ask if she wanted to go for a ride in his carriage, or if he could see her home, but he didn't.

He opened the door to a drawing room, sent for someone to feed the fire and bring tea, and waited. "Well?" he said. "What is it I must explain to my father to persuade him to admit you?"

"I have something of his," she said. "Sam and I plighted our troth with it very solemnly when we were thirteen or so. I ought to have given it back to Sam when I saw him at Cinnamon Hill, but I put it off too long, and it feels wrong for me to keep it."

"You plighted your troth with Sam?"

"We were playing, that's all."

"I'll happily give it to my father for you," he said, and he turned his head aside to clear his throat.

She waited politely and said, "I know you would, but I'd rather give it to him myself."

"That only shows you haven't met him. He can seem brusque, and I don't want you to be needlessly offended. He doesn't like to be interrupted when he's working, and the subject of Sam itself . . ."

"I will be sensitive to that, Mr. Barrett."

He smiled faintly at the formal name, which she always used archly, so that it had the opposite effect, bringing them nearer rather than farther. "It's not a question of your delicacy, but his. He is not the same since it happened. It's best not to bring any of it up. You must understand what I mean."

In the same year that Sam had died of yellow fever, Edward, the eldest, had drowned while sailing off Torquay. Sam was twenty-eight and Edward barely thirty-three. She knew it all, and she grieved it all, but she had promised Miss Hawthorne she would come here and pave the way.

"I'm afraid your father knows I have other business, too. I have written to him."

The room went cold as George set down his cup. She had dreaded it, but it would have been worse if, when the three of them were in the room, she'd sprung it on the old man without warning.

"What kind of business?"

"I will tell you both at the same time. It's best that way."

"It will not be best. Why did you not ask me before you wrote?"

"The friend I'm trying to help had already written to him, so it couldn't be helped. I couldn't direct her to start with you."

"Tell me who she is and what she wants."

"I have to speak to him, and then I can."

"Lenore—" He lost his voice and coughed again.

"Are you sure you're all right?"

He ignored the question, rubbing his sideburn again. "Are you sure you want to attack my father?"

"It will not be an attack."

George left the room, and she heard him clear his throat in the hall. She had never seen Mr. Edward Moulton-Barrett in person. He had been away from home all those years ago—she had counted it up, and it was now nineteen years since her visit to Hope End in Herefordshire. She had been born in Jamaica in 1813, so she had known the island Barretts first and best. The island Barretts, cousins by illegitimate birth, had sued the Moulton-Barretts long ago, and the suit had never been resolved. "Why not?" Lenore had asked her brother, who still lived in Jamaica. "Because to divide up the money differently," he said, "both sides would have to agree on the value of slaves who were sold with the land forty-odd years ago, and what somebody who is dead meant to do, and meanwhile more of the original plaintiffs die, the yield drops and drops, and it gets harder and harder to make sugar pay. Edward'll be ruined by it. Trust me. He lost Hope End, and he'll lose Jamaica bit by bit."

The fire was not as warm in Mr. Barrett's study. The walls were papered in amber, a deep, yellowish gold overlain with a complicated pattern that was large and full of swirls and feathery notions, and light from the window blotted the pattern out where it touched the wall. Old Mr. Barrett's eyes, when he glanced up, were dull and dark brown. His hair was bristly and grayish, he wore no beard or sideburns, and he did not attempt to smile. He flicked a hand at his cane but didn't use it to stand up.

She made herself stand straight and firm as George introduced her. "I'm sorry for your loss, Mr. Barrett," she said. "I should have called to tell you how lively and hopeful Sam was when I saw him at Cinnamon Hill. I confess I can hardly believe he is gone, he was so—"

"There is no need," he said. There might be something wrong with his cheek, red as it was, and swollen. In the painting behind him, she saw a trio of young Barretts: the younger Edward, probably, and the girl Genius, her hand holding a scroll, and Henrietta with a blackbird on a string. Sam wasn't there—Lenore bet he refused to stand still.

"I have something to return to you," Lenore said. She faltered, and she wondered again if there was something wrong with the old man's cheek. Mr. Barrett moved his cane sideways in a slow arc, as if in moving it he could open a trap door where she might fall and disappear.

"Sam gave it to me," she said. She reached into her silk bag and felt it, the hard oval and sharp gold rim. She fumbled with it longer than she meant, flustered by Mr. Barrett's air of malice. Was it meant for her, or did he radiate it always? She took out the brooch, walked forward, and set it on his writing table. "Sam gave it to me," she repeated. "Long ago when we were barely older than children."

Mr. Barrett picked up the cameo and held it for a moment before his eyes, glasses balanced on his nose. He squinted at the carving of the four horses of Apollo, pale cream-colored animals on a field of pink. She could hear his breathing and the ticking of the pendulum.

"He said it was his granny's," Lenore said. "Your mother's, I understood it to be."

Mr. Barrett set it down and stared at it a few seconds more. It lay there among his pens, ink, papers, folios, a teacup. "I don't remember it," he said flatly.

"Let me see," George said brightly, as if he might take her side after all. He lifted the cameo and turned it over in his hands. "It's quite beautiful, but I don't remember it, either."

A pain started in her lower stomach and spread. They had never missed it. It meant nothing to them. They would drop it into a drawer or a box and forget it, and she would never see or hold it again—could not sentimentally pour it out of the silk bag when something (a Jamaican accent, the taste of cinnamon) reminded her of Sam and she longed, as she sometimes did, for the sound of his voice in her ear.

"I confess," she said, "that I thought you would be wondering where it had gone. I have felt guilty all these years, keeping it."

"Needless," Mr. Barrett said, but he didn't say she was forgiven.

George asked, "When did you say that you were at Hope End with your mother?"

"Twenty-six."

"I ought to remember that," George said. "Did your brother come with you?"

"No," Lenore said. "He had already gone to Little Egypt." That was the name of their estate in Jamaica, as she was sure the elder Mr. Barrett knew. "To take over for my father."

"If you will excuse me, Miss Goss," Mr. Barrett said. "I have my work."

George had warned her, but she was still surprised at the blunt edge of his rudeness, the way he turned away from her and looked at his papers.

"Naturally. I'm very sorry to intrude but there's one other matter. I recently sent you a letter. From a friend." The bright blurry patch of light on the wallpaper dimmed as she tried to project confidence. "She wrote to you from Jamaica, she told me, and wants to convey to you that she is here now."

He did not turn his head.

"I thought perhaps her first letter was misdirected," Lenore continued, "and I told her that as I knew your family and had experienced kindness, I would come to you and make a preliminary introduction, as it were. I'm speaking of Miss Hawthorne, as I'm sure you know."

Mr. Barrett pushed his cane forward slightly and rocked it forward an inch, then back.

"She and her father worked at Cinnamon Hill," Lenore said. "Before abolition and after."

"So Stormie would know her?" George asked. Stormie, named for the storm during which he was born, had been there when Sam died and was, she'd heard, the main representative now.

"I think so," Lenore said.

Mr. Barrett took the cane firmly in one hand and pressed the other hand on the arm of his chair, pushing himself upright. "I haven't time."

"She has come here with two letters and a child," Lenore said. "The child is four." Sam had died in February of 1840, and it was now January of 1845. She waited for Mr. Barrett and George to infer what she was implying. Mr. Barrett still sent out his waves of malice. "I feel certain that Sam would want—" Lenore said.

"What Sam would want," Mr. Barrett said, "is to rest in peace, having taken our Lord and Savior as his Redeemer."

Lenore did not like defenses of that kind. "There is only one path to redemption," she said, "and that is to assist the living."

There was a little silence after this pronouncement. She stood inside it and felt Mr. Barrett arming himself for a fight.

"You consider yourself on that path, I suppose, because you have taken her in. Listened to her story."

"I have listened to it, yes."

"And you think I will listen to it and come to the same conclusion."

"I do. If you meet her and the child."

"I read your piece, Miss Goss. The one in the *Post*."

"Which one?"

"Are there many?"

She had written, in the last month alone, one about unwed mothers, one about entailments that exclude daughters, and one about the barbarity still rampant in Jamaica. "Your type is quick to complain that you lack the power to earn money," he said, and she stopped herself from asking if he meant the lack of opportunity in commerce or in education. "But *that* is what saves you from the taint of actually earning it. You criticize a system from which you benefit every minute of your life, on which you survive as a hypocritical parasite. Or has your brother sold the estates in Jamaica? Do you live on manna from heaven instead of—what did you call it—sugar mixed with blood?"

"I went to Jamaica to attempt to improve our management."

"And did you?"

"I found you cannot improve a system that depends on hellish toil for small wages."

"The wages might be small on your estate, but they are not small on ours."

"If I may redirect," George said. "What does the Jamaican plaintiff want?"

She turned her gaze from old Mr. Barrett to familiar, once-friendly George. He did not look friendly now. "For her son, who is Sam's son, to have an education here," she said. There. She had named what had been implied before. The windows did not break. Nothing struck her.

"And you know this how?"

"She has proof," Lenore said.

"What kind?"

"Letters, mainly."

"Letters. One of the easiest things to fabricate. This is not a new game, Miss Goss. Nor am I a new player."

"Will you at least look at them? And at the boy?"

"No. George will see you out."

The cameo was not ten feet away, and she fixed her attention on it. She had nothing to remember Sam by, not a hair of his head, not a drawing, not a letter. If she had been a child, she would have snatched the brooch and run out of the room. Instead, she walked to the door and rested her gloved hand on the knob while her eyes touched things that brought her nearer to Sam than she had been in a long time: windows he had opened, doors he had closed, carpets that contained particles of him yet, those bits of ourselves that float in clouds of dust when the light shines sideways into empty rooms. She wished, thinking back on it, that she had delivered a magnificent exit line, that she had said what she thought of in the carriage: *If you will not hear her, others will.* [Exeunt. Applause.] But she was not a character in a play, and she had simply said goodbye. George had stayed where he was, blaming her for the mess they were in. Mr. Barrett had turned to his desk, where the cameo faced the ceiling with its bone-white horses.

And now here she was, confronted with it all again. George had returned to the party, and she was left alone in the Talfourds' schoolroom, or nursery, or whatever it was. A bust of someone's head stared at her. Drawing paper spread across a table, and pencils, and a globe. *NORTH AMERICA*, she read on the globe's dull surface. *New Albion*. The continent was new but the names were old. They had been carried from the place people couldn't abide to the place they thought to start anew. She turned to observe the street outside, the coaches dim with their sleeping drivers, the shiny, ice-edged leaves of the trees, here and there a silvery cap of unmelted snow. She thought she heard a noise, as of someone in the room, so she held herself still. She studied the curtain that enclosed the children's theater. No, she decided. It was someone in the hall. When she had given George enough time to reach the ballroom, she turned the knob, opened the door, and went out.

"MISS BROWNING?" A man behind Sarianna said. His red skin was rough as seeds, and he had no eyelashes at all. In his hand was a glass of punch, and by his high spirits Sarianna thought it was likely not his first.

"Mr. Chorley," she said. "How good to see you."

"From what do you recoil, my dear?" Mr. Chorley said. "You look like you're about to run all the way home."

She tried to perceive the eloquent soul Robbie claimed Chorley had. "I'm not used to the crush."

"Your brother is the perfect mix. He sees into one—" he took a drink "—into the deepest, darkest parts. And yet he is still so merry. Is he like this at home?"

"Are any of us like this at home? I hope not. I feel as if I can hardly breathe."

Her brother didn't look merry. He looked nervous. She wanted to pull Robbie aside and tell him Henrietta Barrett had seemed to be issuing a warning of some kind. But if she told him what Henrietta had said—that poets named one another in poems all the time, inducting each other into the Living Poets' Club—that would depress him again.

Mr. Dickens and—was it? yes—the magnificent and notorious Caroline Norton emerged then from the crowd, and Sarianna must have stared at them too long because Chorley said, "Rob said you were keen to meet Charles."

Friend enough to call him Charles. Sarianna tried not to resent him for his bit of brag.

"Charles is another idealist in his work, like your Robbie," Chorley said.

"Indeed, though it is his sufferers I love most."

"Oh, I quite agree. I can introduce you."

The energy of the people pulsed, their conversations half-heard and nonsensical. The party was overpowering in its noise and closeness, and each smiling, laughing, or smirking person seemed engaged in a performance of some kind, an unpleasant and false and desperate one, it seemed to Sarianna, but was that because she was nervous herself? The feeling of the party was not at all how she had imagined it. It was too real, and too grotesque. "I can't," she said.

"Can't what?"

"If I have to see him looking at me it will break the spell."

Chorley settled into a quieter, more thoughtful mode, the one that made her like him better. "You mean he might disappoint you? I don't think he could."

She was not being clear. "It's the place—" She spread her hands, and he nodded, waiting for her to go on. "When I'm reading his books, that's all he is, and it's as if I know him. But when I'm here, I see the truth, which is that he's a stranger. I won't know what to say to him about anything, except what others have already said, and that will bore him." She didn't add that he would see how badly dressed she was, a spinster from a cider farm in Hatcham. He might, being who he was, forgive all that, but the famous Mrs. Norton, regal as a queen, a thousand times more beautiful in person than in the caricatures, would be looking at her, too, judging her clothes and hair.

Mr. Chorley took this in and understood it, she felt it in his pause and the dip of his head. All the candles flickered, a gorgeous amber miasma. "We are none of us his equal. But some writers are charming to know both in person and on the page, however different those two beings might be. Your brother is the same."

The musicians were warming up, and Chorley lifted a hand to a man who raised his bow. "Forgive me," Chorley said, "but I promised to play the piano tonight. It has been a great pleasure, Miss Browning."

ROBERT WAS TELLING some men about the Whistling Oyster of Vinegar Yard, and what songs it might be whistling as it trotted over to the shell that had been made up for it like a little bed (everyone, including Robert, laughed at this detail) and whether he had been over to see the little shell-singer for himself ("Not yet! Have you?"), and then they asked, as they always did, what he had been writing lately ("Dribs and drabs"), which led, as everything did, to Italy.

"How did you travel?" George Barrett asked, suddenly part of the group.

"I walked."

"From Rome to Asolo?"

"From Venice," Robert says.

"But tell me, how did you travel when it was too far to walk?" George pressed.

"I went post."

"Is that as awful as it is here? If one were traveling with ladies, I mean, would it be reasonably comfortable?"

"Ladies were present, and they seemed happy enough. Some people bring their carriages," he added, thinking the Barretts might be in that realm of wealth, for all he knew, especially if their money came from the West Indies. "That way one doesn't have to share with strangers. Are you planning to go, Mr. Barrett?"

"Not at present."

Talk turned to the play Macready was rehearsing, bills before Parliament, how sweet the punch was, the beauty of the Talfourd's oldest girl, and, worst of all, the Corn Laws, and as Robert was wishing he were home writing to Miss Barrett, Dickens said, "What's this about an 'Ode to Hypocrisy,' Robert? Will you be the next to speak for the Irish, I hope? "

"I've added nothing to the page yet," he said. "Did Chorley tell you what happened?"

"He did. I think he knows I write much faster than you."

"Who doesn't?" The incident had been disturbing: during a visit to the British Museum, an Irish boy, all of eighteen, extremely gaunt—and seemingly tipsy, though one hated to add that—had asked Robert if he could borrow a pencil, then had stood in front of the Portland Vase writing something. As he left, he'd handed his notebook to Robert and said, "*You* do it." All that had been written in it was a title, *An Ode to Hypocrisy*.

"Did he know who you are?" Dickens asked.

"Who I *am*? Certainly not."

"But didn't it have the start of a poem?"

"It's rather like a beggar handing Charles a notebook with the word 'Chuzzlewit' at the top," Chorley said.

Dickens smiled a little. Chorley mentioned his own novel every time they met, called *Pomfret* something, and Robert knew there would come a day when he'd be asked to read it. One was never asked to read a draft by Dickens. They came out of him like the Thames.

"My sister is here, Charles," Robert said. "She and my mother read every word you write aloud to one another, it's almost sacramental, let me fetch her—she's just there by the door."

Dickens nodded and turned to Talfourd, and Robert crossed the room. "There you are," he said to Sarianna. "Have you been hiding?"

"I have been right here."

"Have you been having a good time?" he said, urging her across the room despite her hesitation.

"How could I not? But Robbie, I must—"

They had reached the man himself. "Charles, as I was saying. This is my adored sister, Miss Sarianna Browning."

Sarianna was at last seen by him who made Sam Weller / Oliver Twist / Nancy Sikes / Tom Pinch / The Ghost of Christmas Past. She was struck dumb, and she was honored, and in being struck dumb and honored, she curtsied.

Then she felt like a fool.

Treat the famous like everyone else, that's what you do, she knew that! She couldn't help but touch her hand to her scorching face, laugh as if it were ironic.

"You see, Charles?" Robert said with his deep, encouraging chuckle, "I told you she is your harshest critic."

Dickens smiled across the gap made by her humiliating and helpless awe. "You do me too much honor, Miss Browning," he said. "But you are very kind."

When he clasped both of her hands in his and nodded gently, she couldn't say a single word, and to her relief, Mrs. Talfourd clapped her hands together to silence the crowd and Sergeant Talfourd struck a goblet with a fork and announced that dinner would now be served.

HENRIETTA HAD VERY little time to make her move. "Please, Rachel," she said to Mrs. Talfourd. "Please, seat me beside Mr. Browning."

"But I've put him by Mrs. Norton. And you by Mr. Chorley. Mrs. Norton doesn't like Mr. Chorley."

"Can you keep my confidence, Rachel?"

"How can you ask?"

"There is a romantic reason."

"Hetty! You and Mr. Browning?"

"Certainly not."

Mrs. Talfourd leaned closer. "Persuade, dear Hetty."

"Mr. Browning has written my sister an extraordinarily passionate letter."

"Passionate?"

Henrietta nodded gravely. "He has quite turned her head."

"Have they met?"

"How could they? And yet he has already told her he loves her, and she is mad for his poetry. She behaves as if he's Byron! Which he's not."

"But I think that's very exciting, darling."

Henrietta shook her head. "I must see what kind of man he is."

Mrs. Talfourd took this in. She didn't want to make changes, probably because Mrs. Norton was such a glittering catch for her party. But a chance for gossip overruled this.

"You'll tell me what you learn, of course?"

Henrietta nodded.

Mrs. Talfourd listened to what the serving woman had to say about the duckling, grimaced, and went to switch the cards.

ELIZABETH WAS AWAKE and telling herself that whatever Henrietta was doing, she would do, and nothing could be done to stop it. Mr. Browning was there, and Henrietta was there, and George, and all the people she knew only by their books. They had no faces except the ones she made up. It was a curious kind of blindness. She didn't mind it most of the time; if only everyone had to be judged by what they wrote and said and not by their faces, bodies, carriages, or homes. One thing and one thing only: the quality of your mind. Not whether fat or bristly or ugly or old or female or Mrs. or Miss.

She had written Mr. Browning, she reminded herself, so he had her own response already: she wanted to write to him about his poetry, and hear what he thinks, and how he does what he does when he makes these far-off places and people exanimate. *Don't*, she willed Henrietta, *don't make too much of it. Don't make him think I see "I love you" as that kind of love.*

AS THE SOUP was served, Henrietta turned resolutely to Mr. Browning, who sat loosely in his chair, a glass of wine in his hand. He had a manliness she did not expect. Was he as old as Ba? That he was unmarried in his thirties was no surprise. You could not expect to marry if you had no living but poetry and a cider orchard.

"How do you know Mr. Talfourd, Mr. Browning?"

"From the theater. We have a mutual friend in Mr. Macready."

"And you write plays, I believe my sister said?" She watched for any change in countenance at the mention of her sister, but there was none.

"Oh, yes. I enjoy that form."

"I'm afraid I cannot talk intelligently about serious plays. I prefer the opera."

"I love the opera."

This led to a brief discussion of *The Bohemian Girl*, and when that talk dribbled to an end, she felt it was time to tell him she had read his poem. "Do you dread talking about your poems with ladies, Mr. Browning?"

"I only dread talking about my poems with anyone, lady or not, who finds them obscure, and wishes me to change my subject, my style, and my habit of writing at such intolerable length."

"I didn't. And I don't."

"Then you are my ideal reader, Miss Barrett."

"If I may confess something," she said.

Browning, all wariness in the eyes, nodded.

"I'm not sure I completely understood the poem that I read," she said.

He took a drink of his wine. Like most men, he ate and talked at the same time, while Henrietta moved her food gracefully around on the plate.

"If you mean *Sordello*," he said, "you're in vast company. If the readers of *Sordello* could be said to be vast at all. Which in fact they are not."

"I mean the one about Pippa."

As far as Henrietta understood it, Sordello was a twelfth-century man in Italy, and his soul developed, or the reader acquired access to his soul via the language, which was like something out of Genesis, Ba claimed; but Pippa was a cheerful Italian girl who worked in a silk factory, and she went around singing on her day off and saw all kinds of sinful business.

"She's an easier subject," Robert said. "And a shorter one." He buttered a piece of bread with neat strokes and bit into it.

"I confess I still hesitate. One doesn't grow up with my sister," Henrietta said, "and not know there is a difference between saying smart things and foolish ones, however polite the author may be."

Mr. Browning wiped his mouth and said she must feel completely at ease.

"Well, then. Is Pippa someone you met in Italy?"

"Not one person. I would say she is the incarnation of a principle."

"What principle?"

"The power to change others inadvertently by the way we live."

"Do your poems express who you are, Mr. Browning, and what you think?"

"That is too small a cage, Miss Barrett."

All around them people ate, as candlelight glinted on their knives and rings, on the bare shoulders of women, on the knuckles of Henrietta's own fingers. The voices had grown louder as the wine disappeared. "I don't understand. Doesn't Pippa speak for you when she says, 'God's in his heaven, all's right with the world'?"

"What did your sister say?"

"She said it was ironic but had more sincere power as such."

Mr. Browning glowed as if she had succeeded in lighting another candle. "I would like to talk to your sister about such things," he said. "I confess that I would. About these subtleties and nuances, most of which I cannot discuss with people."

"Do you know much about my sister?" she asked.

He held his glass, recently filled, but he didn't drink from it. "I know what is generally known. One day Mr. Kenyon and I stopped at your house. He offered to introduce me, but she was ill."

That awful word he'd used in his letter, referring to her room as her *crypt*. "But not dead," Henrietta said. "She isn't dead in a crypt." An awkward silence fell, and she skewered a pair of peas, chewed, and swallowed. "She is able to go out, you know, when the weather is not filthy. When we lived in Sidmouth and Torquay, where the doctors sent her, she was much better. She could walk by the water, go for donkey rides, even. This repulsive air has made her worse. Don't you think it's worse all the time?"

"It does seem to get no better."

"So tell me," she said, "something you liked in *her* book. And remember you mayn't say that you liked the part where she said your name."

Mr. Browning laughed. "I did find that part extremely moving."

"The letter conveyed that."

"They are infinite, Miss Barrett, the things that I loved in your sister's book."

Henrietta waited for him to prove this.

Mr. Browning studied his fork. He said, "'She could never show him— never, / That swan's nest among the reeds.'"

Henrietta watched the candle wax drip. At home she would touch the warm windings, pull a glob of it into her fingers to play with, form a sphere and then a cube, but of course she couldn't do that here. She watched the flames bisect the faces across the table, light the edges of their hands and silverware, prick the liquids in every glass. "Did my sister write that, Mr. Browning, or did you?"

"She did."

"Then that is an example of what I said. About her speaking from the heart, as her own self."

"And I speak from mine."

"The crypt can be a dark place to live, Mr. Browning." Let him answer for the word, she thought.

"You've read my letter, and you don't like it."

"You must know this if you are to correspond: she is exceedingly sensitive. More than exceedingly. *Dangerously.*"

"Do let me explain, as I will to her. I was thinking of a place I went in Rome, an actual crypt of the Capuchins that I regretted not entering. After the letter was sent, I realized the comparison might be terribly offensive. I will explain and beg her pardon at once."

Henrietta reached out to the candle and broke off a piece of wax. It was cold and hard. She let it fall, and she shook her head as if to tell herself, as her mother had a thousand times, *don't be such a fiddler.* Drawing lessons had been an attempt to cure all her bad habits—*Give her a pencil and paper,* the tutor said. Henrietta sat up a little straighter, and she turned to face Mr. Browning. "It didn't trouble *her*, Mr. Browning. She understood it in the way you meant. But a declaration of love. To a woman you have never met. Was that not rash? The way you put it—"

Mr. Browning appeared to be thinking very soberly as he took the knife he had left in the center of the plate and turned it slightly, as if adjusting the hand of a clock. He nodded, perhaps to her, perhaps to himself. "Did you think me rash, or did she?"

"I did. *She* said you did not mean it except as a colleague."

"You think me careless. Apt to say such things whether they're meant or not?"

Henrietta nodded.

"Do you know the swan's nest, the one she describes in the poem?"

"Of course. It was there every spring, at Hope End. We all went to see it, but it was her particular haunt, hers and my father's. She was the eldest, and the most able to command his attention." She did not add that she was her father's darling, the favorite, the pet, and that all of them resented her for it a little bit and then told themselves to stop it because what could be worse than having been an invalid your whole adult life.

Browning rearranged the napkin, making what was neat and square more neat and square. "Do you remember how it ends, the poem?"

Henrietta crossed her hands in her lap. "I confess I don't."

"The line I quoted is the last one. The girl in the poem, Ellie, she's called—perhaps you remember . . ."

Henrietta took her hand from her lap to sweep a piece of duck through cold sauce.

"Ellie is hoping to find a lover to whom she can show the swan's nest, which is, to her, the world's great treasure. She likes to go and check it, that nest, and see if there are any more eggs—any more hope. But one day when she goes to check, the nest is spoiled. A rat has been there gnawing the reeds. It has sucked on the eggs or killed the nestlings. The wild swan has deserted the nest, and nothing will hatch."

"It was often that way."

"That is not the saddest part, though," Browning said. "She says that if she ever found her lover, she couldn't show him the nest, this vision of the world full of life and hope and wonder. She could never show him the ugly truth, which is a world spoiled by predation and premature death. 'Then he'll ride among the hills / To the wide world past the river'—"

George Barrett, far down the table, looked up at that moment with his knife in his hand. The rest of table fell silent, perhaps because Mr. Browning sounded so serious, or because the lines didn't sound like conversation, but like what they were.

> "There to put away all wrong;
> To make straight distorted wills,
> And to empty the broad quiver
> Which the wicked bear along."

Mr. Browning stopped. The room waited. "What is that, Mr. Browning?" Dickens said.

"A poem by Miss Elizabeth Barrett. 'The Romance of the Swan's Nest.'"

"I thought it was your 'Ode to Hypocrisy,'" Mr. Chorley said. "Done already!"

Mr. Browning waited for Henrietta to say something, but she didn't know what to say. He had unmoored her opposition. And yet she waited, frozen by the attention of so many eyes.

"I could not hope to write something as pure and light as that," Mr. Browning told Mr. Chorley.

"To Miss Elizabeth Barrett," said Mrs. Talfourd, her eyes on Henrietta, "and her poems."

Everyone at the table, including Henrietta and an unreadable George, lifted a glass, the warm glow of light quivering briefly inside the wine, and they drank it, the poem and the wine and the light together.

"And the rest?" Mr. Dickens asked.

"Now?" Mr. Browning asked.

Would he really? If he knew the whole poem, did it mean he loved Ba too much? And what would the people at the party think, knowing, as they probably did, that her sister had crowned him in another of her own poems?

"Just one stanza more," Mr. Browning said, standing up and nodding at Henrietta, and then he seemed to notice George's somber expression before he turned to address what might have been the wall or the two windows that faced the dark street.

"But my lover will not prize
All the glory that he rides in
When he gazes in my face:
He will say, 'O Love, thine eyes
Build the shrine my soul abides in,
And I kneel here for thy grace.'"

The silence was brief but it vibrated all around him, the collective charge of an audience that has been moved by a player on stage, that waits a mere second before spontaneous and hearty applause, which now came. "Bravo," someone added, and Mr. Browning said, "For Miss Barrett," as he sat down.

Henrietta kept her eyes away from George's face as people returned, slowly, to what they were eating and saying before the performance or declaration or whatever it was. She wanted her heart to settle, and for nothing that had just happened to be a lie.

Mr. Browning waited, too. He smiled at something the person on the other side of him said, and he said something Henrietta couldn't hear, a word of thanks, it seemed like, or a word of praise for her sister's poems. When there had been time for the noise to rise up and cover the table, Mr. Browning said quietly, "What I wrote to your sister may have seemed impetuous, but it sprang from what I truly feel when I read her poems. Love, Miss Barrett, is the only word for what I feel, and once I love, I am only that which she imagines love to be."

Henrietta was assaulted on all sides by laughter and the clink of dishes and the jarring voices of many people telling jokes and gossip at the same time. There was a spot on her gown—when did that happen? She straightened her back, the dress binding at the waist. A man was not words but flesh, and on his flesh, on the two hands she saw before her, was the hair Ba would feel if he reached out to touch her, and the blunt fingernails, one stained with ink. There were, beside her, not words but trousers and legs and—she raised her eyes again—pale lips and thick beard and flattish nose and smooth cheeks. "But you can't *know* that you love her if you haven't met," Henrietta said, "and you oughtn't say it, in case you are wrong."

"But that's just it, Miss Barrett. I *have* met her in the sense that matters to me. I know her better than many people ever know one another. Our minds are, in poems, open water. Crystal pools." Mr. Browning touched his beard with the stained index finger and thumb. She allowed herself to meet his eyes, and to search for evidence that he was an honest being, that he went clear down. The blue eyes did not shut her out. They let her in to judge for herself.

"Should I tell her that?" Henrietta asked.

He reached into his waistcoat and brought out a letter. He let her read his name and address in her sister's hand. "I brought it with me merely to hold it. I am in earnest, Miss Barrett. Whatever I say to her is the truth, and whatever she needs from me will be hers."

It was too much. A serving man waited to ask if she could surrender her plate. No one said such things and meant them—Heavens, he was like Ba. Like her in his declarations of infinite and eternal and undying and forever. She leaned back, let the plate go with half of the duck and peas still on it, and smiled at young Alice Talfourd, who was mouthing something to her as she stood up to go out of the dining room. *Dancing!* Alice's lips said.

Mr. Browning was being asked a question by the great Mrs. Norton, and all around the long table, the guests were noisily beginning to rise.

SEVEN

∞

It was only in the hired cab that Sarianna remembered her pelerine. She'd taken it off, ashamed to see that no one else wore a shawl, and she'd never gone back to the room where the cloaks and mantles lay.

"Did you have a good time?" Robbie asked.

Sarianna would not miss the pelerine, but her mother would feel its loss so deeply. The lace had been made by a great aunt, who had carefully detached it from an old dress and sewn it to the edge of the shawl for Sarianna when she turned sixteen. How she had loved it then.

"It was not quite what I expected," she said, the wheels beginning to move, the chance to stop the driver rolling away with them.

"You charmed Mr. Dickens. As I knew you would. And Chorley said you were quite disarming. He never says that."

The horses' hooves quickened and they left the square.

"Mr. Chorley sees into one," Sarianna said, watching the wide houses go past, thick and grand, their windows swathed with velvet and satin and yellow light. It was not too late. She could tell Robbie that she ought to go back and ask if the maid would let her look for the pelerine.

"I saw you talking to Miss Barrett's sister," Robbie said.

"How did you memorize that poem so quickly?" She could not go back into the house and admit she had forgotten such an old ladyish, unfashionable shawl. "It seemed very deep, your conversation," she said, and the carriage was nearing the bridge already.

Robbie's hands in his yellow gloves lay at rest on his lap. He never lost things, and he never fidgeted. "She wanted to know if I am serious in my admiration," he said, "and I persuaded her, I hope, that I am."

"I think you persuaded everyone of that." She could never question him, but she wondered what it would do, how it would help or hinder him. Would people think it was a love affair or a poetic toasting, something like what Henrietta said poets were constantly doing in their poetry club? Perhaps people did that all the time, or writers did. "Do you often recite at dinners?"

"I don't. People do. Talfourd's is like that."

Hooves clopped unevenly on wet stones. Just as hunger had moved into something like its opposite before she could sit down to eat, Sarianna's fatigue had moved into restlessness.

Earlier, while Robbie had talked to Henrietta, Lenore Goss had been talking to Sarianna.

"Do you know," Sarianna had dared to ask Miss Goss, "what Miss Barrett's illness is?"

"It could be consumption," Miss Goss had said, "but they say it isn't. I sometimes think—this is very unscientific—that she was too brilliant to be a girl. But now that she's been sick so long, I fear the cure is part of her problem."

Sarianna had seen the cures tried on their mother. Bleeding didn't help. Leeches didn't help. Only rest did, but resting made her mother feel useless. That was not, however, the cure Miss Goss meant.

"One of the more curious effects of opium," Miss Goss had continued, "is the way it makes a small place seem infinitely large. You seem to travel, they say, in rooms that lead to other rooms, and all the rooms seem far grander and taller than any actual habitation, and all the while you're nowhere except the same little bed. You see people who aren't there and become quite nervous. I have heard that she is dependent on it, and I shouldn't wonder, being kept inside so much."

"Do you know Miss Goss?" Sarianna asked Robbie now, picking at the button on her glove, sickened by the idea of Miss Barrett taking opium.

Robbie grimaced. "I do. She is a good friend of Mr. Chorley's. I was surprised Mrs. Talfourd considered her fit company."

"Why?"

"She spent her youth in the West Indies. Not all of it, but too much."

Sarianna pulled too hard on the button, and it came free. "What does that mean?"

He was silent as the carriage turned a corner, rocking them both, and she dropped the button, which fell to the floor. Robbie felt around for it, and she did, too, her fingers brushing dirty water and bits of gravel. Finally, she said, "I found it," and tucked the little pearl in the deep pocket of her cloak.

"She behaves differently." Robbie said. "I don't disapprove of her. I only mean to say that others do."

"Do you mean differently in that she is outspoken?"

"And that she disdains the rules."

Robbie tried and failed to close the window, through which air that stank of something animal and wet and foul rolled in.

Sarianna put this aside for now. Miss Goss alarmed her, but she had a tantalizing air of being in charge of herself. Some of that, or all of that, might come from her money and her looks. Sarianna herself believed mostly in the safety of following rules. She asked, "Will you meet Miss Barrett, do you think?"

His face was unreadable as the lamplight turned it yellow, then it fell once again into deep shade.

"You have secrets now," she said. The sadness she felt was unexpected and disappointing. She clutched the tiny button like a seed inside her pocket.

"No, Rinny. I don't. I'm tired." He gave her a look of the old affection and sympathy, and then he rubbed at something on the finger of one of his gloves. "We are as united as ever."

The carriage bumped and clattered, and Sarianna tried to wrap her cloak tighter against the cold and to make a joke. "What if it's like meeting Mr. Dickens was for me? What if you curtsy when you meet the *great poetess*?"

Robbie took her hand the way he had always done, touching the place where the button had been and where the little threads still obtruded, holding on to nothing. She felt, for a second, the old alliance and calm, the assurance that her brother knew things that carried them both into a realm beyond material wealth and gossip and toil, and the carriage eased onto the smoother road of the towpath.

EIGHT

∞

THE FIRST THING Elizabeth heard when she awoke was George's voice in the hall.

"I intend to see her first," George said, "so I'll hire a cab and meet you."

"Why?" That voice was their father's.

"To see for myself."

"Don't make her think we believe her."

Believe whom? Flush leaped off Elizabeth's lap and ran to the closed door, his body rigid, his hackles up. What George said in response was inaudible because of Flush's barking. "Come, Flush," Elizabeth said, "I'll give you a little of this," and back he came, but her brother and father had descended. The voices came no more.

Elizabeth had on her plate the assortment her father had ordered she be given from now on: cold beef, two boiled eggs, fish, bread, and butter. She could eat nothing but the toast, as usual, and she gave a pinch of that and an egg to Flush before opening Aeschylus. The words she had translated yesterday before dinner were—ha—"Are any of those that have tasted pain, Alas! As sad as I?" And then Henrietta was bursting, as she liked to do, into the room.

"I sat by him!" she said proudly, pointing at the framed portrait of Mr. Browning. "Don't you want to know what we talked about?"

"If you talked about poetry," Elizabeth said.

Henrietta wrung Flush's ears with both hands and kissed him. "More than that, Ba."

Elizabeth stared at a Greek sentence to show she was indifferent.

"Ask me what he looks like," Henrietta said.

"No," Elizabeth said.

"His beard is thicker than that picture. His hair is much more lionish. His face-bones are thicker, not so prissy as that makes him seem."

Elizabeth had not thought he was prissy. "Could you eat any of this?"

"Ask me what the best part was."

"The best part would be him thinking I did not send you to talk me up."

"Why would he think that?" Henrietta said.

Elizabeth wondered if "Alas" needed the exclamation point.

"Never mind," Henrietta said, slicing the beef into spears. "I'm glad you don't care what Mr. Browning said or did last night." Henrietta swooped a rubbery hunk of meat into her mouth and took her time with it. "He quoted a line from one of your poems to me, and then—" she stopped to chew some more "—he told me what it meant. Which ordinarily would make me hate him."

Elizabeth wrote Greek letters on the side of her paper for *theta omicron omega*. The prettiest letter: *psi*. "Which poem?"

"Which do you think?"

Elizabeth began the second letter of ψυχή. "I don't know."

Henrietta cut the next piece of meat into a squarish blob. She salted it before she said, "It was the one about the swan's nest." To think of him, of all men, reading it. She petted Flush's ears anyway. "And the way he talked about it, Ba. I felt all my hair rise up like this. These little arm hairs here. They rose up and sighed."

Elizabeth breathed the letter χ in her mind as she drew it, *Hgee*.

"Can you guess which line he quoted?"

Elizabeth shook her head.

"It was something about a man on a steed. He recited, Ba. He recited two stanzas of your poem before everyone. The whole room. Spellbound."

Elizabeth had to dip her pen again to trace the long leg of *eta*, which was dipping its toe like a girl at her bath.

"You can't hide it from me," Henrietta said when she had swallowed. "You're glad. *But!*" She buttered a triangle of toast, dabbed jam on top, spread it out, and took a bite. "There is a worry. Future tense. They live in I can't remember where. On a farm. They make cider."

"Hatcham," Elizabeth said. She had written the name of the place on his letter. "And Kenyon told me about the cider. You were there."

"Did he? Well, there's nothing wrong with that, of course."

"No, there isn't."

"Except."

"There is no except. If he admires any small thing about my work, I have all the happiness I need." Elizabeth studied the dull dry words that made a dull dry Prometheus. Nothing about the play was alive because she did not know enough, had not lived enough, had not any crimes to expiate. "What you're talking about is not a consideration I will ever have."

Marriage, men, courtship, flirting. Any talk of such things made them both feel their father was listening. He had left the house—Elizabeth heard him go—and yet his ears never stopped hearing, his voice never stopped speaking, his disapproval of men and marriages never stopped being what it was: illogical and cruel to everyone except himself, benevolent and protective in his own mind. He couldn't help it, so she forgave him, and yet young men went on existing and believing in marriage, and they courted Henrietta all the time.

"Do you know who else was at the party?" Henrietta said softly. "Do you remember Miss Goss?"

"Yes," Elizabeth said.

Henrietta lowered her voice even more. "Georgie has seen her before. They seemed to know each other already, and I felt a certain—I don't know what it was—a certain bond between them." She did not tell Elizabeth that they left the ballroom together or that George came back alone, looking cross, or that she had asked Mr. Chorley if George admired any of the ladies present and Mr. Chorley, with a slight nod of his head in Miss Goss's direction, had seemed to confirm the guess she'd made. Anything that worried a normal person would grow to enormous size and menace in her sister's head. "You will find it incredible—I did—but Mr. Chorley said Miss Goss has become an abolitionist. Would you have thought it?"

"That's an improvement."

"And," Henrietta continued, whispering now, "she has a woman staying with her from Jamaica. Chorley hasn't seen her, but he said other people have. They walk every day in Russell Square, this woman and her little boy."

Elizabeth took this in as the clock began its chiming. "From where in Jamaica? Why?"

"I'm late," Henrietta said in a normal voice. "I'm to meet Surtees." Henrietta still blushed when she said his name. She would have to stop doing that if she wanted to pretend he was nothing but a dull cousin. "Shall I ask Wilson to bring you anything?"

"Coffee, please."

"I love you, dearest thing. And so," she dropped her voice back to a whisper, "does Mr. Browning."

"I love you," Elizabeth whispered as she left, "but you are wrong."

Flush lay with his head on Elizabeth's chest and breathed his hot, meaty breath on her, whimpering and trembling his legs in sleep. She allowed herself to think of it and be pleased: Robert Browning had said her words aloud to a room of people. Her words in his mouth, his mind caring what her mind had made.

NINE

∞

GEORGE CAME IN to her room unexpectedly moments later, fresh-smelling and full of some sort of worry, perhaps connected to the person he had been to see and the fact that he wasn't supposed to make her think he believed her. He pulled the blind back to look at the cold roofs, every thread of his fine coat illuminated, his whiskers neat, his chin sharp. "I saw your Mr. Browning at the party last night."

"Not mine," she said very softly, hoping he would take the hint and lower his own voice, too.

George went to her bookcase next and pulled one of her new books out, opened it, and began to leaf. When people did that, it always made her uncomfortable. She didn't like to see them reading her poems.

"I thought it had his name in the title," George said.

"What do you mean?" she said, her voice still quieter than his.

"The one they say has his name in it."

He kept turning the pages, so she told him the poem was "Lady Geraldine's Courtship." George did not read poetry, but now he was reading it in front of her, probably because of Mr. Browning's recitation.

Mr. Browning looked serene in his portrait, and he did not have prissy cheekbones. She could, without much effort, feel his whiskers, coarse and springy, under her fingertips. The edge of his bearded jaw, where the hair stopped and his neck turned soft and naked, like a boy's. Warmer still, the skin of his chest where, perhaps, there was more hair, thick as his whiskers. Sometimes, in the flickering light of a candle and a crumbling fire, Mr. Browning's head could seem to turn and show her the other half of his face, the fullness of his mouth and chin. Certain lines of his she had committed to memory, in part to study them, to understand what effect they had on her and why.

> The castle at its toils, the lapwings love
> To glean among at grape-time. . . .

The image was of birds—the same kind she had seen at harvest time at Hope End—descending among farmers bringing in the last of the grapes. She wasn't sure if she loved it because of the image itself—the landscape, the birds, the castle—or the memory, or the way the words sounded: *lapwings love to glean among*. If called upon to recite lines of Mr. Browning's at a dinner, what but confusion would come of her saying those words? She would rather say them, she thought, to him alone.

"George," she said. "What's this I hear about Miss Goss?"

He looked up. "What did you hear?"

"She has become an abolitionist, Addles said. Is that true?"

He went back to reading. After a moment, he coughed and said, "I think so."

"What does she do? Besides write for the *Post*?"

So impassive was George. So unperturbed. His whiskers were a pair of bookends, a pair of hedgerows, a screen hiding thoughts.

"Tell her I want to help."

"Help whom?"

He kept his eyes on her book, and he turned the page.

"The abolitionists, George."

"I am unlikely to have the chance to tell her that," he said. "And I must go. You're keeping me from reading poetry." He closed the book, leaned over to kiss her, and asked if she needed him to take any letters down. "Any for Mr. Browning, for example," he said in such a low voice, and with such a small change of expression, that she studied him for signs of approval.

"Not just now," she said, and he took her book of poems out the door.

TEN

∞

EARLIER THAT MORNING, in the largest of the large houses facing Russell Square, Mary Ann Hawthorne had not been at ease.

"One of them is coming here," Miss Lenore said. "His younger brother, George. Did Sam talk about his family with you?"

Mary Ann's son was eating everything on his plate and eyeing hers, so Mary Ann pushed her plate toward him. "Yes," she said. "Henrietta the most."

"I saw her at the party last night. Would you like more bread, David?"

Mary Ann's son nodded, and Miss Lenore sent for more bread.

Each afternoon, they went to a park in the center of the square. It would have been a provision ground at home, but here grew trees and bushes that bore no fruit. The park was private and you had to have a key, which Miss Lenore carried in a red velvet bag. Sometimes other people walked in the cold and they always stared at her. Women pushed hand carriages, and David ran back and forth on the yellow grass, the only Black child who ever, it seemed, was let into the park by a key in a red velvet bag.

Sometimes Mary Ann closed her eyes to remember how it felt to be warm. *This is why*, she thought each frigid, foggy day. *This is why the English took Jamaica.*

"Mama," David said. "I'm done."

His nose was running, and he wanted to go to the park. He did not want to meet Mr. Barrett and prove to people with his green eyes that his father was their relative.

"Mrs. Young will bring you anything you need," Miss Lenore said to Mary Ann. "And I will receive Mr. Barrett."

Mary Ann nodded at the continued strangeness of a white woman bringing her anything, and the strangeness of Miss Lenore thinking it was not strange, and she dreaded the look Mrs. Young would give her when Miss Lenore was not there.

Mary Ann watched David hold his hands near the white parrot, but not all the way in the cage. "'David,'" he told the bird. "Say 'David.'"

"Remember not to put your fingers in," Lenore said. Whenever she sat with David and his mother, she felt the pressure of her sacred duty, the finding of it, and the doing of it, but without having her friend Jessie here to tell her what that meant:

> Please receive this woman and her child in the name of the Lord and do your sacred duty by them.
> In His Holy Name,
> Mrs. Jessie Waddell

That was the message Mary Ann had arrived with from Jamaica. The maid had brought the scrap of paper in, and Lenore had asked what the woman and child looked like.

"They are Black, Miss."

"Is the child a boy or a girl?"

"A boy."

"How old?"

"Not five, I would say, Miss."

"Is it hers?"

"I would think, Miss."

"Based on?"

"His skin, Miss."

In Jamaica, when Lenore left, she had told Jessie she longed to do something, and now Jessie was testing her to see if she meant it. She had sent

Jessie some of her published articles—one for an American paper about
post-slavery Jamaica, one for the *Post* on inadequate housing for apprentices
on former plantations—but had received no reply.

"Send her in," Lenore had told the maid.

New visitors tended to look upward in awe the first time, as in a cathedral, and take in the brass rail of the upper story, accessed by a black ser-
pentine stair, and then to notice that the rows of glass cases on the lower
story were filled with bugs. The Jamaican woman and her child stepped
uncertainly forward, eyes flitting from the specimen boxes to the stuffed
sable and the live parrot, and they stopped. The woman's beauty was a radi-
ant thing, both quiet and unquiet. She wore a red and purple dress, a yellow
turban, and a little straw hat—normal for Jamaica but strange for London;
how people must stare at her, Lenore thought.

"You have come from Mrs. Waddell?" Lenore asked.

"Yes."

The boy had extraordinary eyes. They shone like mirrors.

Lenore motioned to a little red couch, but they didn't sit. "Are you hungry?" Lenore asked the boy. What his eyes meant made Lenore more awake
than she had been for days. "Well, *I'm* hungry," Lenore said, "so please—"
she turned to the maid "—bring all the salts and all the sweets. What is
your name?" she asked the boy, trying for warmth but sounding false in her
own ears.

He looked to his mother, and his mother nodded. Her nod was a sideways thing, somewhat on the diagonal, a way of not quite acceding.

"David," the boy said.

"Ah, my favorite hero. David what?"

"That's what we have come to see you about," his mother said. "His
name."

"I see." Lenore felt an unwillingness to go straight in that direction.
"What news do you have of the Waddells?"

"Reverend Waddell has gone to a new mission. In Nigeria."

"Without Jessie?"

"Mrs. Jessie has gone to the Lord."

"Oh, no," Lenore said. Of the white women Lenore had known in Jamaica, Jessie was the only one whose death could pain her. Jessie was too young to have died already, and too good. Lenore sat still for a moment, composing herself. "Was it the accident? Complications?"

"Yes." Jessie had been thrown from a carriage on the way through Lucea. The recovery had been slow, that much Lenore's brother had written to say.

"Did you know her well?"

The woman gave her a forward nod this time, not the diagonal half-yes. "Reverend and Mrs. Jessie took care of me while my father worked."

"Who is your father?"

"A carpenter at Cinnamon Hill."

"He worked for the elder Mr. Sam Barrett?"

"Yes."

The maid came in with a tray and Lenore smiled at David. "I eat the most enormous lunches," Lenore told the boy. "But I can only enjoy them if people help me. Are you a helpful sort of person in that way, David?"

The boy nodded. He didn't smile, but somewhere in the deep cave of his not-smiling she thought a smile might exist.

"Let's put that to the test."

Lenore sliced the ham, opened the mustard pot, and began to prepare a half-salty, half-sugary plate. She told him there was a small table, just his height, over by the parrot, and if he wanted, he could take his plate and cup over there. Her friends' children were terribly choosy and tended to hate almost everything, but when she gave David a sticky green sugarplum, an iced biscuit, and two slices of ham, he sat down at the table and devoured it all.

"Do you know him?" Lenore asked the woman. She pointed at the portrait of her brother in a blue militia jacket, tight flannel trousers, and riding boots. The foliage around him was tropical, not English, and two figures in the background were bare-breasted slaves.

"He might have been at church?"

"Definitely not."

"That is a militia coat."

"It is."

"Every gentleman have . . ." the woman stopped. "Has the same."

"That's true," Lenore said. "Regrettably. Well, I suppose we ought to talk about your name, then. What is it?"

"Mary Ann Hawthorne," she said.

Lenore nodded. This did not answer the question of David's name. "I wonder if you might also trust me with the reason Mrs. Jessie wanted to send you here."

"For David," Mary Ann said simply. "That he might go to school."

There were planters who sent both their legitimate and their illegitimate sons to England for an education. But not lately. And not often.

"When did you arrive?"

"Sunday last."

"Where are you staying?"

"With a woman who gave money to the missionaries."

"Did Mrs. Waddell say the father's family would educate your boy?"

Mary Ann nodded. "She said the English want to help us now."

This stretched out between them and it was such a beautiful idea that Lenore didn't want to say it was only that: an idea.

"Mrs. Jessie said to come here first. She said you wanted to help us." Mary Ann felt in her skirt for something. She found a way into a pocket and drew out a bag sewn of blue oznabrig, the cloth meted out to slaves. Whatever was in the blue bag was heavy, and Lenore thought it might be coins, but it was a watch on a chain.

"His," Mary Ann said.

"Whose?"

"The father's." Mary Ann held it out to her, and Lenore felt the heavy warmth of it in her hand for a few seconds before she turned it over and saw the back was engraved with the gryphon rampant. Lenore had seen it on all their things at the house in Cinnamon Hill: brass buttons, headboards, china, trunks.

"A Barrett," Lenore said. That meant it could be Sam or Stormie. It could be one of the cousins who claimed they had been cheated by the legitimate heirs. It could even be Sam's uncle, who had been living at Cinnamon Hill before he died, and who had revealed, by a gift in his will, the existence of a mistress—the sort of admission many planters made and people liked to gossip about. At the end of the watch chain there was a locket, and inside the locket was a braid of hair coiled like a brittle baby snake.

It was not necessarily Sam's.

"I hope the family will receive you, and do what is just," Lenore said.

"It opens," Mary Ann said of the watch.

David came over just then with his empty plate.

"Would you like more?" Lenore asked in her friendliest voice, and she pointed to the tray, which was still full. Mary Ann had taken nothing. "Choose whatever you like best," Lenore told him, and she watched him take one sticky green candy plum. "Those are my favorite," she said, and he started to put it back. "No, what I mean is, please eat them all. I can't digest them anymore, so you must give me the pleasure of seeing them enjoyed."

He checked with his mother, who nodded, and he took his plate back to where the parrot stood on its swing, saying not a word, but regarding the boy with the eye of a schoolmaster.

She must open the watch now; there was no help for it. She depressed the button, but Mary Ann said, "Wait. Let me."

Mary Ann held it level, like a pot that had something liquid inside, and she opened it. Lying on the glass was a scrap of folded paper, quite worn, and Mary Ann unfolded it to show a few words, or marks in the shape of words.

"What does it say?" Lenore asked, and when she brought it closer to her eyes she saw the language was Greek. Well, she knew one thing. Sam Barrett would never have written something in Greek and kept it in his watch. He was as bad at Greek and Latin as she was.

"It says, 'Odysseus came home,'" Mary Ann said.

Lenore scanned the shelves for the toy she meant to show David, sure that it would intrigue and distract him.

"David?" He was still eating candied plums. She felt a kinship with him when he turned. "I have something to show you." Lenore motioned for them both to follow her to a corner of the enormous room. "Let me see your hands, David."

His hands were very small and bashful when he held them out, as if they were creatures that had no protection.

"Here is a handkerchief to wipe them off."

She poured water on it, handed it to him, and kept walking, trusting him to rub at the honey from the candied plums.

"In the war," Lenore said, "my father lived at Plymouth. French soldiers were brought there by the thousands and put in prison. You can imagine that they had a bad time of it, though my father always claimed that the men were delighted to be taken by the English. The Spanish and the Portuguese prisons were worse, he said, but you know how people are about their own country. Blind!"

It might easily be the old uncle Barrett who was the father of this child, she thought. Or Stormie, despite how sympathetically he spoke of the apprentices and their need for land and money. It seemed to Lenore that English men in Jamaica felt themselves unobserved and unchecked and utterly free. And the first thing they often did with that freedom was to find a woman or two.

Lenore leaned down to open a cupboard. Inside the cupboard was something that looked like a white castle or a white church—a square around a sort of tower that seemed to have spires—and lying inside the miniature white building that had no roof were carved figures—crude but recognizable as men—lying askew or leaning like clothespins on various railings. It was only when Lenore picked up the structure—very carefully—and set it down on the thick Brussels carpet that the window light was bright enough to reveal the blade.

"But these prisoners were allowed to make things and sell them, and by selling them, they made enough money to improve their lives a bit, to buy warmer clothes, better food, paper, and ink. Because the prisoners came from France, and France had just finished its revolution, they often carved these."

"It's a guillotine. A toy one. Carved from—I find this part touching, too—mutton bones. And see, here are the soldiers, the revolutionaries, I suppose you would say, and here is—" she held out a soldier that looked broken, only he wasn't a soldier. His coat had more buttons and his shoes had square buckles. The place where his head would have been was empty. "This is King Louis! And here is King Louis's head." She found a little round bit of bone that had hair, two eyes, and a nose painted on it.

David knelt down and began to line up the soldiers.

"Don't smack them together or all their heads will likely fall off, and then who will run the country?" she said to David.

Mary Ann's expression was somber. "Do not break it," she told him.

David touched the ivory lever that allowed the ivory blade to slide slowly down, but he didn't make it slide down. He picked up King Louis' head, studied it, and set it on the carpet. It occurred to her that he might have no idea what a guillotine was and that she didn't want to tell him. If only the French prisoner had carved some halved cabbages out of mutton bones, or toy timber split neatly in two. She should ask someone to do that. There were scriveners still, weren't there?

"We will be right over here, David," Lenore said, and when they had been seated, she felt in her throat an obstruction. She swallowed just the same. "Which Barrett," she finally asked Miss Hawthorne, "gave you his watch?"

ELEVEN

∞

GEORGE'S SHINY HAT was perfectly correct, as were all his clothes, and
Lenore wished, for a second, that he would slouch into a chair and put his
boots on a cushion as Sam had, but that was perverse of her. George made
such an effort to be obedient to the rules, and wasn't that what she wanted
men to do? To obey the rules?

"Are you all right?" George asked.

"Yes, thank you."

"Did you tell her I was coming?"

"I did."

"What did she say?"

"What did you expect her to say?"

"Please, Nora. I don't see why you're angry."

"Do sit down."

George took off his hat, but he remained near the window. "I thought
you said she came all this way to ask for our help. To show us why she is
entitled to it. Do I have it wrong?"

"No. But I would rather she didn't have to go through it twice. Now she
will have to tell you, and then your father."

"If I believe her, she won't. I will talk to my father."

Instead of sending the maid, she went to their rooms herself. She hoped
Mary Ann and David would be asleep and then she could tell George they
could not be disturbed, although he would think they were stalling and
doubt them even more. She knocked, and she received no answer, and she

knocked again, and after a polite pause, she opened the door, saying, "Miss Hawthorne?"

A fire was burning, as she'd directed, but the room was empty, and their cloaks were gone from the hooks on the wall.

She found the maid and asked if Miss Hawthorne had gone out.

"Yes, Miss. She said she left something on the table for you."

Beside a washbasin and a towel, neatly folded, sat the watch and two letters in Sam's hand. Lenore collected the watch and stared for a moment at the letters before deciding to leave them alone. Miss Hawthorne would need to keep something in reserve in case George did not remember Sam's watch or find it significant.

George was not happy to see that Lenore returned by herself.

"They have gone out," she told him.

"You gave them a chance to avoid my questions," George said.

"I didn't. I gave her notice so she could prepare, and she's not ready, I think. She left this for me to show you."

She held out the heavy watch, the chain and locket coiled beside it, and George took them. The gryphon rampant on a golden curve reflected her window, then George's face. Once again the paper inscription was exposed to air, lifted between fingers, examined for meaning.

"That part seemed odd to me," Lenore said. "For Sam."

"Is this what you meant when you said 'letters'?"

Lenore shook her head.

"And?"

"She must show those herself. Will you ask your father to see her now?"

"Because she has Sam's watch? No. Beg her to come and see me. Tell her this is the last opportunity."

"I don't know where she is, and we both know it isn't."

"The watch belongs to us. My father asked for it when Stormie brought Sam's things. We were very distressed."

"Well, now you know Sam gave it to her."

"She has no way of proving that. To you or to anyone else." He put the watch into his pocket and did not explain that Elizabeth had written the Greek sentence. He remembered it the minute he saw the watch. Elizabeth had asked them all—brothers and sisters—for the longest hair possible, and she had commissioned the braid, "made of everyone who loved Sam," she said, a charm to hold him close and bring him back. The Greek words were hers. "You'll come home," she had said, "like the great Odysseus."

"I hope I will not be gone as many years as that," Sam had said to her. He'd been out drinking, from the smell of him, but they had all pretended not to notice. George, in fact, had thought it natural, given the long journey Sam faced.

"Did George really contribute?" Sam had continued. "I don't believe it. I'll bet you gave Ba a horse's hair instead, Georgie. If I don't come back, it's your fault for ruining the Greek spell."

He did not come back. That's what the watch said; the spell was ruined or, more logically, had no power over death.

"Until someone is ready to show me the letters," George said to Lenore, "I'll tell my father I've seen no proof."

TWELVE

∞

WHEN LENORE HAD been in Jamaica for a year and had begun to write secretly for the American press, her brother Andrew announced, "Sam Barrett has come over."

She'd pretended that meant nothing. She wiped her mouth, cut a piece of salt fish, and ate it.

"Did you hear me?" her brother asked.

"Come over to Little Egypt, you mean?"

"To Cinnamon Hill. From England. With his self-righteous little brother." Andrew was spearing hunks of papaya with his hunting knife.

"Which brother is that?"

"Stormie."

Her memory of Stormie was a blank, but all the little brothers were a blank.

"Stormie is the one who said Parliament ought to give compensation to the slaves instead of to the planters." Twenty million pounds had been paid to the planters in 1834, when the slaves were freed. The seeds of the papaya were greenish in the morning light and as slippery as frog eggs on Lenore's plate.

"Good," Lenore said. "I would love to meet him."

"Yes, you can whip each other into a righteous froth."

"It's odd that Mr. Barrett would send him. Why not send Brozy-Bro, I wonder?" They both found the Barrett family nicknames a bit much. Edward was the eldest, and had been in Jamaica before, not without troubles, but who could come to Jamaica without troubles?

"Why?"

"Nothing. I just thought it was the eldest's turn."

"Brozy-Bro's with the great poet*ess* at the seaside, so they sent the next. Sam has been sick, apparently, since he arrived."

"How sick?"

"I don't know. The last time he came here, he was sick as well. I don't see why they sent him again if the climate is too much for him."

"When has Mr. Barrett ever done the logical thing?"

"Indeed. I'm glad we can have common ground on that. We're to call on them, is why I mention it."

"I thought you said the roads are closed."

"They are open again. The militia has found the man they're looking for."

"And done what?"

"I don't know, Lenore, and don't ask. And don't write about it. Not even in your diary."

She asked the cook to make that tincture of hibiscus flowers, the one with ginger in it, for Sam, whom she would ask about the militia as soon as they were alone, and then, if she wanted to, she *would* write about it.

They set out the next morning with the hibiscus tincture, a basket of fish, and a bottle of Little Egypt rum. The dew dropped from Ackee trees. Green forest unlike any forest of home grew thick on either side of the red clay lane. It attracted and frightened her in equal measure.

"I have a proposition," her brother said.

Lenore was glad they were in an open carriage so she could look straight up and watch the birds. It was, as always, a warm day, and when the sun rose a little more she would need to open her umbrella. "A proposition," she said.

"As you are forever saying, we must seek radical change."

"I thought you were against radical change."

"The kind of change we need is not blaming and apologizing. We need consolidation. To bear the cost of labor, planters must have more acreage."

When Andrew talked about labor and consolidation, she always wanted to change his terms. "Cost of labor" ought to include housing and low-cost land. "Consolidation" ought to mean workers owning what they sold. There was a path to the side of the road, and it led upward to a patch of sunlight. When Andrew was not around, she liked to take such footpaths into the forest behind Little Egypt, and, waving a stick in front of herself, she would lift the webs of spiders and gently place them to either side so she could pass through. The spiders became invisible again among the ferns as she stood very still and felt what it was to hide.

"My idea is that you should marry one of them," Andrew said. "I think it's our best hope."

"Marry one of them?"

"The Barretts are not universally hated. None of *their* houses were burned down. If Little Egypt and Cinnamon Hill were joined . . ."

"Is that why we're paying a call?"

"You're always saying how isolated you are. Always scribbling in your abuse diary and sending mysterious letters to America. Mother told me how taken you were with Sam when you were at Hope End that time, and the idea fermented in my brain overnight."

"I can't marry one of them, even if they asked me. I don't want to stay here for the rest of my life."

"Why not? There is so much for you to criticize! So much reform for you to recommend."

"You don't *do* any of the things that I recommend."

"Because I have been here much longer than you have, and you recommend the silliest things." When she had told Andrew about her grand scheme, a utopia in which the races were equal and Little Egypt was held in common, he had laughed. "You couldn't kill and cook a goat, Nora. Or wash clothes in the river and wring them out with your soft little hands. Or cut the heads off our dinner fish. And if you say that you could, which I can tell you're about to do, believe me when I say you couldn't cut cane for a single week without killing yourself."

Instead of reviving that discussion now, she said she preferred to be in England, where she could pay people better wages.

"And what, dear girl, do you think enables you to pay those better wages? West Indian money. West Indian money builds the houses, funds the banks, sails the ships, sweetens the tea."

The carriage smacked into a hole, and she lost her balance for a moment. They had reached the edge of the forest. The green infinity of trees and vines opened wide for a view of the limitless sea.

"We ought to sell," Lenore said. "Not join up with some other family so we have even more people to manage."

"No one buys a sinking ship, Nora. Selling now, while Cuba and Brazil and the American states are still making cheap sugar with slaves, is impossible. The land here is almost worthless."

The sea was violet blue in the distance, a vivid green up close. A light rain began to fall through sunshine and she opened her umbrella. That such a beautiful, bright place should be full of misery never ceased to confound her. Why could they not all live as though in Eden, picking fruit, cooking fish, bathing in the warm sea? Why must she wear so many layers of clothing, the long skirts and petticoats that were comforting in the cold of England but were suffocating here? She wondered what Sam thought about it all. At fourteen he had been the most mischievous of the Barretts, an irresistible clown and mimic. Perhaps he would like her idea of a utopia where Little Egypt became Little Eden.

Here and there on the island a banyan or cotton tree commanded everything around it. They were approaching one of these as the road ascended, a soaring, thick-limbed ficus. Beside and far below the enormous tree was a gray house—the rudimentary kind, she quickly saw, made of limestone, a plain rough box covered with lichen and moss, a hundred years old or more. But the tree on its lawn was the gem of the property, the part that made it seem consequential and grand. Roots wider than her own waist crept along the grass and ducked down into the ground. Far above her head, in the colossal limbs, leaves rustled, and sunlight split into streaks of gold.

When the carriage stopped, she saw two men on the verandah. One was obviously Sam: tall and disorderly, his curly hair still curly but much longer now, and with a beard. Stormie was clean-shaven, shorter, and neatly dressed, the less animated of the two, watching with a pleasant expression that was neither a smile nor a frown. Lenore prided herself on not caring if a man were handsome, and Stormie was not handsome, but he had a way of holding himself, she could see right away, that made him seem steady and reliable.

"Well, look at that," Andrew said. "I should think you'd be glad to have either one of them. At your age, especially."

She glared and he said he was joking.

The whiskers—why was she surprised to see Sam had a beard and whiskers? The smile was the same, though, a little amused, a little devious, though it might have been the lightness of his green eyes that made him arresting. Stormie had a cleft in his chin.

Sam reached into the carriage to help her out, and the touch of his hand disturbed her. "Too many years have passed, Miss Goss."

"Look at your beard," she said.

"Fine, isn't it?"

Stormie said he was sorry to say he did not remember her.

"I think you were very small," she said.

The two qualities Lenore had resolved to nurture in herself as a West Indian resident were to be humble and obliging. The Barretts' servants came to take the reins, their trunks, the basket of fish, the rum and hibiscus tonic. She was supposed to pretend not to notice them, but it was her intent to do the opposite of that. "Good afternoon," she said to the old woman who took her carpetbag, and she said it again to the middle-aged man who took her trunk. "Thank you," she said as they walked away.

Andrew pretended, as at Little Egypt, that the luggage moved itself.

They stood on the verandah together, admiring the view of the sea. Clouds had formed on the horizon, and she couldn't help being stunned by their size and the majestic way they floated in unison at the edge of the world. "What do you think of free Jamaica?" she asked Sam.

"You haven't even asked after their health," Andrew chided her.

"True. I've brought you the nicest tonic, Sam. I heard you have been ill."

"That is nothing but gossip," Sam said. "I'm very well."

"It's made with hibiscus flower. Look."

She found where the bottles had been placed in the shade and showed him the ruby color.

"We can mix it with rum," Andrew said, "Little Egypt's strongest. Which is the best tonic of all, I think you'll find."

A green glass decanter had been placed on a small table, and to Lenore's relief, Sam didn't summon a servant to do what he could do perfectly well himself. He thanked Andrew for his rum, held it to the light, tasted it, and poured three of the goblets half full. He hesitated over the fourth glass and asked if the lady would prefer sherry.

"You'll find the lady drinks rum," she said. "Having been here a whole year."

Sunlight glittered on the wide expanse of sea, so wide that it felt as if there could be no England anywhere. A breeze lifted hair on her bare arms. Sam lifted his glass and said, "To the isle of our hearts."

"Is that ironic?" Lenore asked.

"I am never ironic," Sam said, "about the heart."

"Drink up, dear sister," Andrew said, and he swallowed the whole pour.

A dog crept into the yard, its spaniel nose lifted hopefully, warily, and Lenore watched it as she took a sip. He or she—she could not tell which yet—was soft and spotted with white and brown, the sort of dog she liked most, though this one was quite dirty.

"Shall we sit outdoors?" Sam asked. Carved wooden chairs were arranged near small tables covered with ironed white cloths, and as soon as Stormie and Andrew began talking about yield and wages, Lenore yearned to get away. She saw that the chairs matched one another and had been carved with the gryphon rampant.

"Do you have trouble getting them to work?" Andrew asked Stormie.

The old woman who had taken Lenore's bag was sitting just inside the open door and other workers were nearby as well.

"Will you show me around?" Lenore asked Sam, before Stormie could reply.

"I would be delighted."

"How are you settling in?" she asked as they walked away. Behind them, Stormie tried to answer her brother without criticizing his own staff, and she heard that Stormie had a stammer.

"The house is rather rough and plain," Sam said, "but I love the views beyond anything. And how I'm never cold, not even at night. It can almost feel like paradise if I forget everything I have to do in order to succeed."

"How does Stormie like it?"

"Truthfully?"

"Isn't that how we used to talk?"

"He can't decide whether he wishes he could run things without me or he wishes he had never come."

"Without you? Why?"

"He doesn't like to make anyone work, and work is what we're here to make people do."

"You disagree about wages?"

"And other things. It's natural to fight a bit, though. My father sent us both so we would compete to please him. It's still a thousand times better than being in London, don't you think?"

"It would be if I didn't feel hatred directed at me everywhere I look."

"Everywhere?"

"Don't you feel resented? For being in charge, still, and not having made things better?"

"Perhaps I'm too obtuse to notice."

"You were never obtuse."

They had now walked out of range of Stormie and Andrew's conversation, and all they could hear was the wind in the palms and the soft thud of ficus berries falling out of trees. She watched the sharp edge of the sea and the clouds that were gliding away and she felt happier than she had been since she set foot on the wharf at Falmouth. "I think I should warn you there is a diplomatic reason for our visit. Andrew has a scheme for me."

"Does he."

"He thinks I should marry you. Or Stormie. Either one, doesn't matter which. For the economic benefit."

"How are you to choose between us?"

"A duel, I think. That's my preference."

"He's a terrible shot."

"Ah, how sad."

"So you ought to choose me outright and save him."

She tried to smile but found she could not. His body near her was too unsettling, his eyes too searching, the scenery too exquisite. "Perhaps you could charge at one another on horses," she said.

"He can't ride that well, either. You must be merciful and say you have chosen me."

Sam reached out to the trunk of a pimiento tree and scraped the bark with his fingernail, loosening the scent of cinnamon. Even as she wanted to go back to England and live in her house and write articles about what she had once seen, but was forced to look at no longer, she also wanted to walk on the grounds of a great house and flirt quietly with a handsome man. Smoke rose from the cookhouse nearby: part coconut oil, sweet and rich, part meat, savory and enticing. The cook didn't raise her face, but went on stirring what was in her pot, the smoke rising all around her, sweat visible on her arms and forehead, fish guts on a slab beside her, a goat grazing in the grass. There was no shade and no seat except an upturned bucket. Lenore looked away, reminded of what Andrew had said about goats and fish heads. "How long are you and Stormie staying this time?" she asked. A shift in the wind carried the scent of Sam to her: tobacco, meat smoke, skin. His shoulders were a bit hunched, the curve of his chest almost concave.

"A year, I suppose. I won't stay here permanently unless I am given the attorneyship."

"Given it by whom?" she asked.

"My father."

She stood with him and listened to the palms clacking. It was her favorite sound, better even than the crashing of the waves.

"What if he picks Stormie?"

"I don't think he will. Stormie is a radical. He despises the society here, so he makes too many enemies."

"Ah, then as a radical myself I will have to marry him."

"You know, you already promised to marry me," Sam said. "You accepted my token when you were thirteen. You can't go back on it now."

"Is a mere brooch binding?" She still had the cameo he had given her, had even brought it with her to Cinnamon Hill. It was in her trunk, at the ready for reminiscence.

"Ah, the lady wants more jewelry. It is always thus."

His body was gaunt and somehow luxurious, his eyes, when he turned them on her, sure of what he could accomplish. He reached out for her hand, and her hand let itself be taken. He held it loosely, with all his old confidence. She tried not to feel that her hand, and all of her, was attracted to the wrong brother.

"Stay here, Lenore. You might learn to enjoy being a planter's wife."

"Only if the planter promised not to have a housekeeper. All of that pretending about what the housekeepers keep—I couldn't."

The breeze picked up in the palm trees, whacking fronds against each other, while a John Crow bird circled, making a slow arc with silvery, outstretched wings.

"Who would make the bed and set the table?"

"Not someone with a little girl who looks like my husband," she said, "and another on the way."

"Who says that's the kind of husband Stormie would be," he said, touching her palm softly with his index finger. "There are exceptions, you know."

"Can you think of one?" she asked.

"Reverend Waddell."

"But the reverend isn't a planter," she said. "He doesn't own anything."

"Stormie doesn't own anything either. Nor do I."

"But you will," she said. "You just said that is your ambition."

From where they stood, she could see the back of Stormie's head and her brother's profile. They had taken out pipes and were smoking them on the lush green lawn. They were still talking peacefully, it appeared, though if Stormie actually believed in reparations for the former slaves, peaceful discourse with her brother could not last long.

"Look," Sam said, wrapping both arms around her waist. "Look at the tree and tell me what you see there."

"Is this a game like finding figures in clouds?"

"Yes."

She sank back against him like a piece of silver in a satin-lined box.

"What do *you* see?" she asked. He kissed the back of her neck, and she knew she should pull away, but the sea glittered, the palms clacked, and the air was as warm as her skin.

"On the left is the man," Sam said, pointing. "On the right, the woman."

The gray mass of the ficus was shaped, she saw, like conjoined lovers. Emerging from one trunk was the sculptural likeness of a male leaning back, and the other trunk—how plain it was, how strangely deliberate and unashamed—the other trunk was a female arching back in rapture, and the bark that covered her vegetal body was as thin and taut as skin. You could see torsos and legs and but no heads or necks—those were somehow buried inside the tree—and the place where their bodies united was hollowed and curved like hips, thighs, rounded buttocks, even the beginning of the man's sex was there. The shapes were so anatomically precise that she thought everyone must see it the instant they approached the tree from this side of the lawn.

"I'm surprised no one has cut it down," she said.

"They can't," he said, his mouth a millimeter from hers. "That would be immoral."

She wanted what he wanted. His mouth grazed hers as she caught a movement in the upper window of the house. "We're being watched."

Sam turned to look, but whoever it was had stepped away.

Lenore squinted into the bright sunlight—she did nothing but squint in Jamaica—and said, "We ought to go back and see if my brother has begun to disagree with your brother."

"May I come to you?" he asked. "Tonight?"

Was that what happened here? You felt as bold as that? "No," she said. She stepped away from him and went to the tree, getting close enough for the illusion of human embrace to disappear, for what she saw to be tree knots, gray bark, and rising branches. "We must go back," she repeated, and she hurried away from him across the green lawn, feeling the ficus berries round and hard under her feet.

THIRTEEN

∞

ELIZABETH HID THE letter she was writing when George put his head into the room, so he would see "Act I, scene ii" instead of "Dear Mr. Browning."

"You look well," George said. "Is the translation going better?"

"Not at the moment."

"May I see?" He read what was on her desk.

"It's very rough, of course."

"May I take it all and read it tonight?"

"I would be miserable if you did."

He stepped away. "Do you remember Sam's watch?"

George never mentioned Sam to her. Henrietta liked to talk about him—it made her feel better—but George never brought him up.

"Yes."

"You don't think he would have given it away, do you? Someone has come over from St. James, and she brought it. A woman who worked at the house."

"Like Treppy? How thrilling! When can I meet her?" Treppy, born to a slave and a Jamaican planter named Trepsack, had become the ward of their great-uncle at Cinnamon Hill and then their grandmother's companion, helping to raise first their father and then each of them.

"Not like Treppy, no. And you can't meet her."

"But where did you meet her?"

"I haven't yet. She's staying with Miss Goss."

"How does Miss Goss know her?"

"From the time she spent at Little Egypt. A bit ago."

That was the freedom Elizabeth would take for herself if she were well. To go see for herself and tell the world what she witnessed and did, rather than just what she read. "I will write to Miss Goss, then. Did you know she's become a friend of Mrs. Stowe?"

"That wouldn't help," George said, without answering the question.

"With what?"

"Determining how the woman came to have Sam's watch."

"Can't you simply ask her?" Elizabeth said.

"I went to Miss Goss's to do that, and the woman left to avoid seeing me."

"Try again, George. You will feel whether she is telling the truth."

"You trust people too much."

"Or maybe I merely trust you," she'd said.

"Don't write to her until I've sorted it out. Promise me." He'd waited for her to promise, and then he'd gone away.

FOURTEEN

∞

"Who is Miss Goss?" Sarianna's mother asked. She held a letter in her hand.

The beets were too hot but Sarianna pushed the skins off anyway, working fast so the meat, round and plump, couldn't burn her. Her hands were bright red and her fingernails were purple. She took satisfaction in the way the knobby root broke free and slid into the bucket for chicken feed. The bright naked beets gleamed in the clay bowl when she finished and she didn't mind the smell of them, for once, sweet as blood. The fire crackled, eating up the apple wood, and her mother went to sit by it, leaving the letter from Miss Goss on the table. Outside the world was a square with a tree inside it: the window wet with rain.

It had been a month since Talfourd's party, but it seemed longer, time to read the end of *Martin Chuzzlewit* aloud to her mother, for the ice to freeze and melt on the canal and in the orchard, for her to recall afresh, each and every morning, that she must think of how duty to her parents sufficed. A life of single blessedness was a full life indeed. She'd heard it said and had copied it into her diary. Then she'd added quotation marks and closed the book.

Sarianna washed her hands too quickly and dried them not enough, so the letter got wet where Miss Goss had written *Please come for tea on Thursday at two.*

"Well, Rin?" her mother asked. "Have I heard of Miss Goss before?"

"She is a friend of Robbie's. She read the book I mentioned."

"Which?"

"Miss Barrett's."

"I should like to hear that poem again. About Lady Geraldine and Robbie."

Sarianna rubbed at the pink dye in the whorls of her fingertips. The quartered beets were beginning to dry, their hearts like fine-grained wood.

"Is that all she said?" her mother asked.

Sarianna was weighing how to answer without lying when her mother said, "The pelerine is not in the cupboard. I was going to freshen it for Sunday. Did you put it in your room?"

The part of the sky that was bright blue was dissolving into a cloud that was misty all along the edges, and the wet tree was dripping onto a crumbling toadstool. Sarianna saw a spot of bright pink on her sleeve. Drops on the other one, as well. She pretended not to have heard the question and said, "Oh, look what I've done. I must hurry and dab these spots or they'll set."

Her mother's hands were in her lap, her eyes on the fire. Mrs. Browning turned to see the stains but didn't rise immediately, as she once would have, to bring soap and kettle. The house felt thick and small. The beams in the low room, dark on a winter's day, seemed lower and more crooked than on the day before. Sarianna rubbed a handkerchief on the cake of soap, then rubbed at the pink spots. What would she wear if she went to Miss Goss's house? She should not go, and yet the idea of it shone.

"Is it not coming out?" her mother asked.

"Not yet," Sarianna said, applying her thumbnail to the stain.

Sarianna said she was going to feed the chickens and see if a storm was coming in, her eye on the narrowing circle of blue, the white cloud closing, then the blue obliterated.

"And be looking for the pelerine when you come back, Rin," her mother said.

If she went to visit Miss Goss in Russell Square, she might also call at the Talfourds' and say she had left something there after the party—had anyone found it? "Which party?" she imagined the servant saying, if it would be the servant, or she might have to talk to Mrs. Talfourd, and Mrs.

Talfourd would be too polite to ask why she had waited so long, and—ah, she couldn't do that in secret, because wouldn't Mrs. Talfourd say to Robbie that his sister called the other day?

"It isn't there," she said to her mother, after pretending to look for the pelerine upstairs.

There was no answer.

"Mother?" she called, and all she heard was the cat, mewling in the cloister, where, to her horror, her mother lay facedown on the floor. "Mother," she said, "did you fall?"

"I didn't fall. I oughtn't bend my knee that way, and I won't again. Let me wait for it to stop throbbing. I thought the shawl might be in that box." Beside her mother was a box of old linens.

She held tight to Rinny's hand, and Rinny took one of the linen handkerchiefs and dabbed at her mother's cheeks.

"Have you any of the turmeric?" Rinny asked. It was the latest of a string of remedies.

Her mother shook her head, eyes closed.

MRS. BROWNING WAS no better on Tuesday or Wednesday. The possibility of going to fetch more turmeric, and the pelerine, too, on Thursday, grew more and more likely. If she happened to be in Russell Square on Thursday afternoon, she might reasonably stop at Miss Goss's house and say she was sorry she had not replied to the kind invitation. Because she didn't reply. She couldn't. She couldn't say yes, and she couldn't say no.

She was seized, on Thursday morning, by a desire to be better coiffed if she did stop in Russell Square. She had a paper with step-by-step illustrations: separate the hair at the back of her head into six sections. Braid, loop, pin. Braid, loop, pin. She held the mirror to see the back of her head, and instead of two swanlike loops of neatly braided hair, she saw loose tails and an off-center part and many unsightly pins. Sarianna threw the pins on the floor one by one and dragged a finger through the misshapen braids until her hair was loose and wild. She made an inner vow not unlike what she imagined a nun took upon entering a convent: *of the Puerile World I am not a member; for its vanities I care nothing.*

She boarded the diligence that left from the crossroads, and stepped, not long after three o'clock, into Miss Goss's library. "So many insects," she said, astounded by the array.

"My father collected beetles."

Sarianna studied them politely, walking case to case. "He ought to visit us in Hatcham," she said.

"If he were living, I assure you he would be there tomorrow."

Lenore showed Sarianna the beetle that had the name *Gossicus* in his honor—"a dubious honor, it seems to me," she added, "and it looks nothing at all like him." They sat down to eat things the maid brought: cold slices of parsleyed pork in gooseberry sauce, currant buns, walnut cake, a slab of creamy cheese. The maid was better dressed than Sarianna (*for the Puerile World I care nothing*). A white parrot in the corner scraped its beak on a cuttlefish bone. The spines of the books all matched one another, Sarianna noticed, as if they were a single argument divided into a thousand volumes. It was a shame to realize she couldn't go home and describe this room to her parents. If she had come here under other circumstances, she could have told her father about the books and her mother about the porcelain cups with faceted sides and the gooseberry sauce on cold slices of parsleyed pork. Miss Goss's very quick black eyes snapped with an almost audible attention to everything that Sarianna said. The neckline of Miss Goss's dress was not as low as it had been at the party, but her collar bones were still bare, as were the tops of her shoulders, and around them she had strung a beaded and embroidered capelet that was the same icy pale green as the dress itself (*For the Puerile World I care nothing*). In contrast to the ice green dress, Lenore wore a red gemstone on a red velvet ribbon around her neck. Her hair had been divided (by a maid, it must have been) from one ear to the other in a perfect arch, not as the equator but as for a tiara, and then the front locks had been made perfectly smooth, as if enameled, and pinned invisibly under a curl that was also ingeniously and invisibly drawn back and secured under a trinity of garnet flowers. The back of her head was a coronet of evenly braided nearly black hair, with not a single tuft refusing its place (*for the Puerile World I care nothing*).

"How is your brother?" Miss Goss asked.

"He is well."

"Does he visit Miss Barrett?"

"No." Letters came to the house from Miss Barrett, and letters left the house with Miss Barrett's name on them. They wrote not once a week but several times. Robbie was happy—he hardly seemed to hear what anyone said or to mind what anyone did. Miss Goss bent over to pour more tea, revealing that the three garnet flowers in her hair were made of velvet, but their seed parts were yellow glass.

"Do you have time for a short walk?" Miss Goss asked.

"Oh, I should have told you at once—I have very little time. My mother is ill, and I have come to buy a powder for her."

"What is the powder, if I may ask?"

"Turmeric."

"I know just where you can find that. I promise we will not be more than half an hour—please?"

Sarianna nodded, and Miss Goss took a large key from a bowl beside the door and dropped it into her purse. She took from the manservant a muff made of fox fur for herself and took another for Sarianna that was entirely white. The inside of it was like holding a cat.

Sarianna soon saw the purpose of the key. It fit into the gate that led into the park the houses on Russell Square faced. It was far larger than Sarianna had realized when visiting at night. Like a large house, the grand park awed her by making her feel small, and then made her feel pleased and important because she was inside—she, who was no one. Miss Goss kept walking, and they followed a path along the outside edge. Black birds flitted here and there in the bare trees. Water poured out of a carved lion's mouth and fed a mossy fountain. When they had passed through a long tunnel of privet, Sarianna heard a dull pock, as of an axe being buried in a tree. A boy ran across the path, shouted, and as he ran back—he was perhaps twenty yards ahead of them—he turned his face and saw the two of them. The boy was not white but Black, and he waved at Miss Goss, who returned the wave. Sarianna kept walking, waiting for Miss Goss to say something, to explain why they were here. After they passed under some low-hanging vines, some of them still holding dark berries, they came to a large open space in the park where there was a tall statue of a man in an iron cloak, a wintry lawn, and a woman who was throwing the ball to the boy. Her face was young, narrow, large-eyed, and Black, like the boy's. She, like the boy, recognized and acknowledged Miss Goss.

People came to London from the West Indies more and more often now, and Sarianna read of them in the paper sometimes, their life stories told by abolitionists, and upcoming lectures and benefits announced. Sarianna had seen a Black man near Hatcham only once, on a barge, gliding past toward London, sitting very still on a box, and he had been just ten feet from her, so that he could see her clearly and she could see him clearly. He had nodded, and she had nodded back, so she did that now.

"David," Miss Goss called. The boy waved to her and went on running while the woman held still with the ball. "This is my friend, Miss Sarianna Browning," Miss Goss said to him, unbothered by his continuing to run. Miss Goss turned to Sarianna and said, "Miss Browning, this is my friend Miss Mary Ann Hawthorne. And her son David."

"Good afternoon," Sarianna said.

"Good afternoon," the woman replied.

All around the field and the brooding statue, the air was still and gray. On the far side of the park, a uniformed nursemaid materialized, pushing a wicker pram. David grabbed the ball from his mother, ran a short distance, and threw it to her, but she missed. Miss Hawthorne—it was not Mrs. Hawthorne, but Miss—walked slowly to where it lay on the cold grass, picked it up, and threw it back, the small bat in her ungloved hand. The boy looked as though he wished for a different partner, or for the audience of ladies to go away, and instead of throwing the ball to his mother, he threw it into the air, catching it himself when it fell.

"Carry on," Miss Goss said, and she resumed walking, and Sarianna, surprised, had to take an extra step to catch up. "We'll not bother them now," Miss Goss said.

Sarianna was perplexed. They walked further, and when they were beyond hearing, Miss Goss said, "I have told you I knew the Barretts in Jamaica."

"Yes."

"*He* is a Barrett."

The gravel crunched under their feet. A branch of a cypress tree curled down, limp and broken. "David's father," Miss Goss said, "is Elizabeth Barrett's brother, Sam."

The gravel went on crunching, and Sarianna's fingers inside the fur were sweating now.

"Sam Barrett died of yellow fever five years ago."

Sarianna could not connect these facts to anything sayable.

"Miss Hawthorne and her son have come to ask the elder Mr. Barrett to pay for his education."

Sarianna heard another pock as the boy went back to batting. "Will he?" Sarianna asked.

"I don't know."

Sarianna wondered what she was expected to do with this knowledge, and she took one hand out of the muff, letting her hand feel the true temperature of the air.

"I intend to make it known, if necessary."

"Known?"

"I write for the *Post* sometimes. And other places. Do you know the *Liberty Bell*?"

"No," Sarianna tried to imagine what this visit between herself and Miss Goss, and this conversation, meant. "Do you mean that you will name them as ..."

"I will name them as an example of our legacy in Jamaica. Our hypocrisy. Can we say that the enslaved women of the island are free if they still bear children who are not acknowledged, who are unequal in opportunity? Mr. Barrett should take care of his son's child and any woman who bore him a child. The people ought to know if these things are done, or they are not done, having paid twenty million pounds to recompense the slave owners for their lost income. The English people will be indignant if they hear of Miss Hawthorne and her plight. They will want to help her, I believe."

They had overtaken the young nurse pushing a pram, and as they passed her, Sarianna nodded and smiled at the woman, and she saw the baby tucked inside, sleeping serenely, unafraid of such things as this.

"If I may say," Sarianna said slowly, "I don't understand what I'm to do."

"Encourage them to help us with their talents. To write something that will make a difference. This key?" She held up the little bag. "This park?" She waved her hand at the trees, the wide path, the tall houses beyond. "If you knew how my ancestors earned the coins that bought us this key and the house where I sleep each night . . . I have been there. I have seen it, and I must *do* something."

Sarianna felt mainly confusion. "My father, our father, I mean, Robbie's and mine, had a relative in Saint Kitts. He was sent there to work when he was young and he hated it. He gave up the shares he was given—I think that's how it worked—and took the job he now has in a bank, and his father was furious with him."

"I didn't know that. I'm very impressed. Miss Barrett's story is quite different."

Behind them came a faint cry, and the nurse stopped to reach into the pram.

"But is it her story?" Sarianna said. "Miss Barrett herself, I mean. Is she to blame for what her brothers do, or her ancestors?"

"I ask myself that question. What did I have to do with any of it? When my mother married my father," Miss Goss said, "she had never been to Jamaica. She knew absolutely nothing about what awaited her. She left her entire family behind, and they thought they had done their duty, which was to secure for her a large and steady income. When she saw what my father was about, keeping his housekeeper in jewelry and dresses . . . She had two children, my brother and me. She wanted to bring us both away, but she was allowed to bring only me."

So deliberate did each footstep seem, so intent was their attention on the mottled gray stones strewn with dead leaves and broken seeds and lichen, that Sarianna felt as if she were trying to read her fortune there, but couldn't.

"People get trapped every day," Miss Goss said. "They walk willingly into a place they have been told is good for them, or into the only place they are allowed to go, and then they're trapped. It happens to all women, all children, most men, I would say, though rich men, and a few powerful women, have more power to extricate themselves and, if they choose, to extricate others." A pigeon cooed inside a bower. "When I saw you at Talfourd's party, I thought you would be sympathetic to the cause. I thought you might help us."

A horse was pulling a two-seater beside the park, its feet ringing out on the stones. A crow cried from the top of a tree that bowed under its weight. The light behind the crow was starting to wane, no longer gray but amber.

"I am sympathetic," Sarianna said, "if you mean the cause of abolition in the States, and elsewhere. And I sincerely hope Mr. Barrett will do right by the child."

"And your brother? If he heard of this, would he help?"

"How?" she asked. Robbie did not talk to her about such things.

The black iron gate stood beside them, and Miss Goss explained that *Liberty Bell* was an annual magazine in the United States with which she had connections. Perhaps Mr. Browning, or even Miss Barrett, would write a piece for the next one. Then she pointed down the street. "Go to the left and take the first turning," she said. "The apothecary is on the next corner."

"Thank you," Sarianna said, uncertain what she would tell Robbie, if she could tell him anything at all, and what he would think. She was eager to leave and yet anxious, feeling all around her an unfinished subject. Without another word, Miss Goss let her out of the park.

The lamps were glowing in the houses and on the street though it was just four o'clock. She glanced behind her as she climbed the steps to number 24, afraid she would see Miss Goss and Miss Hawthorne and the boy coming out of the park together, and they would wonder what she was doing at

Mr. Talfourd's house, but that didn't happen. Only strangers saw her, and they didn't care.

A servant asked whom she wanted to see, and she said, "I don't know. I was here for a party, a month ago, and I forgot something of my mother's."

He waited for her to tell him what it was.

"A lace pelerine. A little cape. It's white."

Her feet were cold from walking in the park, and her nose was threatening to run. As she reached for a handkerchief, she saw that she still had her hands inside the rabbit fur muff of Miss Goss's.

"Your name, Miss?"

She told him, and he said she might wait inside the hall while he spoke to the housekeeper. There was no one in the hall, just the red and white tiles and an umbrella stand and the grand stairway going up to the rest of the house. A housekeeper appeared and she had to describe it again, and say where she had put it, and the housekeeper said she could leave her card, and she would ask the serving girls and the lady of the house if anything of that description had been seen, but she thought it hadn't been, or she would have seen it herself.

"I don't have a card," Sarianna said, embarrassed.

This caused another delay as the servant went out of the room again. When she returned, she had a bit of pencil and someone else's card, which the servant turned over, saying, "It's an old one. You can write your name here."

She wrote it, and she said goodbye and thank you, and soon she was outside again, the borrowed muff on her hands, in a hurry to reach the apothecary and go home.

FIFTEEN

∞

ROBERT WANTED TO meet her. They should be in the same room and talk in person. But Miss Barrett wasn't well enough to go out, or to see anyone, not even him. Not until spring, she said, *late* spring, what others called summer. And it was only February, that endless month when people threw dinners and dances to keep out the dark and forget the fog. Chorley, especially, hounded Robert to go out and see people. Come to my dinner, he wrote, only a little one, just George Barrett, Ben Haydon, Lenore Goss, and Lenore Goss's West Indian friend.

A more explosive combination was hard to imagine. Ben Haydon's paintings were a disaster, financially, and that was his own fault. He persisted in his mania for large, overpopulated canvases that took forever to finish and then earned hardly anything. If it had only been Haydon, Robert would have declined, but he was curious to see the woman George Barrett and Lenore Goss had discussed so unhappily at Talfourd's party.

Mary Ann had been told a poet was coming to the party, the very one whose poems Miss Goss had shown her. He arrived late and was unexpectedly small. Mary Ann had imagined a great big man with wild hair and a wild beard. This man could not strangle anyone, Mary Ann thought. He didn't have the arms for it. Mr. Browning sat in the empty chair beside her, which she didn't like, and he smiled in a disturbingly polite way. "Is this your first stay in London?"

"Yes," she said.

The other artist, the one Miss Goss said was a famous but bankrupt painter, leaned forward and said, "Robert, excuse me, but I must ask Miss Hawthorne if she will sit for me."

Before Mary Ann could say no, Miss Goss interrupted. "No, Ben, she will not, but you have fulfilled my prediction. Hasn't he, Miss Hawthorne? I told her Ben Haydon would admire her so much that he would ask her to sit for him before the soup was served."

"I do admire her, and she must sit for me."

"She will not, Ben," Miss Goss said.

"Are you jealous, Nora? You might come as well, and I could paint you as someone heroic—Daphne, say."

"Is that your idea of the heroic?"

"Let Miss Hawthorne answer for herself," the painter said.

"No, thank you," Mary Ann said.

"Perhaps you'll change your mind," the painter said, and a serving girl brought in the soup. As she waited for what would happen next, she heard the poet say, "From which island do you hail, Miss Hawthorne?"

"Jamaica," she said. Miss Goss had said the poet might help turn public opinion in favor of Mary Ann's "suit," but Mary Ann didn't like calling it a suit. She was beginning to think that nothing would make Mr. Barrett help her and David. If Sam's father wanted to help them, he would have met with them by now.

"Jamaica is Lenore's island, too," Chorley said. Chorley was a good man, Miss Goss said, because he cared not how you looked but how you spoke. This was a ridiculous idea. Everyone noticed right off how you looked and made decisions before you spoke. If Miss Goss were Black, she would know this.

"Is your brother still in Jamaica, George?" Chorley asked. "Perhaps I ought to have called it the Barretts' island, as well."

If Chorley had asked Mary Ann, she would have said, yes, it was the Barretts' island. She lived on Barrett land, went to school in a church built by the grace of Old Barrett, ran her hand along the banister of Old Barrett house while wearing the heavy coral necklace Sam Barrett had fastened around her neck, was kissed by Sam Barrett, held in her palms the watch of Sam Barrett, heard her father say, *Where did you get that, what did I tell you about him?*

"Yes, my brother is still there," George Barrett said. "But it's not our island."

The painter stood up, picked up his chair, and moved it directly under a large oil painting of a man in a riding costume, a whip in his hand. The painter climbed onto the chair and all of them watched to see what he would do.

"What in the world are you doing, Ben?" Chorley asked.

Without a word, the painter lifted the portrait, tilted it, staggered with its weight, found his balance, climbed down, and turned the frame around so the painting faced the wall. Then he hung it up that way and they looked at the back of it. "I couldn't stand it anymore," the painter said. "It's simply too terrible."

"Don't mind him," Chorley said to the white serving girl, who had stopped serving. "Continue. Is my art too good or too bad for you to look upon, Ben?"

"Abominable," the painter said. "It will drive me mad to see you display such errant taste." His hand shook when he picked up his spoon, and he slurped it as they all stared.

"It's my great uncle," Chorley said, "and we none of us can answer for what our relatives deemed in good taste." Chorley smiled and held up his glass until the others, even the painter, raised theirs. "To art," he said.

"Or its censure!" George Barrett countered, raising his own glass. Mary Ann feared he was the one who would decide if she was lying. He had taken Sam's watch back, but he had not visited again, nor had he asked her to come and meet his father, and day after day David grew more uncontrollable, saying he hated England, he hated the cold, he hated the park; why had she brought him here?

"How are you, George?" the poet asked.

"Busy," George said. "I have been talking to my sister about you."

"Have you?"

You could learn, by watching animals, the meaning of what they did. See the doctor bird sip from the ixora, its long tail quivering, see the John Crow circle high above, the cat stalking, the snake coiling, the ant gathering. In such a way did the voices veer in and out.

"I asked her to tell me what *Sordello* means," George said, "and she offered to read the whole of it to me on successive nights."

"Have you that many nights left?" Chorley asked. "To live?"

The poet was the object of their joking and he didn't seem to mind. The serving woman gave Mary Ann her soup—turtle, from the scent and color. Her father hated turtle soup and had taught her to think it defiling.

"Well," George said. "Ought I to accept, Mr. Browning?"

"If your taste runs to what so many have deemed obscure."

"Your sister is a genius, my dear sir," the painter said to George.

"Do you know, Robert," Miss Goss said to the poet, lowering her eyes confidentially and reaching out with her pretty hand, the skin perfectly clear and white, a little pearl ring gleaming on her pinkie. "I have given some of your poems to my visitor. We read 'My Last Duchess' and 'Porphyria's Lover' last night before bed, so you can forgive us if we wonder where the bodies are."

The poet leaned back in his chair to let the serving girl give him soup.

"Is Porphyria someone real?" Miss Goss persisted. "Was it some awful story I missed when reading the *Post*?"

"What awful story?" George Barrett asked.

"Porphyria seduces her lover, or he seduces her, and then he strangles her with her own hair," Miss Goss said. "The man sits up with her body all night waiting for God to say something, but God doesn't speak. I was hoping Mr. Browning might tell us where he got that terrible idea."

The walls were silver, the carpets red, and the soup in her bowl smelled of wrongdoing. A horned-beast head on the wall watched them with an eye of hard glass. Here she was sitting in London, being served by a white girl, remembering her father say *Don't ever eat that*.

"It was reported in *Blackwood's*," Chorley said. "Wasn't it, Rob?"

"It was," the poet said. "But he didn't strangle her."

"Stabbed?" Chorley asked, and the poet nodded.

"Is that what you often do, Mr. Browning?" George asked. "Do you write the news, as it were?"

"The situation may come from anywhere."

"Miss Hawthorne," the painter said, studying her with his horrible frog eyes. "That expression on your face. Carry on Hank, while I get my pencils." He pushed his chair back for the second time.

"Ben," Miss Goss cried out at him, "you may not spoil my guest's dinner by sketching her," but the painter was rushing out of the room. "Don't worry," Miss Goss said to Mary Ann. "I will stop him when he comes back. Enjoy the soup. Chorley has the best cook in London. Better even than mine."

"Ben," Chorley called, "You're going to miss my story, which involves a crime of the most perfidious kind. It's a crime against art!"

"Please stop him," Miss Goss said in a low, angry voice to Chorley.

"He's harmless," Chorley said. "Don't worry."

The spoons went dutifully into bowls all around the table, so Mary Ann went ahead, as she felt she must, and dipped a bit of something into her spoon. The light was dim, but the chunk of flesh curved, had a texture and shape like the end of a turtle's foot. It would not kill her. She put it into her mouth and chewed, then swallowed. Like fish but not fish, like meat but not meat, slightly rancid and horribly rich.

The painter distracted them all with his return. He held a sketchbook and a pencil. "Do not sketch Miss Hawthorne," Chorley said, and Mary Ann took the chance to pretend her soup was too hot to eat. She blew on it lightly and lowered the spoon again, letting another bit of speckled leg sink back into the broth.

"Sir William Hamilton," Chorley said to everyone, "was the ambassador to Naples, and he collected a great number of relics from Rome and Pompeii, including a small, exquisite, extremely old cameo vase. Sir William Hamilton had a beautiful wife, as you *will* remember. But did you know that before she became his wife, she was a housemaid called Amy Lyon, put into service by her family when she was twelve? Her father, a blacksmith, had died when she was two months old."

On he went, the man with his story-voice, and Mary Ann ate only the broth, none of the chunks, taking sips until the broth—too salty for her taste, but endurable—was gone.

"The girl's art can hardly be described here, in the company of ladies, because her employer asked his housemaid to pose for his friends as Io and Venus and Diana and Daphne, wearing nothing more than an artful sheet. Who was there to protect her? Not the men she posed for, among them Sir Harry Fetherstonhaugh of Uppark.

"Miss Amy, whose name morphed into Emma, gave birth to a baby. When Emma begged the father of that child, Sir Harry of Uppark, to keep her and her child together, and support them, he passed her to a friend. That friend made her send the baby home to her grandmother and great-grandmother, who taught her all they knew: to be a cook's helper and maid and seamstress. Emma, meanwhile, was presented to the painter George Romney, who made her his muse. She became a famous beauty and a problem for her lover, who wished to marry someone respectable. An arrangement was made without Emma Lyon's knowledge: if her lover's uncle, Sir William Hamilton, would pay his debts, Emma would be his wife. Sir William quickly paid the debts, and Emma was sent to him. She had to go with him to Naples, and there Sir William Hamilton bought a glass vase.

"The ashes of the emperor Severus Alexander, who departed this world in Anno Domini 235, had been poured into this vase at its creation, and they sat for a thousand years in a marble sarcophagus. In the sixteenth century, when the vase was exhumed, the ashes were poured out, and the vase was sold, and sold, and sold again, until at last it sat in the drawing room of Lord Hamilton and his unhappy wife.

"It was blue glass with white figures. On its side, carved in the overlay of white glass, was a seated woman, naked except for a Roman sheet, one breast exposed, her arm outstretched to a young and handsome man, and they were menaced or protected by a cherub floating overhead, who wielded a sword. From her lap sprang a snake with open fangs. An older man watched the pair of lovers while two monstrous heads, horned like the devil's, upheld the handles.

"It's uncanny how much the story depicted on the vase resembled her life. She who so often stood half-naked in a sheet to pretend she was a Roman goddess took a lover, Admiral Nelson, and her older husband permitted that, but he never let her live with or acknowledge her first child. I used to wonder, whenever I saw the vase in the British Museum, which is where it is now, why Emma never took it from the shelf and shattered it. Yesterday, a young Irish student stood before the same vase. It's kept in a room named for the Hamiltons—the old cuckold and his miserable captive. The Irish boy standing in the Hamiltonian Room heard voices. They told him to do something, and he did it.

"A museum guard named Hawkins heard the crash and came running, as did a group of tourists. They found a river of broken glass on the floor and a boy in a great coat, young and thin, with dirty yellow hair, his face barely old enough for whiskers, his eyes pale and wild. 'I did it, Sir,' he told the guard.

"All of the other visitors stared at him. On the sleeve of the boy's coat a jagged bit of glass—cobalt, one corner frosted white—shone. The boy looked down, held out his arm, and picked it up carefully, between two pale fingers, and held it out to Hawkins. Shards sparkled at the edges of his vision, hundreds of pieces of priceless glass on the floor. The boy's eyes were so full of contrition that Hawkins could hardly believe the act had been intentional. Who would break such a precious thing?

"'Filth,' a woman said to the Irish boy. 'All of your kind are.'

"'I hope they flog you into as many pieces as you've made here today,' said a man, raising his walking stick.

"'They ought to hang you,' the woman said, and the others agreed.

"The boy told police his name was Billy Lloyd and he was a student at Trinity. He had family troubles at home in Ireland. In his pocket he had just nine pennies, and that, he said, was all he had left.

"'What family troubles?' the policeman asked.

"He wouldn't say.

"'Is this what you do when given a chance to better yourself?' the police-man demanded. 'Go into places that are open to all and sundry for their edification, and break what's been treasured for centuries? Since our Lord and Savior walked the earth, this vase has been kept care of, and now you take it upon yourself to smash it like it's no more than a bottle in a pub?'

"It reminded him," the boy said.

"Reminded him of what?" Hawkins asked him.

"He shook his head. Not another word could they get out of him."

"Will they hang him?" Miss Goss asked, her hand at her throat, her eyes wet with tears.

"Don't be absurd!" George said.

Mary Ann's soup was cold. There was a scent on it that she couldn't abide, and as Chorley told his story she saw she had been a fool to think she could bring David here and get what he deserved.

"Why doesn't George tell us," Chorley said. "You know the law, George. What's the punishment for vase malfeasance?"

George took time to wipe his mouth. He pushed back his chair and began to turn the ring he wore on one hand. "The Willful Damage Act would apply here," he said. "The owner would receive compensation. A fine of some sort would be paid."

"By the boy? He only has nine pennies," Miss Goss said.

"What is the vase worth?" George asked.

"They value it at a thousand pounds."

"By whose reckoning!" the painter said. "It is worth far more than that. I ask you—"

"It doesn't matter. He could never pay it," Miss Goss said.

"Unless he's lying," George said. "Before you conclude he's a poor inno-cent victim, recall that he might be of the landowning class in Ireland. Or from a family of middlemen who ratchet up the rents. Chorley is calling him a boy, but he's not a child. And he even lied about his name, he's really 'Mulcahy,' it turns out."

"He might be the same boy I met last month," the poet said. "Same color hair, same manner. If he's the one who handed me his notebook, he isn't a landowner and he isn't lying about money." He said something more—a boy had given him a notebook with a title of a poem in it, one the poet was meant, for some reason, to write.

"You can't know that, Robert, without knowing all the facts. But if he is poor, and he can't pay the fine," George said, "the Trustees of the Museum would have to pay the damages to his Grace. And he would go to jail for a bit."

"For how long?" the painter asked.

"Two or three months, not more, for willful damage."

"I've served longer than that," the painter said, "for *making* art."

"So, Robbie," Chorley said to the poet, spreading his arms wide. "There are sure to be new developments, but what an Ode to Hypocrisy it all makes! Perhaps two! Perhaps an entire poem cycle."

"All you care about," Miss Goss said to the table, "is what you can make of it. How you can profit from it with your stories and your art. What if that's why he did it?"

"I object to the assumption that we *profit*," the poet said.

"He's Irish," Miss Goss said. "So it's obviously an attack on Englishmen and their all-consuming love of *things*, which they take for themselves at will, all over the world, with no thought for the consequences."

George shook his head and leaned forward. "Because the Irish are hungry and poor, Miss Goss, you're saying Billy Mulcahy came here to be their champion? Are you saying he's justified in breaking whatever upsets him?"

Miss Goss studied George through half-closed eyes. The black beads that dripped around her neck caught the candlelight and made her unusually beautiful, or perhaps it was the knowledge that George felt something for her that made her beautiful. They were lovers, Mary Ann thought, or George wanted to be Miss Goss's lover and was not yet.

Miss Goss turned away from George to the poet. "You should make Emma's abandoned daughter the heroine of your ode," Miss Goss told him. "Miss Hawthorne and I would like that."

Mary Ann did not agree, but no one asked her to say anything.

"What happened to the poor girl?" Miss Goss asked Chorley.

"Which one?"

"The abandoned daughter."

"I don't know."

"Of course you don't," Miss Goss said.

The poet declined the next course with a polite smile. Chorley motioned for the serving girl to continue offering it, and Mary Ann shook her head.

"It's to be reconstructed, you know," Chorley said. "Hawkins says the museum has a chap who can put the vase back together."

"Why?" Miss Goss said. "It will be of no value now."

"I suspect the value will go up, actually," the poet said. "The trustees will reconstruct it to prove a barbarian cannot destroy something they hold dear."

The poet took his knife from the table and set it across his plate, balanced over the emptiness, as he had wiped it clean. When the dessert came at last—a pineapple pudding flecked with cinnamon—Mary Ann had to eat it and smile because it was expressly for "Miss Hawthorne," Chorley said, "for our guest of honor." She ate it and thought of the museum men gluing a vase back together. She thought of Sam fastening the coral necklace around her throat: *for my darling*, he had said. Her father had yanked it off in front of the Reverend, in front of Miss Jessie, in front of all the people standing around the church before the service. Her father had thrown the necklace down and picked up a large stone.

Why, her father had shouted as he pounded the pink beads of the necklace into dust, *must he teach my daughter to be a bad girl?*

Mary Ann took another bite, and another, and another. They would never be able to put her beads back together, not even if she went back and picked the pieces up. The pink bits were still there, most likely, or had been carried into the holes of ants.

"What if it were something *you* had made, Robert?" the painter said. "It's easy enough for a poet to say art is worth more when it's in pieces. What if I tore *Sordello* to shreds?"

"Tennyson already did that," the poet said.

"And yet it remains intact!" the painter shouted.

"Does it?" the poet said calmly.

"What do you think, Miss Hawthorne?" Miss Goss said. "You can bring a viewpoint none of us has."

They turned toward her, all of them. The room was at once too small and too big, too hot and too cold. She had only one more bite of pineapple pudding to endure.

"About the poem?" Mary Ann asked.

"About the vase," the painter said.

"I have never seen the vase," she said.

"I'd rather hear," Miss Goss said, "how you feel about the boy that broke it."

"It is not for me to say," Mary Ann said.

"Because you are a woman?"

Mary Ann shook her head.

"Being a woman never stops Miss Goss," George said to Mary Ann. "As you've no doubt heard. She gives her opinions on all sorts of topics."

"Just tell us who you care more about," Miss Goss said, trying her nicer voice. "The lewd old vase or the boy who broke it."

"As if you're not telling her which to choose!" the painter said.

"It's not for me to say," Mary Ann said. She stared at the pudding and her fork and the silver edges of the candlesticks. The necklace she was wearing tonight had been loaned to her by Miss Lenore. It was ugly, and she hated it.

"You twist your argument, Miss Goss," George said. "We were talking about the force of law. Where would we be if people were allowed to slash and burn the possessions of others when they're angry? How best to prevent it—*that's* the question."

"You naturally care for the legal aspect," said Miss Goss. "Mr. Haydon cares most for the vase. Mr. Browning, I think, cares about—let's see."

"All of it," the poet said.

"And you, Miss Goss?" George said, his voice sharp. "About what do you care?"

"I wish for Miss Hawthorne to have her turn. In this, and in everything."

Again the force of the room was directed at her. Tall birds in a circle around a fish.

"I don't know," she said.

"But if you had to choose."

"I cannot choose."

"Out there," Miss Goss said, and she pointed out the windows, "you're not permitted to choose, nor am I. But the glorious thing about Chorley's table is the chance to speak your mind."

"It has nothing to do with me, and I would like to go home."

They were disappointed, but she didn't care. The horned animal on the wall kept his glassy eye upon them, and the carriage was sent for, and when they were seated inside it she closed her eyes so that she would not have to hear Miss Goss ask if she was feeling unwell, nor see the passing of stone houses, nor be asked to speak her mind. It was over, this time in England. It was over, and she must find a way to go home.

SIXTEEN

∞

ELIZABETH WISHED TO unravel the days as Penelope unraveled the cloth. There must never come a day when Mr. Browning saw her as she was, a person, a body instead of a mind. There must never come a day when she had to see him being disappointed in what she was.

The weather is too cold. The weather is too wet. I am not well.

She was afraid he would give up, and she was afraid he would get bored, but he simply kept writing to her. He asked her what she thought of his play and of his new poem. He said that he had kept all her letters and numbered them.

He astounded her with his patience and what he kept calling love. It made her want to write something in honor of it, this *thing* that a man said he felt for her. A sonnet would be the right vessel for a love of this kind: restrained by convention, tied up as tight as a corset.

She calmed herself with the ABBA of it, the stressed and unstressed syllables. Each sonnet had the requisite ons and offs, the ends and beginnings, *octet, sestet, volta,* the words holding up their hands to the partner, who held up his in turn, spun, turned his back, and showed his face again. *Belovëd,* she wrote. *I am thine.* Winter fogs left black specks on the windowsill and on the sheets hung out to dry. *Let me in,* said Robert Browning.

> He wished to have me in his sight
> Once, as a friend . . .
> To come and touch my hand . . . a simple thing

But it was not simple. A man in her room would not be an octet but eyes. What would she see in his face when he saw her, and if it was horror, or disappointment, or a mask trying to hide those feelings, what then?

SEVENTEEN

∞

FIVE MONTHS HAD passed since she answered his first letter, and no one, not even Elizabeth, could say it was not spring. There were bees, butterflies, and larks in the air. Skies blue, bluer, and bluest. When he woke up on Friday, the day had come at last.

Between two and three o'clock, her letter had said.

He trimmed his beard. He shaved his cheeks and the part of his neck just below the beard. He cleaned and cut his fingernails. He heated water and carried it into the room off the kitchen.

"Do you need anything, Robbie?" his mother called. There was no need to tell them yet. He didn't need to tell them she had written to say he might call on May 16 and it was May 16.

"I have everything, thank you."

All of him was as clean as it could be. In the little mirror with a crack in the corner, he saw himself blink, and adjusted his tie and his waistcoat. Nothing more could be added or taken away. What he was, he was, and what was she? Confined to a chair, likely. He was quite sure she couldn't walk, and he didn't care.

"Where are you going?" Sarianna asked.

"To town."

She was shoving her hands into a ball of bread dough, turning and scraping what stuck to her fingers and pushing stray gobs into the dough again. Robbie sent unfinished poems to Miss Barrett these days and told Sarianna he had nothing new for her to copy. She was angry about him sharing his work with Miss Barrett instead of with her. She was disappointed, too, that he had not written something about abolition for Miss Goss.

"Don't wait for me at supper," he said. If the visit went well, he would walk in Regent's Park. If it went poorly, he would walk in Regent's Park. He would need plenty of time to think afterward, and he didn't want to be expected by anyone.

"Why are you taking that?" Rinny asked.

He had a jar of perry in his hand, and he bundled it up in a cloth before setting it in the bottom of his sack. "I might get thirsty."

"No, that." The rolled-up painting in his hand.

"It's the painting that father did. Of the broken vase. I thought my friend might like to see it."

"Your friend."

"Yes." When he bent to kiss Rinny's cheek, she didn't move. Her fingers were buried in the dough, stuck as in a mire.

"Is it a woman, your friend?" she said quietly. "A woman you have never seen before?"

"Yes."

A moment passed. "I hope it goes well, Robbie. I do."

Birds sang along the towpath, tulips bobbed in meadows. The day was cardinal and chartreuse. She might smell of flowers. She might smell of musk. She might let him say that he loved her. She might hear him say all the reasons he must make her his.

A falcon floated as if the wind took it and held it in its hands.

He crossed the Thames near the spire of St. Marylebone. He had walked down her street more times than he liked to say, wondering what it would be like to stop and go in, to climb the stairs, to have the door opened, to sit beside her, to hold her hand.

EIGHTEEN

∞

"I CAN'T RECEIVE him," Elizabeth said.

"Don't be silly," Henrietta said. "He's on his way by now."

"I feel dizzy."

"That's love."

"It's not love," she whispered. "It's the natural fear of bringing a strange man into my room. Does it seem clean enough?"

"Wilson cleaned it. I cleaned it. You cleaned it."

The room was too small for what it had to do. It was not a room where you brought a man to a couch beside your bed that had been stripped and scoured and washed and ironed and made so smooth that it seemed no one had spent a whole winter coughing in it. She felt, herself, like the sheets. As if Wilson had taken her down to the charwoman and the charwoman had boiled her in the pot and wrung her out and hung her on a line in a stiff wind and attacked the wrinkles with a hot iron. You could not be both flesh and spirit. Either/or. Word or body. And she had given up living long ago, when the pain shut out the pony and the garden and the river and the sea.

"Does it smell fresh?" Elizabeth asked. She kept her voice low and wondered if Robert ought to have been told that low voices were best, but why? How could you tell him why?

"We have flowers. It smells like those."

"What if he doesn't come?"

"I will kill him," Henrietta said.

"He could decide it's too momentous."

"He's been hammering at your door these five months. He would have broken in already if he were less of a gentleman."

"I'm too old."

"Don't be silly, Ba. You look as young as anything in that dress."

"It's strange to be wearing so little."

"Why? It's the middle of May. Do you want the shawl?"

"I don't want to look like a granny. Should we go downstairs instead?"

"We talked this over a dozen times. I'm here with you. We have this sitting room here—" Henrietta pointed to the chairs, the low table, the couch, the tea. "This way you don't have to walk up and down stairs in addition to the excitement of a new guest."

Neither said that in her room they also could avoid brothers wandering in and out with friends, or their father, who if he came home this early— they both hoped he would not—he would go into his study but would not likely come directly upstairs, and thus Mr. Browning's visit might not have to become a topic of conversation. Not just yet.

NINETEEN

∞

WIMPOLE STREET WITH its oxblood bricks lay like a corridor before him. Clouds of white floated in a sky of blue. He felt that everyone on the street must be watching and waiting for it to happen, for the long-awaited meeting, the moment when what had been word became flesh.

A man opened the door—not a brother, but a man in livery, blue jacket, silver buttons, red stripes. His face was young and friendly. He knew already whom to expect and what to say.

Robert willed the sweat in his hair and on his back to dry. He studied the hall that was the hall of her house. Umbrellas huddled in a stand, a rack held a half-dozen hats, and when he turned he saw a life-sized portrait of a young woman in a white dress. A pink ribbon cinched her waist and the pink ribbons of her bonnet were untied, floating in a breeze that might, in the next moment, send the bonnet flying. She stood as if on the brink of everything, her arm raised before her in the familiar posture of a dance, serious and direct. It was a Lawrence, no less. She did not smile, but she did not frown.

A door opened behind him, and when he turned it was not the young man in livery but a maid. She said, "Mr. Browning?" Her cap was crooked, as was her charming slender nose.

"Yes."

"She's waiting for you."

He stood for a second more. "Is that she?" he asked.

"Her?"

"Is this," he pointed at the girl in pink, "Miss Elizabeth."

"I don't know, sir. It was brought here from Jamaica, though, so I don't think it can be."

His shoes creaked and the stairs creaked, the sweat on his back and neck wet and warm, and he took in the framed sketches of graphite churches, watercolor seas, inked dells and lazing cattle. On the third landing, the maid stopped.

"Here we be," she said softly.

There were three doors, all of them closed. She turned as if to ask, *Ready?* and when he nodded, she lifted her small fist to strike the nearest door.

"Wait," he said softly. He wasn't ready.

The maid's caramel hair was combed and braided tightly and it was soothing to consider it. When she smiled at him, she showed a dimple in her cheek. She turned her head slightly to the other side, crossed her arms loosely, and lowered her gaze to the carpet.

Robert breathed in, then out. Boiled onions and linseed oil and wool. A lark trilled. He could not make the maid stand here all afternoon. He gave, at last, a nod.

"Mr. Browning is here, Miss," the maid called, knocking. She opened the door a little and put her head in. As she did so, a little dog leaped from the bed, scratched and skittered, barking, then needled its head into the gap between door and frame. Before the maid could block the dog with her foot, he had wriggled into the hall, snuffling and shaking itself in a rage at Robert's feet. From inside the room a woman's voice called, "Flush! No! Come," but the dog went on barking and pawing Robert's legs. Robert heard his own voice saying the foolish things you would say on this occasion, "Good boy, good boy, hello." Her room, not yet entered, was brighter than the hallway, as if it held the sun.

And then the moment of seeing and being seen was there, both eternal and never remembered again quite as it was, overlain by other days.

She was standing up. She could stand, and she did stand. She could walk, and she did walk. Her sister Henrietta was there, too, smiling. "That is Flush," said the standing woman. She was Elizabeth, and she could walk. "No. No, Flush. This is Mr. Browning. Please forgive him, Mr. Browning. He doesn't see new people very much." She walked easily toward the dog and bent down and stroked the dog's head until it stopped barking.

He smiled at the dog, but with glances here and there, he took her in: dark eyes, dark hair, small chin, wide mouth. A small, thin body in a white dotted dress. She stood up again, beckoning to Flush, who followed her movements with his eyes, the windows open, the light pouring in, smelling of summer. She stood three feet away from him after all this time, eyes trying to be steady and unconcerned. Not steady. Not unconcerned. Henrietta seemed, he thought, equally tense.

"Mr. Browning," Elizabeth said. She was—must be—the incarnation of the voice in her letters, with its long self-effacing sentences. She was a whole person waiting to be seen and judged, stiff with the strain of it, as if she had climbed to a great height at his insistence and was afraid she would fall. "Please do sit down," she managed to say, pointing behind him.

He stepped forward instead of back. He took her hands to steady himself. She smiled again, waiting, their hands linked. "You do me such an honor," he said, and the dog barked to say there was no permission to touch the hands he held.

"Come here, Flush," Henrietta scolded. "What are you doing? Can't you see this is our friend? Stop that."

"Hush," Elizabeth said. "I'm so sorry, Mr. Browning. I will hold him and he will settle down." Elizabeth withdrew her hands and sat down on a couch, drawing the dog up into her lap, and from that fortress the dog felt safe to glare. "See? All is well, Flush. Mr. Browning is a welcome guest. Greet him properly."

He smiled in the dog's direction. "Is that a painting of you downstairs?" he asked, trying to remember the painted face, whether it had the same eyes, or whether he was simply seeing the face before him. "The girl in the white dress. Standing on a hill."

"No, that is Pinkie! Our father's sister."

There was as yet a very slight delay in every response, a caesura between question and answer. He thought it was the awkwardness of having to speak instead of write. His body felt like a puppet. "Do people remark on the resemblance?"

Again the delay, summer air, a paper ruffling, his euphoria.

In unison, Elizabeth said, "Sometimes," and Henrietta said, "Constantly."

"Not always," Elizabeth said, having the last word.

He loved her utterly, and there was nothing to fear.

"It's true, Ba," Henrietta said. "People always say it's you. Mrs. Graham said it was you exactly."

"And the sketches framed along the stairs?" he asked in his happiness of loving her utterly. "Whose are they?"

"Henrietta's!"

"Some are Alfred's," Henrietta said. "The best ones."

"That's not true, Mr. Browning. All of these drawings are Henrietta's as well . . ." She pointed to her wall. "And you can see that she is extremely talented."

"You have a charming style, Miss Henrietta. Speaking of art . . . I brought something to show you." He opened the rucksack and felt a rush of dread. Had he ruined it? What an idiot he was. The perry had leaked onto the cloth where the painting was. "Oh, dear," he said. "I brought you my mother's perry, and it seems to have leaked." He held up the jar and tried not to show how worried he was about the painting.

"How delightful!" Elizabeth said. "I've never tasted it. She makes it herself?"

"Yes." He reached into the bag and felt the edge of the rolled paper.

"Will you have some with us?" Henrietta asked.

Henrietta poured the cider into teacups that had been left on a tray. Among the remarks on the flavor—the way it resembled apple cider, but was richer, somehow—he drew the painting out to check the damage. Not too bad, thankfully.

Elizabeth, seeing this, smiled at him. "What is it?"

Would she recognize it? Would she think it odd or nice? He held it out to her and she unrolled it.

"It's the pieces," she said.

"Pieces of what?" Henrietta asked.

"The Portland Vase," Elizabeth said. "How marvelous. Did you do it?" It was signed Robert Browning.

"No, my father did. We have the same name."

He explained that he had met who might have been the vandal, an Irish boy who had thrust his notebook at Robert with the title of a poem written on the first page, "Ode to Hypocrisy." How another Irish boy, or the same one, Billy Mulcahy, had stood in the same room before the same vase and smashed it to pieces. As the winter wore on, a painting of the shards had appeared in the Hamiltonian room, commissioned by the museum so the public could see the atrocity and the task faced by the restorationist. Robert's father had gone with Robert to see the painting, and then, on his own, his father had gone back and made a copy. It was not his father's usual subject; he was a sketcher of faces, a caricaturist. He sat by the fire many nights, doing what he'd wanted to do as a young man—draw and paint— before yoking himself to the dreary desk of a bank.

"My father wanted my mother to be able to see it. She couldn't go herself, so he made this."

"It looks like a mosaic, doesn't it," Elizabeth said.

"Yes." That's why Robert liked it. Because it looked like a mosaic or a puzzle rather than a dull piece of crockery, interesting not because of its famous provenance but because it was broken. On some pieces, half a body reclined without a head, on others, a head was separated from the body. An arched foot was by itself, the raised texture delicately rendered with a stroke of gray paint. A broken image came nearer to the truth, somehow, and to the obstacles in telling it, which was what interested Robert in his own work. He felt he would be able to talk to Elizabeth about this. "I tacked it up in my room," he said. "That's why there are pinholes in it. And this, see—" Robert unrolled a much smaller piece of paper.

"Is that the Irish boy?"

"As my father imagined him."

"He's very talented, your father."

"I will tell him you said so."

"He must love your mother very much."

Henrietta kept sewing to pretend she was not listening, and in truth, she stopped listening, distracted as she was by the birds, the voice of a maid in the garden, a man's ringing laugh.

"Are you tired? Should I go?" Robert asked, afraid that Henrietta's abstraction was a sign that he should leave.

"Not yet," Elizabeth said eagerly, and Henrietta said, "Oh, no, not yet," so he stayed in the place he felt he had always been meant to go, talking about art, poetry, the boy, and their meaning.

When Henrietta walked him downstairs some time afterward, he felt even the maid must know it had gone well—anyone seeing his face would know it. He no longer carried the fear about him. The dragon was slain.

He glanced, as he put on his hat in the vestibule, at the painted girl in white slippers, her arm uplifted, her dress white against a stormy sky, and she seemed to know it, too. All that remained was to see if she felt the same about him, and they could marry.

He stood for a dizzy moment on the steps of her house. Her house, which he could and would visit again. He turned at the sound of a whistle, made by someone's driver, and he thought he saw Sarianna on the other side of the street. When the street was clear, he crossed it, but the woman rushed away and turned the corner. "Rinny!" he called, but the woman made no indication that she had heard, and when he followed, she was gone.

TWENTY

∞

LENORE WAS SURPRISED when Miss Sarianna Browning was announced, and more so by her red face and disheveled hair.

"Was someone chasing you?" Lenore asked. "Are you harmed?"

"Please excuse my appearance. I do apologize."

"You look quite worn out."

"It's very warm."

"Come and sit down," Lenore said, leading her into the library. "Bring some tea," she said to her maid, and then turned to ask, "What brings you to town?"

"My mother. She is unwell."

Lenore felt there was more to say, but that Sarianna felt unequal to saying it. They sat together, waiting for tea, and it was not very long before Lenore realized that David's shoes were on the rug near them, as were his stockings and strewn pieces of the toy guillotine. The maid ought to have seen them and cleared them away, but she was new and not at all observant.

"Is your brother well?" Lenore asked Sarianna. "I have not seen him since the winter."

"He is much occupied at present. I told him about the *Liberty Bell*. He said he could no more write about this than he could about the poor Irish boy who broke the vase. I'm sorry."

"Don't be. Is that why you've come all this way? To tell me that?"

The tea came, and Lenore said to the maid, "These things. Please clear them away."

The girl picked up the shoes and, after a moment's confusion, piled the bone soldiers in her apron, but her expression as she did so was disapproving. Lenore noted it—she must speak to the girl or to Mrs. Young, but not now. The bones in the girl's apron clicked as she left the room, and Lenore did not call her back, though the soldiers belonged in the cabinet, not in some other place, wherever she was heading. In a few minutes, the girl returned to lift the larger platform of the guillotine. She carried it to the far side of the room and stopped, turning in a slow circle.

"You may set it there," Lenore called. "There, on the table."

The girl did so, frowning, and hurried out, wiping her hands on her apron.

They sat. A fly had come into the room, and it buzzed, lighting on her hand, so she flicked it away. It settled on the sofa and rubbed its forefeet together.

"Is there something I may do to help you, Sarianna?" Lenore said. "Because I would truly love to do so if I may."

"I followed Robbie," Sarianna said at last. "I shouldn't have, but I did. He went into Miss Barrett's house, and he stayed for such a long time."

The maid came back in and asked if she might have a word.

"Excuse me," Lenore said. "I will only be a moment."

"It's the boy and Miss Hawthorne," the maid said quietly. "They are trying to steal your dresses. Mrs. Young told me."

Lenore turned to Sarianna and said, "I will be a bit longer than I thought. Please do wait here and help yourself to tea. Do I have your promise that you'll wait for me?"

"I don't want to intrude. I'm refreshed and ought to leave you in peace."

"I beg you to stay."

Lenore had only just come in herself. "Let's take David out," she'd said to Miss Hawthorne earlier in the day. "We have been too much at home."

They would go, Lenore had decided, to the Mechanical Museum and let David ride the dobbie. But the man who operated the carousel had refused to let them in. Lenore saw that some of the children astride horses were accompanied by parents, who kept a protective hand on their backs, so she said, "His mother can go with him. Is the fare the same for her?"

"Not for such as them," the man said. "I can't allow it."

Mary Ann instantly withdrew, stepping out of the queue and pulling David with her. Lenore scanned the faces of the mothers and nurses and children and lovers who waited for their turn or who were still walking on the platform, pretending to study the merits of the various dobbies but really watching the three of them and seeing what would happen. The museum smelled of mildew and rust. The bright carnival colors took on a macabre aspect, as if the horses reared in a rictus of pain.

"It is 1845," Lenore said. "They are free."

The man turned his back on her. All Lenore could see of Miss Hawthorne was her yellow turban as she disappeared into the crowd.

The operator of the carousel spoke to the next woman in line as if Lenore had ceased to exist.

"You must sell me two tickets," Lenore said.

The man flicked his eyes at her and said she could ride if she wanted. To the next customer, he said, "Just the boy? Very well," and he took a shilling.

She had thought of making a speech. Of asking if any of the people in the Mechanical Museum had supported the cause of abolition and bought porcelain plates to free the people whose images were on the charity plates, and if so, did they care what happened to those people once abolition had been achieved? She thought of standing like a preacher and calling them "whited sepulchers," but she was a coward, and her legs carried her out of the pavilion to the bridge, where she found David crying, Miss Hawthorne angry and cold and silent, and passersby staring at them all.

In the carriage at last, Lenore said, "He is a stupid brute, that man. I will report him."

When they reached the house, she'd asked them to follow her, and she led them downstairs to the kitchen. The long marble slab was dusted with flour. Pie tins lay empty beside bowls of stewed fruit, and Lenore studied them. She must do something. She said to the cook, "David, Mrs. O'Connell is the best baker in London. You know that, don't you?"

He nodded.

"See the little cutters there?" She pointed at a tray of tin leaves and circles and squares. "Mrs. O'Connell will show you how to cut the dough with them. Then she'll give you sugar and you can spread sugar on top. She will bake all the pretty things you make and you can eat them all up or you can serve them to us, whichever you fancy."

David shook his head.

"Why not?"

He shook his head but gave no answer.

Mrs. O'Connell frowned at David. She frowned at Lenore. Lenore wanted to break something into a thousand pieces. Miss Hawthorne was listening and watching and absorbing the cook's disdain, which was exactly like that of the ticket man for the dobbie ride, so Lenore said to the cook in her firmest voice, "For the next quarter hour you are to show him how to do that."

Mrs. O'Connell had a roller in her hand, and the ball of dough lay thick and pale on the table. Something about her manner felt like a cracking in the ice under Lenore's feet. Mrs. O'Connell, being an excellent cook who didn't drink or have any children of her own, could quit and have a new job tomorrow. Even if she did what Lenore asked, David might refuse or pout and Mrs. O'Connell could say she tried. Lenore had never been in charge of children. Andrew was the father of at least four in Jamaica, but she was the named aunt of none. She could remember, from her own childhood, what it felt like to be told to make something you didn't want to make, so she ought not to force David, and yet she had issued the order to Mrs. O'Connell.

"Where is Tim?" she asked. Tim was the boy who helped light fires, clean out the ash, trim candles, and the like.

The cook shrugged, the rolling pin in her hand, but something restless in her feet, as if in a moment she would lay down the roller, walk out the door, and never return, willing to go so far as to resign her position rather than entertain this boy. "I don't know, Miss," she said.

Miss Hawthorne's expression was plain. It pleaded for the episode to end. *Please*, it said to Lenore, *please let us go away.* The favorite "away," lately, was not the park but their room upstairs. But there was so little for David to do in there that he kicked the wall or kicked the floor or shouted about going back home.

"Where is Mrs. Young?" Lenore asked. She had decided that Mrs. Young must be made to find Tim and set him down at the table with David. It had not been a command, initially, not for her. It had been intended as a treat. She felt hot all over, and her feet hurt.

Mrs. Young appeared, Tim was found, and it worked, a little. When the other boy began to play with the dough, David took a piece in his hand. Lenore had watched for a moment and then asked Miss Hawthorne to follow her. "Mrs. Young will stay here with them," Lenore said, and because there was something softer in Mrs. Young's face and voice, and because Tim was Mrs. Young's nephew, she believed this was true. She must speak confidently and win Miss Hawthorne's faith again, and they must try again with Mr. Barrett. "Come," she said. "Let us write to him again. We'll tell him what you told me about the coral necklace. Perhaps that detail will touch his heart."

Miss Hawthorne shook her head. "It won't work," she said.

"It has a chance."

"You said that about the news piece." Lenore had sent a description of Mary Ann's journey and her claim to the *Post*. In it, Lenore had named the Barretts and Cinnamon Hill. Weeks had passed before she received a letter. The *Post* had initially insisted on changing the name of Mr. Barrett to "Mr. B" and the name of the estate to "a profitable piece of ground in Jamaica where by all accounts the freed workers are well-treated and happy," and Miss Goss's byline to "a Planter's Daughter." After all these changes, the story had been killed at the last minute for "legal reasons."

"They will not care," Miss Hawthorne said.

"They must be made to care. We can't give up."

"You saw how it is at the dobbie. Everywhere we go, it is the same, and nothing will change for him even if you make Mr. Barrett pay. Everyone will turn away from the money and they will say it is not for such as him."

Miss Hawthorne's face had anguish in it instead of hope. "I want to go back," Miss Hawthorne said. "I will take him back."

How magically easy that would make Lenore's life in contrast. She could read her paper each day, with its stories of abominations suffered by others, and she could give money here and there, to others, who knew how to fix things. She could give money to Miss Hawthorne, and Lenore could call *that* her sacred duty, not this daily struggle. But no. Mrs. Jessie would not agree. "It will never change if we do not insist that it change," Lenore said.

"It will not change fast enough for him. He will be unhappy all the time, every day, and it will not change. I saw it. I saw it by the dobbie horses."

"We can talk about it another day," Lenore said. "When you feel brave again."

"No. It is like saying I should push him into boiling water to cool it off. How many boys would have to die before the water became cool? And what if the heat went on and on because they never turned it off, because they didn't want the boiling water to come cool? That is what would happen, Miss Lenore. I see it now."

Lenore did not know what to say.

"You don't even do for me what you do for your friends," Mary Ann continued.

"What do you mean?"

"Calling me Miss Hawthorne. You call that man 'Robert,' and that man 'Hank,' and that man 'George.' You call women by their first names but not me."

"It was, it is . . . a mark of respect."

"You're afraid of me. Because I'm not like you."

"I would be honored to call you Mary Ann."

"We should go home. We should never have come."

WHEN LENORE HAD followed the maid to Miss Hawthorne's room, Mrs. Young stood waiting in the hall. "I will talk to them myself," Lenore told her.

"She is packing the dresses. I told her that isn't right."

"It is right."

Mrs. Young wanted the dresses for herself. In the past, Lenore had given her old dresses to Mrs. Young, and now she felt entitled.

"Mary Ann?" Lenore said, knocking. "Let me in, please." To Mrs. Young, she said, "Ask Tim to bring my trunk."

When Mary Ann had opened the door, Lenore found them standing together. They had nothing but a small bag. The wardrobe was closed, and she opened it. Inside were the dresses she had given Mary Ann to wear in London, and her shoes, and her new coat.

"These are yours. Whether you stay or go."

"Mrs. Young says they are not mine."

"She misunderstood."

Mary Ann didn't move, and David twisted his hand out of his mother's and went to the window.

"I should write to Stormie if you insist on going back. He, at least, will give you shelter and work and anything you need."

"No."

"What will you do?"

"What I will do."

"I have a visitor. If you will wait until I have said goodbye to her, I will come with you to see about a berth."

Mary Ann nodded, and Lenore went back to the library, where Sarianna sat holding her empty cup.

"Thank you for the refreshment," Sarianna said, standing up. "I am interrupting."

"Do tell me what has happened, Sarianna. Please."

To her surprise, Sarianna began to cry.

"Oh, dear," Lenore said.

David sometimes crept out of his room. Lenore would find him exploring the house, hiding behind the furniture, playing games with things he had gathered. Now Lenore saw him tiptoe past the open door and drop to his knees to hide behind the couch as Sarianna told Lenore of standing outside the Barretts' house for a long time, nearly an hour, and finally seeing a lady appear in the window. She wore a white dress and she had dark hair. Right after this, the front door opened, and Robbie came out. "The lady was . . . I'm sure it was Miss Barrett, because of the nervous way she watched the street, hiding a little in the curtains, as if she wanted to observe him but didn't want to be seen. She was smiling, and he was smiling, and neither noticed the other, but I saw what they felt, Miss Goss. I *felt* what they felt. It was obvious by the way Robbie walked and the way she looked down at him, smiling."

"It sounds as if they are in love."

"I know," Sarianna said. The parrot scraped its beak slowly on a cuttlefish bone. "But don't you remember what you said about her."

"My dear, I don't remember."

"You said the cure was opium, and that it had allowed her to accept being a prisoner."

Sarianna walked to the cage. The bird stopped scraping its beak and watched her, and she watched him, and Lenore could sense David's presence, but Sarianna still didn't seem to notice him. "I don't want my brother to be in love with an opium addict."

"Think nothing of that," Lenore said. "I am sure Miss Barrett takes nothing more than a sleeping draught. It's very common in the city."

Sarianna gave her a reproachful look, and Lenore felt tired. So much and all at once.

"You don't know," Sarianna said. "How much we love and depend on him. How much he has disappeared from us. He thinks only of her now. And if she is, as you said at the party, an addict . . ."

"I must have made too much of it. And perhaps they haven't fallen in love at all."

David popped his head out, and now Sarianna saw him. "Hullo," she said. "Hullo, David."

David retreated.

"I brought your muff back," Sarianna said, "and I gave it to the man who opened the door."

"You might have kept it! I will see you to the door. Let my driver take you," she said. "The heat is too much, and I have worried you unnecessarily." She sent the servant out to summon the driver, and they were alone.

"Have the Barretts accepted him, then?" Sarianna asked. "David and his mother, I mean. I didn't know they were still here."

"No," Lenore said. "They have not."

"What will you do now?"

"I have no idea." She had an idea, but it was impractical. She wished she could go to France or Italy and be done with England all together. She could only do that, though, if her obligations here were done.

TWENTY-ONE

∞

IT HAD NOT occurred to Sarianna until she was climbing into the coach, which had the Goss coat of arms painted on the door, that if anyone in the village saw such a carriage, they would pause to see who stepped out of it. They would notice, and they would talk. They would tell her mother, or more likely, her father, how shocked they'd been to see Sarianna emerge with the help of a footman in livery. Such extravagance! What connections had they been making?

When they were still half a mile from her house, she asked to be let out and walked away swiftly, turning to look over her shoulder, willing the green carriage with the gilt crest to disappear. She saw no one, and she turned where the road turned, and she walked under the cobnut tree and practiced what she would say if Robbie asked where she had been all afternoon. "I bought this," she would say, and from her bag she would produce her alibi: the remedy a neighbor said would aid their mother's rheumatism, but which was not sold in any of the near apothecaries. She'd bought it shortly before knocking on Lenore's door.

It was butterfly season, and she tried to feel what she used to feel when small wings floated over the road and lighted on the soft green leaves and flowers blooming. White and yellow and black and pale blue butterflies were rising and settling on flowers lost in the gold brilliance of the spring sunshine. But their constant movement, so suggestive of happiness before, made her think of herself, the way she had spent the whole day darting here and there, afraid and looking backward, running away.

She tried to read the house before she entered it, as you might try to see, from the way a person's jaw was set, whether he was angry with you. Had Robbie left the door ajar? Was the cat walking from the door because it had been rousted from its place on Robbie's chair? But no. He was not within. Rather than call to her mother and possibly awaken her, she decided to go, like the butterflies, from one place to another, and to try, like the butterflies, to make no noise. Check the letter tray: nothing. Wash the dust from her face. Tie an apron. Check the dough she had left where it would be cool enough, she hoped, to rise slowly. Risen, it had. She was not, like the butterflies, completely silent, and when at last she decided to climb the stairs, her mother called out, "Is that you, Robbie?"

"It's Rinny," she said. She felt in her pocket for the vial of distilled turmeric.

"Where did you go, dear?"

Sarianna went up the remaining stairs quickly and stood in the doorway. The shutters were closed, the room gray. "May I come in and show you? It's a surprise."

"Yes," her mother said.

"You're missing the butterflies," Sarianna said. "Don't you want the sun in?"

"I was sleeping."

Sarianna opened the shutters, and the sun made a long, gleaming column on the plank floor. "See? Let me help you downstairs. But first, this," and she took the vial out of her pocket, saying, "Look what I found for you."

The liquid was a dull bronze, as if what Sarianna had done was fill the little jar with silty water.

"The turmeric tincture Mrs. Craythorne told you about. I found it."

"Where?"

"In town."

"Was Robbie with you?"

"I didn't want to waste his time with what I could do myself."

"You mustn't. You must not go there again, Rin. Not alone."

"And who will do such things for us if Robbie goes away?"

"Is he going away? What have you heard?"

"Nothing. I mean some day he will, surely. Are you having pains?"

"Not much," her mother said, but her book was not beside her, which meant she had not been reading at all.

"I'll get you tea, and you can take some, and while the bread bakes we can walk in the orchard. It will do you good to see the butterflies."

Robbie didn't come home for supper, after which her parents went to sit in the garden together (it was the distilled turmeric, she liked to think), so Sarianna took her chance.

She brought the broom and bucket and a cloth into Robbie's room so that if he came home she could say she had been tidying up. The bed was already tidy. The desk was neatened, too, as if Robbie had finished what he was working on and put away, or thrown away, his drafts. Listening for the door downstairs, and hearing only the evening songs of birds, she lifted the wooden slat of his writing desk and there they were. A pile of letters addressed to him, all in the same hand, all from Miss Barrett.

She could still stop herself. She could put the letters back, close the desk, and clean the floor before the light failed.

Leaving the door open a crack, she sat on the chair and proceeded to count them. It had started to seem that a letter came almost every day and went out as often, so she was surprised to count only thirteen. The last one was dated May 6. When she turned them over, she saw the counting had been done for her. Robbie had written a number on the back of each, sometimes underscoring it or adding a period, for emphasis.

The late-afternoon sun came in through the thick bubbles of glass with a medieval glimmer, as if she were locked in a tower.

She arranged the letters on the bed like cards for a game of Patience. She'd likely not have enough time or light to read more than one. With a pang she thought of her letters from Mr. Arnold, which she had kept despite his marriage to a young widow on the Isle of Wight. She ought to tear Mr. Arnold's letters to pieces and burn them in the fire so that no one could do what she was about to do. Staring at Miss Barrett's letters to her brother, she decided to start with the most recent one. It was likely to be more passionate, if passion there was.

It always took a while to adjust to the way a person formed the letters. She could instantly read anything Robbie wrote, but Miss Barrett's pen must be small and sharp. The line of ink was thinner than the legs of the tiniest fly. *Slow down*, Sarianna told herself as she tried to learn the code of shapes: the tall sloping *F*, the long dangling *g*—no, it was not a *g*, it was an *s*. Once you knew how a person wrote one letter, you could teach it to yourself. Slowly, too slowly, she fed on the miniscule fly-legs: *I think better of sleep than I ever did, now that fee?* . . . no, it was *she*.

I think better of sleep than I ever did, now that she will not easily come near me except in a red wood of poffies.

"Red wood of toffies"? *Red hood of poppies.*

Poppies.

So she did use it. Miss Barrett needed opium to fall asleep. Miss Barrett was not ashamed of that because she talked about it to Robbie. The room grew dimmer, and the fly-legs of ink blurred, and just as she neared the end she heard the front door opening, her father's voice, his chair creaking as he sat down to rest. He did not call out for her, so Sarianna had a little more time. She tiptoed to the door and gently, quietly closed herself in.

The red hood of poppies glowed in the gray room, as if it were a garment a ghost wore. She read: *Mr. Kenyon's on the 12th, brother and sister to meet you and four sister there one day to dinner. No—Four sister* was <u>your</u> *sister.*

The twelfth?

Today was the sixteenth.

Mr. Kenyon had invited Robbie and Sarianna to dine at Mr. Kenyon's on the twelfth, but Robbie had never mentioned it.

Why not?

Sometimes Robbie whistled to himself. When he was happy, he whistled or sang. That was the sound she heard now, distinct from the birds, whose flight she saw when she looked through the clearest part of the curving window—the black wings of birds hurrying home for the night.

She returned the tiny letter to its tiny envelope and gathered the others from the bed, taking care to order them as before, the most recent on top.

She tucked them inside the desk, and she saw what she had not seen before, just barely visible in the dim light: two more envelopes.

"Hello," Robbie said downstairs, and the door scraped on the flagstones.

She took those envelopes to the window and read the dates. Newer than the rest. She put them back, closed the desk, set the desk on the table, smoothed the coverlet, and went to the corner, where she took the broom into her hand and listened to Robbie's footsteps, which were coming nearer and louder on the stairs. She opened his door for him and said, as if everything was normal, "Hello, Robbie." The broom was her defense.

"Now? In the dark?"

"You know how I am. I put it off."

"You ought to have been outside enjoying the evening."

"I did! Did you have a good walk?"

"Splendid. The best I can remember." He took off his gloves, set them down beside the desk she had just opened, and said, "I thought I saw you today."

"Where?" she asked.

"Near Regent's Park. I called you but you ran away."

She told him about the turmeric.

"Why didn't you ask me to get it?"

"I wanted to be of use," she said, and she lifted the bucket. The stairs were too narrow for her to hold it at her side, so she held it before her, and the bucket sloshed water onto her dress and the broom scraped the wall. *A red wood of poffies* went the ominous, misread phrase in her head, a garbling of the truth. In her mind she saw Miss Barrett standing at her window, looking down on her brother with a knowing smile, and now, in her house, she saw her father standing near the stairs with his teacup. "What are you doing with a bucket at this hour, Miss Rin?" he asked, and she said it was all done now.

TWENTY-TWO

∞

SARIANNA WAS UP before Robbie the next day. She was arranging flowers when he came downstairs and set a letter in the tray. He was going riding, he said, and was she going to be there when the letter carrier passed?

"Where would I go?" she asked.

"Would you like to go somewhere?" Robbie asked. It fairly shone out of him, the sunshine of his hope and happiness.

"Riding would be nice," she said, poking the dahlia stem into the vase.

"I know," he said. "Soon! Soon. But I'm seeing Mr. Kenyon today."

"Oh?" She pretended to be engrossed in the search for a stem of just the right length and color.

"He's always asking if I might bring my charming sister to his house."

"How very kind of him."

"I'll get us an invitation, I promise."

Out he went, and in she stayed. She listened for her mother, who snored sometimes when she took an afternoon nap, and there it came: the ragged breathing, so like a man's. Their mother had married very late in life, at thirty-nine, borne Robbie at forty, then Sarianna, and now she was seventy-two. Though only ten years older than their father, she was much weaker, much sicker, and consequently much more removed from everything. At times it seemed as if their mother were their grandmother, and their father, her doting son.

Sarianna picked up the letter Robbie had left for the post and let it sit in her hand. It weighed so little and took up so little space. Whatever it said was to Miss Barrett alone.

Her mother's snore erupted with such violence that Sarianna thought it would wake her, but another snore followed, proof that she was still asleep, oblivious, and Robbie was still gone, also oblivious, and she was still herself, standing three steps from the top, her brother's letter in her hand.

If Robbie meant to marry, it would affect all of them.

She took the letter knife and gently picked at the wax. She didn't want to tear the paper. The sense of violation warred with her determination to know what her brother was thinking and feeling.

Sarianna could see, through the thick glass of the ancient window, a dark shape moving. When she pressed her face to it, the shape became not Robbie but Quig, the mail carrier. He reached the wall and disappeared, but he was there, walking beside the orchard, headed for their house.

She had promised to send this letter. Robbie would wait, as she had once waited, for the next post, and the next, for the beloved person's reply. Any extra hours were a torment.

A knock came, and she went below to open it.

"Good day, Mr. Quig," she said. His carrier's red coat was too big for him. Someone had cut his hair recently, and not well.

"Can you wait while I fix this seal? It's come open."

Quig nodded but he was not pleased.

She went to her mother's table while Quig stood shuffling his dirty boots. "Would you like a bit of cake?" she asked.

He nodded, so she fetched that, and he went to stand under the wisteria, to her relief, and she set about heating the wax, pouring it slightly to the right of the old seal, and driving the brass end into it, finishing as her mother said, "Rin?" She went out the open door and held it for Quig with the address on top, the messy seals below. "Here it is. Thank you, Quig." She would have handed him a coin if she had had one, but of course she didn't. He brushed the crumbs from his mouth, nodded, and was at the gate by the time her mother stood in the room, watching her and him, and Sarianna hoped that her face was not bright red.

"Any letters today?" her mother asked, and Sarianna pointed to the ones Quig had left.

Robbie loved Miss Barrett. That was plain without reading the letter. He would probably marry her, and if Miss Barrett were an addict they would be ruined.

"I'll milk Hilda," she said, walking mechanically down the path, feeling the bright summer sun on her head and reaching out to touch the wisteria that was just starting, she saw, to wither. When she turned the corner to the well, she nearly ran into Robbie.

"Was that Quig?" he said.

"Yes," she said.

"I am too late then."

"For what?"

"I decided to walk the letter to the city myself." Robbie pumped water onto his hands, rubbing them together before he pressed them on his face. She watched his back as he went up the path, through the gate, and into the trees after Quig.

TWENTY-THREE

∞

"Mr. Browning," Arabel said. She held open the door for him. "I'm just going out."

"I was bringing this."

He held the letter. Six miles' walk to bring a letter he might have handed to the carrier. She would wonder what the hurry was, but he didn't care.

"I hate it when I miss the last post," Arabel said, pretending it was normal. "Shall I take it up?"

"Or set it inside is enough, thank you."

Arabel was the gentler of the two sisters, and was more often present during his visits. Elizabeth said she'd always had the gift of knowing, almost without a word, whatever it was you wanted.

"You might go up, you know," Arabel said. "Since you've come all this way. I was just with her. Wait a moment."

He ought to say no, he thought, but he couldn't. He had thought of kneeling before Elizabeth, and perhaps this was better than, more direct than, more irrefutable than, the letter he held.

In no time at all he was there on the green couch, beside the unruly red convolvulus, summer air inside and outside the open window. He collected a fallen blossom from the floor and held it.

"Shall I read it now?" Elizabeth asked, the letter on the table beside her.

"No," he said emphatically. His tension spread to the dog, who growled. The red blossom in his hand was starting to wilt. "I ought to go."

"But you just arrived."

"I am not myself."

"Is it your head again?"

For a moment, he could do nothing but look at her. Arabel was not in the room, nor Henrietta, nor Wilson. Then he said, "I'm sorry to come so suddenly." The dog studied him, waiting to strike.

"Have you been able to work?" she said. "Is *Luria* glad that you have given up the polka, or *have* you given it up?"

Luria was the play he was writing, and he had promised to stop staying out all night, dancing, and finish the last act for her. The room felt like a lake into which he had not dropped, but was about to drop, a stone. The unbroken surface of the water shone. He didn't care about the play just then. What he wanted was *her*, and an end to waiting. "I should like," he said, "to speak to your father."

"He isn't home," Elizabeth said quietly.

"May I wait for him?"

"Oh, no," Elizabeth said, softening her voice even more. "I've told you before. If he allowed us to invite our friends to dinner you would be the first."

He softened his own voice. "I need only to speak to him alone."

"'The castle at its toils the lapwings love,'" Elizabeth said, rubbing Flush's head as if to silence the dog and Robert at the same time. "I have told you, haven't I, that it's my favorite line? I was reading it again today. The birds made me think of it."

"I have made up my mind, Ba."

"*Luria* is not unlike *Sordello*, it seems to me."

"Tell me I may put the case to him."

"*Luria* is all I can think of, or talk of, and you refuse to send him to me. I will send you home and keep you there until you finish it."

"Open my letter first."

"Only if it tells me that you have finished it."

"Could you read it now?" He set the red blossom on the letter he had addressed to her and waited.

"It's five o'clock. You must start for home, and I must prepare for dinner. I'm well enough to go downstairs, you know."

"Ba—"

A knock came, and it was Wilson. Elizabeth's face was bright and strange enough that Wilson became as stiff and unnatural as the two of them, bustling about. Robert had no choice but to leave. His walk home was one of self-flagellation, every step taking him farther away and yet no farther from the certainty, the absolute certainty, that she was reading his letter and receiving it not in the swell of love he'd felt as he wrote it, but in the outflow of the tide that drained and drained and drained the river beside him, leaving the boats that had once been ready to sail, their hulls and decks shiny with purpose, dirty and helpless on their sides in mud.

TWENTY-FOUR

SARIANNA LIKED THE butter to go all the way to the edges, but it had been chilled in the well to suit Robbie, who liked it cold, so it did not spread. Her mother was taking mutton from the tray, and her father was eating.

"I need to ask you all to do something very important for me," Robbie said.

Sarianna's bread tore on a shoal of butter, and she pressed the jagged opening closed.

"If you could please not speak of my visits to Miss Barrett. Or the letters we exchange."

"Why not?" Sarianna asked.

"Because it is of no interest to anyone other than ourselves."

Sarianna bit into her bread, and Mr. Browning took a piece of mutton from his plate to feed the cat.

"I send her my work," Robbie continued, "and she sends me hers, and we are able to help one another because our intellectual aims are the same."

Sarianna's gaze was downward. She was the one who had to answer everyone's questions about Robbie. The butcher's wife, the drover's daughter, the baker—everyone that Sarianna met in the course of her daily errands—had at one time or another asked what Robbie did for a living, and she had told them he was a poet. They didn't think much of it. They were wondering, she knew, what would happen when the elder Mr. Browning could no longer work at the bank. A poet for a son, and not a successful poet, either. How would they live? The one benefit to Robert marrying Miss Barrett would be a change in how they viewed him. No one in Hatcham had ever married anyone famous.

"The news is likely known already," Sarianna said. "Quig is not deaf and dumb, and he sees how fast you write one another."

Mr. Browning took another bite of mutton, fed it gently to the cat, and said, "I believe I may have spoken of it, Robbie."

"To whom?" Robbie asked.

"I was proud, you know. I *am* proud. And why not?"

Mrs. Browning pushed her bread into the sauce and left it there. "Mrs. Larch had heard of it already," she said. Mrs. Larch was the pretty widow their father visited as often as he dared, always with gifts of cream or perry.

"I don't speak of that to her," Mr. Browning said.

"What you've said," Robbie said, "you have said. For the future, though, if you would be discreet."

"Is she consumptive, Robbie?" Mrs. Browning said. "Mrs. Larch said she is."

"No."

"Are you sure?" Mrs. Browning asked.

"Yes."

"Because it may develop," his mother added. "It so often does, when one has it in the family."

"They do not."

"How many are there in her family?" Mrs. Browning asked.

"There were twelve all together."

"As many as that!" Mrs. Browning said.

"Two of her brothers have died in adulthood."

"Of consumption?" Mr. Browning took a bite of meat and began to chew.

"No."

"What was it, then?"

"An accident with one. A tropical fever for the other."

"Where was he?" Mr. Browning asked. "The one that got the tropical fever, I mean."

Robbie said, "Jamaica, I believe."

Their father believed that one's hands, once dirtied by profit from the West Indies, could never be clean. He had given up his own chance to be rich long ago when he'd been sent to Saint Kitts, where he was punished for teaching a young slave to read. He usually cried when he told the story.

"In sugar, are they?" Mr. Browning asked.

Robbie nodded.

"Have you seen her?" Mrs. Browning asked. "Miss Barrett?"

"I have." He turned to his father. "I showed her the pictures you made, of the Irish boy and of the Portland Vase, remember? And she said you were very talented."

Their father nodded. "That's right, that's right, I remember. Is that whose carriage was bringing you home, Rin?"

Sarianna's stiffened. "No," she said.

"Then whose?"

"A friend of Robbie's, Miss Goss."

Robbie looked as if he might dispute that she was his friend, but he didn't, and Sarianna was grateful.

"I went to fetch a tincture mother needed. No one had it here, and Mr. Dill said it could be had in town. I saw Miss Goss, who insisted on sending me home by carriage. Who was telling tales about me?" she asked. "Was it Quig?"

"I don't remember, dear. Don't be so upset," her father said. "Why wasn't Robbie with you?"

"He has visits of his own to make."

"I'll take you, if you wish, Rinny," Robbie said. "You need only ask. Or I will buy anything mother needs."

"It's fine" was all Sarianna said. "I don't need to go. I don't have any reason to go anywhere."

TWENTY-FIVE

∞

AND AT THAT moment God came to the garden and said you are cast out.
Cover your nakedness. You have sinned.

As soon as she had read the letter, Elizabeth wrote:

> *I intended to write to you last night & this morning, & could not,-*
> *you do not know what pain you give me in speaking so wildly- ... You*
> *have said some intemperate things ... fancies—which you will not say*
> *over again, nor unsay, but forget at once, & for ever, having said at*
> *all,—& which (so) will die out between you & me alone, like a mis-*
> *print between you & the printer.*

The warmth of the sun became the heat of the sun. Scarlet flowers wilted
in the window box, and new buds crumpled inside themselves. Elizabeth
kept writing, desperate to make Mr. Browning understand what he ought
to have understood already: a single woman could not receive a lover in her
room—only a friend, and even then, it was delicate. If he were to say these
things, she must shut him out.

The humilities of her position.

The prosperities of his.

A cerebral, intellectual, platonic exchange, far above the grossness of
mortal love, that was all they were doing—

"Ba."

Sweat dampened her dress and lay slick on her face. Her hands felt like
they were made of molten wax.

It was dark, the room was hot, she felt the aura.

"Ba, don't."

She was alone in her room, and yet a voice spoke.

"Why are you telling him that?" the voice asked her. "What is this madness, you silly loon?"

When had she taken the drops? It was not just a voice but a man in the corner. His skin was yellow and his beard was unshaved. His hair wet and matted. It was Sam. She felt afraid and exhilarated at the same time. To have a visitation like this, to see that life continued, that people were not far away from you but this close.

"Tell him," Sam said, "what I will dictate. Take a new page and write this."

She had already taken a new sheet of paper so that she could tell Mr. Browning, again, the absolute necessity of unsaying. She sat very still so he wouldn't vanish.

"My darling Rob," Sam dictated, his eyes fixed on the ceiling, as if that were where he saw the words, "I beg you to come here immediately. I need you. I need you like I need air and light. Do not stay away from me or I shall die of my wounds like an eviscerated unicorn."

That proved he was Sam. Every serious business ended with a joke.

"You're jealous of my phrasing," Sam said, "but it's all right. You may steal from me just this once." His familiar—so very familiar—face was wet when he leaned forward. He looked terrible. He stood up and walked over to her writing desk, and he took the pages she had already written. "Listen to yourself, Bazy," and he read one of her paragraphs to her, then said, "I fail to see why you torture yourself this way—you're ordering him to keep *away* from you."

She pointed to the wall between her room and their father's.

"Let Mr. Browning take you away from here if the Pater objects. Let your lover take you to Malta. You'd be better off."

If only a breeze would start. The teacup was empty, the laudanum corked. It had been dark when she counted the dose, or was that yesterday's darkness and yesterday's dose? What if she were only imagining him, and he were not real?

"Write that you love him and tell him the doctor said another winter here could kill you. The filthy fog could kill *me*, and I'm already dead."

She didn't move or speak.

"Marry Mr. Browning. Go to Malta, or Rome, or Naples, or Pisa. Any of those beguiling cities will do. Exeunt."

Her hand wrote, *And this you will do <u>for my sake</u> who am your friend*

"He asked you to be his wife, Ba. In the letter you are telling him to unwrite."

Her hand wrote, *You remember,—surely you do,—that I am in the most exceptional of positions,—& that, just because of it, I am able to receive you as I did on Tuesday.*

"No one else knows he asked you. No one would have to know."

Your influence and help in poetry will be full of good and gladness to me

"Do you know, Ba, when I'm waiting for the eagle, I ponder this. When I'm chained there and I think I hear his wings and I know his shadow is about to cross the rock, I think to myself, *What is it that I did to deserve this torment?*"

It was not Sam. It was Prometheus. A breeze touched her face lightly, and then was gone.

Her hand wrote *On Tuesday week you can bring a tomahawk and do the criticism and I shall try to have my courage ready for it—Oh, you will do me so much good—and Mr. Kenyon calls me "docile" sometimes I assure you; when he wants to flatter me out of being obstinate—and in good earnest, I believe I shall do everything you tell me. The* Prometheus *is done—*

She was almost done. She, the letter, the night, and Robert's letter were real, but Sam was dead and absent. Invisible, like all the dead.

And if in the unsilence, I have said one word to vex you, pity me for having had to say it—

Sign it, send it, keep him without losing him. Friend unfriend refriend not lover.

Your friend in grateful regard,
E.B.B.

TWENTY-SIX

∞

ROBERT WENT IMMEDIATELY outside with the letter from Miss Barrett.

Apple blossoms pear blossoms cherry blossoms peach blossoms plum blossoms. Between the forked trees in the garden the grass was a visceral green. On the visceral green of the greenest grass fell white blossoms that the wind tumbled and carried like snow.

SHE REFUSED HIM, and to see her again he must forget that he had ever asked.

> . . . *forget at once, and for ever, having said at all*

> *Your friend in grateful regard,*
> *E.B.B.*

"What's wrong?" his mother said. She sat at the end of a row of blooming trees, in the shade, a piece of cloth in her lap, a needle motionless in her hand.

"Nothing. I'm going for a ride."

He resolved to do the forgetting. If there was asking there was unasking. Why had Adam and Eve not tried this? Why did they not say to God, We *have* no knowledge. It has not happened. It does not exist, not in us, not here, not in the garden. We are not naked. We do not love. We are *friends*, Adam and I. We are *friends*, Eve and I. We wish only to discuss poetry.

Adam asked Eve to return his profane letter. Eve sent the letter back and Adam stood beside the fire in the Garden and he burned the letter so they would not be cast out.

The ash of the letter mingled with leaves and rotting fruit, and rain fell steadily throughout the afternoon, turning it to sticky flakes. The flakes, white as the ash of apple wood, attached to the feet of beetles who crept slowly under the carts of horses pulling vegetables to London.

TWENTY-SEVEN

∞

"I HEAR YOU are at fault for your condition, Miss Barrett," Dr. Chambers said.

"From whom?"

"Your father says if you would drink porter and eat beefsteak for a month all your ills would vanish."

"He did tell me that."

Dr. Chambers took her wrist. "Poppycock," he said. "I will tell him the same in a more deferential tone. You couldn't possibly digest such things. Half the men in England can't digest them, and yet they go on recommending them to others. Breathe for me."

She breathed. She could hear it herself. The little wheeze. The faint rattle.

When he had finished listening, he went to the window.

"Have you discussed a winter spot?" he asked. "It isn't beef that will help you but pure air."

"Malta has been raised, and Alexandria, and Pisa. Alexandria seemed the safest, but my father heard from a friend that Malta was better because it's in British hands, and there are troops. I'd rather not go to an island, troops or not. So I like Pisa."

"I like Pisa, too. Set the dates, book your passage. You'll never go if you don't book your passage."

The door opened and her father came in.

"Good afternoon, Mr. Barrett," Dr. Chambers said. "Your daughter and I have been discussing Pisa. I suggest she cross no later than October."

Her father's glance blamed her. "Have you gone there yourself?" he asked Dr. Chambers.

"Many of my patients have. I remain here, unfortunately, to do my work. They assure me Pisa is perfectly safe."

"Provided she can survive a month in carriages," said her father. "Over the alps."

"She needn't go by land. If she goes by steamer from Marseilles to Genoa, she would avoid all that."

"Except the part from here to Marseilles. I remember talk like this of Torquay, Dr. Chambers. It was the same promise then."

"She *was* better there. Much better."

Neither added "until." Until Elizabeth begged their father to let Edward stay and keep her company a little longer in Torquay. Until he took up sailing. Until the boat did not come back. Until they found his body.

"I want to see trunks packed next time I visit," Dr. Chambers said. "I want to hear the date you'll sail."

Elizabeth paid the doctor's fees with her legacy, so he made the mistake of thinking she could direct her own life.

"Go out to the park while it's still warm," he continued. "Go every day while the weather is fine and extend the time bit by bit." He didn't mention cupping. Or leeching. Or bleeding. She was relieved that he hadn't asked if the itching had gotten any worse. She never wanted her father to think of any part of her that was not her brain.

"How is the itching?" he asked after all.

"Not quite as bad," she said.

"What itching?" her father asked Dr. Chambers.

"Side effect of laudanum. Can be quite a menace if the scratching leads to open wounds."

"Has that happened?" If there were open wounds, that would be her fault, for scratching.

"No," she lied. She didn't think they were entirely open. Not now.

"Shall I add something? You could try this," and Dr. Chambers began to write something down.

Her father frowned. It was a scandal, he often said, what the doctors in league with apothecaries earned on potions and unguents.

Dr. Chambers gave the slip of paper to her because, as with his fees, that was the arrangement. "You're otherwise well," he said, "and will be until the first frost. So you should make haste."

Elizabeth nodded.

"Good day, then," he said, and she sat very still, smiling falsely, knowing that her father would stay to attack the Pisa plan.

"I was not aware we had progressed to naming a city," he said as soon as the doctor left. "Have you read what's in the *Times* about Italy?"

"Not today."

"More unrest. More and more and more fighting among the duchies. I prefer Malta."

"Malta seems more difficult to me," she said. "At the whims of the sea."

"It's no better to be at the whims of dukes and soldiers."

"I have a friend who thinks Pisa perfectly safe," she said.

"And which friend is that?"

Mr. Browning was her friend, and nothing but, and her conscience was clear, so she might say his name. Why not? "Mr. Browning."

"Who?"

He had forgotten. For once it was a relief that he cared so little for poetry. "A poet."

"Does he live there?"

"He went last fall, and he means to go again."

"Has he a wife?"

"No."

"A single man may travel as he likes."

She must make some kind of concession. "If you prefer Malta, we should see if the house is still for let. The one Mr. Kenyon had heard of."

"I don't prefer it. I prefer that you stay here. That is by far the safest plan."

The thought of driving through the park with Henrietta and Flush flickered before her, fluttering like a bright flag. She might have the energy to get out and walk. She might sit on a bench if she tired, close her eyes, and picture Italy.

Once her father had shut the door, Flush hopped down, rolled over on his back, and let the sun be a blanket for his whole being. He closed his eyes in the ecstasy of warmth.

TWENTY-EIGHT

∞

ON THE NEXT Sunday, Sarianna came upon Robert in his old thinking place, under the chestnut trees. He was lying under the farthest tree, staring up as he liked to do.

"You look contented," she said, arranging her skirts and picking at clover. Her fingernails were stained from the plum juice.

"I am not."

"Why not?"

"I heard from my Roman friends. They know of a flat I can have for almost nothing in Pisa."

The houses in the distance had a fat, dull look this time of day, bleached by the noonday sun. She could see the orchard where she had spent August, and she could see the kitchen where she would spend September. He would leave, and she would stay.

"There's nothing for me here," he added.

She split the stem of a clover.

"Except you, Rinny. And our parents. I mean there is nothing for my work. I have used up all the fruit I gathered."

All year she waited for the long bright days of August, and all week she waited for Sunday afternoon. Now the thought of him going, and of herself being the one who had to stay and ease their mother's burden, swirled in the clouds of gnats.

"When will you go?"

"Soon."

"And how long will you stay?"

"Forever, I hope."

She watched the gnats with green fields behind them, the gold bits of their bodies in transit. He said it so carelessly—"forever"—as if he had always wished it. Her throat felt thick, and her vision of the gnats clouded.

"It will free you," he said, "from the neighbors who say hello and then pick me apart over fence posts when I'm out of hearing. In Italy, I can be the English poet. Here, I can only be Mr. Browning's idle son."

"Is that why Byron and Shelley stayed abroad? So the neighbors wouldn't gossip?"

He sat up and put his hat back on. "Maybe."

"It gave people a lot more to gossip about in the end." She decided to ask him. "What about Miss Barrett? Is she part of this plan?"

"That is the problem," Robert said, his blue eyes absolutely opaque when they met hers. "Her doctor has said it's a necessity."

"Then you will marry her, and you'll both go?"

He leaned back on his hands so that he was looking straight up at the leaves of the chestnut, a view they had both loved when they were children. It had been his constant suggestion that they look up while walking, not down, and she had tripped so often that finally her mother said she must be going blind.

She lay back and pretended to enjoy the shapes of the leaves, the color of the sky, and the smell of grass and clover, but how many times could you look at the same view? The view that would be hers next year, and the next.

"I can't say a word about that, to her or to anyone," Robert said, "I swore I wouldn't. But if I settle there, I'll send for you."

"That wouldn't work, you know. If one goes, the other stays to help."

"They could do without you for a month or two if it were the right time of year. I could show you Florence and Rome. You would love it there."

"I would rather go to Paris."

"Italy is better."

"I don't understand what you're saying. You would go without her, or not?"

He put his finger to his lips.

"Not without her."

"But you might go."

"It's hard to say what will happen. I shouldn't have said anything. I will likely be right here next year, and the next."

She would like that just fine, though it was selfish. She ought to stop being afraid. She put her head back and closed her eyes and tried to think only of this year, this August, this warm and benevolent sun.

TWENTY-NINE

～

WHY HAD ROBERT gone silent?

Four times a day, the mail came. Four times a day to expect and be disappointed. What had Elizabeth said to make him disappear?

It had felt like she might, or must, explain what it was that made her so obedient to her father, and to be truly obedient was to defend. If she could only make Robert see her father as he had been in July of 1840. So she had written "For three days we waited . . ." For the sailboat to return with her brother in it, alive.

> And the sun shone as it shines to-day, and there was no more wind than now; and the sea under the windows was like this paper for smoothness—and my sisters drew the curtains back that I might see for myself how smooth the sea was, and how it could hurt nobody—and other boats came back one by one.

They found three bodies, not four, one at a time, over a period of weeks, miles from where *La Belle Sauvage* was last seen. The two of them, she and her father, had sunk together into Edward's grave at the bottom of the sea. Her father had climbed back out and reached down for her, insisting that she take his hand and climb into the world of the living.

Forgive me this gloomy letter I half shrink from sending you, yet will send.

Robert probably hadn't responded because she had covered the ground all around him with ash. She had shown him how depressed she was, and he had wanted to go somewhere brighter and happier. She had always known he would. He said he could never tire of her words or company, but when a person liked to dance, as he did, and walk a dozen miles, and ride a dozen more, and stay out all night talking to theater people and critics and artists and writers, and could say to himself, *I will go to Italy*, and then leave whenever he liked, what would keep that person from politely reducing the speed and length and warmth of his letters, and going gracefully but everlastingly away?

She would have to paint different scenery and write him a letter about his poem "Saul." She did it at once, as if she hadn't written him a long letter about death. She was well into her argument about "Saul" when Wilson brought the next post.

He was most grateful, he said. There was a better thing than being "happy in her happiness" and she must blot out of her mind forever the fear that he would be tired of her. All she had to do was write him a letter about normal things—the exact thing she was at that moment doing—and equilibrium would return. The normal letter about normal things went into Wilson's hand and from thence to the mail carrier's glove and from thence to Hatcham.

She used to cut the hours into bites and wash them down one by one with tea and laudanum. Now the days were divided into first post, second post, third post, last post, insomnia. If he didn't write, or he wrote less, she had this room, her sisters, the dog that breathed in the crook of her arm, and the disgust she felt for her published poetry. In two days it would be September, and in thirty days after that, the cold would shut her in.

"Ba?" said a voice. It was George. He never came outside of his regular time—Wednesdays at half past seven—for sitting with her and talking about his work.

"I asked Wilson," George said to Elizabeth, "how often Mr. Browning is here."

"You might have asked *me* that. I would have told you."

"How often is Mr. Browning here, Ba?"

"Are you asking to see if I will tell you the same as Wilson? Is that fair?"

"Let's not do it this way. I know that he visits often. I know that he writes often. I know what he makes."

"How?"

"Your publisher and his, Mr. Moxon."

"You asked Mr. Moxon how much Mr. Browning makes, and he told you?"

"I didn't. A friend did."

Elizabeth kept her fingers buried in Flush's fur. "Why?"

"His intentions, Ba. I want to know what they are."

"We are friends."

How things changed as your life ran along. A gap that seemed enormous disappeared—she the older sister, George a little boy. She had been the one in charge, teaching and consoling, now she was nothing.

"I heard from Chorley he is going to Pisa," George said, making his voice quieter, as if he were on her side.

"Chorley is going to Pisa?"

"No, Mr. Browning."

"Some friends of his said a flat was available there. He might go."

"But you are also interested in Pisa."

"Dr. Chambers believes Pisa to be the simplest and the best."

"But if he were there, and that's where you went," George said. "I'm sorry, Ba. I feel I must ask if that is entirely safe."

"What do you mean?"

"Say it were a French novel, Ba. The unmarried lady of means is thinking of going to Italy for a cure. An unmarried man with an impoverishing profession says he is also going there. Ought her brother to be concerned?"

Elizabeth laughed. "If the lady were eighteen years old."

George didn't laugh. "Say the lady was renowned, and the gentleman was not."

"Say the gentleman was a genius who walks twelve miles a day, and the lady a hermit who walks, on a good day, downstairs. Say he was younger than she."

"Might the gentleman think that of no importance if she had an income that would support them both? In Italy. Where the gentleman would prefer to live."

"Would the brother trust his sister? Her mind, her perceptions, her good sense?"

George stood up and went closer to the window, where the fine yellow light made everything seem easy and charmed. "He would never forgive himself if he did not."

"Then we remain in safety."

The dog looked soulfully at her, waiting and waiting, and George went out, and Wilson came with food and a letter from Mr. Browning that said nothing except he did not have a headache and would see her on Monday.

Flush's paw lay on her dress, and she felt the grains of sand flow like a cataract. It was going, the summer. The cold would come and the light would go out and a layer of ice would trap everything just as it was, thick and dark and soundless, the room small as a coffin, with as little air.

But Mr. Browning wrote again. It came in the morning post. It made her stand up, wash her face, put Flush on a rope, ask Wilson to send for the carriage, and go to the park. Arabel was at a meeting for something, Henrietta was shopping, and she didn't care because all she wanted was to go for a ride in that letter, to sit within and upon it as a swan sits on a lake.

> Can you understand me so, dearest friend, after all? Do you see me—when I am away, or with you—"taking offence" at words, "being vexed" at words, or deeds of yours, even if I could not immediately trace them to their source of entire, pure kindness; as I have hitherto done in every smallest instance?
>
> I believe in you absolutely, utterly—I believe that when you bade me, that time, be silent—that such was your bidding, and I was silent—dare I say I think you did not know at that time the power I have over myself, that I could sit and speak and listen as I have done since? Let me say now—this only once—that I loved you from my soul

and gave you my life, so much of it as you would take,—and all that
is done, not to be altered now: it was, in the nature of the proceeding,
wholly independent of any return on your part.

What it meant to be loved by him was for another day. This morning
was the crunch of gravel under slow-rolling wheels, the horse plodding, the
bright sun, the still water glazed with swans.

"I'll go down at five," she told Wilson.

"Shall I do your hair, miss?"

She said yes. For this meeting with her father about Pisa, she must be
in her going-out dress, with her hair set, sitting upright in the library, pre-
senting to everyone the figure of a person who could walk from a coach to
an inn, an inn to a packet, a packet to a dinghy, a dinghy to the next inn,
the inn to the train, and so on, all across France and half of Italy. Kenyon
suspected the sheer number of embarkations would be her father's argument against it. Her father would say that she didn't know how strenuous it
would be, and she must prove she did.

"Shall we try it, miss?" Wilson said.

Henrietta's picture from a magazine was on the dressing table. In the
illustration, the woman's hair was pulled back, and the curls were pinned
up behind three flowers, instead of left down to frame her face.

"No," Elizabeth said. She didn't want everyone to wonder why, after all
this time, she was following new fashions for hair.

Wilson's face in the glass was disappointed. "Gloves, miss? You have
these new ones."

"I won't be going out."

"But to look as if you were," Wilson said.

So she held in her lap the new gloves, embroidered with bluebells near
the wrist, the fingertips white as snow, unstained by travel but ready for
it. Her fingers were what they always were: dirty things, the ink having
seeped into the cuticles and under the nail, even under the left thumbnail,
she saw. She never bothered about that because she never need bother: who
would see, as she sat in her room, or at her family's table, that her hands

were stained with ink? Only Mr. Browning, who knew it was not grime but a sign of progress.

Kenyon was let in. Arabel sat knitting. Her father was finishing some letters. George had not yet arrived. The gloves were silly, just sitting there on her lap.

"Will you stay for dinner?" she asked Kenyon. She wanted him to stay. He must stay. She tried to say that to him with her eyes. If he said he was staying, it would indicate he thought they would all be happy after the meeting ended, and it would be possible to enjoy the pheasant their friend Miss Mitford had sent. "She told me we must share it with you. You can hardly decline when you know it's your favorite," she added.

In the faintness of his smile, she saw he had come to the opposite conclusion. "Miss Mitford should never be disappointed in anything," he said, assenting, and she loved him for the smile he gave next, which was brighter. He did not believe this would go well, but he wanted to pretend they would win the fight.

HER FATHER LOOKED up from his letters. "And you leave for Dover when?" he asked Kenyon, setting down his pen, turning in his chair, moving his bad leg with a grimace they all pretended not to see.

"Right away," Kenyon said.

"Have you a house?"

"Yes. The same one as last year."

"I don't like Dover much," Mr. Barrett said.

"You haven't been there in ages," Kenyon said. "You ought to visit me and see how exhilarating the views are. It would do you good to get out of town."

They were still waiting for George.

"Remember," Elizabeth said to her father, "the men who carried us on their shoulders when we arrived in Paris?"

"On their shoulders?" Kenyon said.

"Yes. I was six. It was when I hid in the carriage so Papa wouldn't leave me home."

She was caught up in the memory of the light on foreign water, on the men speaking to each other in the language she had heard her mother speak, but French in their mouths was different, as were the gestures that seemed to suggest the impossible: *sit on my shoulders*, the gestures said, *and I will carry you to the beach*. How could she! How could her mother? Her father? And yet they had. That was what you did when you traveled. You did impossible things.

"I had forgotten that appalling practice," her father said.

"I'm sure they don't do it that way anymore," she said.

"Indeed they don't," Kenyon said. "The last time I was in Genoa, the passengers were all brought to shore in rowboats."

George came in, and she repeated in her mind what she had told Henrietta when they practiced. *I will go to Pisa.*

George met her eyes too briefly. "I'm sorry I'm late," he said to their father. "Do you have plans, Ba?"

She gave him a confused look.

"The gloves," he said. "You look like you're going out."

"No," she said. "I am out already in being downstairs."

"It's rather hot," George said, and he was about to say something more when their father cut him off.

"This won't take much time," he said.

Kenyon met her eyes warily, as if to ask whether some previous discussion had already occurred.

"It's obvious to me that Ba mustn't go," Mr. Barrett said.

Arabel's needles, with their soft whispery noise, stopped. "Why?" she asked.

"In addition to all the other reasons, which I have elucidated to each of you in turn, I have heard the most appalling news."

George was looking at their father, not at her, and Kenyon smiled at Elizabeth as if to say it would be all right. Elizabeth felt that Kenyon wanted to reach for her hand and give her strength, but he didn't. She gripped the white gloves with bluebells stitched on the cuffs. "And what is that?" Elizabeth asked, remembering her resolve. She kept her voice level, her body straight. She had a glass of water near her, but she didn't reach for it.

"Pisa," Mr. Barrett said, "was presented to me as the city with the greatest health benefits and the least amount of danger in going to and from, though, as I have told Kenyon, it would still mean at least eighteen days of continuous travel and two water crossings. Now I hear that Pisa has been chosen for quite another reason."

Elizabeth sat perfectly still.

"Because of a man who intends to meet her there."

"What man?" Kenyon asked, though Elizabeth was positive he guessed.

"Robert Browning," George said.

Arabel sat with the lump of knitting in her lap, and she seemed to ask, with a furtive glance at Elizabeth, what she should make of this development, and how she should proceed. Elizabeth had not told Arabel that Mr. Browning hoped to be in Pisa because she did not want Arabel to worry.

"Go on," Elizabeth said to George. "Tell us what you heard."

"He," George said to their father, indicating Kenyon, "knows Mr. Browning, too. I believe they're good friends. Aren't you?"

"Yes. I was at school with his father. And it's no surprise that Mr. Browning might be in Italy. And no matter of concern."

"What do you know of his family?" Mr. Barrett asked.

"They are perfectly wonderful, perfectly correct people."

"What does the father do?"

"He is a clerk. At the bank of England."

Mr. Barrett flicked something off his knee.

"They are very religious people," Kenyon added. "Dissenters."

"I would not call the younger Mr. Browning religious," George said. "I've read his poems."

"Oh?" Mr. Barrett said.

"Heretical, at times."

"What of *my* knowledge of his views?" Elizabeth said.

George turned to her, or, as it seemed, *on* her. "During his many visits and in his *many* letters to you, what is your impression of his views?" he asked.

She did not get a chance to answer. "How often has he been here?" her father asked.

Kenyon waited. She and Robert had thought it best not to speak to Kenyon about each other so that he would not speculate about them or gossip, but there was something in his manner that was knowingly benignant, as if he offered his blessing.

"About fifteen times," George said.

"In nine months of acquaintance," Elizabeth said.

"But his first visit was in late May," George said.

Her father did not stand up. Please let it not be, she thought, as it had been when he had shouted at Henrietta to not be a whore, and Henrietta had fallen on her knees in shock, and Elizabeth had fainted. "Arabel," her father said, "when did you first hear of Mr. Browning coming here, or writing to Ba?"

"In the winter."

"*How* did you hear of him?"

"When he wrote to Ba."

"When was that?"

Arabel's face was crimson, and she held her knitting as if it were a broken plate. "In January."

Collusion. Conspiracy. His daughters creeping around behind his back. That's what he saw, suspected, claimed. "And you, Kenyon, when did you hear of Mr. Browning in relation to Ba?"

She wanted to demand that her father's questions be directed only to her, but Kenyon answered.

"He has admired her poetry for years. I can't fix a date to that. There is nothing at all, nothing whatsoever, to blame her—or him."

Her father turned his face to hers. "I wouldn't have believed it. That you would use your illness to excuse an assignation."

"It is not an assignation," Elizabeth said.

"Why have you kept him such a secret? Every night we sat together, and you never spoke of it. Until you told me a friend of yours had suggested Pisa."

"He sends me his poems. I send them back again with my comments. I send him the new Aeschylus, and he sends it back. We talk about the minutiae of language. Why would I report that I have a friend who reads Greek and writes poetry? It is no different from Mr. Boyd."

"Mr. Boyd," George said, "has a wife and daughter."

"I have to correspond with men if I am to discuss Greek or write poems and publish them. There are few men who do both, and none who have Mr. Browning's expertise."

Kenyon leaned forward. "There is nothing to worry about," he said peacefully. "I can see why you wondered about his intentions, George, and why your father . . ."

Her father interrupted to ask her, "Will you persist in these direct lies?"

Kenyon said, "That is too much, Edward. There are no lies here."

"Tell Kenyon the truth," her father said. "Tell him that Mr. Browning has declared his love for you."

"Why?" Elizabeth asked.

"Because it's true. Do you deny it?"

"I have told everyone the truth. He is a poet," Elizabeth said. "He speaks grandiosely sometimes. He says things passionately but that is the poet in him. I told him that I am nothing but my poetry. Because that is all I am or ever can be."

Her father's look was mocking; she could hardly believe that such a look could be directed at her by him. There was nothing in it of the old fondness. "Do you hear this, Kenyon? When he said he was going to Pisa, and that you ought to go as well, did he speak poetically?"

"He did not tell me to go and live in Pisa. Dr. Chambers said that. Mr. Browning merely offered me the assistance of his experience. Mr. Browning has been to Italy in the last year, and so naturally, when we began to discuss it, I asked if he could tell me his opinion of this or that place."

"You asked his opinion. You told him where you might go. And he made a plan to go there as well. How very convenient for him. A place where you might both come and go with no interference or protection. Where he might poetically marry you and begin to siphon off your money."

"No, he had been planning to return to Italy all along."

"Of all my children. The smartest and the purest. To fall into such a trap."

"It is not a trap."

"You ought to be above such things."

"Dr. Chambers said it was a matter of life or death."

"I have long since tired of Dr. Chambers. It was he who sent you to Torquay. And now he thinks you'll get better if you travel hundreds of miles to live in a country torn apart by rebels and mad papists. In this house, you're safe. You can do your work, which you claim is everything to you. I have never thought Pisa a good plan, and now I see it has been pushed on you by a man who wants our money."

"You haven't met him, Edward," Kenyon began, "or you'd see—"

"Don't tell me how to keep my children safe, John," Mr. Barrett said. "You have none, so you don't know."

"That may be. But I know the people in question, Edward. I know and trust Mr. Browning completely. I know his family. It is a misunderstanding to think his motives are selfish or pecuniary."

Elizabeth stared at the gloves in her lap. She opened one of them, and she inserted her hand. She pulled at the thin leather carefully, so as not to tear it, and when she had covered her left hand, she snugged the fingers so that each of her fingernails touched the ends of the perfectly clean, perfectly stainless tips of the gloves. She stretched her hand out flat on her lap. "I can pay for the trip myself," she said. "I wouldn't ask for anything." She had her grandmother's legacy, which was in her name, and her shares in the *David Lyon*. Combined with her royalties it was enough to live simply in Pisa: £300 a year. Kenyon had examined the figures once, and he had said it would work. When she had told Robert the amount, he agreed it was sufficient.

She took the other glove, and she began to slide her right hand into it.

She could go. She could take Arabel and perhaps Alfred. But they would have to cross over the fire of their father's disapproval. If she were to be ill there, or if anything else went wrong, it would all have been her selfish doing. Arabel and whatever brother she took would be forever on the wrong side of their father, and neither of them had an independent income.

"There," her father said. "Mark it, everyone."

George, Arabel, and Mr. Kenyon waited for what they were to mark.

"She dresses to go out."

"Edward—" Mr. Kenyon started.

She stopped mid-glove. *Love me,* she had always been able to say with her actions, with her poems, with her notes and odes and letters and prayers. And always he had bestowed upon her the title she sought: *the purest woman I have ever known.*

Her mind was like a cave out of which bats began to fly.

"Shall we eat?" her father said. She saw it. He did not love her. He once had, but he didn't now.

"I can't stay," Kenyon said. "I'm afraid I will not have time."

"As you wish," Mr. Barrett said.

"Wait," Elizabeth said. Kenyon was standing, and her father had his hand on the carved head of his cane. "I need to ask something, since you feel I deceived you before."

Mr. Barrett kept his seat, head on the cane, expression obdurate.

"Will you be pleased with me if I stay. If I correspond with Mr. Browning, and see him before he goes to Italy, and I stay."

"No," her father said. With a little flap of his hand, he sent that idea to the floor.

"Edward. You do not mean to say you are displeased if she does as you ask?" Mr. Kenyon said.

"A man like that should never have been let in, and he should be called what he is and never spoken of again."

"He is not that man," Elizabeth said. "It is not a true or fair picture." She stood up, and Arabel reflexively stood up to help her.

She faced her father as she spoke, as if only the two of them were in the room. "If I say that as I love you, I choose to obey your wishes . . . can you say that you are not displeased?"

George stood, and Mr. Kenyon stood, and Arabel waited beside her. Mr. Barrett sat. As if the king sat in his chair and his minions waited. A glass rang out, and knives were placed one by one on the cloth-muffled table. The serving girls spoke to one another, a quiet murmuring, and the walls kept their words from being understood.

George said, "Will he go to Italy, do you think? If you don't?"

Through the walls, the quiet murmuring.

"Who?"

"Mr. Browning. To Italy."

"Yes," she said. Her face burned and her bones felt like lead.

"Good," her father said. "May this be the last we hear of him."

No one looked at her. It was best to sit meekly and separately and hold oneself as a small, powerless thing, awaiting judgment. He did not say he was pleased with her, or even that he was not displeased.

"You will all do as you like," he said. "It's time for me to go to dinner."

Kenyon waited for Mr. Barrett to stand up and turn toward the door, and when her father could not see him anymore, Kenyon met her eyes at last. He held out his hands to take both of hers. "Goodbye, Ba," he said. "I will write from Dover." He took leave of Arabel, and George, and lastly, of Mr. Barrett, and she could not help wishing, as she watched Kenyon go out the door, that she were a speck of dust that could float away from the house and land somewhere, it didn't matter where, as long as it was outside. The door closed on Kenyon and his diplomacy, and he was gone.

THIRTY

∞

THE BARRETTS' LIBRARY was to the left, the dining room to the right. Robert had never entered either one in nine months of visiting. The air inside the dark red hall, its paint dull and thick, was nearly as stuffy as the streets, which were molten today. He had stopped under a plane tree on the way to will his body to stop sweating, but he was still sweating as he stood eye to eye with the girl in the painting. Her pink ribbons wafted in the wind, the white skirts of her dress light as the skin of a soap bubble. Her eyes were exactly like Elizabeth's, and she studied Robert, this incarnation, with a strange and bold confidence. *I will*, she seemed to say. And yet the girl in the painting had died before she did anything at all.

Neither the library nor the dining room door opened. If things were normal, he would have eaten dinner with Mr. Barrett, Henrietta, Arabella, and the brothers who were in London: George, Alfred, Henry, Septimus, and Occyta. The brothers would have examined and tried and judged him in the court of the family table; he would have had that chance. He had hoped that would happen still.

The familiar steps on carpet, lightly descending, meant Henrietta or Wilson was coming down.

"Mr. Browning," Wilson said, cheeks pink, smile unchanged. "Hot, isn't it," she said, and she beckoned him to follow.

The usual pictures by Henrietta marked his ascent up the stairs: the lavender seascape, the soldier with the long mustache, the boy fencing in a sailor suit.

"Is her head better?" he asked.

"I'd say not," she said.

No brother stepped out as if by coincidence, to say, "Oh, hello" or "Back again?"

Elizabeth sat with her desk open, the papers limp, ink closed, a tray nearby. Steam rose from the teapot, and he could smell apples in the tarts—the ones he'd brought last week, perhaps, picked in happy expectation. Outside the sun on the rooftops burned.

He sat on his usual chair, and Flush padded over to him—as if in mourning or distress, so slowly did the dog walk—and put a paw on his leg.

"Are you suffering from a headache as well, my poor pup?" he asked Flush. "Or is it the heat? Why does he accept me today?"

"Poor Flush," she said. "He is the heart outside my body."

"What has happened, Ba?"

"You must be thirsty," she said.

"Ba," he said.

"When will you leave?" she asked. "And will you go to Rome instead? I think it's better than Pisa in many respects."

He walked to the window to keep himself from taking both of her shoulders, or both of her hands, or her face, in his two hands. Always before this he had found it easy to sit where he ought to sit, keeping all decorum, knowing he must earn her trust. There had never been a moment between them that could not be interrupted by a sister, a brother, a priest, or God himself. For seventeen visits they had sat apart.

She offered a filled teacup to him. Flush leaped up to sit beside her.

"I'm not thirsty," he said.

She tried again to speak lightly. "You ought to go soon if you plan to take the Jura road through the Alps."

"Is your father home?" The roof tiles and chimney pots baked. Birds baked. Clouds boiled.

He turned to see why she didn't answer, and she simply shook her head. Robert pointed to the passage door as if he and she were prisoners in a shared cell. It was demeaning.

She shook her head again.

Robert walked toward her, intending, God help him, to take both her hands in his—or perhaps more, he hardly knew himself—but then sat down. It was harder to break through the barrier of propriety than he'd expected. Habit was a thick wall. "Am I to understand that he forbids you to go—even though you *can* go, because you are of age, and you have the means—and that because you will not go, you think I will go by myself, and I will forget you?"

She nodded.

He put the chair close to her couch. He sat in it and leaned back. He reached forward and set his hand on the couch. Between her pinkie and his thumb there was no more than an inch. She didn't move her hand closer. She merely looked at his hand and said, "As I said long ago, it's better sometimes to be vexed oneself..."

He kept his hand near hers, willing her to move her hand closer and prove that she trusted him. "... than vex another," he said. "But you are willing to vex me. To say that I could leave you and forget all that I said."

She withdrew her hand instead of touching him. She pressed both her hands together as if pleading in prayer and she didn't speak.

He stood up again, half-suffocated. "You will drive me mad."

"I cannot take my sister and brother away from here without his approval. They would not be let in again, you see. When they needed to come back. They would have nothing. He would never forgive it."

"I'm not disputing that at present. I'm asking why you reject *me*."

"It is too much to ask of anyone."

"Do you love me?"

"Yes."

"Do you think I could go to Rome, or anywhere, and that's an end to it?"

"That's where you will be happy. It's what you would have done if you'd never met me."

"I quite understand the grace of your self-denial and fidelity, but you don't understand me. I love you because I *love* you; I see you once a week because I cannot see you all day long; I think of you all day long because I

most certainly could not think of you once an hour less, if I tried, or went
to Pisa, or 'abroad' in order to 'be happy' . . . I would not be happy. Do you
really think that before I found you, I ever dreamed of marrying?"

Flush moved his head so that it lay directly on her lap. The pigeons, outside on the windowsill, swallowed music that burbled inside them. The first
drops of rain hit the roof, and in the distance, a cloud the color of slate gave
the sky new depth.

"You can't possibly think that I want to be rich or thought I could be
rich, being who I am, or that I could marry anyone, being who I am. It
seemed impossible to find a woman who believed in poetry as I do, and thus
impossible to marry. If you are hunting about in the dusk to see what's good
for me, then the answer is yourself."

The raindrops were single and fat, striking hard and fast, and then suddenly the rain fell everywhere, drenching the tiles and the tangle of green
and red that tumbled out of the window boxes.

"I will conform my life to *any* imaginable rule that puts us together," he
said finally.

Mud from the window box splattered the glass and ran over the sides.

Elizabeth sat like a sphinx on the sofa, the skin on her hands and face
more than normally pale. "Then you will not go?"

He shook his head.

Flush raised his head, regarded Robert, then set his head back down.
The smell of the rain was stony and clear, and the light was clear also, as if it
were made of rain, and she moved her hand up and held it out to him, meeting his where it collected first the fingers, then the palm, and pressed it to
his lips. He kissed her forehead next. And then, because nothing remained
to stop him, he kissed her lips.

"I will be here all winter. Here."

THIRTY-ONE

∞

SARIANNA DIDN'T APPEAR on Lenore's doorstep uninvited this time. She sent a basket of Victoria plums, still yellowish so they might travel well, with a note saying that they would be ready to eat when they were as "pink as an English sunset"—that was what her mother said to say, so she had written it, but with quotation marks that attributed it as such. The basket was returned to the Browning house the following week holding a cured ham and a thick white card.

"She thanks us for the fruit," Sarianna said.

"I suppose she is used to better."

"Not at all. She says they are the best fruit she's had all summer, if not ever in her life."

If Mrs. Browning had asked for her glasses, and for the card, she would have seen that Sarianna's private question—*May I come and see you Monday next?*—had been answered in the affirmative. Sarianna slipped the card into the pocket of her cooking smock.

It rained the following Monday, starting, it appeared, well before dawn. It continued all morning, pausing to give hope as Sarianna closed the gate behind her, but it resumed before she had reached the towpath. Everyone in the half-empty train smelled of wet skin and wet shoes. Rain glazed windows that framed green, soggy views. Rain drizzled into the carriage and puddled beside her dress. Rain was so deep in puddles that she soaked her shoes again walking from Euston Station to Russell Square, and her hem, which had darkened with mud on the towpath, drank more and more water, so that her dress felt bloated and heavy. The rain that her umbrella didn't catch soaked her sleeves and her gloved hands.

This would not happen to rich people. A servant would protect them from water below and above and make sure they did not look weak and desperate on someone's doorstep. But here she was. Here she must present her bravest front.

The servingman did not trouble to accept, or even acknowledge, her apologies for the wet umbrella and mud she left on the parquet floor. Finally, she stood in Miss Goss's enormous library, among the beetles under glass. Miss Goss sat at a desk, pen in hand, and she dipped it as Sarianna approached.

"I thought you might not brave the weather," Miss Goss said, gesturing toward a pink chair. It was upholstered in what looked like silk, and Sarianna feared she would stain it, but Lenore, calm and dry, went on writing, and when she had finished, she folded the paper, wiped the pen, and came to sit in a chair that matched Sarianna's. She folded her hands and said, "I am in suspense. So tell me. Why have you come in such a storm?"

Sarianna watched the water glaze the window and listened to it splatter the bricks as if it sought to batter its way in.

"Is there something that worries you, Sarianna?"

"Would you hear, do you think, if Miss Barrett were engaged?"

"People would talk of nothing else," Miss Goss said. "Why?"

Sarianna relayed the conversation about Pisa.

Another gust of water struck the house, but the room was dry, and being dry, at that moment, seemed the pinnacle of style, from the ribbon fixed tightly around Miss Goss's neck to the carpet under Sarianna's shoes. "Do you think they plan to elope?" Miss Goss asked.

"I used to think Robbie was one of those eternal bachelor men. That he liked things as they were, with his routine, the writing, the studying, all of that. I thought that was why he didn't do any of the things our father suggested."

"What did your father suggest?"

"Law. The bank. We are not Church of England, so Oxford and Cambridge were not possible. He was at the University of London for a time—my father paid the subscription. But Robbie hated it. He thought the other students fools. So he quit it."

"Your brother went to Italy before," Miss Goss said.

"Yes. Twice before."

"Perhaps it's a way for them to court one another," Miss Goss said, "without so much interference, if I may put it that way."

"I have not interfered."

"I don't mean you. I mean *her* family."

"Either way—" Sarianna started but was interrupted.

"Hello, David," a high, metallic voice called. "Hello, David."

The voice had come from the white bird that sat in the corner, which had now returned to sharpening its beak in the gold cage.

"I didn't know it could speak," Sarianna said.

"It never could. The boy taught it." Miss Goss stood up and walked to the cage, and Sarianna stayed where she was, unsure if it were polite to follow. "He was very determined. He used food, I imagine. That's what my maid said. So now the bird is looking for him, and he's gone."

"Did Mr. Barrett send him to school?"

"No," Miss Goss said.

Sarianna waited. She could not ask directly what Miss Goss didn't offer.

"You were saying," Miss Goss said, walking away from the bird and the cage. "You were saying 'either way.'"

"If my brother spends his time in Italy making love to Miss Barrett, or if he elopes with her here, either way . . . I fear for him. Our families do not seem very much the same."

The bird hopped down to a lower swing, saying "Hello, David, hello, David."

"Is Miss Hawthorne well?" Sarianna asked.

Miss Goss didn't turn to face her. She said, "'Everything is for the best in this best of all possible worlds.'"

"Voltaire," Sarianna said. "But he meant the opposite."

At that, Miss Goss did turn.

"It was only Miss Goodson's," Sarianna said, "but it was still a school. Robbie gave me *Candide* and we talked about it."

"How nice."

"I read everything he gave me, and then we talked."

"Did he listen?"

"Robbie? Of course."

"That's a luxury in itself, to think it's a matter of course." The painting that loomed over everything in the room, the one of a sneering young man, seemed somehow to be her focus as the rain fell and fell and Miss Goss stood directly beneath it. It was as if the young man was in the room and Miss Goss was pointedly ignoring him. "That is my brother, Andrew," she said, glancing up at him and then back at Sarianna. "When I heard that Miss Barrett was nearly killed by the loss of her brother Edward," Miss Goss said, "I envied her that she could care that much. I think you can never love a man in the right way if you have neither a kind father nor a kind brother. It warps your vision of what you can expect. Perhaps of what you deserve."

Her brother, taller than anything else in the painting, stood with his attainments on a red clump of earth: a riding crop in one hand. Two women, Black like Miss Hawthorne but bare-breasted and barefoot, carried baskets of fruit across a crescent beach.

"It's their boat," Miss Goss said. "Your father's first, then your brother's. You may enter the boat of a husband but you will never have your own."

Sarianna wanted to say that she had never felt the least bit uncomfortable in her father's boat. He kept it steady, he watched over them, he prayed, he loved.

"Of all the captains you might have had, Sarianna . . . you are fortunate, believe me. Even if your brother were to move to Italy with Miss Barrett, you are among the fortunate."

How could that be true if Robbie married an opium addict in poor health whose brother had fathered a child in the West Indies—a child his family didn't want to know about or help? What kind of people were they? Sarianna had briefly hoped that Miss Goss was right, and Robbie could write something helpful for women such as Miss Hawthorne, and he would stay here. He would show Sarianna the poem and let her copy it for him and they would talk about art and books as before. Everything was for the best in *that* best of all possible worlds.

"Miss Hawthorne and David are going back to their home in Jamaica," Miss Goss said. "I tried to make people listen to them, but I failed."

The bare-breasted women in the oil painting on the wall wore the smiles the painter had given them.

"And I believe that what will happen to Miss Barrett is that she will be taken by her own people to a warmer climate when they feel it is safe for her to travel. I don't know where. So perhaps all is at an end."

Robbie's disappointment would be profound if this were true, and yet it would be safer, much safer, she couldn't help thinking.

"Should I send for my driver?" Miss Goss asked.

Sarianna could not ride in Miss Goss's carriage because her parents would hear of it—again. She must go the same wet way to the station, stand among the other wet people, walk home on the muddy towpath. At least that way she would not be indebted. "No, thank you," Sarianna said. "I will take the train."

THIRTY-TWO

∞

VISIT AS SOON as possible—this evening, if you're free. That's what Lenore's letter to George said. He would come, she knew, because he esteemed her. It was why she liked to be with George—he would do things for her and ask nothing in return. "I esteem you," he had once said, and she had laughed, unfortunately. He had been very hurt, and she had realized that by "esteem" he meant *love*.

"You esteem me because I am too old for you," she'd said.

"You are not too old," he said. "It's only four years."

"You would want something I can't promise."

"Your esteem in return?"

"A nice, conventional lady with nice, conventional opinions."

"Perhaps I don't want that," he said, but he did, and he knew it, and so did she.

It was not yet dark when George was announced. Lenore waited in the library, having eaten nothing since breakfast. He said nothing when he came in, and he sat in the chair he always chose, one with a leather seat and wide arms. Perhaps it was the piety of his life that made him seem solicitous, as if he were a doctor. He had been freshly shaved, but his whiskers were such a grizzled mass of hair and his eyes were so hidden by his heavy eyebrows that she was startled by a wish to stroke them.

"Would you like anything to eat?" she asked.

"I dined at home."

"Was everyone there?"

"What do you mean by everyone?"

"I wondered how Elizabeth is."

"She has a cold."

They had been alone before in this room, but always during her visiting hours, in the day, when anyone might call at any moment, and often did. The twilight, the pair of candles flickering, the cloth that shrouded the birdcage, gave the visit a different, clandestine quality.

"Miss Hawthorne has gone away," Lenore said. "She's preparing to leave the country."

The twilight was a deep lilac. A carriage rolled by outside, and a breeze bent the candle flame. George's fingers, curled on the arms of the leather chair, remained hidden inside his gloves. He studied her face as a doctor searching for symptoms.

"She took the boy, of course. She saw how it all is."

"How what is."

"She doesn't need just *your* acceptance, or even your father's. She needs everyone's. And that seemed impossible."

"Where will they go?" George asked.

"Home. They're staying with the missionaries for now. I said I would find them a berth, but I can't find anything safe. Please say you'll help."

He seemed to be thinking it over. "Where are the letters you claimed were so convincing?"

"She took them with her."

"Nora, I tried. I came to your house to see them, and to see the proofs, and they went away. You brought her to a party and paraded her around—"

"I wanted her to meet some enlightened Englishmen."

"You count Ben Haydon among the enlightened?"

"He used to be brilliant."

"Jamaica is the best place for her," George said.

"Then let her go on your family's ship, at least. She will be alone with no husband and little money. With your people, she will be protected."

"She was alone with no husband and little money on the journey here."

"But now we know. We ought to help."

"It will look as if we are whisking her out of sight. What's to keep her from showing the letters around on board?"

"Your kindness and generosity."

Did George love her? And was she trying to use that for Mary Ann's sake, or to assuage her own conscience?

George tapped the arms of the chair with his fingertips, and it looked as if he were rapping on the heads of the elephants carved there, rapping their wise, wrinkled brows. He wanted something, but it must be something he didn't want to ask. She felt him struggling under her gaze, his brown eyes deeper somehow and more vulnerable as the seconds passed. He stood up and walked to the window. "Tell me, Nora," George said. "What was Sam to you?"

This was an important question. She had loved him when she was very young, and that had been hard to forget. "He was water in which I knew not to swim."

"And me. What am I to you?"

"A good man."

"Does that make me water in which you *do* want to swim?"

They were near enough that she could feel the warmth of his body, and she could smell what it was he put on his skin, anise and bergamot, and she could see where the whiskers ended and the bare jaw began, which made her feel such tenderness that she reached out and put her palm against his cheek. "What are you asking me?"

He closed his eyes, and he bent his head slightly in the direction of her hand, and then, instead of kissing her, which she felt he wanted to do, he reached up for her hand and took it gently and deliberately away from his face. "I can't ask you that. It isn't possible for me to do only what I like. I was hurt, you know. I saw what you wrote for the *Post*." With that, he let go of her hand, but reluctantly, slowly.

"How did you see it?"

"A friend."

"And you told them not to publish it."

He stood up and walked to the window. "They had already decided that."

"So you won't help them get safely back."

"I will see when the ship is going. If it's soon, I'll pay the best person I can find to watch over her and the boy. Is that enough?"

"It's what I asked. I see that I can't expect more."

"Not now. Not this. If things were different."

"Which part?" She waited to see if he would say that he needed freedom to love her, and it existed somewhere in a future where his father let him choose a wife who had her own ideas and wrote about them, and where his father did not require him to be a humble dependent for the rest of his life.

"I don't know, Nora," he said.

They were not suited to each other, she thought again. And yet she hated to see him put his hat on and go back into himself before he even left the room. She would leave, she thought. She would go and see the friend who said Italy was brighter and more impulsive and free.

THIRTY-THREE

∞

THE WEATHER WAS not as fine as the day before, the air milky instead of clear, heavy instead of sparkling. George kept his eyes active all the way to Nine Elms Station, walking instead of taking the carriage. At last he stood in the station, scanning the crowd for Miss Hawthorne and Lenore. Most of the people there were men, or they were obviously servants, several of them old women, standing with baskets, tired and gaunt.

On a far bench, he saw a woman in the kind of dress Lenore liked, figured and shiny, some sort of silk that was canary green. She wore purple gloves and a green hat with a veil. Lenore never veiled her face, not even when she met him for a ride in his carriage at Regent's Park. Above that bench stood the clock, and it showed him to be five minutes late.

He stopped where he was, pretending he was waiting like everyone else for the train. He studied the signs overhead, the times and the names of places, and he flicked his eyes over the other men standing on both sides of the track, but no one paid any attention to him.

The veiled woman didn't move. She didn't stand, as Lenore would have, or beckon to him. He glanced at her again, and the veiled face was toward him, and he thought she nodded at him. She lifted a gloved hand, then replaced it uncertainly in her lap. She turned away from him to say something, and he saw for the first time that a little boy was sitting near her, swinging his legs. The boy's face and hands were wrapped in what looked like bandages, as if he had been burned.

George walked to the bench and said, "Miss Hawthorne."

The boy looked out between the bandages and George saw, or imagined, that the boy was afraid of him. The boy's eyes were light and his skin was, as George anticipated, dark. Miss Hawthorne reached out and took the boy's hand in her gloved one, and he saw more of the skin she had tried to hide with all the bandages, which were trailing down to the dirty floor of the station.

He did not want to talk there in the station. People openly studied the three of them already, waiting to see what they would do.

"Walk with me," he said, and she stood up and, taking the hand of the boy, strode past the curious passengers to the street. The sun had come out, burning the milky clouds away, leaving a thick heat, smelling of the horses and their dung. He had no plan in mind, and he tried to form one as he led them past peddlers and between carriages and around piles of muck and beggars. A sign advertised coffee—that would do. He nodded to the man at the entrance, and the three of them sat down. The table was not especially clean. He took off his hat. In here, where they had more light, the veil was less opaque. He could see the shape of her eyes, the line of her jaw. He asked for two coffees and a cup of tea, and when the server had gone he said, "I tried to see you when you first arrived, Miss Hawthorne."

Her little boy was playing with the bandages, peeling them off. "Remember, David," she said to him in a whisper. "The game is to be invisible."

"I'm hot," the boy said.

"Is he hurt?" George asked. "Has he been in an accident?"

The boy looked as if he might scream, but he sat down and put his hands under the table.

"No," Miss Hawthorne said. "Here is what you wanted." She had a small bag, one that he recognized as Lenore's, a little velvet bag with beaded flowers. From the bag she pulled a letter. The edges were worn, and the writing rubbed away as if it had been tumbled and abraded, as if instead of sitting in a desk it had been many days inside a pocket. He could just make out the words *Mary Ann*. He couldn't say whose handwriting it was—Sam's perhaps. Perhaps not.

The room was suffocating. The tea came and was set down, and George asked the serving woman if there was any bread for the child. The woman, who was quick to smile despite her bad teeth, looked at David maternally. "Poor lad. Did ye get burned?"

George put coins on the table and the woman smiled again, waiting for an answer that didn't come from the mother, so George said, "A little. He'll be all right soon." She scraped the coins into her hand and went away.

"Shall I read it?" George tapped the letter.

She nodded, and he heard her sigh. David blew on his tea so hard that it slopped into the saucer. Before George could take the letter from the table, Miss Hawthorne reached into Lenore's rose-beaded bag and put another envelope beside the first, crisp and clean, as unlike the other one as a pair of new shoes would be from a pair worn for a dozen years.

George turned that one over. There was no name on it at all. He touched the one addressed to Mary Ann again. There was a scab of wax on it, and a pink stain where the rest of the wax had been.

David was still blowing on the tea to make it fly.

"Please stop that," George said. He had never been good with children. Even his little brothers had avoided him, and he them. David stopped blowing and began to slurp his tea, so George turned to the letter.

Mary Ann had hardly dared look at George Barrett's face at the ugly man's dinner party, but through her veil she could look all she wanted. She wished she had worn a veil the whole time she'd been in London, so she might study as she had been studied. His eyes were the color of wet rust. His eyelashes short and straight. She dismissed each feature in turn as not like Sam's: not those lips, not that chin, not those pale, doggish hairs in his beard. He was reading the first letter she'd ever received. As soon as the servant from the Great House had brought it to her door, she'd hidden it in the waist of her skirt, where the seam was already open a little for carrying coins. She had checked in the mirror to be sure the square of paper wasn't visible from the outside, so her father wouldn't see.

She hadn't been able to open it all day. She couldn't open a letter on the path to school. Not inside the school, either, because the children liked to come up to her desk and waste time, and if they saw Miss Hawthorne had a letter, they'd be sure to tell someone. She couldn't read it on the path home because the boy watching the cows and the boy tending the pigs and the women carrying ratoons or dung or babies or yams would see and they would tell, or they would ask who had written Mary Ann a letter. She couldn't read it in the house because her father sat to the right or to the left. She considered opening it in the netty, but it stank in there and was full of flies.

A whole day passed without a chance and then someone came shouting for her father to help him get a hog out of the cane piece.

She went behind the cloth where she stood each morning to change her clothes. She undid the button of her skirt and reached into the open seam, pulling out the folded paper that was curved like a sliver of moon. The ink was blurred where it had bled through the paper, dampened by her own sweat. What if she'd erased it by accident? The seal had cracked in five or six places. Three tiny pieces of the red wax fell on the floor, and she threw them out the window so her father wouldn't see them. She touched what was left of the seal and held it close to her eyes. She could make out paws lifted up, the body of the lion that was on all the Barrett things, that her father had carved into wood for a bed that someone, maybe even the owner himself, slept in at Cinnamon Hill. She slid her finger under the lip to break the rest of it away and listened for her father's feet coming back.

The writing was not as clear or easy to read as Mrs. Jessie's. Mrs. Jessie had taught Mary Ann to form each letter as if God would see it, saying, when Mary Ann did her lessons well, that no one would know the color of her skin if she learned to write well enough.

Dear Mary Ann,

I have done as I said I would and found a house for you to be mistress of. It will be your own house, not my aunt and uncle's, not mine, not Vertiline's, not Little May's. It has a piano and china cups. It has a mosquito netting like this one, which I send for you, and it has a whole

length of oznabrig for you to use as you like, and a new dress for you,
and shoes from England. Oh, Mary Ann, I am sick with love for you.
I am dying of it. I lie here at night and I dream of nothing but you.
Please say you'll come to me and love me in return. Let me make you
happy and be happy beside you.

Most humbly and affectionately yours
I remain
Sam

Mary Ann used to stand in the Great House when her father was called to fix something and she would stare at the picture of the white girl in the white dress with long pink ribbons on her hat. It was like being shown a portrait of Jesus and trying to understand Christ crucified. To be noticed by a white man, or for a man to want you, was it as good as a pink ribbon around your waist, slender shoes on your feet, and a new dress all your own, or was it the beginning of sin for which the Savior grieved, looking down at your filthiness?

She made herself fold the letter back up and she slid it into the waistband of her skirt. She liked to be noticed by the man everyone had to please and to have him trail along behind her, telling her jokes. She liked the gifts he brought her, especially the coral necklace. Of all the things men said to her back or to her face, his words were the sweetest. If that was love, how could she not want it?

She sat down where she had been when her father left. She opened a book, and she pretended to read.

NOW THIS OTHER Barrett held her letter. The serving woman of the coffee house brought a roll to the table, not very big and not very fresh, which David began to pick apart. The long strips of cloth she'd used to cover his skin so people wouldn't stare were coming loose as David tore the hard bread. She could do nothing about that now, just as she could do nothing about how people saw them. She watched Sam's brother set her letter aside and pick up the other. He kept his eyes away from her, and his thoughts, and his being.

George unfolded the second letter to find something stuck to it. A ribbon, he thought at first: long, and dark, folded at an angle. Once he held it, he could feel tiny silken hairs along an infinitesimal spine; it was not a ribbon but a long, narrow feather, and it had been bent inside the letter, broken so that it could not be straightened again.

This was the letter to Sam's sister, the one she had expected to meet here in England. Sam had three sisters, and Sam had sworn that all three of them would love and accept Mary Ann if they met her.

Dear Henrietta,

If only you could come to this island with no trouble at all, say on the back of a dog with eyes as big as saucers, or one with eyes as big as mill wheels. If one of those dogs appears in your dreams & fetches you across the Carribbean ~~Carribean~~? prepare for a shock or two! In truth, I could dispatch a mosquito, so strong & vigorous do they grow here in the marsh. You would laugh at the wondrous works I & my good helper Giles have accomplished in our wild outpost! We could use a woman's touch, I'll own, in the furnishing. We have a table now, & two chairs—a third is expected & will have a cushion for gentlefolk such as yourself. I had quite a journey bringing the sideboard from Falmouth, but it looks very grand in the drawing room, as I call it, though the drawing room is separated from my kingly bed chamber by nothing more than a piece of oznabrig. Listen to what Giles & I managed to eat last night: roast conch, roast mudfish with alligator pears, plantains, madeira, and a mango tossed with the seedy liquid of the granadillo. How is that for settled living? Am I not ready to take a wife & begin making little nieces & nephews for you & Ba & Arabella to spoil? I will bring them home to England my own self so I will not be sent a little glove all wet with tears.

Please find enclosed:

- cinnammon bark, as promised,
- the tail feathers of a doctor bird (see sketch)
-the seeds of our very best and most cheering flowers for Ba's window boxes

Tell her I am earning my fortune & preparing to come back & make her go for donkey rides with us.

Your vry most affectionate
Sam

The other Barrett read the letter. David slurped his tea.

"How did you come by this?" George asked when he was finished.

"It was in his things."

"Were you with him when he died?"

She shook her head. "He was at the Great House. Giles took him there to get better."

"But not you?"

She shook her head. "I was at the other house."

George sat still. The handwriting in both letters was Sam's, the way of joking was Sam's, the bad spelling was Sam's. He said, "I have paid for a missionary couple—the Martins, they're called—to help you on the way home. The ship is my family's, so all will be well."

My family's. Not hers. She was not part of their family, and David was not part of their family. "Do you believe me?" she asked.

"About what?"

Mary Ann pointed at the boy. "Him."

He felt the presence of an audience behind him. He heard the scraping of chairs, coughing, clink of china and spoon. He felt the people in the coffee shop watching the three of them and he heard them listening, multiplying, until they spread behind him like the sea, listening to see how he would answer. David was playing some sort of game with a toy he had in his hand, a bit of bone, it looked like. He marched the white thing across the table, bringing it down with little clicks. The letters were in the way, so the toy—it was long and slender, and George decided it was a domino—was made to jump on the paper.

George pointed to the thing in the boy's hand. "What is it, David?"

"Miss Lenore gave it to him," Mary Ann said. "The King of France, she said it was. Made of a hog bone."

The boy set it down, and George saw it was a man, crudely cut and carved, with small knobby feet and what looked like a coat and scepter cut into the bone with scrapes and lines. It had no head, and where the neck ended, the bone was smooth as a domino.

George handed it back to David, and David went back to walking the headless King of France across the table. George knew that all he had to do was reach out his arm, scrape the letters from the table into his hand, pocket them, and put a few more coins on the table. He could walk away without another word, strike out the door, stroll down the street. She would not chase him or call after him.

"I'll write to my brother. Stormie. I'll tell him what's in the letters, and have him talk to you when you arrive."

The boy moved the king made of hog bone.

"But you won't say it now," Miss Hawthorne said. "To him."

David made the king move, *click*, *click*, *click*. The boy kept moving the king as if he heard nothing and cared for nothing, but that was how boys did things, George remembered.

She must want him to say to David, *You're my nephew. You're a Barrett.* But he was not legally a Barrett, so he was not really a nephew at all.

George felt in his pocket. He had, as usual, a few guineas. He could not help scanning the room. None of the men smoking, nor women drinking from cups, were familiar, and yet he felt any one of them might know someone who knew his father. He must not hand money to Miss Hawthorne as if she were his mistress.

"I will draw something from the bank for you. You'll have it when you sail." He waited a few seconds, and then, as if collecting his own hat and gloves, he picked up the letters. He kept his eyes away from her as he put them in his coat, expecting her to protest.

She watched him and considered what to do, she a Black woman, he a white man. "I don't need them," she said. "They mean nothing to me now."

The few patrons who looked up from their cups, exhausted in the heat, watched the boy in his bandages, the woman in the green veil. They thought their thoughts, whatever they were, and George took Miss Hawthorne and her child to the wharf.

THIRTY-FOUR

∞

FOR THREE DAYS, the wind died and the sails hung slack at Gravesend. The tide went in and covered up what was drowned, and the tide went out and showed half wheels and buried jars, liquor bottles and twisted cloth, dead birds and broken paddles. Clouds unclotted, clotted, and unclotted again. At night George lay awake waiting for the *David Lyon* to depart. He waited for wind to find his open window and blow papers off his desk, for his morning walk to the Thames to reveal the round sails of freighted ships, carrying Miss Hawthorne and David permanently away. He ate breakfast with Henrietta each morning, knowing that he had her never-seen letter from Sam. The storm of crying it would unleash as she remembered Sam all over again, the river of questions—the questions. *Where did you get it? Why now?* It was best to leave it all as it was, to let the tide cover it up. After three days, he threw both letters in the fire and told himself it was right.

On the 25th of September, 1845, the *David Lyon* sailed. The news was in the paper as he ate currants from a roll. Crumbs fell on the table. The fragments of broken tea leaves, small as ash, settled in his untouched cup. He could not be sure, as he walked in the morning air, half-liberated, half-full of dread, that Miss Hawthorne had been on the ship—he would have to wait for the Martins to write and say all was well. For a few days more he continued to imagine, as he walked home from work, the eyes of his brother's son meeting him as he turned the corner. For a few days more he walked up the steps of his own house at the end of the day preparing to hear *A woman stopped by to see you, Sir, a Black woman, very well-dressed, with a child.* For a few days more he sat with his father in the morning and evening, Sam's watch on the writing table holding the little braid of hair, the one that meant Odysseus came home, and he expected his father to say, "A friend of mine said he saw you in a coffeehouse with a Black woman and a little boy all covered up in bandages. Tell me what I should make of that, George."

The danger was past. The ship was gone. George went to Elizabeth's room that night, having not visited at all for at least a week.

"Ba," he said. She had no papers around her but sat with a book in her lap. Her writing desk was closed. When she had a headache, she put her tea-cup to her temple, and that's where the cup was when he opened the door.

"George," she said, bringing the cup down.

"Are you unwell?"

"Do I look unwell?" she asked.

"Where are your papers? It looks as though you have retired from writing."

"I have nothing to say just now."

"Then you are very unwell, and Dr. Chambers ought to come."

"I went outside a week ago Monday with Flush."

"That sounds better. I'm glad to hear you felt like going out."

"No." She touched Flush's head and Flush blinked. "A woman came to sit by me, George. A Black woman with a child."

The shock of this made his eyes twitch. George found it difficult to nod calmly.

"She said she saw me come out of my house. She asked if my name was Barrett."

Steady now, he told himself.

"She said she had brought her child to see me. 'He is your nephew,' she said. 'David Barrett of St. James Parish.' She asked if I would tell the boy that I was his Aunt Barrett."

"What did you say?"

"She said she worked at Cinnamon Hill, that Sam was the father."

"How—" he couldn't think of a suitable word. "Bizarre," he said.

"Her boy did have eyes like Sam, George."

"Many Englishmen have green eyes."

"But she knew so many things. She said there was a picture in the hall at Cinnamon Hill of a girl in a white dress with a pink ribbon. She told me that my family calls me Ba."

"That's proof she worked there, not that Sam fathered a child."

"Reverend Waddell's letter said Sam had sinned, George. He said Sam had sinned and repented of it before he died. He didn't say what the sin was."

"Sam's sin was drinking," George said. "Waddell thought Sam was an incorrigible drinker, and a gambler, too, if you must know."

"Why would the woman come all this way if it weren't true?"

"She saw an opportunity."

"Could we give her one?"

"We have. She came to me as well. She wanted to go back, and I helped her. She's on the *David Lyon*."

"So you did admit it? He is Sam's?"

"It's not an admission. It's a kindness to someone who worked for the family. I helped them as much as I could without involving him," he said, pointing in the direction of their father's room.

"Did you ask Arabel?"

"Ask Arabel what?"

"If she knows a school for boys."

"They wouldn't take him. He'd need a private tutor."

"I could afford that, perhaps."

George shook his head. "You could not," he said. "And they are gone."

She didn't drink from her cup or lift it. "I think we should have done more. If the boy is Sam's, he is a little bit of Sam still walking the earth, and we have—"

"Don't presume what you don't know. He is better off among people he knows, in the place he was born. You must see that."

She said nothing and stared out at the roofs, difficult to make out in the darkness. There was no moon. George noticed for the first time that Mr. Browning's portrait was gone. A painting of Henrietta's filled that space.

"When all this emotion has settled," he said, "when the trip may be considered as a thing apart and unconnected with this Browning business, I could help you go to Pisa. Next year. I'll arrange the berths, the lodging, the transfers. Arabel will still be willing to go with you, and one of us can also go, Henry or me or Alfred. If Dr. Chambers still says it is for your health, of course."

"Next year," she said.

"We'll start early," he said. "In June."

"I don't want to talk about it now, George," she said.

"Understood. But later."

Arabel came to the door, and George said good night.

THIRTY-FIVE

∞

WINTER CAME AS it always had. Winter never offered any gifts. It was not a time of expectation or choice, merely of enduring. That spring was the most miserable she had ever spent because it did make promises—*this time you could go*, it said—*it would be easy*. She went downstairs to see if it made her tired. It didn't. She went outside with Henrietta. "How are you feeling?" her father asked.

"Very well," she said.

"See?" he said.

She began to ride through the park with Arabel, who said they ought to go a bit farther every time. "In case you might go—" she said, and stopped herself. "Again tomorrow," she finished.

The unusually warm weather turned into unusually hot weather, days and days of blue skies and clear air.

"How are you feeling?" Robert asked.

"Very well," she said.

"Well enough?" he asked.

"I don't know," she said.

In mid-June, Ben Haydon sent a trunk of papers to Elizabeth, asking her to keep them for him in case his creditors came to take away his house, and on the same day, without being summoned, Dr. Chambers was shown in. He smiled as a form of punctuation, and then he opened his leather case. "We are getting on towards autumn," he said. "Again."

"But it is only the end of June," she said.

"At my time of life, June is the start of autumn."

"You are too young to use the phrase, 'at my time of life,' Dr. Chambers."

Again he wielded the smile as a punctuation mark, and he put on his stethoscope. "If a patient cannot follow my advice, I am still bound to give it. If I give it, and it's unheeded, and I find myself in a position, thereafter, where I must repeat the advice again—" He listened to her heart. "Nothing has changed since we sat in this room a year ago, except that, in my opinion, the conditions that prompted me to deliver that opinion have deteriorated further. More houses go up, the population rises, manufacturing increases, more coal is burned. We must have heat for more and more people, and as a consequence, more and more people succumb to the effects of smoke. For the strong, it is a challenge. To the weakened, it is a death sentence."

"Not if I stay inside on bad days."

"Look how well you're doing with exercise and a bit of sun. What would behoove you is to have air moving in and out of the place where you spend most of your time. Indoors and outdoors. Dry, warm, clean air. If you wish me to take my conclusions to your father again, and to say that you must quit this impossible city for a more salubrious climate, I will. But if I do so, and I am once again told that I know nothing of the dangers to which you would be subjected and that others know better, having cared for you longer, I see no alternative. I must resign my post."

"I would not like that, Dr. Chambers."

"I wouldn't like it either. But I won't take responsibility for your health if you don't take the step I regard as essential to preserving it."

Elizabeth was silent.

"Could you let me think?"

"For how long, Miss Barrett?"

"I like to hope he will have softened," Elizabeth said. "That we ought not to regard this year's answer as being the same as last year's."

"Has he said something? Given you some hope?"

She wanted to say yes. "I always believe there is hope."

"It's possible that he would make the decision for me," he said. "That

I would not need to resign, I mean. He might dismiss me for bringing to him a matter he views as closed once and for all. I know he has a doctor he prefers."

"He may. I don't. But I don't like to tell you that he would receive you well, and then subject you to his recriminations."

"That's nothing to me. If I could not bear to hear it when a man disagreed with my convictions, I could not be a doctor. But, as I said at the beginning, where I can no longer aid, I will desist."

"But you do aid me, Dr. Chambers. You have aided me always."

"I suggest that you decide immediately. Whether you are to tell him what I have said today, or whether I am to tell him. The plans must be started at once. If you have the means . . ."

"I do have the means. It is the other . . ."

"Would your brothers help you in the absence of his approval?"

"They would. But I would not let them."

"He could not fight you all, Miss Barrett. If you were united, he might be forced to see reason."

"Whoever helped me would face the same retribution, but without the cushion of my legacy."

"He could not cut all of you off. It would be monstrous."

"No," she said, though she wasn't sure.

"I see in your eyes that you're afraid to talk about it. You think it is sedition—a filial wickedness. If you're afraid to harm your sisters and brothers, consider asking your friends. If any of them are traveling, you might join them . . ."

Kenyon had proposed this to her already. "Did Kenyon suggest that?"

Dr. Chambers nodded. "I could provide you with the name of a doctor friend in Pisa. I could give you what you need in tinctures and remedies to go that far. It need only be carefully planned. The journey must be slow so that you rest during and between ports and cities. If each segment is short and comfortable enough, and you stay in well-furnished inns—"

"Dr. Chambers, to talk this way . . ."

"There, you see? This is what makes it difficult, Miss Barrett. One may not even talk. If I am to be censored from giving my best advice, what use is my consultation? Why should I be paid to tell you things you are rebuked for believing?"

"I must think about it."

"Think quickly, Miss Barrett. The winter is predicted to be especially cold and dry. Conducive to days upon days without cleansing rain or snow-fall. You ought to start no later than the first day of August."

"August?"

"You should plan to take twice as long as the ordinary traveler. So you can rest in between stops."

And with that, Dr. Chambers took his leave.

THIRTY-SIX

∞

DR. CHAMBERS WOULD have to make the case to her father, she decided, and she would ask George to be present. But she had only written "Dear Dr. Chambers" when she changed her mind. If George were present and her father specifically said she could not go, and then George helped her, as he had offered, George would be compromised.

"What madness this is," Robert said.

"I cannot call my father mad."

"What shall we do?"

"Give me your poem," she said. "I need to clear my head."

"Have you told George?"

"Not yet."

Robert thought they should tell George they loved one another and planned to marry. Elizabeth thought it best to proceed as if she were unattached—to tell no one, especially not George. "Will you give me the poem to read?"

"After you tell me," Robert said, "if you think I should take the job as a French tutor."

"You would lose all and gain nothing." Whenever Robert said he would give up writing and teach French instead, because then her father would see that Robert had a dependable, steady income, she despaired. Her father would not think a French tutor could provide a better living than a poet, but what was the good of pointing that out?

"Then we must marry. And go," Robert said. "The only question that remains is the timing of my conversation with your father."

"What conversation?"

"When I ask for your hand."

"That is impossible."

"It isn't. It's essential."

"He would throw me out of the window."

"You don't mean that."

"He would view it as betrayal."

"Why?"

"I said that we were meeting only as friends."

"So you are never to fall in love and marry because you can never go out and meet people in the ordinary way?"

"It doesn't matter if it's rational. I can't bear to hear him say how disappointed he is and how faithless I am."

"But that is wrong."

"He isn't entirely wrong. You don't know what it means to worry so over a person. If you gave me things, as he has—space and time and protection—you'd expect me to respect your feelings and wishes, not go to someone else, behind your back, to do the opposite."

"But marriage is a natural change. For each of you to leave your parents and be with another person and care for them and they for you. Why would he prevent that?"

"He can't trust anyone but himself, somehow. He thinks no one will do it well enough or understands the burden. It's an expression of love, truly—"

He was shaking his head impatiently. "Then I will change his mind. He'll see that I love you, and that we were right to do it."

She could not tell him how unlikely that was. She should not speak of her father that way—as if he were beyond hope. She studied the trunk containing Haydon's memoir and journals, words she had read and then shut up inside the darkness where they belonged.

To her surprise, Robert paused his case. "Are you worried about those?" he asked.

"Yes. He wanted to know if they could be published."

Haydon's last exhibition had been not just a failure, but a tragic failure.

For a shilling, people could choose to see either Haydon's historical paintings or Barnum's "prodigious midget," Tom Thumb. Tom Thumb had grossed £600 the first week, and Haydon had watched every single person who declined to enter his gallery go instead to gawk at the man next door. Instead of telling his wife and daughter that he was ruined and all their furniture and their house would be taken away, Haydon had fired a bullet into his head. It hadn't killed him, so he had slashed at his throat with a razor. His daughter had found him like that, in his studio, dead.

"He wrote to Chorley," Robert said, "and Chorley said Haydon knew exactly, to the half person, how many more people went to see Tom Thumb than went to see his paintings. A little girl being the half."

"I can't send the papers back to his wife and say they're worthless."

"I'll think of something. Chorley will have an idea."

"And there's this," Elizabeth handed him a letter. "From Miss Goss. She wants me to write a poem for the next *Liberty Bell*."

"Have you an idea for it? That might be a good distraction."

"Not a full idea." She had nothing but a face in mind, the face of the Jamaican woman who said Sam was the father of her child. She had not told Robert about her yet. George said it wasn't true, that there was no proof, and she didn't want to tell Robert that her brother had denied what the woman claimed. She fell silent. She stood in her mind as if in a room with no windows or doors. But Robert was there with her, and he didn't know she imagined Sam stuck in another room, invisible and final, completely dark, unable to tell anyone anything, and the Jamaican woman left outside it, told she had no right to knock or mourn. Robert smiled and touched her hand. She heard herself say, "How much money do you estimate we'll need to reach Pisa?"

She waited to hear the amount, fearful of what it meant to take such a step.

"A hundred pounds."

"That much? I couldn't get that much without saying why. I would have to ask George to withdraw it," she said.

"You don't have to. If you choose a date for the wedding—soon—I will do the rest."

Had she just agreed?

"I'll try. I don't know if I can."

"You can, Ba. We have all of July and part of August."

Two months to pull up all of her roots, so deep and heavy, enlaced with her family, and to do it without disturbing a leaf or stone.

"I'm so glad," Robert said.

"I am, too," she said.

THE NEXT DAY, George brought her a note saying Dr. Chambers was resigning as her physician.

"Dr. Chambers tried to keep you out of it," he said. "He swore to Father that you had no knowledge of his visit."

It was still oppressively hot. The windows were open. She had placed last year's *Liberty Bell* on top of Haydon's trunk and covered it with a shawl so that her unfinished projects might not leer at her all day. She could not edit Haydon's life story, she could not send his diaries to his penniless wife and daughter, she could not think of a poem that would make the Americans end slavery, and she could not plan a wedding that was a secret from all the people she loved.

George said, "He's not wrong, you know. It would be far more expensive than anyone admits. You would need at least two of us and a maid. The journey *would* be treacherous. None of us speak French except you, and the states in Italy are still fighting one another. It's cheaper and safer, from his point of view, to keep us all here, in one house."

"I have my legacy. I have the shares on the *David Lyon*. And what the poems bring. If I want to risk it, it ought to be my choice. I'm the one who will suffer if I am mistaken."

"You can't believe that, Ba. If you're ill in the middle of France, should we leave you there? Do you think we wouldn't suffer, worrying about you? It would be better if I accompanied you, but I can't leave. I must watch everything, review everything, and count everything or your legacy will mean nothing."

She could not deny it. Her legacy was a gift from her father's mother and thus came from the same place as the family income: the land in Jamaica, the pimento crop, sugar, molasses, and rum. "I hate it. I hate what we depend on to eat."

"Why? We pay a living wage to workers who are free to change employers. We can't all live upon poetry, Ba, and you *don't* live upon it, not really."

"I would have to if I were there."

"If you want to try that angle," George said, "we must calculate the cost and present it to him. I assume it would be passage for four: you, Arabel, Wilson, and I don't know who. Alfred, perhaps. We must calculate the cost of inns, and horses, and, beyond that, daily life in Pisa, how many rooms, which house, if the house can be found in advance. The biggest expense of all is the carriage. I will ask if anyone is selling one."

"Five," she said. "It would be five with Flush."

"You can't."

"I must."

"You could get another dog as easily. In Pisa."

"I couldn't."

"Very well."

"You sound like Father."

"I *feel* like Father."

He went on talking, but she could hardly hear him. She had not said, *I don't need you, Robert will take me, we are engaged.* If she told him, he would tell her father. The snake ate its tail and formed a circle.

"Two weeks, I estimate," George was saying.

"In total?"

"Perhaps three, if connections are missed, as they inevitably are, or the weather is bad, as it inevitably is, or if a wheel must be repaired or if you—"

"Fall ill."

"Yes."

"Perhaps it would be better," Elizabeth said, desperate to find a more honest way to proceed, "if I went with a friend."

"What friend?"

Say it. Say, *Robert*. Say, *I could marry him*. "Mrs. Jameson," she said. "The writer. She has gone to Canada by herself. She is traveling to France for a book, she says. That would be simpler than all of you risking his wrath, and receiving it, as you surely would, on your return."

"But how would you get from France to Pisa?"

With Robert. "I believe the book takes her also to Italy."

"Mrs. Jameson travels with her husband?"

She did not. They were estranged. Her husband had remained in Canada after they had formally separated.

"She has done so, yes."

"And she will this time?"

"I think not. He is still in Canada."

"Far worse, I should say, than my plan. I would rather send Alfred. Or go myself."

"I thought you couldn't."

"That's the problem. I'll see what I can learn from friends. About taking spoiled little dogs on carriages and trains." He stood to go, and he petted Flush fondly to show he was teasing.

"George, I fear what would happen to you if we failed. If we had to turn back. How could you face him?"

"Let me gather intelligence. We must gather intelligence before we decide."

"Wait." She set Flush on the floor and stood up. "I have started that already." She went to her bookshelf and slid out two heavy books, one by Virgil, one by Aeschylus. Behind them, flat, was the popular travel book by Mrs. Starke. "I have been consulting this," she said. "To imagine the route more realistically, and to estimate costs."

"Who is Mrs. Starke?"

"A thorough traveler." People said Mrs. Starke was not actually married and never had been, but George didn't need to hear that. "She has advice for women and invalids. She confirms what Dr. Chambers says about Pisa. That it is the best winter climate in Europe."

"Do not let Father see you reading that."

"You have seen my method of storing it."

"All right. Good night, Flush. Good night, Ba."

"Good night, Georgie."

AT NIGHT SHE read of Pisa and the Arno and the danger of standing too long in the sun. The distance by sea from Lerici to Genoa was twenty leagues. The fare by felucca was five or six sequins. It sounded like nothing! Nothing at all. But the time to travel twenty leagues by sea in a felucca was twelve to fifteen hours. *Unless there be no wind.* If there be no wind, or if the wind be contrary, travelers are compelled to land and spend the night in Portofino, *a pretty, but comfortless, little fishing town.* She tried but could not imagine that a town called Portofino, reached by handing sequins to a man in a felucca, could be in any way comfortless. She *tried* to imagine how hard it would be, how long, how tiring, but she was always a paper puppet in a paper boat on a paper sea, being carried, bodiless, to the fine port of Portofino and from there to Genoa, also called La Superba, with its capacious but unsafe harbor, exposed to a wind called (gloriously) the Libecio, which blows from the southwest, but within the unsafe harbor of La Superba (fear not) was another harbor, wherein the boats could dock, so her paper self, alongside paper Wilson, paper Robert, and paper Flush, sailed gaily into Genoa.

Listen, she wanted to say to Arabel, sitting by her side in the hot afternoon, knitting for the winter, because winter was coming. *The hotel in Genoa is cheap but gloomy. The bridges and churches and palaces are made of marble. The staircases and floors are marble. The streets are called Strada Balbi, Strada Nuova, Strada Nuovissima, can you imagine? But the older buildings have all been torn down because the streets were not wide enough for carriages. On Strada Nuovissima, the porters charge half a franc to carry even a small parcel from carriage to apartment. But we will make sure to save half a franc for that purpose because we are prepared, Arabel. We will be offered the products of Genoa but we won't buy them: silk, velvet, damask, and paper. We will ask where the water comes from before we drink it because some of the water of Genoa has been injured by passing through leaden pipes. We will ask, Arabel, how long the plaster walls of a house have been drying because they must dry five years before they are healthful. I will line the crown of my hat with writing paper several times doubled if I must go about in the sun. I will sponge myself daily with vinegar to prevent malaria. I will not go without you, Arabel. I could never, never, never go without you.* These were the things she wanted to say, but could not.

THIRTY-SEVEN

∞

On Tuesday, Mr. Kenyon appeared at Elizabeth's door.

"I have been talking to Henrietta and Arabel downstairs. I have told them, and they agree, that Mrs. Jameson is the perfect solution. I have told her everything."

"Everything?" She and Robert, in their dealings with Kenyon, had vowed never to mention each other, but he had a coy way of writing, in his letters to Elizabeth, that he had seen "our friend RB."

"I have told her," he said quietly, "that you need to go to Pisa, and your father stands in the way. That his reasons for doing so are unreasonable. That I worry, in fact, about his being not quite in his right mind—"

"John."

"I know you don't want to hear it, but it's true. And Mrs. Jameson is completely ready and willing to assist you. It was her idea, not mine. She can take you to France, and from France to Pisa. It is her intended route in any case. She needs to go to Chartres, and the Louvre, and I don't know how many cathedrals for her book about the artworks, but all of them lie on the road to Pisa. It's the most delicious coincidence! Two such similar minds, traveling together, it is meant to be."

"I thought she wished to bring her niece with her," Elizabeth said. "I understood it to be her greatest hope, that this time her niece would travel with her and be able to help her with the drawings."

"Miss Bates will be with her. But what of that? A more felicitous grouping yet. The ingenue, the art historian, and the poetess."

"John, you have a wilder imagination even than I."

"Write to her, Ba. Write to her and tell her you accept. Or ask her to visit and talk it over. Let her convince you."

"Let's talk of something else. Tell me about your own poems, why don't you?"

And then it was August, the month when Dr. Chambers said she must embark, but nothing was fixed. George had a case, he said, that was taking all his time. He had to finish it, and then he would go to the booking office and inquire, and he would see if the friend who was selling his carriage still meant to sell it, but paying the friend depended, he said, on the sale of something that had not yet sold, she didn't hear what, she was too alarmed to listen. She could not tell George that she was proceeding without him.

"Did you tell him when you wish to go?" Robert asked.

"I told him to focus on his work, that it could all wait until September. He said he wasn't giving up, and I said I understood how busy he is."

The farther it went, the more secrets she had. *What are you working on?* everyone asked. *A poem for the Liberty Bell. What is it about? A Black mother and her white child. Is it set in Jamaica? No, in America. Who is the mother? She is representative. How is it going? It's very difficult.* Haydon's trunk stayed in the corner, words of a dead artist in a box, a problem Robert said he would deal with, he would entrust it to someone.

The things one must do to get married. It ought to have been exciting to order visiting cards that said *Mr. and Mrs. Robert Browning.* It ought to have been nice to choose a minister. Even the announcement for the newspaper presented a need for a lie. They would marry at the nearest church, St. Marylebone, on September 12, and they would return to their separate houses as if nothing had changed, and only *after* they had left the country (a week later, no more) the newspaper announcement would appear, so it should, if possible, omit the date. Could one omit the date? Yes, one could. It could say "Saturday." And how to put the rest of it? *Robert Browning, Junior, Esquire, of New Cross, Hatcham, to Elizabeth Barrett, eldest daughter of Edward Moulton Barrett of Wimpole Street and Cinnamon Hill, Jamaica.* No, not "of Jamaica." Just of Wimpole Street.

Robert had written down the estimated costs. George's plan of buying a carriage, even an old one, and sending it by ferry to France, where they would arrange to hire fresh horses at each stop, was impossibly expensive, and Robert didn't know anything about hiring drivers and horses. He said a diligence would be cheaper.

"Robert," she said. He was sitting with her as they dared to do now, thigh to thigh, his hand on her knee, her hand sometimes on his shoulder, sometimes in his, the better to keep their voices low. "I don't know what that is."

He told her it was a cab for hire, only bigger, enough room for nine, with the different seats being reserved ahead of time. The best seats were private, and inside rather than up on the box. The *coupé*, it was called.

"How many people sit there?"

"That's the only problem. Three persons and a dog," he said. "I asked."

If Elizabeth brought Arabel and Wilson, there were four persons.

"Someone would have to sit with strangers," he said. It could not be one of the women, so it would have to be Robert.

She studied the list of numbers Robert had made. The price for four people and a dog was written down and multiplied by the number of days and French towns. The price for the inns had not been written in yet. Each town had a question mark beside it. The steamer from Marseilles was another question mark.

"Ba," Robert said, "It's entirely your decision. But you could, if you think about it, hire a new maid in Italy."

Robert did not have a servant to brush his clothes. He did not have a servant to brush his horse. He did not own a carriage. His sister and mother had a maid of all work to do very hard things, but they did for themselves nearly all that was done by servants at Wimpole Street. Robert acted as if he didn't judge her, as if he understood, especially in her condition, why traveling with a maid would be essential. He did not understand how hard it was to find someone you understood and who understood you and who wished to be paid what you could afford to pay, and who did not need to be corrected very often and who could be trusted to see you in private, to know all about you, and not resent you or make you resent them in turn.

"You would have me," Robert said. "And Arabel. We would be happy to do everything you need."

She tried to add and divide and subtract and multiply. Three hundred a year, which was her income, divided by sous. By sequins. By francs. Usually, she had but one expense, or call it two: the doctor and her laudanum. That bill came to £129 last year. Her father paid all the rest of her expenses: servants, food, coal, clothing, books, paper, postage, and ink. The house, their carriage, the driver.

"You must bring whomever you need," Robert said. He kissed her and she didn't even listen for footsteps on the stairs. "But I will do whatever is needed, gladly."

She couldn't ask Arabel to do what Wilson did, and a husband didn't do a maid's work. It was impossible. "You're sure the coupé can't seat four?"

"I asked if I could buy four. It's too small."

She wished—she shouldn't, but she did—that somehow George had found a carriage to buy and send over on the ferry, and that she had a little more money so she could pay for the use of horses. Then the four of them, with Flush, could ride all together, and not worry about strange men sitting beside Arabel or Wilson.

"My cousin agreed to be a witness," Robert said, "and he is free next Saturday. We will need another witness. Will it be Arabel or Wilson?"

"I still haven't told Arabel anything. It's better if she doesn't know anything about it so that when we leave, she can be genuinely surprised. She can say that she didn't know, and she didn't help us."

"But she would need time to prepare if she's coming with us."

"I know."

She put it off, and she waited, and she reasoned that it was best to tell Arabel, if she told her at all, on the night before the wedding, or perhaps even the morning of, but two things happened to complicate what already seemed an impossibly complicated plan. First, the entire family was invited to go to a picnic in Richmond, and they accepted. The picnic was on Saturday, and the departure would be in the early morning, at eight, well before the time Elizabeth planned to leave for the church. Then their father announced that they must all move house. The workers who had been hired to clean, paint, paper, and refurbish their present house would be available on Monday next, so they must all go to the only place that would accommodate all of them within easy reach of town, a rectory in Little Bookham.

As soon as she could be alone, Elizabeth wrote to Robert. The Rectory at Little Bookham was farther from St. Marylebone Church, where the wedding would be, and it was farther from the station that must be their embarkation point. Ought they to wait to be married, she asked, until the move was completed?

No, he wrote. We can't wait any longer. It was all arranged—the minister, his cousin, the tickets on the ferry to France, the inn in Le Havre, seats in the first diligence. The later they started, the later in autumn the final stage of the trip would be, when they crossed over the Alps or went by sea to Genoa.

Elizabeth turned the possibilities over as if in a game of Patience. Each time through the deck, she had nothing. The cards she needed were nowhere to be seen. If she told Arabel now about the wedding, Arabel would need an excuse to miss the picnic, and the only possible excuse was sickness. If Elizabeth said she was sick, Arabel might be left to take care of her, but Elizabeth's excuse for missing the picnic was her promise to visit a friend in St. John's Wood, an engagement she had made so she had a reason to get dressed and go out in the carriage, which was to take her to St. John's Wood after she married Robert in St. Marylebone's. And the more she thought of taking Arabel to Italy, the more selfish it seemed. Arabel would have no friends there and no work—her work at the school for impoverished girls was her main occupation. Arabel had no income of her own to add. Their father would provide her with nothing if she were to follow Elizabeth into an illicit marriage.

"Wilson," Elizabeth said when she came to take away the supper things on Friday night, the 11th of September.

"Miss."

"I want you to sit down."

"Sit, Miss?"

"I need to ask something. You are welcome to refuse—you are absolutely free to refuse, I mean that most sincerely—but if you do refuse, I must beg that you speak of it to no one."

Wilson nodded.

"Will you sit?"

"I'm more comfortable standing, Miss. If you will allow me."

"You understand that Dr. Chambers has advised me to go abroad."

Wilson nodded.

"My father disagrees with this advice."

Wilson nodded.

"I intend to go anyway, and the safest way—" Elizabeth stopped. The plate on which her piece of mutton sat, cold, cut into pieces that were meant to suggest she had eaten, had a disgusting clarity. "The safest way is to avoid involving my sisters and brothers. I intend to go with Mr. Browning."

"To run away with him, Miss?"

"No, not that! I do not intend to *run away* with him. He and I will be married tomorrow. At half past ten."

This was absorbed, and Wilson managed to say that she was happy for them.

"What I have to ask you is more than I have ever asked of anyone, and I can hardly hear myself ask it without hearing all the reasons you have—excellent reasons—to refuse." Elizabeth felt a great pressure in her head. "It is not just to the wedding that I ask you to accompany me, though I would be very grateful if you could perform that office tomorrow while everyone is at Richmond."

Wilson nodded.

"I hardly know how to put it," Elizabeth said, faltering. "It is such an extraordinary request. Would you go with me and Mr. Browning to Italy? To Pisa."

Wilson's family lived in the north. She had just taken a holiday and visited them all, which was good luck, Elizabeth thought, but perhaps that would remind her of how much she missed everyone, and of how much she would like to visit them again soon.

Wilson touched the edge of her apron. She reached out to the tray and put a spoon on a saucer. Inside the cup the tea was a very shallow pool. "When would it be, Miss?"

"As soon as it can be arranged. I'll act as if I have not married, and I, or we—you and I, not Mr. Browning and I—will come back to the house. We will go to Pisa in a week."

"If I may ask, Miss: Does Miss Arabel know?"

Elizabeth leaned forward and Flush lifted his head. What she had to say she didn't want to say. "She knows that we wish it, and how we feel, but not that we have set a date."

"Will ye tell her also, Miss?"

Elizabeth shook her head.

"And she'll not be there, then? In the church? When ye wed?"

Elizabeth shook her head. "I want her to be there, more than I can say. But it would be selfish because it will make my father angry at her, too. I mustn't make her part of it."

"I see, Miss."

"You needn't decide about going to Italy tonight. But the wedding. I need to know if you can do that, so that Mr. Browning will know if we have enough witnesses."

"How could I not, Miss? So romantic it is. And Mr. Browning is a good man. I have felt it from the first."

"He is. He is that."

"What shall ye wear, Miss? What shall I get ready?"

"Nothing but my usual dress. I don't want to look as if I am doing anything special. I will go to see Mr. Boyd after. That is what I am doing tomorrow, if anyone asks, which I doubt they will. I am going to see Mr. Boyd in St. John's Wood."

"What ought I to tell Mrs. Orme, Miss?"

"Tell her you will accompany me to St. John's Wood. To see Mr. Boyd. Because Arabel and Henrietta are going to the picnic with the others."

"I understand, Miss."

THIRTY-EIGHT

❧

SHE HELD HER pencil in expectation, the point on the page, her muscles loose, so that another being, in that invisible place, might move it and say what mattered. If Sam's spirit took the pencil, what might he say? *I approve.* Or her mother? *I approve.* She heard her father go to his bed. He didn't rap on the passage door and ask, as he used to, before the breach, if she wanted to say a prayer with him tonight. He was a smattering of rustles and footsteps and sighs and throat clearings and sniffs, the thud of shoes, and stillness. Then snores.

Tomorrow, I wed, her mind said to itself. Morphine said it. The pencil waited.

She left the warmth of Flush to go to the window. It faced not the street but the back roofs of other houses, and down below, in darkness, the knife edge of a sheet hung to dry. *Tomorrow I wed*. She felt something prickling her arms, the skin of her cheeks, a tingling and lightness. *Tomorrow I wed*.

She stepped out onto the landing and saw that Arabel's door was open. No light shone there, and when she stepped to the doorway, she could see Arabel asleep on the bed, the sheet all that covered her, her face barely visible in the light that was gray lace. Elizabeth could still awaken her and say she was getting married in the morning. *Come with me,* she could say, and Arabel would consent and be happy.

Or she could do what was best for her sister. She could allow Arabel to say, truthfully, when all was revealed, that she'd had no idea Ba was getting married. No idea that Ba was going to Italy with Mr. Browning.

The armor of ignorance would protect her best.

Henrietta slept through all noises and disturbances, but Arabel was a light sleeper. The distance to Arabel's window, which faced the street, was elongated, and the slightly tilted feeling Elizabeth had as she walked, as if on a bridge strung from ropes, meant the morphine was working at last and she might sleep if she said the Greek numbers to one hundred followed by the Greek alphabet and if that wasn't enough, she would walk herself through the rooms at Hope End while holding a little brother and singing "Bye, Baby Bunting." She stood very still in Arabel's tilted room so that she could look for the last time at the place in the street where she had seen Robert Browning going away from the house after his first visit. She reached the armchair and steadied herself on the wall, peering down.

A shrouded figure sat on the stones. She studied it, waiting for it to move. It might be a woman or a man. The minutes passed without any movement. No matter how hard she stared, she could not see a face.

"What's wrong?" Arabel asked from the bed. "Are you ill, Ba?"

"Is that a woman?" Elizabeth said. "Can you tell?" Arabel stood beside her. Elizabeth pointed.

"Come and sleep," Arabel said. "You must have a fever."

"I can't sleep."

"You can sleep if you lie down, but not if you roam the house. Say the Greek numbers to me."

"Do you see her?"

"Who?" Arabel said. "It's nobody. It's bundles of rags."

It looked more like a woman, but she went back to her room with Arabel.

IN THE MORNING, carriages banged and clattered through the streets. Arabel offered to stay home from the picnic in case Elizabeth was ill, but Elizabeth said she was perfectly well, and Arabel must go to the picnic and bring back news of everyone they hadn't seen since Christmas.

"If you are well," Arabel said, "you ought to come with us!"

Henrietta agreed. "You can sit on a rug the whole time. It will do you good."

Elizabeth said she had promised Mr. Boyd.

"Poo. Mr. Boyd doesn't deserve a visit, and Treppy does. Surprise her!"

"I can't. I promised Mr. Boyd."

"I think you're making a bad bargain. Look what a bright day it is! Don't waste it in a grumpy man's parlor."

"What did you eat last night?" her father asked.

She said she had eaten nearly all the mutton and all the toast.

"If she doesn't wish it, she doesn't wish it," her father said, and they left one by one, George last of all, his eyes like a magnifying glass and she the specimen.

At last they were gone. Wilson steadied her as she stepped into the hired carriage. Flush barked because he was left behind, barking every word of the plan to Mrs. Orme and Hingston and the neighbors and the place where she had seen the sleeping woman. All down the block, she thought she heard his plaintive yips.

Robert was there in St. Marylebone Church, handsomely dressed, carefully shaved. A man stood with him. "My cousin, Mr. Silverthorne," Robert said. He called her dear and darling, and she clutched his hand and the flowers he had brought her. In his buttonhole, too, a flower. Mr. Silverthorne wore glasses. Trim black clothes. Square cut fingernails.

"With this body, I thee wed," she repeated.

It was a triumph of clouded joy. Four people, a nearly empty church, and her head ringing as he kissed her. And then down the aisle, thinking the whole time of how when they stepped out of the church the ring must be off her finger again because if someone saw Miss Barrett coming out of the church on a Saturday, she must not look joyful. She must not be wearing a ring or holding rosebuds.

Mr. Rabelais's man was watching as they came and went. Smoking and watching as if smoking and watching who came in and out of St. Marylebone Church was his occupation.

"Do you see him?" she asked Wilson when they were in the carriage.

"That I do, Miss."

"Will he tell, do you think?"

"Who, Turnip?"

"Is that his name?"

"He won't tell anything, Miss. All he sees is a woman coming out of church with her maid, and that's not of interest to Turnip."

"But he's seen Mr. Browning come and go."

"Mr. Rabelais is not a friend of your father's or of anyone else, either. Be glad, Miss. Be glad you have married a good man." She reached to secure the latch on the door, but it stuck. She tried again, removed her gloves, and it clicked into place. Wilson folded her hands, appeared to be thinking hard about something, and said, "If ye still want me, I have decided. I will go."

"I do, Wilson. I do."

"It will be an adventure," she said. "That's what my mother said when I left to come here. She never thought I should go with Mrs. Goodin Barrett to Jamaica. 'London is adventure enough,' she said."

"What will she say about Italy?" Elizabeth asked.

"It doesn't matter. Whatever it is, I'll be there by then."

The carriage turned to go to St. John's Wood, giving her one more glimpse of Turnip smoking his cigarette, and then he was gone amid the mass of black coats, brown coats, ladies' bonnets, the bricks of houses, and the green beginning of the green park.

THIRTY-NINE

∞

THEIR TRUNKS HAD been sent to Vauxhall and would be collected. They would board the train to Gravesend, find the queue for the Southwestern steam packet and cross the Channel to Le Havre. Le Havre to Rouen, Rouen to Paris, Paris to Orléans, Orléans to Avignon, Avignon to Marseilles, Marseilles to Genoa, Genoa to Pisa.

Beads on an abacus, dots on the map. There was absolutely nothing to worry about. Robert had it all arranged and would meet her and Wilson and the dog at Hodgson's Bookshop.

The week had been a play in seven acts, starring herself as a married woman. The audience knew but her family did not. Wilson knew, but only Wilson. When they were alone they could whisper about it. "No one saw me, not even Mrs. Orme," Wilson said. Wilson had packed this, she had pocketed that, she had sent this, she had arranged that. On the day of the seventh and final act, Wilson was securing tongue and sorrel sandwiches for "a picnic in Regent's Park."

"Isn't it lucky," Wilson said, "that all is in turmoil about the house just now?" The move to Little Bookham and the imminent arrival of a horde of workmen provided excellent cover for whisking away her mistress's belongings. No one could find anything anyway, and no one would be suspicious if trunks were being packed and sent away.

There was no time left to start again on the letters Elizabeth had written, to explain it better. She had sealed all but one so she wouldn't reread her explanations and tear them up to start over. One said her father's name, another was George's, there was one for each sister and brother, another to

Miss Mitford, another to John Kenyon. At the bottom of each, the same message: *Forgive me. Forgive me. Forgive me. Direct your replies to "Post Restant, Orléans."* Only Arabel's remained to be sealed.

Flush thought the trunks and bags were proof she was going without him. *We are one creature*, said his whimpering and pacing. Elizabeth whispered that it was fine. "We're going for a picnic," she said out loud. Flush leapt into the bag where she'd tucked Robert's letters and the feather-scraps of sonnets she had not told him she was writing and the poem she was supposed to be writing for the *Liberty Bell*.

Quarter past, said the St. Marylebone bell. Time to go.

There were men already in the rooms downstairs, the thud and scrape of heavy objects.

Now was the time to go, while Arabel was at the house in Little Bookham, Henrietta was shopping, her brothers and father were out on unknown errands. The green velvet drapes of her room were pulled down and folded. The blinds Henrietta had decorated were rolled up so that all she could see was the dingy border of Souvenir de la Malmaison roses and a church steeple. Her books were stacked in boxes, every one of them to be left behind. "There are books in Pisa," Robert said. Books in Venice.

The shells Sam sent from Jamaica filled a sack, the chalk drawings Edward did at Torquay leaned against the wall. They must be left. All must be left.

She wasn't leaving forever. Next summer, cured by a winter in Italy, she and Robert would visit as man and wife, forgiven by everyone.

Flush trembled, watching her stand and stand and stand—*Why don't we go now?* he begged to know—because why was she wearing shoes and why were the bags packed and why were men moving in and out of rooms downstairs?

She lit the wick, melted the wax, and poured the wax on Arabel's letter. It caught fire and she tamped it out with the seal. Before the wax was cold, she put the letter with the others into her pocket for her last act of strangeness: taking letters addressed to all the people inside the house and posting them outside the house to be delivered to the house once she was gone.

As she expected, tying her bonnet made Flush leap and bark. He barked as she arranged her shawl, he barked as she picked up the bag, he barked as she held the rope over his head and said, "Let's go." He barked as she walked down the stairs, and she dropped his leash so he wouldn't drag her. He barked as she faced Hingston coming into the hall with Arabel's birdcage.

"Good afternoon, Miss Elizabeth," he said amidst the barking. "Are ye going out?"

He barked as she said she was going for a picnic and Wilson was bringing the sandwiches made by Mrs. Orme.

He barked as Hingston turned the knob of the door that she might, or might not, see when she came back next summer, forgiven. Sunlight blazed through the open door as Hingston called, "Good luck, Miss!" and she thought, *He knows*. He would have seen the increase in letters from Mr. Browning, and he probably was a friend of Turnip, friend enough to hear gossip about a lady from his house coming out of the church with her maid and a man wearing a red flower in his lapel, the same man who has been coming to the house every single week for over a year.

She couldn't think what to say so she waved at Hingston and stepped down into bright sunlight, the hot smell of horse dung, the glitter of light on a mirror a man was carrying to the other side of Wimpole Street. She nearly ran into another man who stopped to avoid Flush squatting to relieve himself. He glared and said it was cruel to keep dogs in the city and she said nothing to him, either, but let Flush drag her to the next Smelling Place, thrusting his nose at bits of pavement and soil, leaving his own water everywhere they went.

The ring. Might she put it on now? She had hoped to feel Robert slip it on her hand once more. "Are you ready, Miss?" Wilson was there now, young and blond and clear-eyed and happy. She was taller than usual because she wore a stiff bonnet with a high crown, and to her relief the bag she'd packed was in one of Wilson's hands, full of the sonnets, a heavier shawl, a second skirt, all of Robert's letters. In her other hand was a basket containing plums and jars and oil-stained paper.

"Did Hingston say anything?" Elizabeth asked. "Did he wish you luck?"

"No, Miss."

She felt almost as if she had summoned George with her fear of discovery, and there he was, staring at them, his face sweating in the heat.

"Where are you going?" he asked.

"A little picnic is all. Flush barks at everyone who comes up the stairs. He has barked the whole day long."

"What have you got?" he said, poking a hand into the basket. "I'm famished."

"There is one for you in the kitchen, sir," Wilson said, so calm and fearless. "I saw Mrs. Orme set a whole plate of others aside."

"I'd rather go to the park," George said.

She thought she'd go mad. They would miss the train if George insisted on walking with them to the park. Robert would be at Hodgson's, wondering what had happened. A horse clopped by, a child shouted in the park, the sun blazed.

"I don't dare, though. You look very warm. Ought you to be out?"

"We'll be well enough in the shade. If we move on."

"Count the swans for me," George said, leaning in for a kiss.

"I always do."

"The Rectory will be a nice change," he said. "Flush will like it."

"Yes," she said.

Wilson said nothing as they walked away. She waited until they reached the gate, turned around to make sure he was nowhere to be seen, and they prepared to go back the way they had come to meet Robert at Hodgson's. "He'll understand, Miss. He'll understand when he knows everything. He's been in love."

"I don't know that he has," Elizabeth said, stepping into the street.

Almost there, Elizabeth thought, almost there, and the goblin of deceit was a light in the windows, bobbing beside them, a streak half-seen and glittering at the edges of the day.

Robert waited outside Hodgson's Bookshop with a small bag. His trunk had been sent to Vauxhall and he knew the timetable for the *Southwestern* ferry, where to stay in Le Havre, where to exchange the passports, in which pocket he had put the tickets for the coupé of the diligence, how many shillings equal how many sous, and where not to put money in his portmanteau. He had the letter of credit from Rothschild's, the hundred pounds borrowed from his father, the names of inns where a woman would be comfortable. He did not have a good night's sleep.

"Mr. Browning?" said a man's voice behind him. A young man blinked, his freckled face smiling, his whiskers trying but failing to make a firm line, his blue eyes aqueous. It was Hodgson's assistant, Michael. "I have the book you were looking for, sir. It arrived today."

He could not remember what he'd ordered, it had been so long.

The freckled boy held the door open to the shop and waited for Robert to go in.

"I'm in a bit of a hurry, Michael," Robert said "I'm going abroad again. Heading out tonight."

It was all right. She would not leave the meeting place if he went in for a moment.

"Where to this time, sir?" Michael asked.

"Pisa."

"Is it more material you're after?" Michael asked, just as Hodgson stood up and smiled. Robert wanted to say he had married Elizabeth Barrett and was taking her abroad. There were her books, right there, a whole row of them, on the same shelf as a single copy of *Sordello*. "Robert, I want to say, and I'd say it to anyone, they're wrong," Hodgson said, seeing, perhaps, the way Robert's eyes went. "Take it for what it is. Envy. Pure and simple."

"What is?"

"Moxon didn't send them back to you? I thought he would."

"I'm not sure."

"It's a measure of your importance, remember that. They wouldn't be writing about you if they didn't think you had the stuff, so you keep the copies. Don't burn them in a pyre."

That's why it was one copy of *Sordello*. Not that it sold out, but that the unsold copies had been returned to him.

"I only keep copies on the shelf for a certain period, it's the same for everyone. Don't take offense."

There were only two lines in it that I understood! went Alfred Tennyson's review, *and they were both lies!*

"Not important," Robert said as Michael wrapped up the book for him. He hadn't even seen what it was.

There she was at the window. The dark bonnet, the spaniel in Wilson's arms, a basket, and a small bag. They were staring out at the street, looking for him, no doubt, and he must go.

"Ah, there they are," he said quickly. "The ladies I'm meeting. I must hurry to the station," he said, putting a coin on the counter. He hoped—he couldn't help it—that Hodgson knew what Elizabeth Barrett looked like, that he saw Robert go out the door and touch her hand, be smiled at. He hoped that once the advertisement of their marriage was published in the *Post*, Hodgson would say to people that he saw the two of them, poet and poetess, right there in front of his shop, the lovers on the verge of their departure.

FORTY

∞

THE TRAIN HAD begun to roll when a woman stopped in the aisle beside them. Elizabeth was trying not to feel a surfeit of blood, as Dr. Chambers called it when she felt like this, a surfeit that demanded release by cutting or leaches. Her body was used to its cycles; the nightly tea, the drops of morphine. The wedding ring and a bottle of morphine were together in her pocket, the bottle wrapped in a twist of cloth.

"Mr. Browning?" The woman said.

"Miss Goss," Robert said, standing up at once. "How good to see you!"

"And to see you," Miss Goss said.

So that's how she looked now. The woman's beauty had a force that everyone must feel.

"Do you know Miss Barrett?" Robert said.

Miss Goss must be thinking the same thing, *So that's what she looks like now.* Older, thinner, frailer.

"Miss Barrett she was before, I mean, but she is now Mrs. Browning, I'm proud to say. I present to you my wife."

"Wife? Have I been so very out of touch, Mr. Browning?" Miss Goss asked.

"It is the newest of news," Robert said, and he turned to Elizabeth as she absorbed the pleasure and strangeness of being called "wife" in public before they had quite left London. "Miss Goss is a friend of your brother George," Robert said.

"I know," Elizabeth said. "You have written to me," she said to Miss

Goss. To Robert she turned and said, "About the *Liberty Bell*. And we knew each other when Miss Goss came to see us at Hope End."

It was the same Miss Goss as before: confident about things the young Elizabeth had not liked. Her pale green jacket and dress were perfectly tailored to fit her tight, slim waist, and they matched, exactly, her silk bonnet and exquisitely embroidered gloves. And yet she was a serious person now.

"I'm sorry I've not finished the poem," Elizabeth said. "I think I'm too late now. I meant to write you and explain." Was Miss Goss in touch with George? Might she write to him at once and say, "I saw your sister!" The letters were supposed to inform and explain in her own way. The news must not travel by some other means.

"Oh, there's always the next edition," Miss Goss said, bracing herself against a turn with the skill of a frequent traveler, barely needing to adjust her balance. "You have been busy, that's plain. I didn't hear a word about it from your brother!"

"No," Elizabeth said. "You wouldn't." Why did she put it like that?

"He ought to have told me the good news."

"Indeed." Should Elizabeth say it had been a secret and was still unknown?

"Where are you headed, Miss Goss?" Robert asked, pressing her hand.

"A friend has invited me to Venice."

"We hope to go there later—to Venice, I mean," Elizabeth said. This meant they were traveling to the same country so they might meet again and again. Miss Goss asked where they were going, and Robert began telling her about the weather in Pisa.

The sunlight was tangerine, and the train moved faster and faster past gray stone and red brick, into open spaces, and Elizabeth wanted to give herself up to the scene outside the windows, to the fields, and not think about George and the arrival of her posted letters.

"Do you know Lady Layard?" Miss Goss asked. "Or Mrs. Jameson?"

"We know Mrs. Jameson very well," Robert said, and Elizabeth nodded, desperate for Miss Goss to go away.

"Then we'll have the pleasure of meeting again. She's in Paris, you know."

"Yes, we hope to see her there," Robert said.

"I will leave you two alone."

Thankfully. "We must talk again soon, Miss Goss," Elizabeth said. "Do forgive me my distraction."

"There is absolutely nothing to forgive. My sincerest, deepest congratulations on your marriage." Miss Goss's skirts rustled expensively, a row of ribbons tied in perfect bows down the back of her tight green jacket.

Released. Robert took Elizabeth's other hand, and he folded it—how she loved the way he did that—into the warmth between his body and his arm. Wilson leaned over to say, "Remember when you said you thought George had never been in love, Miss? That's why I said he had. Because of that lady."

"Do you think so, Wilson?" Robert asked.

"I know it. I am sure."

"But how?" Elizabeth asked.

"How do I know?"

"How do they meet?"

"Everyone finds a way, Miss. And it's a good thing, too."

Elizabeth leaned her head on Robert's shoulder, and he kissed her hair, and she watched the last bit of sun going down on a world red as a rabbit's ear.

FROM HER CAR, Lenore began at once. Her maid was occupied with setting the table, and Lenore had just enough time if she hurried.

Dear Sarianna,

You were right: they meant to wed, and they have! I have encountered them myself on the way to Venice. They are settled in the car with her little dog and her maid, and though the new Mrs. Browning seemed tired I could tell they are very much in love. Where was the wedding? I hope you were there. I have heard nothing about it from anyone so perhaps it happened yesterday, or even today. I will watch over them for you if I can—I know you worry. They are heading to Pisa (as I'm sure you know) and I to Venice, but I will likely stop in Pisa on the way as I have never seen the Torre Pendente. The route to Italy is the same for all until you reach the Apennines, and I doubt they would go that way.

Write to me at the Hôtel de Ville in Paris and I will tell you whatever I can.

Your friend,
Lenore

What she didn't mention to either Sarianna or the Brownings was her intention of staying abroad. She was tired of everything to do with England and furious about the way the *Post* protected men who were friends of the editors. She must tell the Brownings that the move was permanent, more or less, when she had the chance. Mrs. Browning might send the antislavery poem to the wrong address, if indeed she ever wrote it.

The car was nearly dark now: the sky a blazing streak of orange just at the horizon, and Lenore would just have time to post the letter before she boarded the ferry to Le Havre.

FORTY-ONE

∞

THE BOAT TO Le Havre chugged toward the mouth of the Thames, the sea-smell mingling with smoke, the steam of the engine blotting out the purple sky. Tiny lights gleamed ashore, and the globes of lanterns on passing ships made yellow trails on black water. Robert wished it weren't dark for Elizabeth's first crossing. Better to see it all as you left: the soft shoulders of the river, the whitecaps and seabirds and steeples and hills, the country made smaller and more innocent as you left it behind. Instead they were stealing away like thieves, as if they were afraid George would rush to Gravesend. They hadn't had a single moment alone since they took their vows, the kind of delay that in the theater would mean someone standing up and shouting about an annulment.

"Did you bring a change of clothes?" a woman asked.

It was Miss Goss again, and she wore a cloak lined with fur. "I don't mean to intrude," she said, "but I have crossed before at night, and I sat where you are, and it was astonishing how wet I got. I think you should move astern."

"How thoughtful of you," Robert said, not wanting to seem like a novice traveler, "but I have crossed before."

"Do you have a sac de nuit?"

"I do," Elizabeth said. Robert had told her the bag would be safer with the other luggage, not to worry. It was the bag with his letters in it, and the sonnets, and the poem Miss Goss was probably wanting to ask more about.

"Then you'll be able to change, at least," Miss Goss said. "I was afraid you'd have put all your luggage together. Once it's marked for Paris, it cannot be retrieved and opened. I made that mistake once and it was terrible! I was drenched and had to endure hours and hours in my wet dress."

Wilson, who was so cheerful and eager before, was gripping the metal slats of the bench, tightening her neck, pressing her lips together, and groaning softly.

"But it *is* marked for Paris. I thought that's what they said to do." Robert said.

"The sac de nuit?" Lenore asked.

"Yes, they put it below."

"Oh, no. They ought to warn people. I don't know why they don't!" Lenore said.

"They will make an exception, surely," Robert said to Miss Goss, "if the weather is bad."

"I fear they won't, Mr. Browning. Here, Mrs. Browning, you must take my cloak." She unhooked the silver clasp.

"Oh, that's kind of you but I have my shawl," Elizabeth said.

"That won't be enough," Miss Goss said, shrugging it off and holding it out to them.

"We mustn't deprive you," Robert said, removing his own coat.

Miss Goss stood with the splendid cloak over her arms, and Robert told her to please put it back on, she must, they would be fine, Elizabeth would wear his coat, but Miss Goss remained where she was. "If you won't take my cloak, please join me in the more protected seats." She motioned for them to stand up and follow her, asserting herself in a way that was unexpected, crossing a line, it seemed to him, though maybe it was because he had made an error already in telling Elizabeth to surrender her small handbag. It was the dog who made him suggest it, the dog who had to be held. If anyone was sick, as the maid was starting to be, they did not need to have extra luggage. Robert had never taken the night ferry, he had never traveled with a terrified dog, he had never traveled with a maid, he had never traveled with a wife.

"I promise it will be much drier," Miss Goss said.

They followed Miss Goss across the deck with Wilson trailing behind them. She did not want to get any closer to the rail. "It's all right," he said. On land, Wilson had been the adult who reassured Elizabeth. She was calm, careful, and efficient. At sea, Wilson was not Wilson. She stood still and stared at what would have been visible in daylight: water rising and falling, a great dark mass of instability. The boat that had been chugging noisily chugged and churned more noisily. The deck went up and down under their feet. Rain was starting as he took her arm and coaxed her to follow Miss Goss and Elizabeth and the yipping dog.

At last they reached the stern and the seats that were, as Miss Goss said, protected. Inside the windowed area were rows of people wearing cloaks and coats. At their feet were small, handled bags. Every seat was occupied, every face that was near enough to turn and see who had come in turned to see them, and then turned away.

"There were seats when I left," Miss Goss said.

"Where is yours?" he asked.

"Follow me," she said, giving no answer, going back out into the rain, and he had to steer the unwilling maid back onto the deck. The next place had a small, solid barrier about three feet high, beyond which lay the water. It was under the roof, but it terrified Wilson, he saw, because they were so close to the sound of waves.

"Perhaps we ought to go back," he said. He had to shout to be heard.

"The spray on the other side will utterly soak her," Miss Goss shouted. "Do try sitting here. I have my sac de nuit and can change later."

"Dearest," he said, but Elizabeth was already taking a seat, her hands mechanically petting the dog, trying to calm him down, or to calm herself, and Wilson followed her.

Before she left, Miss Goss slid out of her cloak and dropped it over their laps. The deck shone with water, and the rain fell harder, thundering on the roof over their heads and splashing down in thick cataracts that formed a sort of curtain between them and the invisible ocean. He heard a moan from Wilson, who had begun to murmur prayers. The last time he'd sailed anywhere, the passengers were all men, and none of them were seasick. He reached for Elizabeth's hand, tiny and cold, and it felt looser than before, as if she couldn't close it. They should not have crossed at night. A plan, once started, had its own momentum, as if it were a thing apart, no longer in his control. Her tiny cold hand, not gripping his but lying loose there, uncommitted, chilled him. And then Wilson was sick, leaning over her knees to heave.

Elizabeth put her hand on Wilson's neck, rubbing it.

The cloth of her dress under his hand was wet. Her hair was wet. The rain had managed to soak them all.

The tossing and surging convulsions of the boat made Wilson lift her face. "Are we sinking? Shall we die?" she asked, just as a man with a bearish face laid a hand on Robert's arm. "Monsieur," he shouted, motioning for them to stand, and the three of them staggered after him like a six-legged beast toward a door. The Frenchman unlatched it, and Robert grabbed the wall for balance as the boat tipped them toward the opening. Once they were in, the man shut the door, and the noise dropped. They were wholly enclosed. A lamp welded to a wall shone enough to illuminate what appeared to be a ramp. "La," shouted the man, pointing into the darkness, gesturing and saying the French word for *dry*. Wilson, who was first, didn't move, so the man unhooked a lamp and led them down to what Robert realized were stacks of steamer trunks, carpet bags, and the rounded sides of barrels. The inner ribs of the boat had been painted white and they gleamed as the lamp moved. The man showed them where they could sit and made a shushing motion. In French he said it was forbidden but the lady insisted. The relative quiet of the cargo hold and the dryness seemed to comfort Wilson, silence the dog, and please the bearish Frenchman. They could not refuse the favor and ascend, but nausea gripped Robert even as he thanked the Frenchman who would want, he was certain, to be paid for this.

He willed his body to hold itself steady, and Elizabeth leaned her head back, the dog silent in her arms.

He had felt so very well prepared. His assurance that he was well acquainted with the route to Italy and the safest means to get there was an absurd assurance. That was plain now. They were wet, they were cold, and he was starting to be as sick as Wilson. Cholera could breed in this water.

"Don't worry," Elizabeth opened her eyes to say. "It's warmer down here. Much warmer." She didn't look the least bit nauseated, and there were times that night in between his bouts of sickness that she seemed— astonishingly!—to be asleep.

PART TWO

❦

The Wider World

FORTY-TWO

∞

THE AIR IN France the next morning is as clear as sunlight on a lemon, and you would never know there had been a storm. The harbor is new to Robert, who has never come this way, and Le Havre is larger than he expected, with tall buildings of a rich golden color, as if they had been baked like bread. Many ships, topped by flags, bob in the still water. Squares of green grass, chestnut trees, and statuary are dwarfed by wide lanes for carts and carriages. The private carriages that have been ferried across the Channel are beginning to assemble in front of a grand hotel with red and gold awnings. That's the hotel where Elizabeth would have stayed if she had come with her brother and sister, most likely. She would not have stayed at an inn with a grimy threshold and a peeling door. He watches the coachmen in livery loading brass and wooden trunks, washing and polishing, checking the fittings of clean leather traces, and he forces himself to turn away. He is here, she is here, they are safe. His wife sleeps in the room he has just left, the sun is shining, swallows are soaring overhead, and he has plenty of time to find the post house where they will board the morning diligence.

Miss Goss walks toward him with a stick of bread.

"Another early riser," he says. "What did you do to get us out of the wet last night?"

"I told the captain a very famous lady, with many connections, was in danger of dying on his boat. I said she was the most famous poetess in England."

"Did he ask why this lady was traveling in such a low style?"

"I said her lover was a fellow poet."

He smells warm bread as women and men walk in and out of the boulangerie, carrying their breakfast, rushing to their kitchens and tables with that glorious air of confidence natives have when they pass people they know to be tourists.

"Are you leaving today?"

"Yes," Miss Goss says. "You?"

"In two hours. I'm going to see how far the post is."

"May I walk with you a little?"

He answers too slowly, so she adds, "I find the days of sitting very tedious and cramped, so I walk when I can."

"Please do."

"If I may say," she says. "I applaud your success in winning Miss Barrett. I got the impression that there was something wrong with every match a Barrett might propose."

"Did George tell you that?"

"Not for the reason you're thinking."

"What am I thinking?"

"That I was waiting for George to propose."

"I don't imagine you waiting for men to do much of anything."

"I am delighted to be so well understood."

Miss Goss stands with her face in shadow, her gloved hands laced through a bag of plums. He wants to say more on the subject of George, to say that George knows about the wedding now, but had learned of it afterward, not before. The trouble with saying he had persuaded a rich and famous woman to marry him and had done so in secret to avoid the disapproval of her father was that she might think, as George might, that her father had objected with good reason. In a dramatic monologue, such a man would sound like a conniving rogue.

"George promised to help her do this," he says at last, "to leave London and go to Pisa, I mean, but Elizabeth didn't want anyone but herself to take the blame."

"Blame for what? For going to Pisa? Why on earth should she be blamed?"

"We agree. But it is also the marriage itself."

"George didn't know?"

"Elizabeth won't say anything against her father, so I won't, but she was certain he would refuse if I asked for her hand. Once we decided to marry, she felt that keeping it a secret from her siblings was the only way to make them innocent in the eyes of her father."

"Why is he like that?"

"I might ask you the same thing. You said George mentioned the mania to you."

"George connects it, charitably, with the ruin of their finances. Protecting a smaller and smaller fortune from lawyers and extended family has given him a horror of wills and additional descendants, but I have met him. A more disagreeable person could not be imagined."

Robert wants to hear about Mr. Barrett and at the same time to respect Elizabeth's protective love of her father, so he doesn't question her further. "I must add, Miss Goss, I know how it may look to him, and to others— to you, perhaps. My wife has her own income from an inheritance and of course her books—I will take no part of that. As soon as we can draw up a legal document, it will be hers alone."

"Did you really think I could see you in that light, Robert? I approve of women doing what they like, and you ought to know that. When do you leave for Paris?"

The wind was coming up in the harbor, and a red sail began to flap, reminding Robert of the hour and need to hurry.

"Nine."

"On the train?"

"No. Diligence."

She was surprised.

"We have seats in the coupé."

"I wish I had brought my carriage. I usually do. Then I could take you with me. But I am riding with a friend, and I believe we are four in number. Let me ask her, Mr. Browning, if there is room for you."

"There is no need. It's getting late, Miss Goss. I must run and see that the diligence is on time."

"Of course. Au revoir, Mr. Browning. And bonne journee."

ABOVE THEM, ELIZABETH goes to the window, past Wilson, who is still asleep, past Robert's open case and the rumpled blanket where he had lain all night (he and she in the same room: the wonder of it). He must have gone out already. Flush leaps down and follows her, but Wilson sleeps on. Never has this happened: she awake and her maid asleep. Elizabeth stares at France as it is embodied by the market square. Those who must sell and carry have begun their days of unknown complication, walking, carrying, sitting, polishing. She hears hammering in the distance. There are four small parks within the square, green grass and stubby bushes and chestnut trees. The harbor is full of boats, and that's where the sound is coming from. She can see a barebacked man hammering on the deck of a schooner.

Flush whines.

"Oh, Miss!" Wilson says, sitting up abruptly and beginning to neaten her hair, pulling strands out and untangling them with her fingers. "I ought to have been up before you, Miss. I forget myself, I'm so tired." Wilson searches for her bag, and then rummages within it. "Shall I do my own first, and then help you, as at home?" She has found a hairbrush.

"Nothing will be done as at home. That's what makes it wonderful." Flush rolls onto his back, warm paws upward, dry nose on hers, a small soft lick of her face to say good morning.

"How do you feel, Miss?"

"Ecstatic."

Wilson looks suspicious, as if she couldn't possibly.

"I'm stronger than you think, or maybe used to feeling terrible, so a change of scenery affects me more."

Flush barks and moves into a crouch, as he does when it's time to remind people about food. At home, Arabel did the morning's first walk with Flush, and Arabel fed him.

"We leave at nine, I think," Wilson says, rushing now, braiding her hair before a mirror, pinning it behind her head, and in the mirror Elizabeth sees the rumpled blanket under which Robert slept but a few feet from her and thinks that, in the next town, she and Robert might share a bed.

She turns back to the window, and four stories down, she sees him: her mari talking to a woman. It's Miss Goss again, dressed in scarlet and gold, hair neatly tucked into a striped bonnet, her face fresh and clean in the sun. Miss Goss looks as if she has slept in a palace.

Neither has noticed her and she doesn't want them to. An old woman at the apple cart sits with folded hands. She and her apples, the silvery blue water of the harbor, the dog trotting past, are utterly ordinary and yet they are extraordinary to her because they are French. It cannot be that she is here, in France, with a husband, and yet she is.

"Shall I see if there is coffee, Miss?" Wilson says.

"Oh, yes, yes, please."

Flush puts a paw on Elizabeth's leg and barks, so Wilson thinks to take him, too, and when they have gone Elizabeth touches the pillow where Robert's head had been. The open bag shows his hairbrush and two guide-books: Murray's and Galignani's. She must have made him anxious with her warnings. She has told him too many times how horrifically compli-cated it would be to take care of her, so there are slips of paper stuck every-where in the books.

She brushes her hair, rubs her face with water, finds a handkerchief, sighs. Go back, she reminds herself, to the ecstasy that is being here, being married, in France. Don't hate Miss Goss for being beautiful and talking to your husband before you have even said good morning. Read the pages that your husband, trying so hard to take care of you, has marked with a torn piece of the same ecru paper on which he wrote love letters to you.

The front division is called the Coupé, shaped like a chariot of post-chaise, holding 3 persons. The fare is more expensive than in the other parts of the vehicle.

The Intérieur holds 6.

The Rostande is a "receptacle of dust, dirt, and bad company."

The Banquette or Impériale is an outside seat on the roof of the coupé.

If she were her once-hardy, girlish self, the nymph in the kitchen garden of Hope End, she would demand to sit on the outside seat.

Elizabeth peeks out the window to see if Miss Goss is still talking to Robert. Miss Goss is gone, and she sees Robert a hundred yards off, striding away, soon lost among the vendors' carts.

FORTY-THREE

∽

Du soir, the man at the post stables tells Robert. The diligence leaves at nine of the night. Not nine of the day. He points with a broken fingernail at the ticket and shrugs.

Robert said *du matin* to the seller in London, he's sure of it, but the seller is not here, so his insistence doesn't help. "Are there any seats in the coupé that leaves this morning?" he asks.

Non.

"But if someone doesn't arrive?" he asks in French. "Could we have their seats?"

The man is already walking away.

"I'll wait," Robert calls after him, and the man shrugs without turning around. He ought to go back and fetch Ba and Wilson, because if there were enough empty seats, they would need to take them right away, but if he leaves, the man might give them to someone else. A group of people are assembling for the morning diligence. They seem pleased with themselves, and they ought to be. They have booked the one you ought to book, the one that will have the freshest horses and the cleanest seats. He watches them board as a boy straps the trunks on top, knowing that it is pointless to wait because Ba is not capable of rushing here on foot. And yet he sits in the warming air, smelling manure and coffee and, from somewhere else, a whiff of baked bread.

The man comes back to him with a smile. "Everyone does not arrive! It is available, the Impériale. Would you like?"

The Impériale. Outside, where his wife cannot sit. "Non," he says. "Merci."

The man squints up at the sky, which is speckled delightfully with tiny tufts of clouds. To the west, above the fields, the clouds are thick and iron gray.

Robert walks past French words painted on shop windows and the words are like the thoughts of the flower seller on her stool, her fingers braided together. The painted words and printed words and spoken words and silent thoughts are not English, and in their Frenchness, as a riddle, they invigorate. He tells a girl brooding at the desk of their hotel that the Brownings will stay in their room because they have an evening departure, and she nods, writes nothing down, tells no one, turns her blue eyes again to a young man sitting on a trunk thinking his thoughts in French.

He's surprised and pleased to find Ba alone, beaming at him. He takes her hand in both of his, and then, because they are, for the first time since they left London, in private together, he presses it against his mouth, brushing the small ends of her fingers with his lips. It makes him ache, how soft her hands are, and he has just opened his mouth to speak when the door opens, admitting Flush, who runs straight for his feet and barks maniacally, and then Wilson. "I have coffee," Wilson says, "And cups that are not quite clean."

"I would drink it from a puddle," Ba says, drawing Flush into her lap and shushing him, reminding the dog that this is Robert, the same Robert, but Flush doesn't remember or doesn't care. Flush hates him, or suffers him, and the reason for either mood is never clear. He wants to take her in his arms, gently, of course, so carefully, and carry her to the bed, but there is Wilson. There is the dog. There is the night of not sleeping and the fatigue, thick as a blanket. He cannot banish the maid so he can bed his wife.

"It's ecstasy to be here," Ba says. "Pure ecstasy. You mustn't stay cooped up. What's there to see in Le Havre?"

"Nothing at all! We'll stay in and rest," Robert says. "And in Rouen we'll pay our respects to Joan of Arc." He hands one third of the apple slices to Wilson, apples his mother has given them for the trip, and she is embarrassed to be served by him.

English voices call to one another on the landing. "Hurry, hurry, we'll miss it, Frank, hurry." The carriages and vendors are louder now that the early morning has passed. He aches for it to be quiet. They might touch each other now. They might remove each other's clothes. But Wilson butters her small bite of bread, takes a sip of her coffee, turns her face toward the window with a look like regret, and he sees the lavender bruises of tiredness under her eyes.

If they were poorer, or if they were richer, he and his wife would be alone.

A knock comes at the door.

It's a boy, his pimply chin unshaven, his feet bare, saying *la madame* sent him to clear the room.

"But we will stay until the night," he says in French. "I told *madamoiselle. La fille.*"

The boy says if they wish to stay all day in the room, all day and into *le nuit*, the room must be engaged again and the full sum paid. The rooms are not let midnight to midnight, *monsieur.*

He summons all his French. "We have already paid twice the normal sum for a dirty coverlet and a single room overlooking a public square where the hammering started at dawn and scores of people come and go— it's the noisiest room imaginable. We did not eat supper here, and the room includes *table d'hôte.*"

"*Oui. Mais non, Monsieur. La madame* says you must pay again.*"

If he were alone with his wife and she were not ill, they would storm out. They would find a park or a meadow and spread his coat for them to lie down in the grass, or on the banks of the river, in deep, very private shade, and they would sleep and he would kiss her when they awoke. He would be a pilgrim with a pilgrim wife and they would spend no more centimes in Le Havre.

The rumpled boy holds out his hand, Robert puts sous in it, and the boy says something cheerfully as he walks away. What he says proves correct: "The three of them will be very glad to have the room," he says in French, "because *il pleuvra*." It will rain.

FORTY-FOUR

∞

ARABEL CHECKS THE letter bowl on Ba's behalf, as she always does. If there is a letter from Mr. Browning, she brings it straight upstairs.

The letter bowl is full of letters in her sister's hand, addressed to her and her brothers and sister. *Arabella Barrett. Henrietta Barrett. George Goodin Barrett, Esquire.* So many neatly addressed letters that it feels like birthday mornings at Hope End, when you came in and added your ode to your sister's or brother's plate.

Arabel stands looking at the letters as the clock ticks. She has just come back from Little Bookham, perspiring, grimy, tired, and hungry, anxious to wash her face and hands. She can hear Mrs. Orme in the dining room, Hingston talking to her about supper, the thud of boots on wood. It smells of mutton. Any second now, a brother or Henrietta will come into the hall with a question about what to do with this or that thing that ought to have been sent this morning on the wagon because it's too large to fit in the carriage. Arabel could walk out and leave this alarming discovery for someone else. But the letters look up at her like a child with a secret, and she puts them in her pocket.

It can only have to do with Mr. Browning.

Ba's door is closed. "Ba?" she calls softly. She knocks but gets no answer, so she turns the knob and enters an empty room. The mirror before her reflects the bed, barely visible because her sister who never lowers the blinds in warm weather has lowered every blind. Arabel sees herself, an ash-colored thing, in her sister's mirror.

Ba would never leave her desk behind, but here it is. Beside it on the dressing table is a locket. She opens it, sees her own face represented, the eyes not quite the right shape, her hair thicker and curlier than in real life.

Someone opens the door with a startling click, and Henrietta steps in, eyes flitting to the made bed, the closed desk, the drawn blinds. Arabel pulls the letters out of her pocket and spills them on Ba's bed. They are jumbled and askew.

"She has done it," Henrietta whispers. "She has done it!"

Arabel doesn't say anything as Henrietta takes her own letter from the pile and breaks the seal. "Have you read yours?"

Arabel shakes her head.

"Why not?"

The sun continues to orange itself in the slit between the window and the drawn blinds. Once Henrietta starts to read her own letter, Arabel sees there's no use avoiding confirmation. It's like holding up your hands to stop the rain. She pulls her letter from the pile and sits down beside Henrietta. It's nearly too dark to read, but she doesn't move. Henrietta reads, Arabel reads, and downstairs a door opens and shuts. Their father's voice is a low murmuring while a heavy piece of furniture is dragged across the floor. Arabel has to go and open the blind because she can't make out all the words.

"At least they have married," Henrietta says. "I was worried they would run away first."

Arabel is holding her letter open beside the window, and her hand shakes.

"What shall we do now?" Henrietta asks.

More voices can be heard downstairs, the others assembling for supper, and somebody is swiftly running up the staircase—it will be Wilson, to see what Ba wants to eat. But that can't be. The letter says Wilson has gone to Pisa, just as Wilson went to the wedding, the one that happened last Saturday when Arabel was doing some ordinary dull thing, what it was she can't remember. The picnic. That's what it was. The picnic.

"Perhaps we ought to ask George to come up by himself," Henrietta says.

"No. We should go down and eat as if nothing has happened."

"I cannot," Henrietta says.

"We must."

"Perhaps Papa will not be there yet, and we can tell George."

"He's here. I heard him."

Arabel has never been good at pretending, but she is very good at renouncing. Her father's chair, to her surprise, is empty. Blank as a throne. Stormie is reading something in the paper, Alfred and Henry and Occy and Setty are talking, but George is just sitting there. He sees Henrietta and she bursts out with it.

"She's gone," Henrietta says.

The brothers who were talking carry on, louder, laughing, about a mutual friend named Irey who has done something ridiculous.

"Who's gone?" George says.

Henrietta wears such a triumphant smile that Arabel feels ill.

"Ba," Henrietta says. "She has married him and run away."

Stormie lifts his eyes from the paper and he and George stare at Henrietta while the four youngest go on laughing at Henry, who is acting out what Irey did at the club.

"She wrote to all of us to explain," Henrietta says. "She *posted* the letters."

The brothers who were laughing have finally seen that something serious is being discussed, and they fall silent. "What?" Setty says. "Who posted letters?"

Their father's cane announces him, and then his body is in the doorway. He stops there and takes the measure of the room. "Why is everyone so quiet?" he asks. This is the beginning of their perceived complicity. Each waits for someone else to say something.

Minny comes in with soup and Mr. Barrett says, "Good evening, Minny."

"Good evening, sir."

Minny does not serve on Saturdays. Arabel studies her face for clues to what she knows, and she hopes that her father will forget what day it is and who does what.

"Where's Wilson?" Mr. Barrett asks Minny.

"She took Miss Elizabeth and the dog to the park, sir."

"When?"

Arabel tries to perceive if Minny, too, was let in on the secret.

"I don't know, sir. I heard it from Mrs. Orme."

"Did she tell you she was going out?" their father asks Arabel.

Last Saturday when Ba was getting married Ba had told Arabel she was going to see Mr. Boyd. She kept insisting that she had been there the whole time and that she had told Arabel that's where she was going and that Arabel must have forgotten.

Minny holds the tureen until their father asks her to leave it on the sideboard, thank you, Minny.

"No," Arabel says.

"I saw them on their way to the park," George says.

Arabel waits for Henrietta, but Henrietta says nothing, and Arabel can't help it. She looks at Henrietta for a sign.

"Someone tell me," their father says.

"She has gone," Henrietta says.

Arabel pulls from her pocket the letters, one or two at a time, dropping them on the tablecloth. She pushes them away from herself and toward their father. The brothers who sit farthest away stand up, leaning over, eager to find out what Ba has done. How lucky they are to know nothing. How lucky they are to feel only excitement.

Their father does not rise or reach for the letters.

George takes his but doesn't open it. The other boys take theirs and follow his example. When all the letters are distributed, they discover a strange fact: there is none for their father.

George holds his letter in one hand as if to ask for a sign. Their father flicks his hand impatiently upward, his eyes narrowing.

"Go on," Mr. Barrett says.

George unseals and unfolds Ba's letter to him and another letter falls out. He lifts it and silently reads what it says. Then he places it in front of their father's place, and Arabel reads the words: "To my Dearest Papa." The letter is not lifted or touched.

George begins to read his own letter, not aloud, as they would have done with any other letter from a family member not at home, but to himself. He turns the page, moves to the next page, turns that one over, all the while absorbing what Arabel imagines is like her own letter: *please, I beseech you, forgive me, I beseech you.*

"Evidently she has married Mr. Browning," George says at last. "At St. Marylebone. And they have gone to Pisa."

It is a long pause, and yet it can never be long enough.

"It is done then." Their father's voice is very composed and calm, but that is dangerous. He is most composed when furious. "Arabel, the soup."

She collects her father's bowl. As she is scraping the dipper through the broth—it is some kind of fish, and there's a flexible spine at the bottom, mossy green herbs, sediment of potatoes—the door to the hall begins to move slightly inward, and she sees one of Minny's eyes, silently asking what she ought to do, and Arabel hopes that the tears in her own eyes and the monumental silence in the room will convey to Minny what she ought to do with the blessed freedom that is hers: *Do not come near the volcano.*

Minny allows the door to quietly shut.

They mechanically do what they have been taught to do in a crisis. When Arabel has given their father his soup, he begins to slurp it, and the others stand up with their empty bowls and quietly fill them with the dipper and sit down again and eat, or the boys do. Henrietta merely drags her spoon slowly across the shallow, bumpy broth, back and forth, defying their father with this tiny gesture. George has set his letter aside. The one marked "Dearest Papa" floats on the red table.

When his soup bowl is empty, Mr. Barrett speaks. "How has this come to pass, George?"

"I don't know."

"He came here, and took her to Pisa, and none of you knew?"

They shake their heads.

"How many times has Mr. Browning come into your sister's room?"

"I don't know."

"Can you guess?"

"I can."

"Guess for me, then."

"Weekly, more or less."

"For how long?"

"More than a year."

"How much more than a year?"

"I don't know. A bit more."

Their brother Henry says, "It has been at least two years since Mr. Browning first visited."

Their father's letter from Elizabeth sits on the table, and they all sit in their chairs, waiting. Finally, Mr. Barrett says, "A year ago, we sat and talked about what a danger he was, and you swore, and she swore, that we misunderstood his intentions."

It's not even dark outside. Not yet.

"It's all just *poetry*, you said"—as if the word had another meaning they are all pretending not to know. "Arabel," he says, "go and get the main dish."

When Arabel goes down to the meaty air of the kitchen, Minny and Mrs. Orme are sitting together, and they stop talking. Arabel says nothing except that her father wants the mutton now. Mrs. Orme takes the oval tureen from the oven, lifts the slippery saddle of meat, gray and oily, and sets it on a platter. She motions toward a covered dish of turnips and Minny stands up.

Arabel shakes her head. "I am to do it," she says. "I'll come back for it."

Up the stairs with the platter she goes, and then back down the stairs again, then up the stairs with the warm dish of turnips. The smells collect in a hollow inside her right jaw, and the ragged slabs of warm mutton with their congealed blobs of fat sicken rather than entice. She gives her father the number of slices he always takes—three—and the number of turnips he always takes—three—and she sits down without taking any.

"Arabel."

Arabel nods.

"Did you know of Mr. Browning's intentions?"

Not all of them. She did not know Mr. Browning intended to marry her sister last Saturday and take her to Italy today. "No."

"And you, Henrietta? Did you know?"

"No."

Mr. Barrett takes a drink of madeira from his glass. "All of these years of devotion to her every need and this is how she repays us."

No one, not even George, speaks.

"She has married him," Henrietta says quietly. "She has not sinned."

"Either she told you, and you are lying to me, or she didn't tell you, and she lied to you and to me with her actions. *That* is a sin."

Arabel feels as if a rock is attached to her waist and she has fallen into a deep pool of water. In the past week, as in all weeks, there were many conversations with Ba, dozens, in her case, all of them false now.

"Saturday last," their father says. He eats a bite of mutton, followed by a bite of turnip, and the candle flames go on melting the wax, burning it away to uselessness. When he has swallowed the food, he takes a drink from his glass. Arabel wishes he would at least read Ba's letter. He is still holding his knife when he says, "I have been misled, but it will not happen again."

No one moves or takes a bite. George has his hand around his goblet, and he holds it loosely, the wine untouched. He says, "If I may ask, Father— she asks us to write to her at Orléans."

"There is nothing to say. There's no need to write."

George touches his right sideburn, brushing the hairs down, as if to make them mind. "May *I* write? To convey your entirely justified response?"

"Why? My response is my silence."

"It would kill her, Father," Arabel says.

"Silence is the only answer she deserves."

George says, "With the greatest possible respect, Father, she ought to hear your side of it, and ours."

"Do as you wish."

Arabel doesn't ask if she may write to say she does forgive and she does understand. She eats as little as she can without drawing his attention, and when she has escaped the dining room, she hurries to her own room, which has already been stripped of its pictures and curtains and decorations in preparation for the painters, and she lies down in a bed that hardly feels like her own, so seldom has she slept there, preferring the couch in Ba's room. The sheets are cold and the bedding heavy.

"Babes," a voice at the door whispers. Henrietta comes in without a candle. "Are you awake?"

"Yes."

"Can I sleep here?"

Arabel moves to the cold side of the bed and Henrietta snugs up close. "Do you think they will be happy?" Henrietta whispers.

Arabel is so far from happiness that she cannot imagine it.

"He loves her," Henrietta says. "I know that he does."

"I kept trying to get her to go for longer rides in the carriage, just in the park," Arabel says, "and . . ."

"So did I."

"It tired her so much. I wonder if Mr. Browning even imagined, properly, I mean, what he would have to do."

"He said he expected nothing but to serve her and take care of her."

"But he would say that, wouldn't he? What if he is too much like her?"

"That's why I think they will be happy," Henrietta says. "He is exactly like her."

"He ought to have asked Papa for her."

"Papa would have said no. You know that."

"It isn't that. I know he would have refused," Arabel says.

"Then what?"

"It makes Mr. Browning seem sly."

"But he isn't," Henrietta says. "You know he isn't."

"But it's how he *seems* now. It would have been better to ask and be told no. Then they could have married anyway because they are of age, and she has her own income, and he couldn't have said that she lied."

"Father would have cut her off," Henrietta says.

"He *will* cut her off."

"Then what difference does it make? It is the same no matter what."

"People will talk about her and Mr. Browning courting in secret. Behind his back. And whether the marriage happened before or after. That's what he doesn't like."

"If Father were not always refusing to do everything normal people do," Henrietta says, "Mr. Browning could have come to dinner and this wouldn't have happened. It's his fault, not hers or his."

"Henrietta," Arabel says. "I'm afraid you'll never get to see Surtees now."

"Then I will run away, too."

Arabel sinks through the water, the stone having carried her a great way down. Ba has left her, and Henrietta will do the same. Her brothers, too, will fall in love and never be allowed to come back home. One by one her brothers and sisters will do what is normal, what is right, and fall in love, and their father will say it is not the right match, and they will go away, and Arabel will be left behind. She pretends she is asleep, as she used to do in Ba's room, until she dreams there is yet another depth, a place where the bottom can never be found, and she starts awake.

THE BREAKFAST ROOM is empty when Arabel gets there, stripped of its red curtains, Turkey rugs, and oil paintings. All the scratches and grimy places on the walls have been crudely revealed.

"He acted just as she should have expected," George is saying when he comes in with Henrietta. "And he thinks you conspired because you did."

"I didn't know she was planning to marry him so soon," Henrietta says. "Without asking."

George, who remains calm in arguments, turns to Arabel as he takes a fillet of fish and a plum. "The plan was to do it properly," George says. "We were to escort her ourselves. I said I would arrange it, and she never told me she had decided to do it herself. She promised he was not the reason for her going, and she married him."

Henrietta holds a fork in the dull morning light. The weather is not sunny and gold anymore in the street, luring you outside, telling you to go to the park, to gorge yourself on warmth and color, to not let September get away. A cold haze has fallen and turned everything gray. Henrietta says, "I know that you gave her your blessing, George. In her letter to me," Henrietta says, "she said—"

"I said I would help her go to Italy for her health. I said I would make the arrangements, and she made her own while I was still attempting that. With a man who has no income."

Arabel chooses the smallest plum and sets it on her plate.

"She thought you approved," Henrietta says, scraping butter across her toast.

"Of her desire to try a new cure. Father would have been right to say no to this marriage, and I would have agreed. Robert Browning is as impractical as Ba is, he has no money at all, and such a man cannot run away with a rich, older *invalid* and think the world will believe in his pure motives. He cannot write the poems that he does and think no one will see who he is."

"He is kind and loving and thoughtful," Henrietta says. "I have talked to him many, many times."

"He is a failed poet, has failed at everything, in fact, and now he has all her money. It worked out perfectly for him," George says.

"It isn't like that."

"How do you know?"

"He loves her as much as she loves him," Henrietta says. "I have talked to him many times, as I said. I have seen what he's really like."

"Did Papa ever read her letter?" Arabel asks, holding the ripe plum in her fingers, unwilling to pierce it.

"No," George says. "He says he won't." He butters his toast, and the soft scraping sound makes Arabel hungry.

Henrietta says, "He should at least listen to her reasons."

"I never, never would have thought her capable of such selfishness. And impetuosity," George says, his knife slipping on the cold butter.

"It was not impetuous," Henrietta says. "Of that she cannot be accused. They have corresponded and visited for two years."

"If this is what they've been planning for two years, it's worse."

Arabel bites into the plum. It separates easily from the pit, as if it knew this moment would come. A drop of juice runs down her hand, stains the white napkin chartreuse.

"Why can't you take her side?" Henrietta says.

"Why can't you see his? Or mine? You told me, 'Ba writes to everyone all the time! It is not a love affair.' I distinctly recall you saying that."

"She does write to everyone all the time. You could have seen that things were changing, that this became different. You ought to be on her side. You ought to want her to be happy."

"I do, and that's why she ought to have let us help her and retain her legal rights. For heaven's sake, she has never been to Pisa. She has never been anywhere without us. She has never managed her own money or affairs."

"She has Granny Betsy's legacy. She has her royalties, the ship money—"

George interrupts. "I see her accounts. Sometimes the ship yields nothing. And you forget that while she is here everything is paid. She doesn't have to buy food, pay servants, or deduct rent. What about furniture? Dishes? A carriage? Do you know how much those things cost here? Can you tell me?"

"No, but—"

"She doesn't know, either."

"I'm sure they have talked about it."

"Why are you sure? He's a poet, too!"

"Enough, George. I am tired to death of caution. I'm happy for her. I'm glad she did it, and I will do the same if I have to."

Arabel holds the teacup near her mouth, breathing the steam of her tea.

"Practical matters aside," George says, "you seem not to realize that she could very easily die on the way. If she does, he'll have enough money to stay in Italy forever, writing his ghastly poems about murdered women."

Crumbs absorb the dull light.

"So it's enough money for him to pay all those expenses, but not for the two of them? I would rather die on the way to Italy than live to old age here," Henrietta says, pushing her chair back, "denied what any woman has a right to expect."

"Did you just say Ba is better off dead?"

"No. I said *I* would be better off dead than shut up here forever, getting older and older and older, never able to have a house or a love or a child of my own. As for Ba, I want her to have the chance Dr. Chambers said she needs. She won't die. Mr. Browning will look after her as well as we did."

"Why should he? And if he wants to, does he know how? She has never traveled without at least one of us, without special accommodations, taking the shortest possible routes, with the food thought out ahead of time, the weather worried over. Do you remember the carriage from Torquay? Fitted so that she could lie flat in it the whole way to London? Can he afford that? What if it's too much for him, and he's not what you say he is, and he gets tired of the bother? What if she does survive, and he leaves her after they've settled in? Have you thought of that? What if he takes her money, which I repeat is his now, and he takes up with some girl in Rome?"

"He isn't Lord Byron."

George laughs. "How on earth do you know?"

"You don't know him. Tell him, Arabel."

Arabel doesn't know what to think. She tries to examine, retroactively, Mr. Browning's well-trimmed whiskers, his kind eyes, his perfectly tailored clothes, his yellow gloves. Could he have said and written those things to Ba and be an ogre? The trouble was that Ba saw the mythic in people. What fed her poetry, and what had kept her alive, was the grandiose, the gorgeous, the impossible, the ideal.

"He seemed very devoted," is all she can think to say.

"You really didn't know about the wedding?" George says.

"No."

"I would have thought she would take you, Arabel," George says. "Of us all. I would have thought she'd take you."

ARABEL STAYS AT the table after they both go. The pain rises and spreads and vibrates. It covers the curtains, the mahogany table, the green skins of the plums, the congealed edge of unfinished ham. It covers her hands, her eyes, her hair. How can she absorb it before anyone sees? She ought to be useful. That's how you got through things: by working and forgetting yourself. Jump up, find Mrs. Orme and Minny, ask if there are any baskets left to hold the food that must be carried with them to the new house—these plums, for instance—and if produce and meats should be taken now or later in the day? The china will be broken if they leave it on the shelves, but Wilson is not here to crate it up. Did Wilson crate anything before she went running away to Italy? What about the ewers? Are they to stay on the floors of the rooms, to be smashed by ladders? Will the painters think to cover the piano?

Their mother had died. Edward had died. Sam had died. But Ba had not. It wasn't just due to Arabel, of course. Together, collectively, they had kept out the cold, fought the damp, scoured the dirt, warmed the tea. But her sisters and brothers had always had more to do. School, work, infatuations, fashions, parties, secret beaux. It was she who slept in Ba's room. It was she who stayed home to count drops for tinctures, warm the tea, feed Flush, walk Flush, summon the doctor, feed Flush, walk Flush.

Why Wilson? Why Wilson, and not she?

Arabel tries, with leaden arms, to pour herself more tea, but there isn't more. It was just a simple wedding. A private secret one with no flowers or anything. There had been no wedding breakfast, no weaving of a wreath or selecting a bouquet or sewing lace on a veil. So why does it hurt? It's the feeling she had at Ramsgate when she was three and the rest of them got in the carriage to go home—Ba, Edward, Henrietta, Sam, and their parents. All of them had climbed in, and when she had tried to follow them, Minny Robinson had gripped her hand tightly and said, *Stay with me, dear. We're going to have a holiday of our very own, so that you will get better,* but it was not a holiday. It was exclusion and exile, the isolating of the sick. Arabel became on that day a singleton, an *A* with no *B*. Ba, Bro, Sam, and Henrietta had ridden away with their parents and left her. Away they all went, and away they all stayed. Not just that summer, but the endless fall, the iron winter, the empty spring, yet another summer in the Ramsgate hotel. By the second summer Arabel had given up, by the third she spoke to no one. Not until she was seven had she been deemed well enough to come home. She was so grateful to have their company that she did anything for them. Blessed are the humble. Blessed are the meek. One did get a certain pleasure from it, if it was the only pleasure on offer.

How could Ba do it without her? That is what keeps her pressed in the chair. She has given up everything else. There are so many things she has taught herself not to mind. She is not to mind that she has no honorable man appearing from somewhere to seek the hand of such as her. She is not to mind she has no wedding of her own to imagine, and she doesn't mind, not anymore, because *charity vaunteth not itself, seeketh not its own*. There will be no baby to expect, no christening gown to embroider, no small face that will seek out her own among the others. To take pleasure in the joys of *others* is her only part, but Ba had not needed her. Wilson had awakened on the wedding day and gone secretly to the carriage. Wilson had sat with Ba in the church. Wilson had seen in her sister's face the bliss of pure love rewarded. Wilson had gone with Ba to Pisa, and Wilson would see the Field of Miracles.

She goes out the front door with the intent of seeing to the bedding; it has been stripped for the move and tied in huge, teetering bundles, and someone—one of the men hired for the day, or Hingston—has put the stacks on the street to wait for the wagon. On the street! Where any wandering dog might lift a leg.

Arabel stands beside the bundle and feels the particles of fog bite her face. The day is as slick and cold as an eel.

She sees a wagon coming, driven by the same man as yesterday, with his gray whiskers and bulbous nose, and when she has smiled brightly and pretended nothing is wrong, and the driver has climbed down and begun to load the blankets onto what he says is clean, dry straw, she doesn't scream. She doesn't cry. She turns and walks away from the wagon, swiftly, as if she has a train to catch, and no one comes out of the house, so she doesn't have to hide that she is going to St. Marylebone to read the register, to see it written in ink, the name of the person who sat in the church last Saturday and ate the morsel of joy that ought to have been hers.

FORTY-FIVE

∞

IT'S COMICAL, AT first, how crowded the coupé is, how unexpectedly small and tight. They are pushed against each other and the dog runs back and forth over their legs as if they are one big lap.

The ache starts in her back and goes to her neck. Now and then, as the road curves, she can see one of the horses—a gorgeous thing, to see the white mane of the horse pulling them in moonlight—and she comments on that instead of her neck. The forest goes by at slow pace, followed by a field, a silent house, a river, and pain going up her back and into her arms.

"Can you sleep?" Robert asks. "Try to sleep."

She puts her head on his shoulder and Wilson takes the limp body of the sleeping dog.

Robert falls asleep with his head on the side of the carriage, and Wilson falls asleep next, and Elizabeth, wide awake, remembers the morphine she hasn't taken. They had meant to get tea at the post house, but there had been no tea and the driver had rushed them back inside.

Drink the moonlight, she tells herself, and the moon on foreign trees, and remember Joan of Arc on this very road. Another river, another post house, another undoing of the traces so that tired horses walk away to rest while a man brings new horses and opens their mouths for the bit.

She's awake to see the sharp metal hands of a village clock. Could it only be one o'clock? Could there be so much of the night to go?

"Where are we?" Wilson says when the daylight has crept upon them and the carriage has stopped again. How incredible that Wilson can sleep with her head up and her whole body bent. Robert, too, has been asleep for hours.

"Rouen, I think."

She thought she wanted to see the monument to Joan of Arc, but all she wants is a bed. If she were to lie flat, she might surrender. She sees a row of tables under a slanting roof, travelers seated, most of them frowning and tired and frowsily dressed, but they have cups, little silver pots, and enticing loaves of bread. "Is this the inn?" she asks.

"It might be," Robert says. "We only stop here to board the train."

"Oh," she says. They will not sleep here. She will not be able to lie down.

"I think we have enough time to see a bit of the cathedral. Would you like that?"

"If I might wash and change," she says, "and have some coffee."

"I'll ask them to get the luggage down."

Flush is whining softly, trembling with the need to run around, to relieve himself, to eat, to drink. The man to whom Robert speaks is shaking his head.

"Oui," Robert says. "C'est necessaire."

"Non." There is more headshaking.

"We are not taking the diligence to Paris," Robert tells the man in French. "We take the train."

"Oui, exactement."

Robert stops smiling. He says it again in French, then in English because a group of other travelers are watching the exchange.

An English traveler steps up and says that the whole diligence, with the travelers' luggage, will be hoisted up, so, and placed on the tracks. With everyone seated inside! The Frenchman nods at Robert, throws out his hand toward the English explainer, and says, "Oui."

"Why?" Robert asks.

"That I do not know," says the Englishman, and he bursts out laughing.

Robert returns to the carriage and opens the door. They cannot wash or change. The carriage must be endured a bit more. "We can get out, but we leave in half an hour."

"May we have coffee?" Elizabeth asks.

"Yes, yes, let's do," Robert says, and Wilson nods. Wilson climbs easily out and Flush bounds from her arms, instantly the focus of lucky diners who have bread and coffee and sugar and tea. A French child says, "Look at the dog," and Flush pees at great length on the slender trunk of a leafless tree.

Elizabeth tries but cannot stand. Or bend forward. Or straighten her knees without sharp pain. She watches Flush wander to another French tree, lift his leg, add his water to it. How perfect the word *relieve* is for what he must feel. The shame of being so much trouble makes her put all her energy into the third attempt, laughing, saying, "I seem to have turned to stone," and she rises a little despite the pain, leaning toward the door of the coach, but the pain intensifies and the world is a white circle diminishing the tree and the dog and the cafe to a tiny dark blur, and then nothing.

She awakens on the floor of the carriage, hearing Robert's shouts for help. What a burden she is. A sweating boy climbs over her like a cat, puts his hands under her arms, and pulls her like a doll out to Robert, who thanks the boy and begins to carry her across the square. It's horrible to be watched by everyone: English people, French people, German people, all of them staring as Robert sets her on a chair. She must submit to it, though, and laugh. Laughing is the only way she has ever managed to survive the humiliation of being carried and deposited. You can't do anything but laugh at yourself and say thank you in the three languages that come to mind.

"When we get to Paris, we can have a good long rest," he says over the coffee, which is the best coffee she has ever tasted.

What they do not see: where Joan of Arc was burned. The mechanical figures in the famous clock. The long lanes of medieval houses.

After many pieces of thick, sour, delicious bread with wide pats of fresh butter, Robert carries her back to the diligence and the diligence is lifted, creaking, to the tracks that lead to Paris as she laughs and thanks him in every language she knows.

"WHAT ARE YOU thinking about?" Robert asks as the train speeds on. The sky in France is lime green. At its edges grow green bushes, green trees, ink towns.

"I'm thinking about how happy I am."

"Is that why you look so sad?"

"I'm not sad."

"He will forgive you, Ba."

"I know."

But what she is remembering is the dedication she wrote to her father two years ago, in her acclaimed *Poems* collection, a dedication of nine hundred words. She had labored over the tribute for hours, copying it six times, never showing it to anyone except Moxon before its publication.

Her father's room was next to hers on the third floor, so Elizabeth could hear her father snoring, and her father could hear (she imagined) her pages turning, her pen scratching, the candle wax dripping, Flush's dream-barks. He could hear her if she needed Dr. Chambers to be fetched.

At eleven, the hour he came in to pray with her in the years before he stopped visiting her entirely, she would hear him on the stairs, his cane the first and loudest punctuation mark, his own door closing behind him, the splash of water as he washed, the thumps and clacks of cupboard doors, and coins. Always the coins ringing into the copper bowl, to be collected by him the next morning, dumped there again the next night.

"I was remembering something about him," she says to Robert.

Robert laces his fingers with hers. Flush is asleep, Wilson is asleep, the trees are yellowing in the forest beside the train. They pass out of the forest and into a field, the furrows straight and dark, birds descending to eat.

They gave all of Bro's things to her father after the inquest. The watch, his ring, the coins. Whatever was in his pockets. And when Sam died, it was the same. The unspent coins were given to their father, and after a time it became clear to someone, probably George, that the money their father put in the bowl beside his bed, and the money he carried around with him every day, was that unspent money, what had been on the bodies of the dead young men, an amount that never changed.

They pass a pond, and in the pond is a small red boat, holding a boy who turns to watch the train pass. They appear and disappear so quickly, and the sun is setting, so that the earth itself seems to be dissolving behind them.

"There are reasons for the strange things people do, don't you think?" she says. "But we don't know what they are most of the time."

When her father came to her room at night, he started with complaints. The wrongs done by every person he had met, the imbecilic drivers, the maddening solicitors, the rapacious Brazilian planters, the obtuse customs agents. She had tried to remember, instead, the dry heft of his giant hand, the scent of his clothes: camphor, cedar, cinnamon. To believe he was the same person she had always loved, just more disappointed. *I am yours,* their eyes had always said to one another, *and you are mine.* He'd given her sixpence and dubbed her Poet Laureate of Hope End. He'd insisted Edward's tutor include her in his lessons.

But the memory that repeats, along with the sound of the unspent money in her brother's pockets clanking into the bowl, is the last time he came in to talk to her before she left.

"Everything is ready," he said. "It will be nice to have a change."

He meant the house in Little Bookham. "Yes," she said.

"You didn't send your desk in the wagon today," he said.

"I couldn't be parted from it," she said. "I thought I would carry it on my lap."

"Everyone has something he will carry on his lap, I notice." He settled himself in the black chair with the rush seat. That chair, too, had been saved for the last wagon to Little Bookham.

Her father picked up her bottle of morphine and turned it. In turning it, she supposed he was calculating how much it had contained yesterday. The teacup into which she had stirred the full dose was still there, saved for the very last wagonload.

She was married, and he didn't know. She was leaving, and he didn't know.

"Did you eat the beef tonight?"

"Yes."

In his right hand, her father held the cane, and in his left he held the book she had dedicated to him two years ago. He had promised to read it, but she didn't know if he had because he never mentioned it. "Look what I found in my desk," he said.

She smiled at it.

"I know you wanted to go to Italy."

She nodded.

"You're much safer here with us. I only went against Dr. Chambers's advice because I know you so well. You trust me, and I trust you."

The truth lay over her skin like wet clay.

"I read your dedication this morning," her father said. "And I thought it again. 'Ba is the purest woman I ever knew.'"

The candle flame flickered in the window glass, beyond which the half moon was rising, edging its way toward an obscuring cloud.

"You are the only one," he said, taking his hand from hers and patting her book, "that I trust."

She remembers the reeds around the swan's nest at Hope End, her father reaching out to part them to show her the good news, all the little gray babies, and the way it felt when what they saw instead was a dead cygnet. She couldn't speak or look away. A neighbor, maybe, or a man who worked on the farm, had come upon them at that instant and declared his opinion that the cob—the father swan—had crushed that one because it couldn't keep up. That's what cobs did, the man said, so the others could swim fast out of danger. It was natural. "It was a rat," her father had said. "Or a crow."

"I doubt it! See—" the man said.

"It was a rat," her father insisted. "Or a crow."

The train passes dim fields and silent, glowing meadows. Birds are black things, small and far off, in a race against night. What her father will say about her betrayal rides on the back of the setting sun, flashes from ponds, becomes first acceptance and then fury, it could be one, it could be the other. There is always a chance, she tells herself.

When they reach Paris she can't walk to the hotel room but pretends it's funny when Robert insists on carrying her. She hears a young French voice telling Robert to "go up the stairs, turn just there, Monsieur, *à gauche*, let me open it *pour vous*." She is laid down like a bundle of curtains and sees, through the skin of her eyelids, Robert and the French boy closing the shutters, hears a light clacking sound, and the groaning sound that might be her own breath as it finally happens: she falls asleep.

ROBERT PUTS IT off again, his hope that this will be the place he and Ba will be alone together. Ba will sleep, Wilson will find something for them to eat, and he will learn what has happened to their passports. He surrendered them in Le Havre, as everyone did, and the mayor was supposed to send them to Paris where the Minister of the Interior was supposed to sign them. In the meantime, they each had only a *Passe Provisoire*, which would carry them *through* the country but not out of it. If he could not retrieve their signed passports before leaving Paris, they could be stuck for weeks in Marseille, and the weather would get colder, and wetter, and the nights would get longer, and the journey from Marseille to Genoa would get more treacherous, so although he is hungry, the first thing he must do in Paris is find the police station before it closes for a two-hour lunch.

My dear Mrs. Jameson, he writes before leaving the hotel. *I wonder if you have any advice for a traveler whose passport has not arrived?*

He pushes hard on his temple with the knuckle of his thumb. As soon as he withdraws his knuckle, the nausea returns.

He finds the rest of the apples his mother put in his trunk—three left, so he can eat one. The water in the pitcher is clean and feels good on his face. There is the sight, so soothing, of his wife on the bed asleep, soon to be kissed, to be enfolded, to be taken into his whole being.

Nothing is soothing about the police station, where the clerk says *le Passe* is not ready.

"How long does it take?"

The clerk goes to ask another man, older and more tired, who glances at Robert and listens, then says inaudible things that Robert can tell are versions of "as long as it takes."

The young clerk doesn't have any choice but to come back. "There is nothing you can do but wait. It will be sent," he says.

"When?"

"That we cannot know. Every traveler must wait until it arrives if he plans to leave the country."

"Why?"

"If it is not sent to your place of retiring you may come here again."

"I may? I *may* come again?"

The young man doesn't like his sarcasm. "Oui."

"Why couldn't you have it sent on to Marseilles, so that the traveler can make better time?"

"*Non*. You must stay here until it comes."

"My wife is very ill. We're trying to get to Pisa for her health."

A blank pause. The young man looks at the clock, which says ten minutes to noon.

"Is it consumption?" the older clerk asks, using the English name. He is interested now, and fluent, and officious. "A fever?" He has stood up.

"No," Robert says. "It is nothing. Just a small cold."

"Perhaps you could bring a doctor's note. A doctor here would have to see her."

"Thank you," he says. "I will see to that."

He leaves the station and walks left, toward trees and a wall of crenellated stone, and he finds himself in a park where old men and women sit on benches, where limestone paths curve around a fountain. In the fountain the cloudless sky is reflected, and the hull of a boy's toy boat. The serenity of other people's contentment settles on him, and he briefly imagines his headache vanishing, the day becoming bright with promise, he and Ba coming back here to stroll beside the toy boats and refreshment stands.

"Mr. Browning!" Miss Goss stands before him in yet another bright dress, this one orange and red, with a matching parasol. "You look positively ill. How are your travels?"

He explains about needing to go to Orléans at once, partly because Elizabeth is so anxious to get there and read her family's letters, and more important, because he has paid in advance for specific dates of travel, but instead they are marooned in Paris, waiting for the Minister of the Interior. "Do you think we could go on without the passports?" he asks.

"Definitely not. If you're in a hurry, you must find someone who can talk to Lord Normanby. Perhaps your wife knows him. He was the governor of Jamaica ages ago, before he became ambassador here. If you mentioned George, I'm certain he would help you. He might even remember my name—I could ask."

Robert walks beside Miss Goss through warmth and coolness, through the dappling yellow and deep green stripes of the path, until they reach an iron gate.

"I would be happy to speak to him for you," she says. "Have you seen Mrs. Jameson yet? I didn't tell her, you know. I didn't want to spoil the surprise."

"Thank you. I sent her a note this morning, and I'm going there now."

"Shall I speak to Lord Normanby?"

"Don't trouble yourself, please. It may sort itself out. Perhaps the passports will arrive tomorrow."

"That never happens," Miss Goss says. "Let me give you my card." She writes on a thick white card the name of a hotel, and he takes out of his own case the cards that say *Mr. and Mrs. Browning.* "Where are you staying?" she asks.

"The Hotel Messagerie."

"Where is that?"

"Near the train station."

"Is it to your liking?"

"Perfectly," he says. *If George were here*, she's probably thinking, *Mr. and Mrs. Browning would be staying in a hotel with a gilded drawing room and thick plush carpets near the Tuileries, as is fitting for a Barrett.*

Miss Goss writes the name of his inadequate hotel and drops the pencil into her bag. "Do send word if I can help you. And please give my love to Mrs. Jameson."

Robert takes his leave and stops before a shop window. He waits for

Miss Goss to disappear. Taking his eyes casually from the display of hats, he surveys the street, relieved that the bright orange dress is no longer visible. He finds a place out of the sun, out of the way of tourists and tradesmen and nurses holding the hands of children, to open his map and search for l'Hôtel de la Ville de Paris. The truth is, he doesn't know the city at all. Paris is where everyone goes. What one *must* do in Paris, what one *must* see in Paris, belongs to conversations of a type certain people had at dinners, people who were always dull. He scans the map, up the Seine, down the Seine, but there is no method to the way he takes in the names printed on trapezoids and churches and boulevards and parks. The headache blinds him to what he seeks: *there* is the Île de la Cité, *there* the Champs-Élysée, there the Louvre, green park, blue Seine, pink *église*, but never l'Hôtel de la Ville de Paris. Men and women rush by him, chatting gaily to one another in French, scorning him as yet another English tourist on a street in Paris, studying his Galignani. At last he sees the hotel on the map. It is near the Seine, and he must cross over, or is he on that side already? The Right Bank, if you look away from the Île de la Cité, is here, and there is the Left if you are facing it. He is facing it, though he is still quite far away. He wishes to proceed as he once had, when he was the kind of traveler no one noticed, privately fascinated by whatever he came upon. But Ba thinks they are leaving tomorrow, so he must find Mrs. Jameson in l'Hôtel de la Ville de Paris. He walks beside the Seine, absorbing the sound of the water, the smooth glide of the boats, the fluttering of chestnut leaves as they fall, copper and gold, and swirl across his path, making a dry, courteous scraping sound. If they have to wait in Paris for a few days, he could bring Ba to sit here or to ride in a barouche like those that pass him now, perhaps even ride in a boat. It would not be bad to have a few days in Paris once the fear of losing money is behind him.

He laughs when he sees Mrs. Jameson's hotel, so unlike the hotel where he left Ba and Wilson. He has never stayed in a castle like this one, where the ceiling is painted with angels, pasted with wreaths and flowers and birds and more angels, and gilded. The room is so tall that giraffes could walk to the desk where he is told Mrs. Jameson is not in.

"Would Monsieur like to leave his card?"

"*Oui.*"

He takes the pen from the inkstand because something must be said to explain the addition of a Mrs. Browning to his card.

The clerk waits. The queue behind him lengthens. The angels on the ceiling float.

Come & see your friend & my wife EBB, he writes. He signs it *RB*.

Out he goes, past the well-dressed travelers with matching trunks and hatboxes and carpetbags and maids, past the hotel men in peacock livery, past the marble statues of naked maidens near the doors, and along a line of leather-fitted, brass-trimmed carriages marked with the coats of arms of their owners. In his attempt to be both swift and nonchalant, he goes left. He crosses the river, and for a long time he enjoys the trees. And then, when he thinks he ought to be in the park with the old men and the pond for toy boats, there is a circle, and there is a statue, but it's a man on a horse instead of a woman with a flag. There's an *église*, a narrow alley, another alley, three streets branching off in different directions. He picks a street and walks until he finds the street name, which isn't on the map.

He studies the position of the sun. Based on the angle, he ought to turn around. He turns and goes back the way he came. He looks beyond the bend in front of him, and the next one, and the next, for a tree that has the right shape, for a park with a familiar gate, for a shop window or door that he remembers. Think. Think and calculate. They had come south from Le Havre to Paris, and they stopped at the outskirts where the first group of hotels had been, but the angle of the declining, weakening sun on the long blocks of houses and the meandering, moss-green Seine means he is not going north. The map is either out of date or fanciful or incomplete, and the streets themselves deliberately obscure, designed to confuse the uninitiated.

He stops. He studies. He hates to ask, but he asks. *Non, non, Monsieur. À gauche.* And then at last, like the face of a beloved family member, a shop window he remembers stands before him. He saw this straw bonnet and those slender gloves crossed on a linen pillow before, beneath that hand-lettered sign. He is on the right street: yes, here is another window he remembers, another door, and a stained-glass transom.

When he reaches the hotel, night has fallen. He walks down the narrow, dim hall with its low ceiling and badly patched plaster. They will wonder where he's been. He can't tell them he was lost all afternoon. What would they think of their guide? They would lose faith. This is the other way traveling is different when you're alone. When you're alone it doesn't matter what mistakes you make, how often you get lost. No one knows. But he can't let Ba and Wilson lose faith in him.

He prepares to tell it as a funny story, but when he opens the door, Flush barks and rushes at him, as always, and must be called back, as always, and told *this is Robert, you know Robert.* At a table by the window, with food before them, glasses of something gold from a green bottle, sit his wife and her maid. They are fine. They look pleased and rested. The sky behind them is speckled with chimney pots and apricot clouds.

"Robert," Elizabeth says, "what's wrong?" She stands up.

"Nothing!"

"We must call a doctor," she says. "You look like death."

"No, no, I'm fine. You know how I love to walk."

"I think you went too far."

"I'll be all right in a minute or two."

"Eat," she says. "Sit here and eat."

He has hardly eaten of the bread and chicken—moist and salty and rich together—when a knock comes at the door and Wilson lets Mrs. Jameson into the room.

Mrs. Jameson is lace, taffeta, and girth. The ribbons in her hair are ribbons of a past era, when she was the anonymous writer of a fictitious "diary" that everyone was reading and then everyone was complaining about because the author had not, as it turned out, died tragically at the age of twenty-one. The black cord around Mrs. Jameson's neck is thick enough to use for mountain climbing, and on the end of it dangles not a jewel but a magnifying glass.

She stops beside the table, and she holds out her thick hands to Elizabeth. "Can it be possible?" Mrs. Jameson says. "Is it truly possible?"

There had been no moment like this for Elizabeth at home, no mother in a chair to hold out her hands to her daughter and guess the happy news that was about to be shared. No one to clutch Elizabeth's hands and then turn to the man she would marry, thus sanctifying, with her smile, the change of roles from daughter to wife. What a difference that would have made for her.

Mrs. Jameson kisses and embraces Elizabeth, who is crying.

"You wild, dear creature!" Mrs. Jameson says to her.

Elizabeth collects Flush with both hands and settles him onto her lap at the table. They all blink at each other, smiling. Mrs. Jameson turns her pale, watery eyes to Robert, then to Elizabeth, then to Robert again. "You dear, abominable poets! You must move to my hotel at once. When can you come?"

"We are very well here," Elizabeth says, "and must leave tomorrow. We are headed for Pisa."

"Tomorrow? But how? Do you have your passports?"

"Yes," Elizabeth says. "We got them in London."

Mrs. Jameson turns to Robert.

"That is what I haven't told you yet," he says to Elizabeth. He explains, and Mrs. Jameson says, "Everyone has to wait in Paris. The good thing is that it's Paris. There is no better place to be marooned."

"But we can't," Elizabeth says. "My family is sending their letters to Orléans."

"The letters will wait for you, dear," Mrs. Jameson says.

Robert doesn't say anything about losing the places they had on the diligence tomorrow, or the inn in Bourges, or the inn in Orléans.

"Don't worry," Mrs. Jameson says. "I'll do what I can. But you must come and stay at my hotel. You look utterly destroyed already, and you're not even close to Pisa. Robert, do you have you a fever? You look as though you've had a fever for a week. I wish I had been in when you called. I would have made you stay and sent for the others. As it is, I think perhaps I should let you sleep here. I'll send my carriage for you promptly at nine o'clock. Don't eat breakfast here. You mustn't. You must eat at the restaurant where I know everybody. How have you gotten this far?"

"By diligence," Robert says.

Mrs. Jameson stares.

"It was marvelous," Elizabeth says. "We sat in the coupé, which was a bit awkward because it became obvious that others resented our being more comfortable, but we had paid for the tickets in London, and it was not as though we muscled anyone aside. If I were perfectly well, I would have asked to sit on the bench on top—what is it called, Robert?"

"The Impériale."

"The Impériale. As it was, I was still able to see the country. There was a full moon."

Mrs. Jameson does not appear to envy Elizabeth, or to approve. "What a ménage you will make, with only poets to arrange things!" she exclaims with a mixture of horror and fondness, reaching out to take Elizabeth's hand again. "You should each have married a petit bout de prose."

"Robert has managed things so well," Elizabeth says, "you would almost think him a novelist, Mrs. Jameson."

"Call me Aunt Nina, as my niece Geddie does."

"I would have thought," Elizabeth says, "that you would admire us for traveling by diligence. After all the brave things you did in Canada! This is nothing compared to your travels."

"I was not ill when I set out for Canada. Not in the least. I am made of iron, but you, my dear . . . you are made of petals. And all of your petals have been crushed. You must resign yourselves to being in Paris for at least a week, and to spending the week with me."

FORTY-SIX

∞

THE RAIN HAS stopped falling on the rectory at Little Bookham, and the yellow leaves plastered to the roof outside the window are starting to dry and peel upward in the steamy sunshine. Already Arabel has seen a thrush, a lark, and a squirrel. It's astonishing how much bluer the sky is here, how much farther one can see. But instead she is left with the feeling she had in the church, seeing Ba's name in her own hand, and Mr. Browning's name, then the witnesses: Mr. James Silverthorne and Miss Elizabeth Wilson. The organist had noticed her, she thought, but perhaps he hadn't, because he kept on playing, and she had just missed the reverend's wife, a shadow approaching stained glass, and she had hurried out, not breathing until she reached the steps again.

"Has Father eaten yet?" George asks when he sits down.

"Yes. He's gone to see about the house."

George takes the last rasher and an egg.

"Have you written to her?" George asks.

"Yes." She touches the yolk on her plate with the point of a knife and thick orange liquid oozes out. "Look. They are the same color they were at Hope End. Do we have our own chickens here, do you know?"

"I haven't asked. What did you say to Ba?"

"Would you like me to see if there is bread?" Arabel asks. George likes to put his egg on a piece of toast. To crumble the toast finely and spread it with butter, mashing it with the egg to a rich paste.

"No, thank you. What did you tell her?"

Arabel salts the exposed yolk of her egg and dips her spoon into it. "That I forgive her and wish her happiness."

George picks up the morning *Post* and holds it in front of his face, his disapproval unmistakable, so she tells herself to enjoy her tea and the view of the wood. The teacup is quite delicate, and she is surprised the owners left such fine china for them to use. Henrietta must still be sleeping, she thinks, and the boys, too, and her eyes drift from the window to George's newspaper. Arabel doesn't read papers, generally, because they're full of babies who fall into fires, women who drown themselves, and accounts of boys crushed by wagons, but held up before her face she sees:

MARRIED.

On Saturday, at St. Marylebone Church, by the Rev. Thos. Woods Goldhawk, M.A., Robert Browning Jun. Esq., of New Cross, Hatcham, to Elizabeth Barrett, eldest daughter of Edward Moulton Barratt, Esq., of Wimpole-street.

The gamboge-yellow leaves glisten, and she studies the water drops they hold. A wood lark lands on the branch, sending a shower of drops onto the stones below.

"I'm going for a walk," she says, and he doesn't answer, so she takes her hat and wanders out. The herb garden is overgrown, but she can still see tansy, or is it St.-John's-wort. Ba would know. She passes out of the garden and walks along the stone wall, avoiding the churchyard, which Ba would have wanted to visit, reading the names and dates and inscriptions. The wood is well traveled, with a footpath she can follow in spite of the rain, keeping to the grassy edges so that she doesn't sink into mud. She has found a stump within a circle of beeches and is sitting there, waiting for her sadness to settle into the stillness of the wood, when Henrietta hurries up the path.

"George met me on his way out with this." Henrietta holds the newspaper up.

Arabel pretends she has not seen it, and she reads it again. A squirrel stops beside a tree and regards them, quivering. The fur on its tail ripples softly, as if each hair is sensate.

"I'm going out to dinner," Henrietta says. "George is, too. Everyone will have seen it, and they will have said things to Papa about it, and he will be impossible."

"Where are you going?"

"With Surtees. His aunt is always wanting us to dine with her."

"Where does she live?"

"Near the museum, I believe."

Arabel sits quietly, watching the fine hairs on the squirrel's tail, its tiny hands going to its mouth, wrapped around something that it wants to eat. Henrietta says, "You could come with us. If you want to avoid—"

"No, thank you."

"Then you ought to say you're sick and eat in your room."

The squirrel runs up the tree, vanishing into the leaves.

"Do you want me to stay with you?" Henrietta asks. "I don't want to, but I will."

It is Arabel's role to do what the others don't want to do. There's a tiny nobility in it, the only kind she has ever felt she could claim. "No."

"Thank you," Henrietta says immediately. "I must write to Surtees or I'll miss the post," and she turns around, leaving Arabel with the absence of the squirrel.

FORTY-SEVEN

∞

IT WILL HAPPEN here, in Paris, in this deep blue room. They are, Robert wants to shout, man and wife. They have been man and wife for twelve days. Nothing need be said. He will know when she is ready. She will know that he is waiting. They will mutually infer.

The trouble lies in his promise of eternal forbearance. He vowed to love her as a brother even if he called her wife. But he loves her as a man instead, and what if every man is Zeus taking the form of a swan to descend on Leda? The drakes at the pond hold their mates down in the shadows, and the ducks stagger away alone afterward.

The rooms Mrs. Jameson has secured for them in l'Hôtel de la Ville de Paris are on an interior wall of the building, without good ventilation or views of the Seine. They have not yet been renovated—paint buckets and canvas cloths lie in the hall after the workmen go home at night—and two small windows look down into a shaft. The walls, conforming to some oceanic color scheme, are midnight blue. The worn sofa and bolsters on the bed are the silvery pale blue of a rippling sea, and stars have been painted on the ceiling—medieval stars, with dots in the center and lines radiating outward to show how they shine. All he wants to do is lie down in the small bed, in this oceanic darkness, and wait for her to reach for him and say she is ready.

"I will rest here," Elizabeth says, "until Wilson gets back with Flush, and we will send for something to eat or go down as Mrs. Jameson suggested and eat at the restaurant." Her face is oyster white, and she smiles at him. She sits fully clothed on the bed, and the dress is not as tight-fitting, he thinks, as it was when they set out. All the more reason to wait, bring her food and coax her to eat it, to be the brother he promised to be, chaste as a priest. "I could send Mrs. Jameson a note and tell her I will stay here with you instead," he says.

"I don't want to keep you from seeing the Louvre. She seemed very keen to have your insight."

"I would rather stay here."

"You promised me you would go out and do everything you used to do."

"I will when we're settled in Pisa. For now, I want to be here if you need anything."

"I have everything," she says. "I feel as if I were inside a nautilus. I would feel terrible if you miss seeing the paintings Mrs. Jameson is writing about. You can't miss everything in France because of me."

"Let me lie here a moment. A half hour. I'm not meeting her until ten."

He sits on the side of the narrow bed. He pulls up his feet, and at first he is on his back, a strange and corpselike pose, but she is curled on her side, facing him, and she puts her hand on his open palm.

"Here we are," he whispers.

"Here we are," she returns.

How much of life is habit? Restraint and forbearance have rusted him in place. The wheels, held in place by the brake, are grown over with vines. Years and years of forbidding, negating, abiding. Her hand is small and warm in his, and he wants to turn over on his side and face her, to stroke her face with his hand, to unbutton the buttons, and yet he lies as if frozen on his back, letting his hand have only her neck. The ways in which he could say it—*we ought to, are you ready, do you feel, may I, may we*—but they are discarded like cards that don't make a pair. They breathe together, and the room, ink-dark at mid-morning, is a charmed place. His hand, like the rest of him, is immersed in the nearness of her, and he wills himself to turn, slowly, gently, to face her, the nearest they have ever been.

Her eyes open when he turns, and he brings his other hand to her cheek. She regards him steadily as he rests his hand gently on the curve of her jaw. He dares to bring his thumb to her lip and stroke it. She kisses his thumb.

"Stay," he wants her to tell him. "Stay."

Something is in in her face, her eyes. Fear? Doubt? Or is it the same inertia, the long habit of denial.

"Come back to me at the end of the day," she says, "and tell me what you saw. I will be right here waiting for you."

FORTY-EIGHT

∞

"It's from a friend of Robbie's," Sarianna says to her parents. "She has seen him on the train and says they are doing well."

They all stand right there, her father not even out of his coat, as she reads them Miss Goss's letter.

They have been bereft since the wedding. Two weeks now, it has been, but it seems longer. Only the night before it happened, Robbie said, "Miss Barrett has accepted me."

Their mother had been genuinely delighted; their father, too.

"When is it to be?" their mother asked. "Will we have a chance to meet her family first?"

"That's the part I hate to tell you," Robbie said.

"Not at all?"

"Nothing has improved."

"He doesn't want to meet the people his daughter will live among?" their mother asked.

"But she won't," Sarianna said, not sure if she was helping Robbie or rebuking him. "She won't live among us. She has to go to Italy and be cured."

"But not right away, surely?" their mother asked.

"Yes," Robbie said. "We ought to have left in August. I would have told you sooner if I could—"

"I expect they don't think we're good enough," Mr. Browning said.

"She desperately wants to meet you all. She sends her love and her hope that she may write to you."

"You have fixed the day, then?" Sarianna asked.

"We have," Robbie said.

There was a reason for his reluctance, she felt it. "When?"

"Tomorrow."

"Tomorrow?" their mother said. "Where?"

"At St. Marylebone."

"What time?" Sarianna asked.

"A quarter past ten."

Near her house, not theirs. It would be a long way for their mother. Would the train be going in the morning on a Saturday? Could it get there in time? Sarianna had nothing clean to wear because it was harvest time. If they did arrive by train, how shabby that would seem to Miss Barrett. They ought to go by carriage and she must wash what she can now, hang it by the fire, then press it dry in the morning.

"It will be over in an instant, and you needn't exhaust yourselves. We will celebrate properly at a future time."

"It won't exhaust us," Mr. Browning said. "We are up to it, aren't we, Mother? We want to show we love her as our own."

"Miss Barrett's family will not be present. It would be unfair, I think, if I had my family around me."

"Are you telling us we can't attend your wedding?" Sarianna asked.

"Not that you can't. That you shouldn't trouble yourselves. It will be nothing much to see," Robbie said. "A formality, and a very quick one. When we return from Italy next summer, we can spend days and days together, and you can talk to her and show her everything here that I've told her about. That will mean more than a few minutes in a cold church."

Their mother didn't speak.

"Truly, Mother," Robbie said. "It will be the barest thing. It will make formal what is already true between us."

Their father put his hand on their mother's shoulder and said, "That's all right, isn't it, Mrs. Browning? We care only that you're doing right by Miss Barrett."

"I am. You can depend upon it."

"When do you leave for Italy?" their mother asked.

"Saturday next. But I will come home after the ceremony and be here all week. She will be with her family as well."

How odd it was to marry someone and then pretend that you hadn't, Sarianna thinks.

"When will you come back?" their father asked, his hand still on their mother's shoulder.

"When it's warm again. Next summer, or even in the spring."

And now this letter, not from Robbie, but from Miss Goss. "It's good to know they are safe and well," Sarianna says, folding it back up.

"Indeed it is," Mr. Browning says. "We will thank God for that, won't we, Mrs. Browning."

Mrs. Browning gives the slightest nod.

Sarianna goes to the paddock without saying that's where she's going. Their father keeps putting off the letter he must write, the one telling his brother Reuben that Robbie has gone to Italy again, and the horse has no one to ride him.

"It's no one again," Sarianna says to York as York trots to her. The horse knows her and crosses the field at once. "No one is here to feed you," she says, "and no one would like to ride you."

York shows his teeth when she offers the apple. He lets her touch the place on his forehead where the hair grows in a circle.

"Would you like no one to ride you?" she asks.

The picking is not finished, nor is anything else she's supposed to do. The orchard waits, the horse chews the apple, and she breathes in the scent of him. "This is just the beginning," she says to York. "No one is going to ride you, and no one is going to go all the way over there, to that hill. You'd like that, wouldn't you?"

The horse follows her as she walks along the fence, and soon, she thinks, she will try the bit.

FORTY-NINE

∞

ELIZABETH COUNTS DROPS of morphine, and each exquisite ruby curl swims to the bottom of the tea, somersaults, and dissolves. It's best to do this out of Robert's sight, as it had been best to do it out of the sight of her family at home. He says she is his morphine and that he understands her present, temporary need of it, but it seems a large dose if you don't know anything. In Pisa, she won't need it anymore. Fini, she has told Robert. Morphine will be fini in Pisa.

Robert has gone to the opera with Mrs. Jameson and her niece. Wilson has gone to her own room on the top floor. Flush's eyes hold the candle flame inside them, two dark pools of readiness and wordless questions.

The tea goes down her tired throat, down with the morphine inside it, and the room is very dark because of the beautiful dark blue paint and the watery pale blue curtains. The air surges like the sea, starfish attaching themselves to skirts and candles.

My beloved Arabel I write you after a thousand thoughts . . . (for I have not heard a breath of any of you yet)

"Don't," Sam says, his long legs draped over the arm of the chair, his face pale and glistening, as if he has been for a swim.

"Don't what?"

"Why is Mr. Browning not here? I thought he loved you."

The dog sleeps beside her, and a long column of light falls across the room, glazing the carpet, the rumpled bed, the dog's fur, and Sam's sweating face.

"I told him to go to the opera."

"He should be here, Ba."

"I can't confine him."

"*Confine* him? Have you had a wedding night?"

She refuses to answer him.

"Are you still ashamed, Ba? Now? When all is sanctified before the Lord?"

People who were healthy thought wellness was an act of volition. As if she had never tried the thing they had always been able to do naturally. The potted plant ought to move itself closer to the sun! *Simply do it*, whatever it was. Be with your husband, as is natural.

Sam walks to the window, and he looks out at the view of the airshaft, narrow as a well, at the bottom of which rubble has turned green with moss. She has stared down into it many times already, and across the shaft at the other windows, curtained, mainly, and empty, though at night perhaps one would be seen by others who have stayed home from the opera.

"Lenore Goss was the first person we met on the train," she says. "The very first to see us after we ran away. She is everywhere, first in Le Havre, then here. Is she following us?"

Sam reaches out to touch the windowpane, and he leaves all ten fingertips pressed against it. When Elizabeth was feverish, she would ask for the couch to be pushed nearer the window so she could melt frost with her fingertip. Sometimes she drank the stale drops of ice, licking them from her skin.

"Sweet Nora," Sam says, letting the curtains fall back over the window. "I sent her."

"Did you see her when you were at Cinnamon Hill?"

"I'm here to talk about *your* husband. Whom you sent to the opera on the first chance you had of a night alone."

"The Reverend Waddell said something in his letter, Sam—"

"Maybe your poet will come back to you, Ba. That would be romantic. If he slipped out of the opera and hired a carriage and came back to you, overcome with desire. If he really loves you, that's what he'll do."

"Reverend Waddell's letter said you confessed something. What, Sam?"

"Don't fall asleep, Ba. Be awake for him. These early days determine everything."

"What happened in Jamaica, Sam? Why did you tell the reverend that you were afraid to die?"

He puts his hands over his head, crosses his wrists, and winces. In a much different voice, as if he is finally considering her question, he says, "What is the crime that hath brought thee to pain? What crime dost expiate so?" It's her own translation of *Prometheus Bound*, the one she hates now.

"Don't mock me."

"I'm not mocking you."

"She came to see me, Sam," she whispers. "She showed me a boy she said was yours."

"The poem is too sad, Ba. If you say anything about what really happens, people will blame you for it. They'll say you're the one who corrupts the public."

"What did she mean to you, Sam? Is she the reason you were afraid to die?" The room is too large, and he is too small, and the dark blue walls are farther away than she remembers. She can't see him anymore, a fish that swims just under her two hands but can never be caught.

Instead of writing to Arabel, she should do her work, the poem she promised to the *Liberty Bell*, even though Sam is right about it being too sad. A white man rapes a slave in it, and she kills the baby because he looks like the man who whipped her. Sad indeed, but no sadder than the stories her uncle had told about Jamaica when no one but family was around.

> And the babe who lay on my bosom so,
> was far too white . . . too white for me,
> As white as the ladies who scorned to pray
> Beside me at church just yesterday

ROBERT CAN'T FIND the right stairway inside the hotel, and because he has just been to the opera, getting lost in a stairway feels like a scene in a farce in which the thwarted lover goes all over the stage, opening doors, turning in confusion as the audience laughs. At last he finds the door that leads to the hall cluttered with workmen's hammers and buckets. He searches in his pocket for the key that would not be there if this were a farce, but the key is there. He unlocks the door, and because it is not a farce, it is the blue room painted with stars. He waits for the dreaded volley of barking, for Flush to leap down from her lap and rush at him, but there is only silence as he approaches the bed.

"Robert," Elizabeth says, and she reaches quietly for his hand. "What was the opera about?"

"What the opera is always about."

Elizabeth's face is hard to see in the darkness. "Thwarted love?"

"Myopia."

"Was Miss Goss there?"

"Yes, in another box. We saw her at a distance. Why?"

"I worked on the poem I promised. I want to let her know."

He has never taken his clothes off in front of a woman. But that's what he must do now, for the first time, and ever after. "Where is the dog?"

"With Wilson. I didn't want him to wake everyone when you got in."

He doesn't really have to take off his clothes. He removes his shoes, but he decides not to remove his stockings. He unbuttons his waistcoat, but feeling self-conscious, he leaves it on. Elizabeth moves over so he can lie down beside her on the bed. He lifts the coverlet and slips in.

The settling of darkness reveals the edge of the bed, the couch by the wall, the medieval stars on the painted walls. He sleeps on his back at home, but he has never thought of the position as a cold one. It feels cold now, corpselike, himself in effigy, held apart. "Were you sleeping?" he asks.

"A little. I dreamed I saw my brother, and he was Prometheus."

"Which brother?"

"Sam." To mitigate the coldness of his prone position, he sweeps his hand slowly across the sheet in search of her fingers. His pinkie touches what he presumes is her leg, and he leaves his hand there, where it is joined by her small, cold hand. "Your hand is ice," he says.

"Cover it with yours."

He does, and the gold stars send their painted gleaming into the corners of the room.

"Are you thinking of your promise, Robert?"

"Which one?"

"To be like a brother to me."

"I do think about it, yes."

"Don't."

"I can wait as long as you like," he says.

"I don't want you to be able to wait."

In the paintings Robert went with Mrs. Jameson to see in the Louvre, medieval paintings by Pessellino, martyrs were tortured with fire, but the flames curled backward and refused to burn flesh.

"You wish me to?" he asks.

"Please."

He turns to her, her clothes like flames in the painting. They peel back under his hands and he hardly knows himself. "Tell me if it hurts," he says, but she doesn't say that it hurts, only that she thought she would never have any of it.

FIFTY

❦

IN THREE DAYS, in the Tuileries, life presents one of its exchanges. *You may have this*, life says, *but only if you also suffer this*. The sufferance, and also the deliverance, come through Mrs. Jameson. Her assistance forms an avenue like the avenue of trees through which the three of them walk, Mrs. Jameson, Robert, and Mrs. Jameson's niece. The pruned trees are a tunnel and a refuge, a graceful constraint on choosing any other direction, and a delightful freedom from having to forge a path.

"Lord Normanby has worked his magic," Mrs. Jameson tells Robert. "I have your passports."

"We can leave?"

"Tomorrow."

Mrs. Jameson sends Geddie to make a sketch of a statue so that they can speak in private, and Geddie skips over the white path, paper and pencil in hand, dead leaves skittering under her shoes.

"Mr. Browning," Mrs. Jameson says when they are alone, "I have something to say to you." She can—*must*, really—travel with them all the way to Pisa.

"But your book," he says, startled. "Your strict schedule." And the constant hovering and listening and directing, the never being alone. In Mrs. Jameson's presence, he is something other than the husband and protector. In her presence, he is nothing more, really, than Mrs. Jameson's dependent niece.

"I have only one alteration to make," Mrs. Jameson goes on, "and that's Chartres. I need to go there instead of Orléans."

"Ah," he says, relieved to see a way out of the narrow path with its severely pruned trees. "We can't do that. Her family will—or has—sent their letters to Orléans."

"Really? Why? Why did she not have them send the letters here?"

"We thought it would go much more quickly."

"If only you had told me, Robert. If you had shared it all with me from the beginning, I could have saved you so much trouble."

"I know." He knows.

They crunch the gravel underfoot, and leaves from the unpruned chestnuts tumble in a disordering breeze.

"But I can't let you do it alone. It's too much," she says.

"We will manage, Nina. You mustn't take on so much."

He turns to see if Geddie is still sketching, and she is a small person now, a small and devoted person sitting at the base of the statue, the devotee of her aunt and the goddess of Art.

"I think," Mrs. Jameson says, "I could make do with just one day in Chartres. A day and two nights. That way, we would get to Orléans with reasonable swiftness."

"She couldn't bear to wait any longer, Nina. You must realize what a strain it is to wonder if they have forgiven her. I have planned everything and we will be fine on our own."

"My dear Robert. Show me what you plan to do."

He doesn't want to show her his plan, but it is all in his notebook, in the pocket of his coat, and she has done so much for them.

"No," she says after a brief perusal. "It's impossible."

"What is?"

"You will kill her, traveling like that."

He folds it up again and turns around on the path. "I must get back."

"Robert, don't be offended. I don't doubt your love for her or your concern, but you have never traveled—"

"But I have," he says.

"Not with a woman. One who isn't well."

"I know she isn't well. That's why we must get to Orléans as soon as possible, and when her mind is eased, hurry on to Pisa."

"Please listen to me. Sit and listen."

He cannot refuse. She shows him, in her own book, the towns where they *ought* to stop for the night. "These are safer places, with more reliable inns. And you can travel by day. What you've planned, with so many nights on the road, I urge against it because she doesn't sleep. If you go by day, she can get out of the carriage more often. She faints because she isn't getting enough air or food or sleep, and she's stiffening up, holding herself in one position, trying not to be difficult."

He resumes walking, saying it's easy enough to change that.

"Why two nights in Avignon, and one everywhere else?" she asks.

"So we can go to the Sorgue," he says, "and see where Petrarch wrote the sonnets. I promised. It's the only thing she asked."

"Oh, no. I must tell her."

"What?"

"It's become a destination for lovers on their wedding trips—vulgar people who don't know Petrarch or read real poetry at all. They have ruined it."

They pass a couple laughing softly with each other, arms encircled. "We would bring our own associations," he says. "You find what you're looking for, I think."

"If you both wish to see it, you must. I do understand. How to see the place itself through and around and *despite* all the people who are looking at it? I have to shut my ears sometimes."

A breeze caught a pile of leaves and rolled them over the path. One of the leaves was yellow, the others dead brown. The cold was catching up to them.

"I can adapt the route," Robert says. "I see your point, and I am grateful to you."

"You can adapt it, or you can let me travel with you and I can make it simpler. Simpler for all of you. Have you thought what you'll do if she gets too sick to go any further?"

How can she ask such a question?

"You must ask her what she wants. Ask your wife, and we'll talk later."

HE TELLS ELIZABETH as neutrally as he can.

"It's very kind of her," Elizabeth says. When he takes her hand, she draws him toward the bed, and instead of sitting up to talk about it, they lie together, her arm entwined with his.

"It's the going out of our way to Chartres that I couldn't stand," Elizabeth says.

"I thought the same."

"But it would be easier on Wilson to have Mrs. Jameson there," Elizabeth says. "She wouldn't have to go out in each new place and find everything with no experience or knowledge, and neither would you. It would be much easier, I think. I am so much trouble."

"You are the opposite of trouble," he says.

"We must accept," she says.

Only the hotel maid can be heard in the hall as she lets him go farther, as she waits for him to unbutton the dress. The first time that it happened in the daytime is represented by a circle, a notation he makes in his diary, a symbol he alone can read.

FIFTY-ONE

∞

LENORE'S ONLY LETTER in Paris is from George.

Nora, she reads, and she is aware that he has not said, *Dear*.

> *If you have ever cared for me, you will do me this favor. Stop them.*
> *You know the poem I mean, Nora. Do not let him kill Porphyria and*
> *say she was in God's hands.*
> *I am*
> *As ever*
> *George*

Stop them?

Because the crossing was wet and none of them had a sac de nuit? Because they had traveled by night in a common diligence? Because Mr. Browning had not asked permission from her maniacal father? Because Mr. Browning was a poet with no income? Or—*this* she had not liked—Mr. Browning had gone without Elizabeth to the opera house with Mrs. Jameson and a red-haired girl of seventeen whose look of adoration was plain even from Lenore's box.

But he did love Elizabeth. He was not a murderer. Perhaps she would see them again, and if she did, she would make up her own mind.

FIFTY-TWO

∞

THEY HAVE BEEN traveling twelve days by the time they reach Orléans.

Robert walks from the post house with seven letters, including one from someone he doesn't know, a Mr. Jago. The others are expected: her father, George, Arabel, Henrietta, John Kenyon, and Miss Mitford.

He opens the door to the room he and Elizabeth occupy—ah, the luxury—by themselves.

Elizabeth is a pale figure in the shaft of sunlight. Before her is the breakfast he fetched: bread, butter, and coffee—no fish, no eggs, no beef, none of the things she says turn her stomach in the morning. The only thing he added to her list is the cotignac, a quince paste, but she hasn't touched it.

"How many are there?" she asks.

She hasn't even finished the coffee.

"Ba," he says. "You promised to eat. Try the toast with a bit of quince." He had spent too much on the small wooden boxes of jellied fruit, then spent too much on sending one to his family. It was the thought of home that did it, or perhaps the age of the woman who made the jelly. Her hands shook when she handed him a sample scraped up with a stick. On the table now the jelly sits as it was: a rose-colored attraction for a fly rubbing its legs together.

"I have to eat the letters first," she says. She turns each one over, reads the writer's names without opening them. She puts her father's on the bottom of the stack. "Where are you and Mrs. Jameson going today? The cathedral?"

"Nowhere. I told them to go without me."

She opens nothing, eats nothing.

"Would you like me to read one? We could start with Arabel as a tonic."

"I would rather that you go and see something. Mrs. Jameson said you can walk where Joan of Arc rode into the city."

"I don't care where Joan of Arc rode into the city."

"I need you to walk there for me."

He has already walked it. He has seen the timbers in the walls, the crooked windows, inhaled the breath of the past.

"I need to read them by myself."

He goes out of the room and shuts the door, but he doesn't touch the cobblestones touched by the hooves of Joan's horse. He goes to the end of the hall, to a dirty window where a spider holds perfectly still. There is another room nearby, and the door is ajar so he can hear a woman speaking French to a child, softly, kindly. She, too, is concerned with someone who is not eating. The child says no in English, and the woman starts again, undeterred, with her list of places they will go, and what they will eat there, and what his maman will say. He can hear nothing from the bedroom where Elizabeth is opening what she kept calling the Death Warrant. The child and the French servant come out of their room, the servant holding the boy's hand, and the woman looks distrustfully at him before she leads the boy downstairs. Through the window, he can see a sleet-gray conical roof, its point sharp in the sun. The spider, no longer afraid of him, fingers a tuft of white.

ELIZABETH OUGHT TO have eaten some of the quince jelly and pretended to be delighted. Robert took such pleasure in eating that he believed she needed only to taste what he liked, and she would love it, and then they would be as alike in body as they were in mind. People who are not sick always think that. The fly rubs its legs and tastes the jelly on her plate, taking its time before trying the bread.

The letters are easy to arrange in order of foreboding—her father's must go on the bottom, with George's, and Kenyon's or Miss Mitford's on top, but setting Arabel's that far down in the stack makes her remember how Arabel had looked forward to seeing Pisa. She had wanted to go to mass just once, if it would not be wrong, she said.

Elizabeth starts, instead, with Mr. Jago. Direct, simple, and precise. He sends his best wishes and the prescription for laudanum with the strength corrected.

Kenyon is next: pleased. Miss Mitford: surprised but pleased. Henrietta: approving and loving. Arabel: approving and loving, and yet warns Elizabeth of how bad things are, how irreparable. There are only two letters left, and the cake of rose-orange jelly, and the buzzing fly.

The one in her father's hand is not addressed to anyone at all. It says only

Witness that upon the day of her marriage, Elizabeth Barrett Moulton-Barrett, eldest daughter of Edward Moulton-Barrett, has turned from God to the things of the world & its regard for Genius. From this day he is no more her father.

Signed
Edward Moulton-Barrett
50 Wimpole Street
London

She takes the stick Robert broke from the box of quince paste. The fly buzzes in circles of annoyance, settles on the bread, and rubs it. It flies away when she drags the stick across the jelly—it is, as Robert said, the color of a conch's throat—and sets a blob of sweetness on her tongue. She swallows it without chewing and rakes her finger under the seal of George's letter.

Dear Elizabeth,

She is not Ba to him either.

Nothing could be more disappointing or galling
Then came your letters. Begging us to excuse & forgive & understand!
Your wound in each & every one of us has been made by calculation & secrecy

You will say that I am hard

Now our father will feel all the more a sense of doubt about the motives of those he loves because of you

But it has often been thus with artists. They prize what they have to give to the world, not what their families have given & sacrificed for their sake.

Do you really know him, your Mr. Browning?

When she looks up from the letter, Robert is at the door.

"What did he say?"

She shakes her head.

"And George?"

"George wrote his letter with a sword."

"I'm sorry, Ba. I—"

"These you may read," she says. She hands him the letters from her sisters, and Kenyon, and Miss Mitford.

They sit together, they lie together, it's several hours before he asks about Mr. Jago. "It will be a relief to poor Wilson. She can simply show it to the apothecaire and not have to know the French equivalent."

The fly buzzes over the quince paste, the surface of it seeming to thicken as she stares at it. He butters the bread thickly, applies jelly, and she tries to eat it.

"Please let me read what George and your father have said," he asks one more time. A brazier must be burning beneath the window, bringing with it the scent of meat.

"No," she says. "They don't mean it. They will feel differently in the future, I'm sure of it."

"What have they said about me?"

"It's me they censure."

"What have they said about me?"

"Nothing. It's me they censure," she repeated.

There's no fireplace in the room and it feels too cold now. When Robert goes downstairs to talk to Mrs. Jameson, she tears George's letter into pieces. The pieces are still distinct, with readable words, and it reminds her of the Portland Vase after it was broken. The boy tried to destroy it, but all he did was strengthen the resolve of those who owned it. The pieces, even the tiniest ones, had been gathered up, as you might do with a broom and a fingertip, and they had been placed like a puzzle that could be—must be—restored to its former shape. Then they had painted a picture of the shards, determined to impose order. She had been inspired by the idea of its restoration, of its salvation. It had seemed like a sign that everything could be fixed. She takes her father's letter and tears it up, too. She pours water on the bits of paper in the bowl. They dissolve, as she rubs them, into clots, and when she can't read any of the words, she pours the mess into the empty chamber pot, which she covers with a lid. Robert must never know what they think of him because what they think is wrong, and she will never again read George's words about her because he is wrong, too. That is not how she is or what she has done or what it means to have married.

SHE DOESN'T MIND traveling with Mrs. Jameson and Geddie, who are cheerfully efficient, but she can hardly get up each morning. She confesses to Robert that she is tired, but when she does that, he carries her to the room instead of letting her walk, which makes her feel she is failing an important test. He buys more food, and he sets it before her, begging her to eat, so she stops saying she is tired.

She looks out the window of the diligence and sees cattle the color of bread. Stone stables. Sunflowers black as ashes bowing their heads. An allée of enormous plane trees forming a tunnel for a flat green slow-moving canal. It takes hours to pass through the Forest of Tronçais and by the end of that day she can't walk; he must carry the burden that she is. The roads lead to a seemingly endless number of other small roads, mile by mile, not flown over, as she had flown to Pisa in her mind. The train is a relief in comparison, and the Dore River has rapids like silk. She wants to make that into a poem but can't.

Mrs. Jameson insists that she get out at every change of horses, that she drink and eat and go with her and Geddie and Wilson to some attraction a few feet away, a stand of trees, sometimes, or a village shop. It's like she is a pony and Mrs. Jameson holds out a lump of sugar to coax her on. "We're almost there," Robert says, but he means Lyon, not Marseilles. After Lyon comes Avignon, and after Avignon, Marseilles, and after Marseilles, Genoa, and only after Genoa, Pisa. She will get there, he tells her, to the Field of Miracles in Pisa. She will stand on earth brought from the Holy Land eight hundred years ago and they will give thanks together.

FIFTY-THREE

∞

THEY ARE DISEMBARKING in Lyon, and Robert is saying that the city has two rivers side by side, the Saône and the Rhône, "as if poets had named them specifically for their own ease," when the carriage beside them produces a maid, another maid, two people they don't know, and Lenore Goss.

Geddie is presented and greeted and talked nicely about. Mr. and Mrs. Something, Lenore's friends, are likewise greeted and talked nicely about and excused to wash and dress for dinner.

"Are you engaged for anything this evening?" Lenore asks.

"We will eat and rest, I think," Robert says.

Lenore is bound for the Roman ruins on Fourvière Hill.

"You must go with her and see them," Elizabeth says to Robert. "How will you get there, Miss Goss?"

"Donkeys, they say."

"Could Robert and Mrs. Jameson and Geddie go with you?" Elizabeth asks.

"Of course! You're all very welcome," Lenore says. "It costs almost nothing."

"Not tonight," Robert says.

"I couldn't either," Mrs. Jameson says. "I must slip into Saint-Jean and see a picture before the sun sets. But Geddie will like it. And Wilson can stay with your wife, Robert. You ought to go."

"I don't want you to miss everything because of me," Elizabeth says, and she says it until he agrees, unhappily, to go.

Elizabeth tries to see the hill from her window but there are too many buildings, and she can only imagine the donkeys picking their way on a path, Miss Goss on one, her husband on another, Geddie in her youthful beauty on the third, as if they were figures in a painting of the Magi.

THEY HAVE CRESTED the hill and have just half an hour, the guide says, before they must begin the journey back down. The city is pale pink and yellow, like Italy. The fulcrum has been reached, the place where France is not quite France anymore but the beginning of ochre walls and flat roofs and cypresses, where every hill seems the last hill before the Mediterranean. Lenore feels as if she has encountered the Brownings on purpose in order to tell him where they are and arrange for their capture. Every sentence she speaks is related to that mission, no matter how brightly she tries to say it. They step over stones that used to be foundations of high walls but now go no higher than her knees. They form rooms where Romans used to sleep, but the rooms seem too small, too full of grass, too much like meadows, to be habitable.

"Where will you go after this, Mr. Browning?" Lenore asks.

"Avignon. And you?"

"Avignon, as well. My friends have never seen the Popes' Palace and insist on stopping. I fear I will have to trudge through it with them, pretending to care about vestments."

"Isn't the city supposed to be beautiful?"

"I find it cold. As I remember, it smelled horribly of drains."

Geddie is walking in and out of the stone remnants of rooms, pausing at each vanished doorway as if the Romans are still there and she hates to disturb them. Her face, when she turns toward them, is full of something Lenore once felt: rapture, delight, astonishment.

"Will you stay there long?" Lenore asks. It's a normal question, anyone would ask such things, she ought not to feel duplicitous.

"Long enough to visit the spring of Petrarch in Vaucluse," Robert says. "I promised Elizabeth."

"I have never been," Lenore says. "Only lovers go, I hear."

"Mrs. Jameson says it's a silly place now. But we will visit just the same."

"I hope it isn't silly," Lenore says, and the guide is waving his arms at them, in a hurry, most likely, to have an end to his long day, and put the donkeys in their stable. They wave back at the guide and stand in the ruins looking down on the pink and yellow city threaded with two pink shimmering rivers, the Rhône and the Saône. One of the donkeys shakes his head and makes the bells jingle. "George wrote me," she says. "He urged me to stop you."

"Stop me?"

"Some people take poetry quite literally, you know. That madman who strangles his lover with her long golden hair has done you no favors with George."

"You don't mean he thinks that of me?"

"He doesn't trust your motives."

"It's absurd. She has written to him, to all of them, and George knows me."

"Not very well."

"It's difficult, I admit it. The journey is far more difficult than I thought. But she's not in any danger with me, and never will be."

"Is that what you want me to say when I write?"

"My motive is love and always has been."

Geddie walks along a row of stones toward the donkeys, her hands held out for balance.

Lenore believes him, but she doesn't know why. Perhaps she merely doesn't believe that George and his father have any better idea how to love. Before the sun has completely set, and before they have dismounted the donkeys and paid the guide and said goodbye, she knows most of what she will write in her letter.

Dear George,

I have seen your sister and her retinue at Lyon, and they are very well. It is love between them, I'm sure of it, and their mutual friend, Mrs. Jameson, is mothering them day & night. How could I stop them?

You overestimate my powers and underestimate Mr. Browning, who is the kindest of husbands.

I might see them in Vaucluse if I tell my companions that it's an essential stop for lovers. If I manage it (I make no promises) I will write you directly, but at present I see no reason for you to take to the roads on your fastest stallion.

Unless, of course, you wish to see me at the lovers' spring.

Your faithful
Nora

FIFTY-FOUR

∞

ELIZABETH HAS IN her pocket the sonnet she's trying to finish, but it feels dead and trite. Real poetry is made by throwing your mind into a stranger's world, by occupying it and having authority there, as Robert does. To do what she does in the sonnets, articulating her love for him in the old, courtly patterns—it's the kind of writing Robert has left behind, a subject he rejects. She hasn't told him why she wants to go to Petrarch's spring because she would have to tell him about the love poems. She wants inspiration. Holy water. A sort of affirmation.

They leave Avignon in the morning, and she can tell it's all for her benefit, that the rest would all avoid the place and the extra miles if they could. The valley of the Sorgue is not as she expected. Stone escarpments without trees loom over the road. The town, shaded and shabby, is almost impassable because of the carriages waiting two deep in the square. "I feared as much," Mrs. Jameson says. Even Geddie, who is charmed by every village, tree, monument, and painting, seems out of sorts.

But they have come, and they have gone around the carriages, and they are near the water, so they get out. The Sorgue is not like the Thames or the Rhône or the Seine or the Loire. It is not, like those rivers, opaque. It's liquid crystal, perfectly clear, flowing over a fluttering green bed of cresses. It is the purest substance she has ever seen, and she wets her hand in it. Beside the river is a tea garden filled with people having lunch, and Geddie is hungry so they go in immediately and wait for a table, lined up on a bench beside the bored and impatient tourists.

"It's a bit sad," Geddie says. "Petrarch must have been the gloomiest man in the world. The ones who dip their handkerchiefs in the sacred water—do they know he was all alone? That Laura de Noves was married?"

"His poetry is better than love," Mrs. Jameson says. "It survives him. Has survived him by five hundred years."

"But he never spent a minute with her," Geddie says. "And he didn't know the poems would last."

"As much as I detest Lord Byron," Mrs. Jameson says, "he said it best. 'Think you, if Laura had been his wife / he would have written sonnets all his life?'"

Geddie laughs, and Elizabeth says, "Will you all excuse me for a moment?"

"Of course," Mrs. Jameson says, distracted by the bill of fare and steep prices, which Elizabeth leaves behind for the riverbank. She steps into the shallow water, testing the stones for stability, feeling the water soak her hem and stockings and shoes. The water gets no deeper than her knees and is bracingly cold. She hears someone sloshing behind her, and when she turns, Robert puts his arms around her.

"Did you come to stop me?"

"Certainly not." He bends over and gathers her up. Geddie and Mrs. Jameson stand watching from the rail of the deck. The men who serve brandy water and stale bread serve more brandy water and stale bread. "Petrarch," Robert calls, "I'm coming!"

There's mud on the stones by the throne-rock, and he slips a little.

"I can do it," Elizabeth says. "Set me down."

To her surprise, he does so.

"The spirits are talking to me, or maybe it's that German governess over there. Nicht something." She has gotten her footing and she reaches her destination, a shoal where a giant rock is shaped like a chair. "Lenore Goss is here," she adds. "I can see her watching us."

He scans the tables for Miss Goss and Elizabeth sits down. Where she thought she saw Miss Goss, there is no one. It feels good to rest and watch the water flow between her and everything else, the green watercress going up and down in the eternal current.

"This is the most wonderful moment of my life," she says. She wants to call out to Geddie and tell her to write in her sketchbook, the one where she sweetly writes down practically everything everyone says, that Petrarch didn't fail. Instead, Elizabeth says she wants to sit here all day.

A policeman is waving an arm and saying something in French that she can't hear.

"Is it against the rules to come out here?"

"I believe so. Hold on to my neck."

"I can walk. Just hold my hand."

He folds her hand into his, and before the thick crease of worry returns to that place between his eyebrows, before the carriage has to be summoned, before they discover that Mrs. Jameson has misplaced her shawl, and it has to be hunted for, the words come to her, the ones she has been looking for, the ones he deserves.

Appendix I: The Barrett and Browning Families

ELIZABETH BARRETT BROWNING, known in her family as Ba, was born on March 6, 1806, in England, to Mary Graham-Clark and Edward Barrett Moulton-Barrett, the heir, with his younger brother, of a sugar plantation in St. James Parish, Jamaica.

Elizabeth's aunt, Sarah Goodin Barrett-Moulton, called Pinkie, sat for a portrait by Sir Thomas Lawrence in 1794, when she was eleven, because her grandmother in Jamaica missed her and wanted to be able to see her face again. Pinkie died of a fever a few days before her portrait was exhibited in London and before it was sent home to her grandmother. The painting, also known as Pinkie, was passed down within the family and was for a time in the hands of Elizabeth's father. It is now owned by the Huntington Library in San Marino, California.

Elizabeth had ten siblings who survived to adulthood, born as follows:

Edward, called Bro, June 26, 1807
Henrietta, called Addles, March 4, 1809
Samuel, January 13, 1812
Arabella, July 4, 1813
Charles John, called Stormie, December 28, 1814
George, July 15, 1816
Henry, July 27, 1818
Alfred, called Daisy, May 20, 1820
Septimus, called Sette, February 11, 1822
Octavius, called Occy, April 11, 1824

Elizabeth's brothers Samuel and Edward died in 1840, Samuel of yellow fever in Jamaica and Edward by drowning, off Torquay.

The coins that were in Sam's pocket when he died are extant, along with a note in the hand of his father that says, "Given to me by CJ [Charles John] Barrett taken by him from the pocket of my dearest Sam after death."

A freed Jamaican slave identified only as "Mary Ann H—" was described in the memoir of Reverend Hope Masterton Waddell, who served as a missionary and pastor in a church on Barrett land. Here are two excerpts from that work, *Twenty-Nine Years in the West Indies and Africa: a Review of Missionary Work and Adventure, 1829–1858*:

> Each estate had its own overseer, who had "book-keepers," carpenter, and mason under him. From the attorney down all were unmarried, yet all had families. A married lady was rarely seen. Some planters had not seen one since they left home. Others knew not how to address one when they met her. The "housekeeper" system had become a colonial institution. It was thought cheaper than the other; but that was a mistake . . . Planters have owned to me that they were shocked at first by the style of living, but were laughed at and ensnared, and became in the end used to it as unavoidable. Others never got over it. Troubled by pangs of conscience, they drank to excess, and died in despair.
>
> . . .
>
> "The day on which it was commenced, 25th August, 1837, was distinguished by a rather remarkable scene . . . The public service was over . . . when an excellent man, Charles H—, who had declined the eldership the previous year because of his daughter—came hastily meeting us, much agitated. He held out in one hand a coral necklace, or what was so called, and a pair of great flashy earrings, and in the other a stout "supplejack."
>
> "See, minister," he exclaimed. "See these things. You know how often I have charged Mary Ann not to go near that great house, and

to take no presents there. Now I find these on her, which she got from _____ yesterday, and what more she has been doing, I don't know. I have flogged her well; and now I want to go and ask him why he must always teach my daughter to be a bad girl."

A letter Reverend Waddell wrote to Elizabeth's father in 1840 describes Sam's death and his fear of damnation but does not state the nature of Sam's sin. David is an invented character.

Elizabeth's brother Charles John (known as Stormie) fathered two daughters in Jamaica with a woman he loved but was not permitted to marry. That information comes from letters written by the younger daughter, Arabella Moulton-Barrett, in which she states that her parents, though not legally married, were true to each other for forty years and that her father took her to London in 1867, when she was seven years old, and introduced her to Robert Browning.

Robert Browning was born on May 7, 1812, in Camberwell, a suburb of London, to Sarah Anna Wiedemann (born 1772) and Robert Browning, Sr. (born 1782). The senior Mr. Browning wanted to be an artist but was sent as a young man to work in slave-owning Saint Kitts for a relative. He refused to stay, returning to London to work for a modest salary in a bank. He left behind many sketchbooks and was an avid book collector and reader who subsidized the publication of his son's poems.

Robert's sister, Sarianna, was born January 7, 1814 and received a copy of Miss Barrett's *Poems* as a gift from John Kenyon in 1844.

After Elizabeth and Robert left England on September 19, 1846, they traveled by train and diligence from Le Havre to Paris with Elizabeth's maid. They stopped in Orléans to retrieve letters from Elizabeth's family and in Vaucluse to touch the waters of the spring where Petrarch wrote his sonnets.

The 573 letters Robert and Elizabeth exchanged between 1845 and their departure for Pisa were published after their deaths and are still in print.

Elizabeth wrote forty-four sonnets to and about Robert during their courtship and kept them a secret for three years. After their marriage, she wrote a poem called "The Runaway Slave at Pilgrim Point" from the point of view of a slave who, after being raped by white men, bears a white-skinned baby that she smothers. It was published in 1848 as part of an American abolitionist periodical called the *Liberty Bell*.

Appendix II: The Wider Circle

LENORE GOSS IS a fictional character inspired by Caroline Norton, Harriet Martineau, and Margaret Fuller. Her family members are likewise invented.

Elizabeth Barrett's maid Elizabeth Wilson was one of seven children born to the wife of a coal merchant in Northumberland in 1817. She was a witness to their wedding and went with them to Italy.

In 1841, Robert Browning dedicated *Pippa Passes: A Drama* to his friend Thomas Noon Talfourd, author of the once-celebrated play, *Ion*.

Charles Dickens reported on the trial of Caroline Norton when her husband accused her of Criminal Conversation (adultery) with Lord Melbourne, the prime minister of Britain, in 1836. Norton became an activist advocating for separated, abused, and deserted wives. Benjamin Robert Haydon used her face for Cassandra in his portrait of the Duke of Sutherland.

Lady Hamilton's first daughter, conceived when she was the servant and companion of Sir Harry Fetherstonhaugh, eventually moved to Italy and became a nun. She lies buried in the same Florentine cemetery as Elizabeth Barrett Browning.

Henry Chorley's novel *Pomfret: Or, Public Opinion and Private Judgment* was published in 1845. Charles Dickens left a snuff box to him in his will.

The writer Mary Russell Mitford gave Elizabeth a puppy called Flush after Elizabeth's brothers died in 1840.

Paintings by Benjamin Robert Haydon are owned by the Tate Gallery, the National Portrait Gallery, and the British Museum. He corresponded often with Elizabeth Barrett, and he slit his own throat on June 22, 1846.

Anna Brownell Jameson's many books about art and travel provided a means of support for her, her sister, and her niece, Geddie. Jameson and Geddie traveled with the Brownings from Paris to Pisa.

Irish student William Mulcahy was ordered to pay £3 for the destruction of the Portland Vase. In lieu of payment, he was sentenced to hard labor. He was in solitary confinement at Tothill Fields prison when an anonymous letter containing £3 was sent to the Bow Street police office and he was released.

The Portland Vase has been reconstructed three times since it was broken on February 7, 1845. It can still be seen at the British Museum.

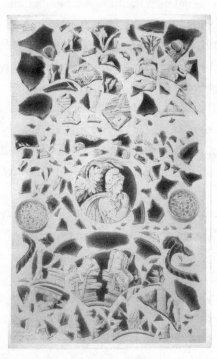

Shards of the Portland Vase
"Drawn from the Fragments by T. Hosmer Shepherd—1845"
"Destroyed Feby 7, 1845, Restored September 10 by John Doubleday"

Robert Browning's first letter to Elizabeth Barrett (two of six pages)

Acknowledgments

SEVERAL YEARS AFTER I started research for this book, I heard a chilling bit of too-late advice: "Historical novelists should be fed on very short rations."

The Barrett-Browning archive includes thousands of letters, drawings, diaries, manuscripts, and objects. It is the opposite of short rations—it is more like a feast that has grown larger over time, about which diners are constantly writing new and conflicting opinions. The feast, furthermore, is not in one banquet hall, but in many rooms spread all over the world. That's because the Brownings' only son, Pen, died in 1912 without a will or an heir. The administration of his estate was granted to lawyers of his eldest Barrett cousin and Pen's estranged wife. Pen's numerous Italian properties were sold and his and his parent's personal effects were dispersed by Sotheby's during an auction lasting six days. The Barrett-Browning papers (and jewelry and crockery and locks of hair) were mostly purchased by dealers, who later sold them, a scattering and gathering that continues to this day—papers are still sought, acquired, and snapped into the million-piece puzzle that is their lives. Some important pieces remain lost: the letters that Elizabeth Barrett Browning wrote to her father after her marriage are missing despite an intense, lengthy, and well-publicized search.

To achieve my goal, which was to tell the story of their romance without contradicting the known record, I needed to enter all of those rooms, and I tried to miss nothing. I ate biographies, letters, poems, forgotten novels, footnotes, rings, brooches, lockets, shoes, diaries, histories, more footnotes, more diaries, and sketchbooks. I went to each place they traveled or lived and I studied what was still there 175 years later. This is a work of fiction, but I have relied on and represented many true things, and for those true things I am most indebted to the work of one extraordinary person, Philip Kelley.

Kelley, a graduate of Baylor University, decided in 1959 to come up with a system that mapped the Barrett-Browning letters for researchers, and he has been enlarging and organizing the archive ever since. He not only made a system that numbered the letters and identified their locations, but he started a publishing house, Wedgestone Press, that has issued twenty-nine volumes of their correspondence so far. These books and a related website, browningscorrespondence.com, have enabled writers and scholars to read exact transcriptions of letters without traveling to New York, Eton, Oxford, London, San Marino, California, Austin, Texas, Waco, Texas, and more. Because of his work, and the website, I was able to read, from home, detailed biographical sketches of everyone the Brownings knew well and to learn which institutions hold the original manuscripts. He is the Google Earth and Sherlock Holmes and Charon of this book and I thank him and apologize to him in equal measure. This book, which he made possible, is fiction, and Philip Kelley deals only in facts. Thank you, Philip, and forgive me, if you can, the things you find amiss.

I am also grateful to the staff and founders of the Armstrong Browning Library at Baylor University, where I was granted two generously funded sessions as a visiting scholar. Jennifer Borderud, Cyndie Burgess, Christi Klempnauer, and Rita Patteson shared their deep knowledge of the Baylor archive with me and made my days there a pleasure.

Although the lives of the Brownings in Florence are not specifically referenced in this book, I wish to thank the Provost and Fellows of Eton College for their continued preservation of Casa Guidi, the apartment in Florence that Elizabeth and Robert called home for nearly fifteen years. The apartment now contains the couch on which Elizabeth was sitting when she met Robert for the first time and many other objects the Brownings owned, including an oil portrait of Elizabeth's father and paintings of her and her siblings when they were young. Despite being a museum that preserves their rooms in period style, it is rented out to overnight visitors under the auspices of the Landmark Trust. It is the best of all the author's houses I have visited, and the only one in which I've been allowed to sleep.

The British Library owns the manuscript of "Runaway Slave at Pilgrim Point," a copy of the 1848 *Liberty Bell*, Elizabeth's handwritten "How do I love thee?" sonnet, and the best newspaper archive I've ever used. I thank them for existing and for letting me sit at their long buffet tables, holding irreplaceable papers in my hands.

In Jamaica, I am indebted to Denton Prendergast of Dengast Tours; to Thomas "Bob" and Ann Betton, the owners of the historical wonder that is Greenwood Great House, once inhabited by Elizabeth's cousin, Richard Barrett; and to Nadine White of Cinnamon Hill Golf Course, who took my husband and me to see Sam's grave in the Barrett family cemetery, which is now in the center of the golf course and is closed to visitors. I am also indebted to the friend, who, as she put it, pulled not only strings but the whole spool to get us access to that cemetery and to the eighteenth-century Barrett family house, Cinnamon Hill, which at that time was still filled with the belongings of part-time residents June and Johnny Cash.

The Clapp Library at Wellesley College owns the love letters quoted in this book and the door through which Robert's letters to Elizabeth were originally delivered. I spent a supremely happy day there with Ruth R. Rogers, Curator of Special Collections, and Mariana Moller, Associate Curator, who stayed late to help me see every single letter I had read in transcription but wanted to hold in person. I thank them for permission to quote from them and use their images here.

The two other institutions that gave me generous access to Barrett-Browning ephemera are the New York Public Library and Eton College. Retired Eton College librarian Michael Meredith knows the Brownings so well that it is impossible to bring up any period of their lives without getting some new, deeply informed insight. His kindness in showing me his personal holdings and the collection he donated to Eton enhanced my perspective on several members of the family, especially Elizabeth's brother Stormie and Robert Browning's father.

Doug Stewart at Sterling Lord Literistic read and represented this book despite, as he confessed, not even liking poetry. The only suitable thanks for his enormous help would be a lock of my hair in a glass pin. I esteem him enough to not give him that.

Janet Reich Elsbach, Sorayya Khan, Lily King, and Dana Reinhardt read this book in messy forms and told me they liked it anyway. They are wonderful writers and even better friends.

Kathy Pories did what great editors do and perceived what was too recessive, what was excessive, and what was missing. The book is much better because of her insight and tact.

Our son Sam went in my stead to the ceremony marking the 132nd anniversary of Robert Browning's death in Westminster Abbey and went with me on many ghost hunts. He and his brother, Hank, have gracefully managed the stress and dullness of being Browning-adjacent for the last six years, and of having to tell their friends why our cats are named Edward and Elizabeth.

Tom McNeal should not be last because he is always first. He was the travel agent who planned every trip to places Where Something Once Happened to the Brownings. He not only got us to Florence, but parked our rental car in a space the size of a shoe so I could see Elizabeth's tomb. He got us from Rouen to Bourges on roads built for horse-drawn vehicles. On one memorably cold April day, he drove us, windshield wipers on high, past a topiary installation that said ENGLISH RIVIERA, and did not curse me as he checked us into a freezing hotel so I could (in the rain) go every place Elizabeth once went the summer that her brother Edward drowned. He read a thousand drafts of this book, and he went with me to college housing at Baylor and to Jamaica (actually, that part wasn't hard, and he should thank me for needing to go there) and New York and London and France and Belgium and all the cities in Italy where the Brownings went in search of happiness. I could not have believed in Robert Browning, who sometimes seems too faithful and good to be real, if I did not have my own writer husband proving himself, over and over again, inexhaustibly good and real.